Dear Reader,

This month we are trying something a little different: *Renton's Royal* is set in 1969 and is more of a saga than anything we've published so far. Do you enjoy this type of romance? Would you like to see more sagas on the *Scarlet* list? Or historical romances? *I'm* a great fan of Regency novels, but perhaps you prefer other historical settings?

Wild Justice is the first part of 'The Beaumont Brides' trilogy, telling the stories of three, very different, sisters. We do hope you'll enjoy the chance to be involved with the same characters over the course of three books. *A Dark Legacy* combines romance with a dash of mystery, while *No Darker Heaven* is the story of a woman who's torn between two men – father and son!

Do write to us with your views on *Scarlet*, won't you, as it's only by hearing *your* opinion that we can continue to make sure that the book

Best wishes,

Sally Cooper

SALLY COOPER,
Editor-in-Chief – *Scarlet*

PS Have you filled in a questionnaire yet? If you haven't, please complete the fom at the back of this book and we'll be happy to send you a free gift as a thank you.

About the Author

Nina Tinsley is the author of many, very popular, romance novels, so we're delighted that we are able to include *Renton's Royal* on the *Scarlet* list. Nina writes very entertaining involving stories which feature women who discover not only true love, but also independence and their own particular strengths as the plot unfolds. Nina's friends and fans eagerly await the publication of *Renton's Royal* and we're sure her popularity will increase as new readers discover the delights in store between the covers of Nina's novel.

*Other **Scarlet** titles available this month:*

A DARK LEGACY – Clare Benedict
WILD JUSTICE – Liz Fielding
NO DARKER HEAVEN – Stella Whitelaw

NINA TINSLEY

RENTON'S ROYAL

SCARLET

Enquiries to:
Robinson Publishing Ltd
7 Kensington Church Court
London W8 4SP

First published in the UK by Scarlet, 1996

A copy of the British Library Cataloguing in
Publication data is available from the British Library

ISBN 1-85487-486-1

Printed and bound in the EC

10 9 8 7 6 5 4 3 2 1

CHAPTER 1

March 1969

'Stop here a moment, please,' Sarah Renton instructed the driver as he swung the taxi through the open gates. He pulled up on the wide drive and, sliding out of his seat, opened the door for his passenger. She alighted and stood gazing her fill at the building before her, which in the dusk of a late March afternoon seemed to ride the air with all the grace of a ship at sea. The brilliant red neon lettering proclaiming the name of the hotel, Renton's Royal, had all the beckoning expectation that must have satisfied travellers years ago, when a humble hostelry had occupied the site.

'Michael,' she called to her companion. 'Get out and look.'

The youth, unfolding long limbs, reluctantly joined her.

'Well,' she said impatiently, resenting his slowness, 'what do you think?'

'It's OK.'

'Of course it's OK.' But she couldn't defend this creation of hers to her grandson.

'It's a winner,' Jack Silworthy, the taxi driver said. His swarthy face betrayed the kind of admiration he reserved for his favourite soccer player. The lady was a professional; he'd been driving her for a long time; he prided himself on knowing her ways.

1

'Thank you Jack. Well, let's get on.'

They climbed back into the cab, and the driver crossed the forecourt, and taking a narrower road pulled up in the space before a cottage. Sarah Renton had arrived home. She had moved into this cottage at the time of her daughter Claire's marriage, thus leaving the hotel apartment free. She hadn't wanted to move, believing that she could control the hotel more easily by living in, but there wasn't any way she could tolerate Jim O'Hara, Claire's husband, other than on a business basis.

The cottage was in darkness, but then she wasn't expected back for another two or three weeks, and she had a feeling her early return from visiting her son in Spain would be regarded with disfavour by the O'Haras.

The driver was heaving out the luggage. Sarah opened her calf-skin handbag, found her house keys, and alighting once again, walked up the short path and unlocked the door. She switched on the lights in the narrow white hall.

She was relieved to see the house hadn't been neglected in her absence. All that was needed, she thought, were flowers from the garden.

'I'll carry your luggage upstairs, Mrs Renton,' Silworthy offered.

She smiled her thanks, and walked into the sitting room, which occupied the whole length of one side of the cottage. On the other side of the hall was a small dining room and the kitchen. All was as she'd left it, and satisfied that Claire hadn't changed anything during her absence, she turned her attention to Michael, who was hovering in the doorway.

'Come in,' she said. His bewildered look amused her.

'It's so small. I mean – '

'I know what you mean. You thought I'd have a large ostentatious house like your father's.'

'Dad said it would be super,' he defended himself.

Silworthy came down the stairs. 'I'll turn the heating on for you, Mrs Renton,' he said, going through into the kitchen.

She followed him, as always touched by his concern. He never seemed to realize she was totally capable of performing such tasks for herself.

'Soon be cosy,' he said as he adjusted the heat control and then grinned his thanks at the size of the tip Sarah added to the fare.

Michael was still standing in the hall. He moved to allow Silworthy to leave and closed the front door after him.

'Come on,' Sarah said, 'I'll show you your room.'

The stairs ended in a narrow landing. Sarah's bedroom was above the sitting room, with an east and west aspect, the two small guest rooms and bathroom being on the opposite side of the landing.

Michael Renton followed his grandmother up the stairs. He felt stifled and afraid. He resented his father's disposal of him, just as if he was a discarded piece of machinery. Paul Renton was a great discarder.

Sarah busily opened cupboards and drawers, but Michael dumped his bag and crossed the room to look out of the window. Sarah joined him. From here most of the hotel was in view. It glittered with lights from many of the windows, and scattered about the grounds were great round globes of light which pierced the near darkness.

She touched Michael's arm. 'Come on love, unpack your bag, and have a wash. You'll feel better then.' The tone of her voice changed. 'No need to worry. You'll be safe here.' She felt a need to fold him in her arms, but resisted it. Their relationship was too tenuous for a show of demonstrative affection. She would bide her time.

'Are you hungry?'

He shook his head.

'Right. We'll eat later over at the hotel.'

3

In her own room she took off her plaid travelling cloak and sat down in front of the dressing table. She switched on the light above the mirror, and studied her face. The Spanish sun had laid a creamy-brown patina on her skin. She had the kind of skin that tanned easily, and without blemish. She reflected the sun had been the bonus of her trip and other than that her stay with Paul had been too tense.

She took off her spectacles, and the blurred vision of herself disconcerted her. She found it hard to come to terms with the realization she would be sixty in a few months time, and searched her face for the beauty which had once captured Gerald Renton's heart.

She sighed. When Gerald had died seven years ago, a part of her had died too. Or so she'd thought then, but now she knew it wasn't quite true. She loved her children of course, but the will to succeed, to make Gerald's hotel the kind of place he'd dreamed about, had been the driving force behind all her actions. And, she thought grimly, she wasn't ready to be replaced yet.

Thinking about the hotel reminded her that she hadn't told Claire she was back. She moved to her desk, neatly set out with paper, envelopes, pens and reference books, and lifting the telephone receiver which connected her directly to the hotel she spoke to the receptionist.

'Hullo, Mrs Renton?' Mavis Blair the head receptionist sounded surprised.

'Home is the traveller, home from the sea,' Sarah joked.

'And the hunter home from the hill,' Mavis added. They amused themselves quoting and misquoting poetry to each other. 'Have you enjoyed your holiday?'

'Yes thanks, but I'm glad to be back. Will you put me through to Mrs O'Hara, please.'

Claire answered immediately. 'Mother. What on earth

4

are you doing home? You promised you'd stay with Paul at least a couple of months.'

'Restless, love, and I feel so much better. I've brought Michael back with me. He can stay here.'

'But Mother, you are supposed to be taking things easy. You are the absolute limit.' Claire's annoyance was only too apparent. 'And why didn't you phone me from the airport?'

'No need. Dear old Silworthy came for us.'

'I suppose you wanted your return to be a surprise.'

'Why should you think that?'

'Because you are afraid that Jim and I aren't capable of managing the hotel in your absence.'

Because that was exactly what Sarah thought, she didn't deny it, and merely said she and Michael would be over for a meal later.

She cradled the receiver thoughtfully after she's hung up and then with a flurry of energy unpacked her small overnight suitcase. This done, she undressed, hanging her tweed suit in the wardrobe, pushing her underclothes into the dirty linen basket. She wrapped herself up in a white bathrobe, and headed for the bathroom.

A leisurely bath restored her, and returning to her room she sat down in front of the west window. Although it was now dark, she knew exactly what could be seen in daylight. She never tired of the view. Beyond her own special garden, walled in to deter straying guests, and beyond the perimeter of the grounds, sand dunes reared up in ever changing shapes, though anchored by the tough growing marram grass; and in the secret recesses of their furrowed valleys was a selection of rare wild flowers.

Beyond the dunes was the endless stretch of dun-coloured sand, rippled by the incoming tide, and scarred here and there by pools of standing water. She loved this uncompromising view. Often when needing solitude she donned a pair

5

of old and comfortable sandshoes, and walked close to the moving water, scaring the raucous gulls to flight.

Restlessly she stood up, suddenly aware that there was no sound from Michael's room. She crossed the landing, tapped on the door and went in.

He lay on the bed, asleep.

Her heart turned over as she stood by the bed gazing at him. He was the only one of all her family to resemble Gerald, and bending over the boy she longed to stroke his cheek, to kiss the soft place in his neck, just as she'd done to Gerald in the heady first days of their marriage. Her throat thickened with unshed tears, and she was filled with compassion. He looked childishly vulnerable, and she vowed not to become over-protective. At that second a vague idea took root. Here was her natural successor: Gerald's grandson.

Michael opened his eyes, and smiled. And because his habitual sulky expression was banished, she saw in him all the charm of the young Gerald with whom she had fallen so desperately in love.

'I was dreaming,' Michael said as he sat up. 'A super dream – '

'Tell me?'

'I can't. I mean it's there and I can't reach it. I only know I was happy.'

Then she touched him on his cheek. He responded, taking her hand and kissing the palm.

'You believe in me, Gran. Dad says I've no backbone. He despises me. But I'll make him change his mind.'

'Your father loves you,' Sarah said with asperity.

'Dad used to talk about you.' He swung his legs off the bed. 'He said you'd set me straight. He said you wouldn't forgive the drugs – ' He stood up. 'I've kicked the habit, really I have, Gran. You see, when Dad married Fortunata after Mum died, I wasn't wanted.'

'Rubbish,' Sarah said briskly. 'Of course you were wanted. And I – I want you more than words can say.'

'Really?' he asked as he looked at her eagerly.

'I think, Michael, we need each other.'

He bent and kissed her cheek. 'You smell gorgeous – not like Fortunata. She smells sexy,' he laughed, and throwing off his shirt headed for the bathroom.

She hadn't liked Fortunata. Paul described her as a Spanish beauty. Certainly she had the looks, black hair and flashing eyes if you like that kind of beauty. Sarah had summed her up as a lightweight. After years of practice she was adept at summing up people. The hotel guests fell into a pattern. There were those to be trusted, and there were the shifty ones. Sarah recognized them at a glance but was tolerant of them nevertheless. Gerald had taught her that. She sighed; she wouldn't think about him now; she reserved those thoughts for the dark and sleepless hours in the night, the lonely walk at the sea's edge, the moments when she wondered if the time had come to pass on the power she had wielded for so long and so well.

She returned to her room, and chose to wear a patterned silk dress, one she was particularly fond of. Gerald had always urged her to wear the greeny-brown of autumn, a complement to her bright hazel eyes.

Michael called from the landing. 'What do I wear?'

'Not jeans and one of those dreadful tee shirts.'

He laughed, and in a few moments appeared in the doorway.

'What do you think of this?'

He wore tight black velvet trousers and a matching jacket.

'Good Lord, did you buy that get-up in Spain?'

'Carnaby Street. Dad and I came on a flying visit to London last year. Head office wanted to see him. They offered him a move to the office in New York but

7

Fortunata kicked up such a fuss, he had to refuse. He'll never get to the top with her round his neck. The travel agency business is terribly competitive now.'

'A pity he didn't take his father's place and manage the hotel with me.'

'He wouldn't have liked that. For one thing he can't get on with Claire. Will I like her? My Mum didn't. She said she was too bossy.'

'Happen she is, but so am I. Michael, you know your father is willing to allow me to train you in the hotel business. How do you feel about it?'

He hesitated so long she had a qualm of conscience. Was she trying to use him for her own purposes?

'Michael, there must be trust between us, and openness. If you are not interested, say so now.'

'I am. But suppose I can't learn it all? I trust you, Gran, but I don't trust others. They let you down.'

'Oh come, Michael. That can't be true.'

He came close to her and put a tentative hand on her arm. 'If Mum hadn't died . . .'

'Would it have made any difference?' she asked gently.

He nodded vigorously. She understood his loss and pain, remembering how desperate she had felt in the days after Gerald's death.

'We have to pick up the pieces and go on. You matter a great deal to us all.'

'I only know *you*, Gran. Not the others. Why did Dad forget Mum so soon?'

She could not explain the unbearable loneliness, nor could she share hers, which was on a different plane to his.

'Fortunata was waiting.' His voice hardened. 'I hate her.'

'Time – ' she began.

'Oh don't give me that,' he said violently. 'Time doesn't heal. It blurs the edges.'

He was right, and for the moment she had no words of comfort. He was occasionally very mature. Sarah picked up her cloak and Michael held it for her while she slipped her arms into the sleeves.

They left the cottage and walked along the drive leading to the front of the hotel. Lights illuminated the driveway. As they approached the hotel Sarah observed the car park was nearly full. They mounted the shallow steps and entered the foyer. This was the moment when Sarah always felt a flutter of anticipation; she was entering into her kingdom.

The hall porter held the door. 'Evening, Mrs Renton.'

'Evening, Bill.' She prided herself on knowing the names of all the staff. 'Looks like a busy night?'

'Yes, Mrs Renton. We've got a conference in the ball-room. Glad to see you back. Not the same without you.' He spoke so quietly she barely caught the words but heard enough to reassure her.

She was proud of the foyer. Often her thoughts slipped back to the first drawings, the first plans. Gerald had been an imaginative architect. His plans took shape and form in his mind before even the first stone was laid. He'd conceived the curved staircase as a central point; and every step of the way he'd consulted her.

She glanced at Michael as they paused a moment beneath the Waterford chandeliers, which had miraculously been saved from the fire which had burnt down the Renton house over forty years ago.

The house had stood closer to the sea then, but Gerald had refused to build the hotel on that site, instead choosing the slight eminence further inland, where the old hostelry had been a landmark for ships sailing up the estuary.

Michael clutched her arm. 'It's absolutely super. Dad didn't tell me what it was like.'

Sarah hardly heard his words. She seemed to grow in

9

stature, assuming the mantle of professionalism she had gained at such cost.

And that was how Claire saw them. She descended the staircase slowly, pausing long enough to notice that Michael in profile resembled her father; and that her mother was back on form, standing straight and commanding.

Sarah's glance swept round and alighted on Claire, chiding herself for observing her dispassionately, as if she weren't her first and beloved child.

Then Claire descended, and putting her arms round her mother kissed her cheek. 'Are you well, darling? You should have let me know you were coming back.' She turned to Michael, 'Dear me, you're a young man. Last time I saw you was when Jim and I were touring Europe. You must have been about ten.'

'Twelve actually. And now I'm eighteen.'

'I suppose you've come to England to attend university?'

Michael shook his head.

'Where's Jim?' Sarah asked.

It was Claire's hesitation, too slight to be noticed or interpreted by anyone else, that warned Sarah her early return was not convenient. She guessed her son-in-law was up to something; and it would give her pleasure to find out what it was.

'He's around.' Claire gestured. Her hands were smooth and white skinned, and instinctively Sarah concealed her own, aware of the telltale signs of hard work.

'It's a busy night,' Claire said. 'A middle management conference in the ballroom, and a birthday party in the Nealey Room. Are you and Michael having dinner in the public dining room? We have a guest, so perhaps we can all eat together.'

'Anyone I know?'

'Yes. He's here on business – '

Sarah's smile was deadly. 'Our business? Shouldn't I be in on it?'

'Mother,' Claire's exasperation spilled over. 'You think no one but you can run this hotel, but let me tell you both Jim and I are more capable than you've ever been, and we resent your interference.'

A slight flush coloured Sarah's cheeks, and her heart gave an unaccustomed bump. 'Interference? Are you hiding something?'

'Don't be silly, Mother. You are so suspicious.'

'So I am. And your guest has just come into the foyer with Jim. Charlie Mullins, I see. That makes it even more interesting.'

'Mother!' Claire laid a detaining hand on Sarah's arm, but she shook it off.

'Sarah. This is an unexpected pleasure,' enthused Charlie Mullins as he held out his hand and grasping Sarah's, raised it to his lips in one of his old-fashioned gestures which mistakenly made business associates believe he wasn't rock hard.

Sarah knew better. She freed her hand.

'I suppose you were told I was still in Spain staying with my son.'

'It was mentioned – '

'Of course it was. Charlie particularly asked after you, Mother.'

'I'm sure he did.'

He laughed, and turned to Michael. 'I detect a family likeness.'

'My twin brother Paul's son,' Claire said. 'He is staying with Mother at the cottage.'

Sarah acknowledged Jim's greeting, and led the way into the dining room. The family table was in a slight alcove, and as they disposed themselves round it, Sarah's sharp gaze swept round the room. The service appeared to

11

be as smooth as usual. She noted the flowers looked fresh, and the waitresses' black dresses and white aprons couldn't be faulted. In spite of Claire's objections, Sarah insisted on the traditional dress.

Charlie's look of approval was unmistakable, and taking a chair on Sarah's right he unfolded his linen napkin and placed it carefully across his knees.

'Look's good, Sarah. No slipping standards here. I reckon you are running neck and neck with the Imperial Hotel in Blackpool. Your dinner at 18/6d is just as good as theirs.' He was keenly interested in prices, and reflected his findings in his own chain of hotels. 'You have a good manager in Jim. I always think family businesses have the edge. Not many left,' he added enigmatically.

'Mother-in-law sets the pace.' Jim's discontent was heard in his voice, and his cold glance met Sarah's. He hasn't changed, she thought, and never will. She reckoned him to be her one mistake. All the staff she'd hired over the years had proved themselves. Had she been beguiled by his smooth talk, his dramatic good looks, or Claire's enthusiasm? He certainly knew his job, and she now remembered with some misgiving he had learnt his craft in one of Charlie Mullins' hotels.

'Still turning out managers like Jim?' She was sure the inference would be obvious to both Charlie and Jim.

'Some good, some bad. I'm looking for promising youngsters. Are you interested in the catering trade, Michael?'

Before he could answer, Sarah summoned the head wine waiter. 'Champagne tonight. A couple of bottles of the Moët and Chandon, please, Albert.'

'Certainly, Mrs Renton. Your return is indeed an occasion for celebration.'

She believed in the loyalty of her staff, and considered it part of the secret of her success.

'Celebrating my return may be premature,' she said, 'but it is indeed an occasion to have my old friend Charlie here, but most of all to wish my grandson well at the start of his career. It's possible he may join my staff. And if he does I'm going to make a great hotelier of him.' She turned to Charlie. 'Think I can do it?'

Charlie smiled. 'I don't doubt, Sarah, you are capable of doing anything on which you set your heart.'

CHAPTER 2

Claire woke early. She lay still in the twin bed nearest the window, listening with rising irritation to Jim's heavy breathing. They had stopped sharing a bed years ago. Claire didn't remember exactly when, but the slow and insidious decline in their marriage had, in retrospect, started then.

The pain from the attack of heartburn which had awoken her increased, and getting up, she padded into the bathroom and took a dose of medicine. At last the pain receded, and she walked slowly into the apartment kitchen to make a pot of tea.

She filled the electric kettle and perched on the stool, waiting for it to boil, feet in mules, housecoat huddled round her.

Last evening had been a disaster. Her mother's early return, accompanied by Michael, had brought into sharp focus her dilemma. She was appalled at the emotions the animosity between her mother and Jim had aroused in her. More importantly, she had recognized Charlie Mullins' amusement; and was convinced he would take advantage of the situation.

Alone, drinking tea, she admitted to herself how much she liked Charlie, and believed that he held reciprocal feelings, and although no word had been uttered, conscious desire was there.

14

She glanced at the clock, surprised at how long her thoughts had rabbited round in her head, and returned to the bathroom to shower and dress.

Early mornings in the hotel had a fascination she couldn't name, but she was sure her mother felt it too. Now, pacing the thick red carpets in the corridors, she felt a vague curiosity about the strangers moving about in the privacy of their rooms. She gave fleeting thought to the circumstances which had brought guests to Renton's Royal Hotel, and if in any way their stay influenced the course of their lives.

On the first-floor corridor she hesitated outside Charlie Mullins' door. He responded immediately to her light tap, and ushered her into the room. He was dressed, and packing.

'Good morning, Claire.'

He looked good in the morning. Clean shaven, thinning pale brown hair carefully brushed, expensively suited, he was the prototype of a successful business man. He offered her the easy chair.

No preliminary fencing was necessary.

'Jim has over-reached himself. I'd no idea he'd invited or arranged for you to come here.'

'And you had no idea fighting Sarah would break up the party.'

They smiled at each other, and he perched on the arm of her chair. She was aware of his masculinity, and his closeness disturbed. He didn't touch her.

'Well?' she queried.

'Jim threw out his usual vague suggestions. Sarah will shortly be sixty. The business is in fine fettle. Claire needs a rest. Not exactly an invitation, just a few random hints.'

'So you came.'

'Naturally, my dear. I wanted to assure myself that Jim

15

was acting without Sarah's knowledge, and if the situation was in any way changed.'

'Mother will never willingly give up.' She leaned back in the chair and closed her eyes. 'She and Jim are at loggerheads all the time,' she added very softly.

'Of course Sarah won't give up. And believe me, Claire, I wouldn't want her to opt out until she's ready. But if Renton's Royal Hotel ever comes on the market, I'd like to be the first to know.'

'You have so many hotels, why pick on this one?'

'Success. Sarah could have owned a chain to rival mine if she'd so wished, especially with the Renton money behind her. Instead she concentrated on this one, making it exclusive, superb in every way.'

Claire resented his unstinted praise of her mother, particularly as she knew it was founded on fact. 'Does that mean – ?'

'It means, Claire, that I desire to add this hotel to my chain more than any other I've acquired in the past, and your mother will know the reason.'

He smiled. 'The cards are down. Let's see how the hand is played. Who has the luck this time?'

'Not me,' she said despondently.

'Your mother is an optimist, and a survivor. I thought perhaps you, Claire, would have the same philosophy.'

'Then you are wrong. She's overshadowed me from the beginning, and I hadn't the guts to get out.'

'What's holding you back now,' he said pointedly, and as she rose to leave he put his arms round her and kissed her on the cheek.

Damn Charlie Mullins, she thought, descending to the ground floor by the staircase. If he thinks he'll ever get Renton's through me, he's very much mistaken. Head high, she marched through the lounges, ignoring the cleaners' respectful greeting, and flung open the office door.

Sarah was already there.

'Good morning, darling.'

'Are you all right, Mother?'

'Never felt better,' she said, tipping the stubs out of Jim's ashtray into the wastepaper bin. 'I've ordered breakfast here, will you join me?'

Resentfully Claire watched her mother clear the mess Jim had left on the desk. Why he had to use an old scribbling pad, and stumps of bitten pencils she'd never know. Sarah made no apology for the removal of her son-in-law's occupancy.

'I don't bother much with breakfast,' Claire said.

'Ridiculous. When you were all little I made you eat a good breakfast before going to school.'

'Go to school on an egg,' Claire laughed. She lifted the receiver of the internal phone and ordered coffee and toast.

'That's better. A smile at last. What's troubling you, darling? Is Margaret all right?'

'I don't know.'

You don't know!' Sarah scandalized tone brought a wry smile to Claire's lips.

'She telephones now and again, but she's quarrelled with her father. She's so headstrong and independent, just like you. She will have her own way.'

'That daughter of yours will go far,' Sarah declared. 'I think you should try and see her. Anything can happen these days.'

'She's twenty. Old enough to look after herself. And she won't thank me for interfering.'

Sarah didn't ask why Margaret had quarrelled with her father, but busied herself putting a cloth on the side table. The waiter arrived with breakfast and unloaded his tray, setting the dishes down with care and attention.

'Sit down, Claire.' Sarah pulled up a chair. 'I hate cold scrambled eggs. Like some?'

17

Claire shuddered, and listlessly buttered a piece of toast and poured herself black coffee, glancing away from her mother's piled plate.

'Mother, you are incredible. Don't you ever feel tired?'

'Often. But I'm like my old Dad. He used to say, "Sarah, my girl, you'll die in the shafts, and that's the best way to go."'

Sarah didn't often speak of Joe Nealey; not because she didn't frequently think of him, but because she had realized the Renton family preferred to gloss over her humble background. Old Mrs Renton had invented a fanciful past for Sarah. Her version of an orphan taken it by the nuns of the Convent of the Sacred Heart bore no relationship to the truth, and had been a source of great amusement to Gerald and herself.

Gerald had teased her about his mother's theory that Sarah had been left on the Convent doorstep by some aristocratic father, when in truth, the nuns had taken her in as a girl of fourteen on the death of her father in 1923.

Sarah had never forgiven his mother such snobbishness. Gerald had said it didn't matter; nevertheless, she had loved her father dearly and it had hurt. Joe Nealey would have been proud of his grandchildren, and perhaps they would have learnt to value his worth too, had they had the opportunity.

Sarah finished her breakfast and poured herself a second cup of the strong Indian tea she favoured.

'Tell me, darling,' Sarah's voice was deceptively mild, 'who or what brought Charlie Mullins here?'

Claire started. 'I don't understand – '

'Plain English, lass. I've known Charlie since we were kids at school. He's rapacious and greedy. He rarely acts without an ulterior motive. Don't think I don't like him, I do. He's part of my past. I understand his ambitions, but I don't like his methods. You've never met his poor down-trodden wife. She's in a Home now, and when he's ready he'll get rid of her.'

'Wife!' Claire said. 'I thought she was dead.'

'Dead to him, no doubt.'

'I think you are mistaken, Mother. If his wife is alive, surely he'd mention her?'

'Charlie's maxim is out of sight, out of mind.'

'I think that is a terrible thing to say. He's not my favourite man, but he isn't deceitful.'

'I'll allow that, but we are straying from the point. I know Charlie wouldn't have come here openly unless someone gave him the wink. So let's have the truth.'

'I didn't know,' Claire muttered. 'I think Jim may have mentioned something – '

'I guessed as much. Perhaps Jim isn't satisfied with his job here. Maybe he'd like to transfer to the Mullins group.'

'He's your son-in-law. You don't think he'd be so underhand, surely?'

'I've never yet been able to discover what Jim thinks, so now is the time. Ask him to come up here.'

Deliberately Claire picked up the diary, and placed it open on the desk. 'It's a busy day. He has appointments. Can't it wait?'

'No.' Sarah had no intention of allowing Claire to brief him. 'Don't bother to look for him. I'll have him paged. Now do me a little favour. Go over to the cottage and see if Michael is awake, and bring him over here. He can have breakfast in the staff dining room, and by then I'll have time to talk to him.'

'Just what are you planning, Mother? You said last evening you were going to make a great hotelier of Michael. Does that mean you are taking him into the business?'

'Happen so.' Sarah lapsed into her Lancashire phrases

19

when she was annoyed. She wasn't ready to be questioned by Claire or anyone else.

'I don't think you can do that without consulting us.'

With great forbearance Sarah kept her anger in check. 'You're wrong, Claire. I can do exactly what I like about the business and you know it.'

Claire flounced out of the room, banging the door after her.

Sarah sighed, and to recover her composure she walked across to the window and threw it open. Gusts of salty air surged in. She breathed deeply. She loved the sea, not just here where it surged speedily up the beach, but in Liverpool, where she had spent so much of her childhood wandering about the docks, her head filled with stories the sailors recounted over strong cups of tea in her father's café.

The ringing of the house phone disturbed her thoughts, and almost reluctantly she answered it.

'Send him in,' she said, and putting down the receiver crossed to the mirror to rearrange her hair, and apply the subtly scented powder she favoured.

She was seated at her desk, pen in hand, by the time there was a knock at the door and Charlie Mullins entered.

'Good morning, Charlie.' She indicated the chair on the opposite side of the desk.

'Morning, Sarah. How are you?'

'Fine thanks. And you?'

'Well enough. We're a tough breed from the Pool.'

'Not all of us. How's Alice?'

'The same. No change.'

'Perhaps time – ?'

He shrugged, and his expression hardened. 'You know damn well, Sarah, her condition will never improve. The doctors call it a slow deterioration. She hasn't forgotten how to hate me, blames me for her condition when she's capable of thinking. Was it my fault, lass?' he asked quietly.

'You picked the wrong girl. She couldn't handle your kind of success. Her looks were a snare and a delusion, and you fell for it. And now, Charlie, what's on your mind?'

'Renton's Royal Hotel,' he said. 'I want it. I can offer you . . .' He paused dramatically, before naming an astronomically large sum of money.

He hadn't changed, coming straight to the point with a kind of deceptive honesty. She could match him with bluntness.

She shook her head.

'Come on, Sarah. You are reaching retirement age. Think what you could do with that kind of money. You always wanted to travel the world. Remember when we were kids hanging about the docks?'

She could well afford a world cruise now if she wanted it. There were her children and grandchildren to consider. There would be enough for them anyway. She didn't have to pretend to herself. Renton's Royal was her life. It was her link with her beloved Gerald, and the thought of the desecration Charlie would create was more than she could bear. The uniqueness of Renton's Royal Hotel would be lost. She imagined his handling of the new brochures. Another Mullins hotel, no different from all the others.

'No. No, never.'

'Why?'

She couldn't put her feelings into words. Charlie would think her sentimental if she tried to explain that Renton's Royal was a precious legacy from Gerald, and the hope for the future of her family. 'The hotel isn't for sale,' she said stiffly. 'Who gave you the idea it was?'

'I've wanted it for a long time. Renton's Royal Hotel.' He lingered over the name. 'The final accolade, the jewel in my crown. Think about it, Sarah. I don't give up.'

'And neither do I.'

He smiled. 'I like a fight. We're well matched. Your dad used to say you've got to be good to get the better of our Sarah.'

'Remember that,' she warned.

'I'll be in touch. Take care, my dear.' He went, closing the door silently after him.

The trouble is, Sarah thought, Charlie is good. He'd overcome prejudice, reached the top grade at Stick Street Primary, and won a scholarship to the grammar school.

She smiled to herself. The enemy without would fight fair with her, but what of the enemy within, the one willing to betray her?

Impatiently she phoned Reception. 'Page Mr O'Hara,' she instructed.

At moments like this she longed passionately for Gerald. His quiet authority achieved so much more than she could ever hope to do. And thinking of him, she calmed herself, arranging her thoughts coherently.

A moment or two later, Mavis, the head receptionist, phoned. 'I'm sorry Mrs Renton, but Mr O'Hara has gone out.'

'Alone?'

'No. He joined Mrs O'Hara and Mr Mullins. I reminded him the builder was due about the conservatory extension. In fact he's just arrived. Will you see him, Mrs Renton?'

'Yes. And Mavis, I'll take all Mr O'Hara's appointments for today.'

'Good. What will be, will be.'

'Mavis, my dear. You're getting enigmatic in your middle years.'

Mavis' chuckle reassured. 'Shall I send in the plans and specifications?'

Plans, Sarah thought. Specifications. Gerald would

have demolished the anomalies at a glance; but she, she had to rely on her quick wits, her assessment of people. Integrity wasn't just a word, it had great meaning for her.

Mr Craig, the builder, was ushered in. He was a short man, with an equally short temper, and the best builder in the area.

He held out a hand as work-worn as Sarah's.

'I'm glad to see you, Mrs Renton. You're a woman I can do business with.' He sat down, and spread out the plans on the desk.

Sarah leaned forward. At least the lines had some meaning for her, thanks to Gerald's tuition.

'How will it be if we change the elevation here?' Craig's stubby finger stabbed the place.

She considered the implications for a moment. 'No. That isn't what I want.'

'Why not?' Craig said sharply.

'I want it like this.' She took up a pen and sketched the shape with care.

'Well now, this other way was Mr O'Hara's idea. He said it would cut the cost.'

'As I happen to be footing the bill, we'll do it my way.'

'I like it,' Craig said. He refrained from mentioning that Jim O'Hara had expected a rake-off, and Craig had told him to get lost.

'Have we had your estimate?'

Craig said, 'I'll check – '

'If it's satisfactory, when can you start?'

'Name the day, Mrs Renton. I always give priority to your commissions.'

She consulted her desk diary, and agreed with Craig on a possible starting date. He gathered up his plans, shook hands, and repeating that it was his pleasure to do business with her, he left.

She turned back the pages until she came to the present

day, Friday, 28 March, 1969, and in the allotted space wrote in her large untidy handwriting the finalized plans with Craig for the new conservatory, providing his estimate was acceptable.

She checked in the diary and saw she had a full day ahead. Her spirits soared; she was in control, and that was the way she wanted it.

CHAPTER 3

Michael lay in bed writing a letter to his father. It was difficult. Already he'd screwed up several attempts.

'Michael – are you up?'

He abandoned his letter, sprang out of bed and went onto the landing.

Claire stood at the bottom of the stairs, drumming her fingers impatiently on the newel post. 'You'll never make a hotelier lying in bed, my lad.'

Michael recognized the resentment in her voice. He'd lived with that tone of voice for two years – Fortunata's – and he'd formulated a defence.

'Who said I want to be a hotelier? I might want to be a pilot, or an explorer, or an astronaut.'

'You'll be what your grandmother wants you to be. Get that into your noodle.'

'You don't want me here, do you?' he said. He'd learnt attack was always the best form of defence. It threw his opponent.

'Get dressed,' Claire said, 'and hurry up.'

She disappeared into the sitting room and Michael shot into the bathroom with commendable speed.

When he ran downstairs Claire was in the kitchen. 'Coffee?' She indicated the mug.

Michael noticed that her hand was shaking, and

immediately he felt a pang as sharp as the ones he'd endured during his mother's illness.

'Are you okay, Aunt Claire?'

'Cut out the aunt, there's a dear.'

He added milk and sugar to his coffee, aware she was watching him. She wasn't quite what he'd expected. There was a petulant twist to her mouth, and her glance darted around without meeting his gaze. He diagnosed a nervousness that surprised him. He was pleased with this assessment, culled from a reading of Freud recommended by his school teacher. Sarah would have arrived at the same conclusion, albeit by a different route.

Claire was unhappy. She held her mug of coffee in both hands, staring into the depths.

'Claire, I'm hungry.'

She looked up and laughed. Her brilliant eyes sparkled with all the glory of sunlit water, her mouth curved and revealed small even teeth. Her face was familiar; she resembled his father.

'Fine. Drink up. I'm instructed to take you across to the hotel and deposit you in the staff dining room. Make friends with the chef. He thrives on hungry people.'

The staff dining room adjoined the kitchen and was reached by a narrow passage. Sliding doors, always open, gave Chef complete command of his territory. He was sitting at the table reading the *Sporting News*.

Claire introduced Michael. Chef looked him over, as Michael studied him back. He wore his tall white hat constantly; it gave him the height he lacked, and hid the balding patch on his head.

'Mother brought my nephew back with her from Spain. As you know, he lives there.'

Chef nodded.

'Mother suggested he has his breakfast here.'

'Right.' Chef folded his newspaper. 'What would you like?'

26

'Can I have bacon and eggs, please? I'm awfully hungry.'

Chef smiled. 'Sit down,' he said as he indicated the chair next to him. 'Set a place for him,' he shouted to a commis hovering nearby, and as Chef rose the kitchen became alive with activity.

'Please see he reaches Mrs Renton's office after breakfast,' Claire instructed him before leaving.

'Are you interested in catering?' Chef asked.

Michael shook his head. He glanced round the kitchen, surprised at the number of people engaged in the preparation and cooking of food.

Chef noted his interest. 'This is your first visit to Renton's, isn't it? We have one of the best equipped hotel kitchens in the north. Mrs Renton ensures we have the latest equipment,' he said with pride.

Michael's interest at that moment however was in the large plate of bacon and eggs which the commis set before him.

'Look after the boss's grandson, Ramiro.' Chef gathered up his newspaper and a sheaf of other papers, and moved into the kitchen.

Ramiro brought a pot of coffee, enquiring anxiously if there was anything else Michael would like. He waited until Michael finished eating, and cleared away the plate.

'I hear Mrs O'Hara tell Chef you come from my country. Do you speak Spanish?'

'Not terribly well. What are you doing here?' Curiosity aroused, he observed Ramiro closely and liked the look of him. He had hair as black and curly as Fortunata's, smooth skin and even features, and sparkling dark eyes. Michael detected an eagerness in his expression and the way he spoke.

'I come here to learn from the Master,' he indicated Chef. 'You understand we have a family restaurant and many English customers.'

Michael grinned. 'Chips with everything?'

'But no,' Ramiro said seriously. 'I learn the best cooking.'

'That's a damn good idea. You will do well.'

Michael was impressed by the boy's intensity. He felt the first stirring of interest, and something more, a desire to be part of this contained world where everyone had a place, and abided by it.

He drank his coffee slowly, but his thoughts were racing. Had his grandmother really meant him to learn the business? His father had agreed only because he wanted the villa and Fortunata to himself. And he had not forgiven Michael for being tempted into taking drugs. His father had a fine contempt for the cosmopolitan crowd with which Michael spent the school holidays, either on the beach or round a friend's swimming pool. At least he hadn't found out about the nightclubs, and a temptation of a different kind. He finished his coffee and stood up. Immediately Ramiro was by his side.

'Please, I take you to Madam's office.'

The extensive kitchens were behind the dining room. Sarah, remembering her father's café and the cellar kitchen he had had, insisted on the perfect layout in her own hotel now. Gerald had been pleased to go along with her ideas, as his grandiose ideas were to be executed where they showed; Sarah's were of a much more important, practical nature.

Ramiro led the way through the cold rooms, pointing out the serving hatches, and passing through the hotel dining room where a few late guests were still breakfasting, and tables were already being set up for luncheon.

'It is so.' Ramiro said gesturing towards the waitresses. 'Like walking, *si*. One step forward all the time.'

Glass doors opened out onto the foyer, which had a used look. People coming and going. Pyramids of luggage awaiting the attention of the hall porters. Michael had stayed in many hotels, and had taken the bustle for granted. Now he had a small insight into the pattern which before had seemed without purpose. It was like being in a grand station, a place for beginnings and endings.

Ramiro piloted him to the reception desk, and catching Mavis Blair's glance, left Michael in her care.

She introduced herself. 'Mrs Renton is engaged at the moment. She suggested you might like to have a walk around. She'll be free in about an hour.'

His heart lightened. For an hour he could postpone any decision he might be called upon to make, and he would find it easier to think, away from all the distractions. The head porter opened the swing doors for him, and he ran down the shallow steps, across the forecourt, now humming with cars and taxis, and in the direction of the sea.

He didn't stop until he reached the boundary fence, and before searching for a gate, he turned to look at the building behind him. Last evening, seeing it for the first time in the dusk, it had seemed to him that it had been imbued with an odd mystical element, perhaps due to the lights which illuminated the walls and gave it the appearance of having withstood for eons.

He knew this wasn't true though. His grandfather had laid the first stone in 1927, and now, forty-two years later, it had only mellowed enough to give it an illusion of age.

He admired the shape. Straight lines, three storeys high, and ornamental turrets at each end. It looked sturdy enough to withstand the strong westerly winds, whipped up to gale force in the winter months.

He found a gate, and leaving the grounds plunged into the soft yielding sand of the dunes. Beyond lay a long and inviting stretch of beach and with a sense of freedom he began to run, heart and feet thrumming in unison.

Breathless, he stopped, and saw a number of horses with riders galloping along at the edge of the incoming tide, kicking up arches of shining spray. He longed to be one of the riders, and vowed that as soon as he was settled he would join them.

Had he made his decision to stay at that moment? Soberly he walked back to the hotel and his interview with his grandmother.

'Michael, love,' she greeted him. 'You were asleep when I left the house this morning. I sent Claire to look after you.' She held out her hand, and he approached her and kissed her cheek.

'She did. And I had a super breakfast.'

He thought she looked different. Perhaps it was the severely cut grey suit with a white jabot at the neck, or perhaps it was merely the setting; the boss at her desk.

She retained his hand in hers.

'Ah, Michael, Michael, I need you.'

'Why? Dad says you don't need anyone.'

She sighed. Did she hide her loneliness so well, that even her son had no notion of the emptiness in her heart created by Gerald's death?

She let go of the boy's hand, and suggested he accompany her on her morning tour of the hotel.

'Super, Gran,' he agreed. 'I want to see everything.'

'I don't want you to be influenced,' she warned. 'As your father says, it is a business.'

'But it's different,' Michael said as he followed her out of the office. 'It's yours. Dad works for a travel agency with branches all over the world.'

'He's very successful,' Sarah reminded with, without having the least idea of the competition in the world of travel. She believed Paul would rise even higher in his chosen career. She only wished he had taken to the hotel business.

Her office was behind the accounts office and Reception. She explained the simple layout of the working area of the hotel which she and Gerald had agonized over all those years ago.

'We've got one chance to get it right,' he'd said. And even Charlie Mullins admired not only the working parts of the hotel, but the general layout for ease of control. In fact, he admitted he'd emulated it in one of his newly built hotels.

Michael was silent as he followed his grandmother through the public rooms. Each lounge served a purpose, and no one could have faulted the furnishings or the decorations.

The ballroom delighted Michael, especially when Sarah suggested he might like to help with the Saturday night dances. The new restaurant, built only seven years ago, after Gerald's death, still pleased Sarah. She had designed it herself, much to Claire's chagrin. But she had consulted Claire and Jim about the public bar, and admitted that she liked the seaside theme they'd chosen.

Sarah explained the plan governing the sixty-five bedrooms, more than half of them *en suite*. At last they arrived at the apartment where Gerald had put in so much loving thought to make it worthy of his wife. After Claire's daughter, Margaret, had been born, Sarah offered the apartment to Claire and Jim, making it easy for Claire to look after the baby, and be on hand if she was needed to help out in the hotel.

Gerald had agreed to this arrangement in view of the fact he had renovated the original gardener's cottage in the grounds, and had suggested that it might be a suitable home for himself and Sarah, now that the children no longer lived with them.

Michael was both impressed and excited by the whole hotel.

Sarah warned. 'You must think carefully about learning the job. It's complex, but so rewarding.'

31

'*You* love it, Gran.'

'It's my life.'

'And if I make it mine?' he asked cautiously.

Before Sarah could reply the door opened and Claire came bustling in. 'I guessed I'd find you here. Well, Michael, how was the grand tour? Your grandmother loves showing the place off; you'd think it was Buckingham Palace.'

Claire was brittle with nervousness. 'Now you are here, we may as well have a drink. Is it a celebration, Michael? Has my mother persuaded you that a hotelier's life is no less exciting than your other options, but safer? Coffee or a drink, Mother?'

'My usual. Michael, what would you like?

'Orange juice please, Gran.'

Claire poured two gin and tonics and a glass of orange juice.

Sarah sat down, placing her glass on a side table. 'What other options?'

'Oh dear, hasn't he told you? He mentioned being a pilot or an explorer or an astronaut. Flies high, does our Michael.'

For a moment Michael thought it was his father speaking. Cutting him down to size, showing him up. He turned to Sarah.

'And why not,' she said equably. 'It proves Michael has the right adventurous spirit. I like that. You know, long ago, when Charlie Mullins and I were kids we used to dream of stowing away on one of the Cunard ships. It was magic to us to see them sailing over the bar. It transported us away from the drudgery of my father's café. I don't expect anyone told you about your great-grandfather's café on the Dock Road.'

Claire frowned. 'Really, Mother, I don't know why you have to hark back to those days, and I'm sure Michael isn't interested.'

32

'Perhaps we are kindred spirits, Michael,' Sarah said.

'She's going to tell you running a hotel is a great adventure. It's not. Be warned, Michael. It's damned hard work, and as for adventure – ?' Claire refilled her empty glass. Her anger was coiled within her, just waiting for the moment of release.

'My dear Claire, I have no intention of persuading Michael against his will. But remember, you wouldn't be put off. At least, not after Jim came on the scene.'

'So that's it!' Her anger was too near the surface. 'You think because I fell in love with Jim, he persuaded me into marriage so he'd have a secure job for life. And I tell you this, Mother. If you've any ideas about getting rid of Jim and me, you'll be unlucky. We haven't worked like stink all these years to be pushed aside. We want what is rightfully ours.'

Michael put down his glass, stood up, and walked out of the room, and out of the hotel. He ran back to Sarah's cottage and opened the door with the key she had given him. He began to pack. His case was almost full when he heard footsteps on the stairs.

Sarah opened the door. 'Running away?' she said.

'Going home.'

He sat down on the bed, suddenly aware of the implication of his words.

'Will you be welcome?'

'About as welcome as I am here.'

'I suppose pilots or explorers or astronauts don't have set-backs. All easy, is it?' She sat down on the bed besides him. 'I've fought my way to where I am now. I need a champion. Understand?' She smiled and took his hand. 'I need you, Michael.'

A champion? That was different. He emptied his case on the bed. 'I stay,' he said.

CHAPTER 4

Sarah's telephone call to her younger daughter, Rachel, left her not only with a feeling of dissatisfaction, but with the thought that once again Rachel was in the middle of a minor crisis.

Rachel's life was a series of highs and lows. Lows predominated.

Rachel's rapturous greeting, 'Oh Mummy, you're home,' didn't fool Sarah. She was needed, and that was of prime importance. She suggested that she visit Rachel the following day.

'Would you like to come with me to Bransfell, Michael? It's time you met your Aunt Rachel and your cousin, Fleur. She's a year younger than you.'

His immediate agreement worried Sarah. Was he already regretting his decision to stay on at the hotel? Perhaps she should have suggested a trial period.

'Dad says Aunt Rachel is soft,' Michael announced, settling himself in the front passenger seat of Sarah's Mercedes.

'Your father's judgement is prejudiced,' Sarah said severely, reversing carefully out of the garage.

Michael was impressed not only by the car which he pronounced to be out of this world, but by Sarah's expert handling of it.

'Dad has a company car and he won't let anyone touch it. Fortunata says if he doesn't buy her one, she'll ask her father. They row about that. Fortunata's father is an arms dealer. I reckon he's a dealer in death.'

Sarah nosed the car out of the driveway, and turning northwards, headed for the motorway. She found Michael's disapproval of Fortunata's father both surprising and interesting.

'Do your friends agree with you?'

'You bet. We don't intend to have our sweet young lives cut short by another war.'

Was freedom no longer an issue worth fighting for, and if it came to the crunch, what then?

'Dad promised I could learn to drive.'

'And so you shall. But not in this car, my dear boy. I'll fix lessons for you in one of the hotel cars.'

'When?'

His eagerness pleased her; his enthusiasm matched her own. Always she had faced each new opportunity as if it were a first adventure. Gerald, much more cautious in his outlook, had envied not only her energy but her supreme confidence. She had accused him of being mother-ridden, hating the autocratic woman who didn't try to hide how much she despised the girl her son had chosen to marry. Michael's mother had never been a problem. She'd been kind and loving. Always the best are taken, Paul had maintained.

'Tell me about Aunt Rachel. Dad says she's quiet as a nun. Mum loved her. She said she belonged to another age. I couldn't quite understand what she meant by that.'

'I know what she meant. She has a contentment of spirit. Very rare these days.'

The journey was gaining in enjoyment for Sarah. She loved the mountains, sharp and clear, shapes she knew, fells already green and inviting. The March winds were cannoning bloated clouds across a sun-bright sky. Summits played along with the wind's game: now you see them, now you don't.

The road followed the curve of the lake, and, turning away, petered out in the village of Bransfell.

It had been just such a March day as this when she had first seen and coveted Verne Cottage. Both she and Gerald were ardent admirers of the Lake District, and it made sense to buy a holiday home there while the children were young.

'The cottage has quite a history, Michael. It belonged to a family called Verne. They occupied it for about two hundred years, and then in 1930 disaster befell them. Their eldest son killed his wife's lover, and the family were so ashamed they moved away. The cottage remained empty until your grandfather bought it in 1935,' Sarah said.

'What happened to them?'

'You must ask Rachel. She's writing Samuel Verne's story. Well, here we are.'

Sarah's critical gaze swept over the cottage as she alighted from the car. It looked spruce on the outside, and the curtains at the windows were fresh. The garden was a sunburst of the Lakeland short-stemmed daffodils. The front door opened and Rachel's daughter Fleur ran along the path to the gate, and bear-hugged her grandmother.

Fleur had inherited the Ashton looks. High forehead, sharp nose, and a thin well-shaped mouth. Her hair was the colour of pale orange tea-roses, growing darker where it curled in the nape of her neck.

'Mother is over at the bookshop. I promised to ring her as soon as you arrived.' Her critical gaze rested on Michael. 'Hullo cousin,' she said.

She led the way into the cottage. Sarah was reassured. She felt more at home here than anywhere else, perhaps because over the years so many happy holidays had been spent in the cottage.

Fleur phoned her mother, and went into the kitchen to make coffee. Sarah followed her. Here were the only changes; new fixtures, a narrow refectory table with matching stools, and a modern gas cooker replaced the old Aga.

'Like it, Gran?'

'Very nice.'

Fleur laughed. 'In other words you preferred it as it was. Dark and inconvenient. The new window was a brilliant idea of Mum's. Look at the cupboards, so roomy.'

Sarah noted the changes. She felt she should have been consulted. After all, the cottage was only on loan to Rachel, and Sarah knew she would have jealously guarded it, if Rachel hadn't left Mark Ashton and needed a place of her own.

Rachel came dashing in, arms outstretched, ready to hold her mother close.

Sarah's heart rejoiced. Rachel always had the knack of giving out affection, of making a person feel special. And there was no one, she admitted, more special to her than her mother.

Impatiently she brushed back her fly-away hair which was for ever falling into her eyes, and holding her mother at arms' length looked at her critically. Satisfied no great change had taken place during the weeks Sarah had been away, she turned her attention to Michael.

'You've grown very like your father,' she said, observing him. 'What do you think, Fleur?'

'Really Mum, I haven't a clue. It's ages since I saw Uncle Paul.' Her gaze settled on Michael, and it was obvious from her expression she approved of his looks. 'Out of my kitchen,' she ordered. 'Lunch will be ready in a few minutes.'

Rachel escorted her mother into the sitting room and busied herself pouring sherry into the Ashton cut glasses unclaimed by Mark.

Sarah prowled round. She loved this room, so full of mementos of the past. Gerald's photograph had pride of place on the mantelpiece; some of his books were still crowded into the bookcase, and one of Gerald's fine pen and ink drawings of the cottage still hung on the wall.

Rachel answered Michael's interested questions about the Verne family until Fleur called out that lunch was ready. Fleur had taken trouble with the table settings. She had massed daffodils in a bowl in the centre, and used matching yellow mats and napkins. The silver was highly polished, and Sarah immediately voiced her appreciation.

Fleur carried in the silver tureen of soup, and placed it before her mother. She handed round hot rolls nestling in a cloth in a woven basket.

'What delicious soup, Fleur. I love home-made soup,' Sarah said with relish.

Fleur's laughter bubbled up and spilled over. 'Don't you recognize it, Gran? Your Chef's recipe. I wheedled it out of him.'

Laughter spun round the table, binding them together as no other emotion could have done.

'You must be a witch,' Sarah said. 'Albert Thornton guards his recipes as fiercely as if they were state secrets. Is your passion for cooking as strong as ever?'

'*Stronger* than ever. I don't want to do anything else.' She collected the dirty plates and took them into the kitchen, and returned with a large brown casserole pot. 'This is my own recipe,' she announced proudly. 'You must all tell me what you think of it. I've also concocted the kind of gooey sweet my darling Gran loves.'

Sarah's happiness rose from the well of her heart. She loved and was loved, and she was content.

Michael's admiration for his cousin increased with each mouthful of food. 'My stepmother should take lessons from you,' he said. 'She's a lousy cook. All oil and spices, I hate it.'

'Doesn't your father complain?' Rachel asked. 'Paul was always a terrible fusspot over his food, wasn't he, Mummy?'

'Complain?' Michael's voice rose. 'If she gave him his boots in gravy he wouldn't utter a word.'

'You must remember Fortunata is Spanish,' Sarah said. 'They have different ways from ours.'

Fleur cleared the table, refusing help, and triumphantly bore in the sweet.

Sarah's eyes lit up. 'I do try and cure myself of my appalling sweet tooth, but all to no avail.'

'Enjoy it, Gran, while you are able.' Fleur cut into the concoction. 'Gran, I was thinking, now I've left school can I come and stay with you?'

'Of course, lass. You and Michael will be good company for each other. But I know what the attraction is – Albert Thornton, my superb chef.'

'How did you guess?' Fleur's happy laugh rang out. She dashed out to the kitchen, returning with a tray of coffee.

'It seems my daughter is set on a catering career,' Rachel said. 'What are your plans, Michael?'

He hesitated and looked across the table at Sarah.

'He's thinking about hotel management,' Sarah said.

There was an extraordinary silence. Rachel frowned and turned to her mother. 'Is that wise?'

'Of course it is,' Fleur said. 'The hotel needs some young blood, and it's time Claire and Jim had a bit of competition.'

'Fleur – ' Rachel frowned. 'You really must learn to hold your tongue.'

'Why? Aren't I allowed to say what I think? We all know

that Aunt Claire isn't going to want anyone else to muscle in on her patch.'

Sarah was troubled. Silently she applauded Fleur's outspokenness. Ever since she had brought Michael back with her, she was acutely aware of Claire's opposition to her plans. Sarah was determined that Michael should have his chance, she considered it his right, but Claire was not willing to have her own and Jim's position undermined.

'Mummy, have you talked to Claire?'

'Why should she?' Fleur said sharply. 'The hotel is Gran's. She can do as she likes. You know, Mum, what Aunt Claire is like. She's selfish and possessive.'

Sarah frowned. 'I don't think that's quite fair. Your aunt and uncle are dedicated – '

'Oh come on. It's Gran who is dedicated to the hotel. It's a success story, and we all know it, and we all like it.'

'Really Fleur, I don't know where you get such mercenary ideas from.' Rachel flushed with annoyance. 'I suppose you've been listening to the Ashtons.'

'My father is quite the most conventional and boring man I know. Only someone like him would imagine heaven lies in the arms of a tart like Else Covett.'

All Sarah's protective instincts surfaced. She couldn't bear to see the expression on Rachel's face. 'You are being rude and unkind to your mother,' she said.

'Mother is an ostrich. It is we young ones who are realistic. Remember, it's the swinging sixties. Times change, and for the better.' She glanced at Rachel, and flung herself into her mother's arms. 'Oh God, Mum. I don't mean to make you unhappy. I promise I won't mention the rotten old Ashtons again.' She kissed Rachel on the cheek and brow. 'There, all right now.'

She turned to Michael. 'Come on, I'll show you the sights of the village. Do you fish? We have a super river chock full of trout.' She laughed. 'Mum doesn't approve of me catching the elusive little beggars. God knows why she married my father – a member of the hunting, fishing and shooting set.'

Their going left an uncomfortable vacuum. Sarah began to clear the dishes. She usually plunged headlong into family arguments, but today she felt a strange flutter in her heart, and she breathed a little faster.

'Fleur doesn't understand. She will, when she falls in love the way I did with Mark.'

Sarah understood. She'd fallen in love with Gerald, with the same impulsive abandon that had driven Rachel into such an unsuitable marriage. She picked up the wedding photograph that was prominently displayed on the wide window sill. How handsome Gerald had looked on that day. He'd been so proud of Rachel on his arm. There had been such an aura of hope and happiness about the seventeen-year-old Rachel, beautiful in her youth. They had wanted her to wait, but Mark was impatient, and Rachel so much in love, and so certain she would always be happy.

Sarah sighed, and put the photograph back. 'I was a fool,' Rachel said, 'I really believed nothing would ever part Mark and me. You warned me, but I wouldn't listen. I wanted Mark and nothing on earth was going to stop me marrying him.'

'Why don't you divorce him? You might meet someone else. You're young enough.'

'It doesn't seem worth the trouble.'

'Rachel, you aren't thinking he'll come back?'

'Oh no, never that.'

As a child, Rachel's delicate skin had always been quick to colour, giving her away when she attempted a lie. The sudden wild rose tinge to her cheeks told its own story now.

Sarah said nothing but gazed out of the window. She

never tired of the view; the descending slope of the fells down to the edge of the road, the moving sheep, and beyond, rising tier on tier, the mountains. The road was still as narrow as in the past, when she'd sat at this window watching for Gerald.

'You love this cottage,' Rachel said, getting up and standing by her mother. 'You'll want it back.'

Startled, Sarah looked up at Rachel. 'Why ever should I want it back?'

'Claire was here. She reminded me it would soon be your sixtieth birthday. She thinks it's time you retired.'

All thoughts of the past fled from Sarah's mind.

'I haven't the slightest intention of retiring.'

'Claire thinks you need to take it easy. You overdo everything. We worry about you, Mummy. The hotel is a terrific responsibility. Claire told me Mr Mullins is offering for it.'

Sarah sat back in her chair. She ached for Gerald. The years since his death had seemed endless. She needed his strength and advice. Was she standing in the way of the family? Had she outlived her usefulness? Immediately a surge of energy possessed her.

Rachel sat down on the wide window sill, and with the light behind her, Sarah wasn't able to see her expression.

'I don't know what to do, Mummy,' she said.

Sarah wrenched her thoughts back to her daughter. She wondered what minor problem was etching lines of worry on Rachel's face.

'Fleur?' she queried.

Rachel shook her head. 'It's Mr Glover. He is selling the bookshop.' The quiver in Rachel's voice warned Sarah her daughter was near to tears. 'I've been thinking and thinking, and there isn't any way out. I can't bear to give it up now. Oh Mummy, I'm safe here.'

Sarah didn't need to ask why Rachel thought she was

safe in Bransfell. The little village off the beaten track was a haven. She was safe from the Ashtons, she was safe from her aggressive sister Claire. Her gentleness could not be violated.

'Does the shop make a profit?'

'Not much,' Rachel confessed, controlling her voice. 'But Mr Glover hasn't bothered about profit until now. He's decided to go and live in Canada with his daughter.'

Rachel sat with bowed head. Sarah's love overflowed for this daughter who seemed so unsuited for the set-backs in life. She admitted both she and Gerald had been over protective. But there hadn't been any way of curing Rachel of her shyness; not even marriage to an extrovert like Mark Ashton had helped her to overcome it.

'I can set you up in a decent shop,' Sarah said. 'Maybe in Kendal or Windermere.'

'Oh no, Mummy, no. I'd hate that. I'm happy in the little shop. I know the customers, they all love the lakes, and everyone says I have built up the best collection of books relating to Lakeland in the district.'

'Does Mr Glover understand the situation?'

'I don't think so. He doesn't really care for Lakeland, and he thinks of the shop as a disposable asset. In fact he has a buyer in view.'

'Perhaps the new owner will keep you as his manageress?'

Miserably Rachel shook her head. 'He won't. I've met him. He isn't interested in Lakeland. He plans changes, extensions. I'm scared stiff Mr Glover will sell it to him.'

Sarah found Rachel's despair unbearable.

'Where does Mr Glover live? I'll talk to him. Mind you, lass, I'm not promising anything.'

Rachel face flushed with relief. 'Oh Mummy, I've been so worried. I asked Claire for help, and she said it was wrong of me to bother you.'

43

'I should have been extremely upset if you hadn't asked me, Rachel.'

'Claire said managing the hotel was a big job. I didn't want to burden you.'

Sarah took Rachel in her arms. 'You foolish, foolish girl,' she murmured, kissing her. 'Now tell me how to get to Glover's house, and try not to hope too much.'

Sarah drove the Mercedes slowly along the narrow village street, and half a mile further on, turned in the gates of Glover's house.

She disliked it on sight. Gerald had taught her the finer points of architecture, and the red brick house was certainly ugly and ungainly. Why red brick, she wondered, descending from the car, when the tawny stones of the county were available?

Mr Glover answered her knock on the door.

'Rachel has just phoned to say you were on the way to see me, Mrs Renton?' He held the door for her to enter a square gloomy hall. Closed doors precluded light. He led the way into a back room and offered her a chair.

Sarah looked round the room with interest. It had a Victorian flavour – solid furniture which included a mahogany desk, bookshelves crammed with books, and one picture. She could not resist studying it closely.

'My wife when she was seventeen. It was painted by an unknown artist. You know, Mrs Renton, I have longed to find out the name of that artist, it is not even initialled, but the essence of my Sylvia is in her expression,' he sighed.

Mr Glover was totally unexpected, and as if guessing what was in her mind he said, 'Some people might call me sentimental. However, Rachel is sympathetic to my quest. Do please, sit down. Can I offer you tea?'

'No thanks. I've just eaten lunch. Did you build this house?' she asked.

His glance was amused. 'You play at matching people up with houses,' he stated. 'Rachel told me her father was an architect. As a matter of fact it was left to me by an uncle. He was a hard-headed Yorkshire man. Tough, bluff and self-opinionated. He made a lot of money out of wool. When he retired he went in for a course of self-education – hence the bookshop. He reckoned it was good business to buy books in bulk – and any books as he felt that knowledge was bound to rub off on him. He spent his lonely evenings reading. After my wife died and my girl went off to Canada I spent as much time as I could with him.'

Sarah pictured the two men sitting in front of a fire in the high old-fashioned grate, discussing the books, making of a second-class relationship, a much closer, warmer one.

'He didn't forget me when it came to the end. And he didn't forget his employees. He prided himself on repaying loyalty, and you know they were a loyal lot. Year after year they visited him, sent him cards, photographs of their grandchildren, even bringing the youngsters to see him.'

Sarah was deeply impressed. She thought loyalty hadn't much relevance in the sixties. And yet here in this ugly house it flourished. She felt sad that if Glover left, the thin thread would be broken.

'Is the house up for sale?'

'No.' He ambled over to a sideboard, and poured sherry into glasses from a decanter displayed on its top.

He carried a glass carefully over to Sarah. 'I'm told you are thinking of retiring. Pity. We need more dynamic women in industry and business.'

'I haven't the least intention of retiring now, and maybe never. I don't understand how such ridiculous rumours get around.'

'I do. Wishful thinking. Don't let them shove you on the scrap heap. From all I hear you've plenty of fight left in you, my dear. Now to business. Your interest is in the shop, I'm sure. Rachel is a grand lass, and she makes a good job of managing it. I'm sorry I had to spring this on her. She's taken it very hard.'

Sarah nodded. 'I understand you have a buyer?'

'We haven't closed the deal.'

'Good. I'd like to look at the accounts.'

Glover hesitated. 'This chap is keen. To be truthful, Mrs Renton, I want it off my hands. I feel bad about Rachel, but – '

Sarah's determination hardened. She had visions of Rachel's total collapse if she failed her. She began to feel she wasn't in command. 'What's your asking price?' she said.

Immediately they were both on familiar ground. It was in their northern blood to strike a good bargain. They enjoyed the preliminary skirmish; the talk of stock, turnover, figures, sales. It was all there being assimilated, and processed into value and worth.

Sarah understood the game as clearly as Glover. She knew when to move the counter forward, and when to retreat. Her blood tingled with excitement. She forgot she was only bargaining over a small bookshop; the acquisition was important to her, not so much for Rachel's sake, as for her own satisfaction.

And Glover played her along. He was as old a hand as was she at this dangerously exciting game. At length a bargain was struck; their clasped hands were their bond. Theirs was the old way of settling a bargain and was more binding than any legal documents.

'Now,' Glover said, refilling their glasses, 'I know you use Verne Cottage as a holiday home, and I am wondering if Rachel would like to live here while I'm away.' He fetched a tin of biscuits and offered it to Sarah. 'Arrowroot, my dear, Good for the digestion.'

'It's true all the family use the cottage at various times,

46

but I don't think Rachel will want to move. However, I'll pass on your kind offer.' Sarah finished drinking her sherry and put down the glass. 'Suppose I hadn't agreed to buy the shop, would you still have offered Rachel the house?'

'Yes,' he said, glancing up at the picture of his wife. 'She would have approved. Rachel has the same sweet contented nature, and I would have walked through fire for Sylvia.'

Sarah stood up and held out her hand. Glover grasped it tightly. 'I know how you feel,' she said.

'I think we understand each other very well,' Glover said, as he showed her out.

CHAPTER 5

Claire and Jim O'Hara faced each other across the desk in Sarah's office. For the first time since her marriage Claire observed Jim dispassionately. He was even handsomer at forty-eight than he had been when she married him twenty-two years ago. He sat back in Sarah's chair, elegantly trousered legs crossed, one of the small dark cigars he'd recently elected to smoke in the corner of his sensuous mouth. His thick fair hair was vaguely sprinkled with grey; his features had sharpened, but his eyes were as brilliant as ever; and the slight Irish intonation in his voice, inherited from his father, had increased, whether by accident or design, Claire wasn't sure.

He had developed a kind of defensive arrogance; a realization that he considered himself a person of consequence in his own right, and not just a Renton hanger-on.

Sarah's holiday had increased his taste for power. During her absence he'd enjoyed the absolute management of the hotel. In spite of Sarah's insistence that Claire had an equal say in any decision to be made, in most cases he hadn't consulted her. At first, testing the water as it were, he had made the excuse that she hadn't been available at the time the decision had to be made. He worked at his popularity, both with the guests and the staff. The guests enjoyed his interest and care, the staff did

48

not. Part of Claire's job was concerned with the welfare of the staff, and she had come to realize that her husband was the cause of most of the staff's dissatisfaction.

She was aware of her mother's firm control; only then was there no contention. Sarah overrode some of Jim's decisions, and annoyingly, Sarah was usually right.

Jim crushed out the butt of his cigar in the ashtray. His action was slow and deliberate, and intended to focus Claire's full attention.

'I've had an offer from Charlie Mullins, for both of us,' he said. 'Charlie is building a fabulous new hotel in Barbados.'

'You won't consider it, of course. That would be disloyal, and anyway it's probably one of his sneaky ploys to force Mother's hand.'

'Oh come on, Claire. This is business.'

'It may be to you. To me it's disloyalty.'

'Your ideas are as old-fashioned as your mother's.' Jim eyed his wife dispassionately. 'I'm too good for here.'

Claire sprang to her feet. 'You have to be joking. You'd be nothing without the Rentons. You still are – nothing.'

She moved to the window and turned her back on him, trembling with an emotion she found hard to define. She was only too well aware that the love trap had been sprung; holding her fast until now.

She heard the door behind her open, and close sharply with Jim's characteristic insistence that doors shut off scenes, unpleasantness. Doors gave privacy to his secret desires. Jim had cleverly shut many doors in his life, but had always made sure he was on the right side of them once he had.

Claire wished she hadn't come to realize her marriage was as featureless as the long stretch of smooth sand edging the sea, receiving the water unmoved, rejecting it with regularity. The first months of happiness had ended with

49

Margaret's birth. She'd pretended for so long all was well; hiding her disappointment from Sarah's sharp eyes. Sarah knew all right. But she hadn't said I told you so.

Claire's despondency was short-lived. A glance in the mirror assured her that her looks were undiminished. Lately she had opted to buy her clothes at a new exclusive boutique in Liverpool. The proprietor, an ex-model, had a flair for finding the right clothes for her customers, and she considered Claire, so much in the public eye, a good advertisement.

With renewed confidence Claire made her way to the foyer to speed some particularly rich guests on their way. This was one of Sarah's rigid rules. One of the family must always be on hand for departures.

Sarah, returning from her visit to Rachel, entered the foyer, and noted with pleasure how smart Claire looked. Together they made their way to the office.

'I need a drink, Claire,' she said as she settled herself in her chair, moving Jim's ashtray away. 'You?'

Claire nodded, and poured two gin and tonics with a steady hand.

'Well, lass. What's troubling you?' Sarah held up her glass to the light.

Claire shrugged her shoulders. 'Rachel sounded in a panic when she phoned while you were away.'

'Why didn't you tell me she'd phoned? And why tell her not to bother me? Her troubles are mine.'

'I forgot. Anyway she lurches from one silly little crisis to another. She's hopeless. I expect you've sorted her out.'

'If you mean have I been able to restore her to her usual state of contentment. Yes, I have.'

'You always do. All of us. You're like a thick white sauce pouring over us, filling in the cracks. Oh sorry, Mother. It's a bad day.'

'Don't ask me to pour sauce over you, Claire.'

50

'I'm not. I didn't mean – '

'I know what you meant, my dear lass. You think I am no longer indispensable. Both you and Jim resent me hanging on. Suppose I do hand over to you and Jim? What will I do with my life?' There was no self-pity in her voice. She genuinely saw the problem in the cold light of reason. She was not ready for retirement. The thought, to her, was like being told she was in the last stages of an incurable illness. Nevertheless, she was unprepared for Claire's violent reaction.

'If you retire soon, it will save my marriage.'

'Claire!' Sarah felt the colour receding from her cheeks; her heart gave an unaccustomed heavy beat.

'You must know Jim and I aren't happy. He wants complete control of the hotel, and he blames me for not forcing your hand. If you bring Michael into the business, Jim sees himself threatened.'

'But that's ridiculous,' Sarah said.

'You're quick enough to run after Rachel, but you don't care what happens to me.'

'How dare you say that! I've always tried to treat you all alike. But I've thought of you as being the strongest, and having an independent character.'

'You like to call this a family hotel, Mother. But it isn't. It belongs to Sarah Renton exclusively. You haven't the least intention of sharing. Well, I'm sorry, Mother, but I may have to make a choice between you and Jim. You've never really liked him. You know he's ambitious, but he's stayed on here because he believed that eventually you'd hand over to us. He knows now you never will. You intend Michael to be your successor in another five or more years. Well, Jim will never accept Michael and neither will I.'

Jim O'Hara's thoughts were running on similar lines. His precipitate departure from Sarah's office drove him straight to the bar for consolation. He realized he drank whenever he sensed trouble. And right now, he guessed he had to come to a decision. Either he eventually accepted Michael, or he bargained. and the latter course was much more to his liking. Would Claire stick by him? Or would she side with her mother and all that waffle about the infallibility of the Rentons?

He sat down on his usual stool at the bar counter, and glanced round. As yet there were few residents in the small and intimate cocktail bar. He ordered a double whisky.

However much family affairs preoccupied O'Hara, he had taken in at a glance that the bar was as it should be. The table tops were spotless, the ashtrays clean, and the bar itself was correct in every detail. Kellett, the barman, was slicing lemons. He was a first-class barman, and the thought crossed Jim's mind that he could work with him if he could be persuaded to move.

'Do you like working here, Kellett?' he asked abruptly.

'Yes, sir.'

'You could do better. Widen your horizon.'

Kellett's eyes narrowed 'Maybe, maybe not.'

'No ambition? You've been here a few years. Haven't you ever thought of a move?'

'No, Mr O'Hara. Mrs Renton is a good and fair boss. She's done a lot for me, and I wouldn't let her down.'

'You know your worth, then?'

'I know my job, Mr O'Hara. Has Mrs Renton any complaints?'

'No.' Jim shoved his empty glass across the counter and watched Kellett push into the optic twice.

'If Mrs Renton has any complaints about my work, surely she'll tell me herself?'

'I had in mind a much better paid job. Interested?'

'Where?'

'Abroad.'

'I have commitments here.'

Kellett moved down the counter and rinsed a glass. He was aware, as were most of the staff, of O'Hara's ambitions and the dissension between Mrs Renton and her son-in-law. So what was his game?

Kellett disliked Jim O'Hara. Mrs Renton was one of the best. What other boss would have stood by him so steadfastly in his despair over the boy? Hadn't she paid for Kellett to take his son to the best specialist in the north? And now the boy's condition was worsening. Kellett dreaded the ringing of the telephone summoning him to the hospital.

He'd talked to Mrs Renton. 'Don't give up hope, Arthur,' she'd said. 'Take time off. Don't worry about the job. It's yours for as long as you want it.' And not a day passed that she didn't come into the bar to ask after the lad.

Her concern was a comfort. It was a ray of light in the darkness of his spirit, but even to her he could not express the fear that was with him constantly. If his son died, what then?

O'Hara pushed his empty glass across the counter and left. But first he offered Kellett a drink. Surprised, Kellett accepted. 'Chalk it up to my account,' O'Hara had said.

Kellett poured himself a double whisky. He thought it might stop the burning pain in his stomach, but it only increased it. His discomfort crystalized into hatred for O'Hara. He watched him leave the bar, and sourly chalked up the drinks to his account. An account that was never paid.

Jim joined his wife and mother-in-law at the table reserved for the family when they dined in public in the hotel dining room.

Claire looked beautiful. The expensive dress shop knew

their job. Jim was appalled at the size of the bills, and glad that he hadn't to foot the account. Claire was at least independent. Her salary was no less than his, which was one of his gripes.

His mind focused on his wife. Her green dress, a perfect fit, accentuated not only her slenderness, but the auburn tints in her hair, and her large sea-green eyes.

He hated green, and she knew it. It reminded him of his father, and he had no wish to remember his many links to the Emerald Isle.

Jim thought it a pity that green suited Claire so well. Reluctantly he admired the simple round-necked dress, neatly belted, and a full skirt, calf-length. Her emerald pendant and emerald drop earrings completed her elegant ensemble. His glance shifted to his mother-in-law, regal in a long velvet skirt and chiffon blouse. Her commanding presence always seemed to overpower him when they all dined together. In desperation he beckoned to the wine waiter and ordered a bottle of Beaujolais. He did not bother to consult the ladies, in the mistaken idea he was more knowledgeable than they were.

Claire was indifferent, and in any case was drinking mineral water, and Sarah held her peace for the moment. Not easy to do as she looked at her son-in-law without affection. He was the weak link in the family chain, and with Charlie Mullins' recent telephone call fresh in her mind, she waited for the right moment to speak to him. Her glance round the dining room was cause for satisfaction. Some of the guests were frequent visitors, but her gaze lingered on the table occupied by two smart young men absorbed in earnest conversation. She was aware of their identity – Charlie's spies, she dubbed them. She didn't fear the reports placed in front of Charlie.

She knew the food was first class, and the service excellent.

'The lobster is very good tonight, Claire,' she said. 'I understand from Chef he is now having them sent direct from Cornwall.'

'Really!' Claire picked at her chicken supreme.

Sarah's glance lingered on Charlie's spies. Was Charlie so enamoured of the little business, that he'd betray her now? Charlie had always had principles of a kind.

'I took a call from Rachel,' Claire said. 'Michael is staying on at the cottage for a few days. It seems he has the same passion for cycling as Fleur.'

'Good. I want them to be friends. Did Rachel tell you I've bought the bookshop?'

Jim's head shot up. 'Bookshop? You don't mean that grotty little place Rachel is supposed to manage. Good Lord, it must be a dead loss. You're losing your grip, Mother-in-law.'

'Why did you?' Claire asked.

'Rachel has set her heart on it. Mr Glover is giving up, going abroad.'

'Why can't that wretched husband of hers do something for her? I suppose he's too high and mighty for that; and probably too mean.'

'Rachel wouldn't ask him.'

'She's quite happy to sponge on you, Mother.'

Sarah frowned.' I don't think you are being kind or fair to your sister.'

'You're probably right. But Rachel has always been able to wind you round her little finger.'

'You obviously haven't the right technique, darling.' The scorn in Jim's voice hurt Sarah. 'May one ask how much the bookshop cost you, Sarah?'

'You may not. You should know I don't discuss family – '

'But we are family,' Claire interrupted. 'Why not be honest and say you prefer not to tell us.'

'I don't understand you, Claire. You've always begrudged anything I've done for Rachel. You know she's less able to stand on her own feet. And you do have Jim.'

'So I have. I'm inclined to forget. You don't exactly treat me like the most precious thing in your life, do you, Jim? So I couldn't be blamed if I looked elsewhere.'

Jim's colour heightened, and with an angry exclamation he stood up and walked away.

'I don't like to hear you two quarrel, Claire.'

'Sorry. It blurs the family image. But let's be honest, Mother. Even if you don't trust Jim, he's never been disloyal.'

'Until now,' Sarah said softly.

Claire ignored her mother's remark, and summoned the waiter, ordering black coffee.

'I shall have a *bombe glacé*,' Sarah declared, indulging her sweet tooth as a sort of compensation for the dissension which she felt she had unwittingly stirred up.

'You'll put on weight,' Claire said disparagingly.

'When Charlie Mullins and I were kids we treated ourselves to penny cornets on a Saturday,' Sarah said.

'You and Charlie seem to have had a great time.'

'It depends on how you look at it. The view from here might be tinged with nostalgia, but in reality Charlie and I slaved in Dad's café every evening after school.'

Claire's nose wrinkled with distaste. 'I'm sure Mr Mullins won't want to recall – '

'He doesn't forget.'

'Do you trust him?'

'See those two young fellows over there? Charlie's spies, I call them. They will likely report back to Charlie.'

'I think it's disgusting,' Claire said, then finished her coffee and summoned the waiter to refill her cup.

Sarah enjoyed her *bombe glacé* in silence.

Charlie was that part of her past she remembered too

vividly. He'd been at her side when Joe Nealey had been found lying on the Dock Road, run over by a horse and dray. Charlie's arms comforted. Charlie had seen her through the following dreadful days. And Charlie had carried her bag to the convent, kissed her and promised to be around.

But times had changed, and now she and Charlie never shirked their responsibilities. They were both bosses; they knew what it was like to be at the bottom of the heap. Gerald, poor darling, had never understood her concern for their staff. Their way of life had been too remote from his, his view too narrow, and yet his loving kindness had in some way encompassed them.

Sarah sighed.

'You look tired, Mother. I'll walk you across to the cottage.' Claire fetched their coats and arm in arm they walked out into the night.

The April evening had a scented magic. The wind off the sea stirred the senses, and the clumps of daffodils and early tulips shone palely in the light from the lamps flanking the drives. Above were stars, and in the east a thin sliver of moon.

Lights were illuminating the drawn curtains in the cottage windows. Mrs Humphries, the hotel house-keeper, had been there to keep it orderly and she took Mrs Renton's comfort seriously.

Sarah inserted her key in the lock. Ricki the elderly red setter ambled into the hall and, satisfied it was his mistress, returned to the hearthrug and the crackling logs burning cheerily behind the high old-fashioned nursery guard.

'Humphries makes a hobby of you.' Claire noted the lace cloth on the table which was set with cup and saucer and the teapot warming in the hearth. 'Will you be all right?' She kissed her mother.

'Of course, lass, there's plenty of life in the old bitch still.'

'Mother!'

Sarah laughed. She never meant to shock Claire; but sometimes she saw a look in Claire's eyes reminiscent of that old bitch, Gerald's mother. God, how she'd hated the woman, putting up with her for Gerald's sake.

She would have liked to detain Claire. She imagined them sitting in front of the fire, sipping tea. She felt a need to speak of the past, to speculate on the future. To fuse them together in relation to the present. But Claire hurried away, and Sarah boiled the kettle, made tea, and removing the fireguard stretched out her legs to the warmth.

Ricki lolled against her knees. Gerald's dog, bought only a few months before his death. She fondled the dog's head. Gerald had always kept dogs. Much to Sarah's amusement he judged people by their attitude to animals. She remembered the bull mastiff her father had kept as a guard dog. Not a lovable dog, but devoted to his master. After Joe's death the dog pined away.

Here, in this cottage, where she and Gerald had known happiness, she was acutely aware of his presence. She fancied she heard a faint echo of his voice. She ached for the warmth of his arms; she longed for his gentle love-making, roused to passion by her response. Her heart was full of bitter tears. She fed on her memories, as if they could assuage the hunger of desire.

Ricki stirred and barked. Footsteps were heard on the path, and there came a knock on the door. Listening, she heard Jim O'Hara's voice. She let him in. He tossed off his anorak and sat down in a chair by the fire.

'You're playing cat and mouse with me. Is there a drink?' He looked longingly at the drinks cabinet.

'Tea or coffee?'

He shook his head. He felt in his pocket and produced a silver-topped flask, and took a swig.

'You know, don't you? Your pal Charlie Mullins is a two-faced bastard.'

'Hold on. Whatever else Charlie may be, he is not a bastard. His father was a docker. Origin Ireland. He stood in the pen with his mates, and if he got chosen for a day's work the family ate. And if he didn't Charlie washed dishes in my father's café for a shilling which he took home to his Mam. And at the end of the evening my Dad gave Charlie a heaped-up plate of Lancashire hot-pot, and the remainder in a dish to take home.'

'What do you expect me to say? Hurrah for the docker's son who made good, and the skivvy who married the boss's son?'

Sarah was speechless with rage. She felt the colour surging into her face, the breathless quickening of her heartbeat.

'I'll accept your apology on condition you never again speak to me in that manner.'

He took another swig from his flask, and replaced it in his pocket.

'I'm sorry, Sarah. I should talk, I come from the same background as you and Charlie. A Renton hanger-on, as my wife frequently reminds me. My family came over from Ireland at the time of the potato famine. Dad had a miserable job as a clerk in a shipping office, and my mother waited at the gates for his pay packet on a Friday before he could get into the pub. Drink killed him.'

'And it isn't doing you any good, Jim. Knock it off. You've got a future before you.'

'I wonder! You going to throw me out when that whipper-snapper of a grandson of yours is in charge?'

'What's wrong, Jim?' Sarah asked gently. 'You know that I treat all the staff fairly.'

'I'm *family*. Your son-in-law. I expect more than just fairness. You know that Charlie has offered me the managership of the hotel he's building in Barbados?'

She nodded. 'Charlie isn't deceitful. He told me. He thinks by making difficulties, that is, the loss of you and Claire, I might be more inclined to consider his offer for Renton's Royal.'

Their glances met in the flickering firelight.

'Will you sell, Sarah?'

'No.'

'If Claire and I go – '

'Be careful, Jim. Charlie is playing a game. He's old-fashioned, like me. He'll reckon if you aren't loyal to me, you aren't likely to be loyal to him.'

'So what. Do you think I'd be fool enough to go without a legal contract? Not this boy, Sarah. Now if you offered me the kind of contract I have in mind, we could talk business.'

'As Claire's husband – ' Sarah began.

'That's just it. Suppose Claire ups and goes? Where does that leave me? It's not good enough, Sarah. I want a ten-year contract on a rising salary, security of my present position, and a share in the profits.'

'And if I don't agree?'

He shrugged his shoulders and leaning forward touched her knee. 'You will, Sarah, you will. If I go, Claire and Margaret go with me.'

She mustn't let anger overcome her, Sarah reminded herself. She must subdue the ridiculous flutter in her heart. Keep calm, my dearest one, Gerald had always advised.

'No deal,' she said.

'You're a fool. You are putting your pride and obstinacy before the happiness of Claire and Margaret. If you lose them, don't blame me.'

He stood up, shrugged himself into his anorak and left.

Sarah sat unmoving. She conjured up her image of Gerald, letting their mutual love fill every part of her being. Her heart and body called out to him. She shivered with desire.

Gerald's dog stirred, and ambled across to the door, wagging his tail. She let him out into the night. The cold air calmed her, and she looked up at the stars and was comforted.

CHAPTER 6

Michael liked Verne Cottage. Rachel reminded him of his beloved mother; and Fleur was as fresh and lively as the April wind sweeping down from the mountains, smelling of snow and earth; and she set his senses dancing.

Fleur's two hobbies interested Michael. She was a keen botanist, and an enthusiastic cyclist. She indulged in both hobbies constantly.

She took Michael into Kendal to her favourite cycle shop, and advised him on the purchase of a good second-hand bike. Her enthusiasm, and the knowledge that she was a prompt payer encouraged the proprietor to offer a Raleigh he'd been doing up. It was painted red, with dropped handlebars, three speed gear, and new tyres.

'We'll cycle to Gran's,' Fleur suggested a few days later, when she was sure Michael's prowess was up to her standard. 'I want to talk to her.'

Michael agreed reluctantly.

'Come on, Mick.' Fleur was impatient. 'We've everything going for us.'

'I like it here. I like your mother, and going round the countryside with you.'

'Oh Lord, Mick, stir your stumps. Mother's a darling. She loves us being here but she doesn't really need us.

She's stopped running now she's got my awful father out of her blood.'

Michael felt he knew a bit about awful fathers himself.

'Was he always busy like mine – always out chasing the next deal?' he asked sympathetically.

'The next willing female more like! And I doubt Daddy ever chased a deal in his life. Ashtons don't, you see, they just *are*. Wealthy, gifted, handsome . . . and doesn't my father just know it? I can't stand to be around him after the way he treated Mother.'

Michael thought about the way Fleur had described her father. It seemed surprising that fey, gentle Rachel had ever made such a *mésalliance*.

'But I suppose he must have had his good side?' Michael probed. 'I mean, your mother's not an idiot. She wouldn't have married him otherwise.'

Fleur sighed. 'No, I suppose not. He can be charming when he chooses and a lot of fun. When I was small, I remember I was quite a daddy's girl. He was so patient and attentive then. I can remember him riding round the estate for what felt like hours, holding me on the saddle before him and introducing me to everyone we met. It was the most marvellous day, I still think about it sometimes. Funny how things turn out, isn't it?'

'You just grew up,' Michael said diplomatically.

'And he grew daily more arrogant and dismissive. Mother couldn't do a thing right for him or his smug, self-satisfied family. Oh, I think he did love her once but that didn't stop him chipping away, constantly trying to mould her in the Ashton image. He criticized her clothes, the way she entertained their friends, even the way she spoke – and always for her own good, so that she need never feel out of place in the exalted family she'd married into!

'Mother tried to please him, she really did, but the

63

constant criticism undermined her until she was practically afraid of her own shadow. And Daddy likes people who stand up to him – or says he does. He couldn't get that at home so he started to look elsewhere. His latest girlfriend has bottle-blonde hair and skirts up to her armpits. Can't see *her* fitting in at Ashton Hall somehow. But who cares, anwary?'

Michael could see she did, very much, but the conversation was obviously painful to her so he turned it to other things.

Fleur was meticulous in her preparations. The bikes were overhauled, food and clothes packed in the saddle bags, money stowed away, and a route agreed upon.

On the day of their departure, the April weather was a bonus. They waved to Rachel standing wistfully in the doorway, her dressing gown pulled tightly around her.

Michael was reluctant to leave her. He didn't understand the nature of loneliness, but he was moved by Rachel's sad little smile.

The clear blue-green dawn stole colour from the burgeoning hedgerows, and lay coldly on the few remaining drifts of snow high on the fells. But as the sun rose, and the sky blossomed into shades of pink and orange, so did the landscape. Colours brightened, the long narrow B road was intensely white.

'Ever heard of Eostra, goddess of the dawn?' Fleur led the way, and when the road widened slightly, she slowed down for Michael to ride abreast with her. 'I'm her reincarnation.'

Michael laughed. 'You're mad. Potty. Goddesses are legends. You're just a girl, and a scruffy one at that.' His glance swept over her bent back, her bare legs, feet thrust into sandals, and her ragged shorts and stained shirt.

'Dear me, the boy has an eye for fashion. You aren't exactly smart yourself.'

The tyres sang on the hard surface. Their legs rising and falling rhythmically on the pedals set the pace. The countryside slid by in ever-changing patterns and moods. Occasionally a car nosed past them and for a time they were caught in a flock of sheep flowing past and round them in a warm surge. The dogs barked, and the shepherd balancing on a cycle called a cheery greeting.

They stopped for sandwiches and coffee in a field gateway. Michael perched on the top bar, Fleur squatted on the grass and poured coffee from a flask.

'The only time my dad is nostalgic,' Michael said as he bit into a thick ham sandwich, 'is in April. He quotes a line from some poem. "Oh to be in England now that April's here." He doesn't mean it. Mother never quoted poetry but she longed for home. When she was so ill, Gran wanted her flown to London, but she wouldn't come.' He sighed, and held out a piece of bread on the flat of his hand to an inquisitive cow.

Fleur stood up and leaned against Michael. 'I couldn't bear to live anywhere else,' she said.

'Not even for love?'

She hesitated, 'How should I know. I'm not in love.'

'Do reincarnated goddesses fall in love?' he teased.

She pulled him off the gate, and commanded him to pack up the remains of the lunch while she disappeared behind the hedge.

'What's your stepmother like?' Fleur asked Michael as they freewheeled down a gentle slope.

'I don't know.'

'Don't be stupid, Mick. Is she pretty?'

'Sure. She's a Spanish beauty, all dark hair and flashing eyes, and speaks quaint English. Dad's besotted with her.

65

He wanted me out of the way, and jumped at Gran's suggestion to bring me here.'

'Was it Gran's idea you should take up hotel management?'

'I think she and Dad hatched it up between them. She has this obsession that Renton's should keep the flag flying *ad infinitum.* and I'm the last of the Rentons.'

'So you are,' Fleur said thoughtfully. 'Do you see yourself as a hotel proprietor?'

'Gran's selling me the idea without saying anything.'

'Me too. I have ambitions to be a superb chef.'

Their ambitions unrolled before them as surely as they spun along the road. Michael was subtly changing his outlook. Talking to Fleur put a different slant on the future. He began to see it had the majesty of some grand fugue. He was going to make his own way, harness his luck.

And riding up the driveway, he saw Renton's Royal Hotel in a kind of rosy light. Gran had hinted that it was his for the taking, and partnered by Fleur anything seemed possible.

'We'd better go to the side door, or Lady Claire will throw a fit.'

Michael giggled, following Fleur to the side door where they left their cycles in the lobby, and climbed the stairs to the family apartment.

Claire, freshly bathed and dressed for the evening, regarded them with horror.

'What a disreputable pair. I hope no one saw you.'

'If anyone did,' Fleur said, 'they'd think the kind lady was taking pity on a pair of hippies.'

'It isn't a laughing matter, Fleur. Is Mother expecting you?'

'No. We thought it was a good day for cycling, and here we are.'

66

'You really are irresponsible, Fleur. I hope Michael has more sense. You'd better go over to the cottage. Mother is out just at the moment; I'll tell her you are here when she comes back.'

'Dismissed without a word of joy or comfort,' Fleur said, ignoring the pathways, and riding across the lawn which caused mayhem among the white peacocks proudly strutting with all the dignity of dowagers.

'Hang on a sec,' Michael called, stopping to watch one of them unfold a glorious fan of feathers.

'Rentons' good luck. As long as the peacocks are here the Rentons will flourish.'

'I thought they were unlucky.'

'For some, maybe,' Fleur said, 'but not for us. One of our ancestors brought the first pair here, and here they've stayed.'

'So far.' Michael remounted his cycle.

'Proper little Jonah, aren't you?'

Fleur reached the cottage first, and waited impatiently for Michael to unlock the door. 'Toss you for the first bath,' Fleur suggested while she propped her cycle against the wall, and Michael followed suit. He opened the door. Ricki growled and came to investigate. A word and a pat satisfied him, and he returned to the hearthrug in the sitting room.

The house was quiet and welcoming. The evening sun slanted in through the west windows. Fleur took hold of Michael's hand. 'We made it,' she said. 'We're home.'

Mavis Blair took the telephone message from the Northern hospital. Before contacting Arthur Kellett she called Sarah.

'Leave it to me,' Sarah said. She sat still a moment or two to collect her thoughts, and then walked along to the cocktail bar in search of Arthur.

He was just opening up. Immediately he saw her, the colour fled from his cheeks, and he put out a hand to steady himself.

'You're wanted, Arthur, at the hospital.'

'Is it . . .?'

'They didn't say,' Sarah said gently.

She waited a moment until he collected himself.

'Come along. Just lock up the bar. Have you a car?'

He shook his head.

'Just as well, I don't think you are up to driving. Can you send for a friend or relation?'

Again he shook his head.

'Right. We'll use the hotel car.'

'We?' he whispered.

'Do you think I'd let you go alone?'

'But . . .?'

'Come, Arthur. Meet me in the foyer in a few minutes.'

She walked briskly back to Reception, ordered the car, and made her way to Claire's office.

'What's the matter, Mother?' Claire jumped up. 'Are you ill?'

'Bad news, I'm afraid. The hospital has phoned Arthur Kellett to go immediately to see his son. I'm going with him. Can you find a substitute for the cocktail bar?'

'Mother, are you fit?'

'Of course I am, lass.'

Nevertheless, she did feel rather breathless as she hurried back to the foyer where Kellett was waiting.

She made no attempt to talk to him during the journey into the city. He was sitting crouched in the corner of the back seat of the car, a hand over his eyes. His anguish was so positive it affected both Sarah and the driver. He drove fast, taking short-cuts down streets Sarah wasn't aware even existed.

The car accident which had partially paralyzed the boy

had happened several months ago. At first young Alan Kellett had seemed to be making good progress, and Sarah had made sure he consulted the best doctors in the north. It had been a bad time for Arthur. His wife had left him before the accident, and his whole life had been centred round his son.

When they reached the hospital Sarah urged Kellett to go ahead, and indeed he needed no urging. He leapt out of the car and through the doors and out of sight. Sarah followed more leisurely, and took a seat near the lifts.

Waiting was an agony. She sat on the edge of the chair, her thoughts inevitably returning to Gerald. His sudden death had stunned her. She had at first been beyond grief; later it surged like a wild tide to engulf her. And through it all Sefton Taylor had upheld her. He was Gerald's friend and partner, and her friend too. Her children had done their best to comfort her, but even they couldn't reach the core of her loss.

Her driver slumped down on the seat beside her. He was a middle-aged bachelor and had been in charge of the hotel garage for several years. He doted on the cars, and he kept Sarah's Mercedes in tip-top condition.

In a little while he offered to fetch tea, and when he returned Sarah accepted the paper cup gratefully.

'Thanks, Terry. Do you know Arthur's son?'

'A grand lad, Mrs Renton. Mad keen on cars. If he doesn't pull through it will near kill Arthur.'

He disposed of the empty cups and enquired at the desk if there was any news.

'Would you like to speak to the ward sister, Mrs Renton? I'll come up with you.'

Sister assured them everything possible was being done for the boy in Intensive Care. The father was being allowed to stay, and he'd asked if Mrs Renton would contact his sister in London. She handed Sarah a slip of paper with the telephone number.

It seemed there was no more they could do, and Terry piloted her back to the parked car. It was the rush hour, and in spite of Terry's skill, the slow journey back irked her.

Back at the hotel she telephoned Arthur's sister, and extracted a promise from her to come north as soon as possible.

Claire was waiting in the foyer for her, and together they went up in the lift to the apartment.

'Well?' Claire asked.

'A set-back. That's all,' Sarah declared, sinking into a chair and accepting the drink Claire poured for her. 'Were you able to find someone to take over the bar?'

She was gradually returning to the real world; the world in which she held the delicate strands that kept everything running smoothly.

'Jim obliged – reluctantly.'

Sarah sighed.

'He thinks *I* should have gone to the hospital with Kellett. I am supposed to be in charge of the staff.'

'Yes dear, but – '

'It's always the same. The staff ignore me and come running to you.'

Sarah wasn't sure how to deal with this new assault. She felt tired and dispirited and frightened. Yes, frightened. The emotions she aroused in others and suffered herself were too strong, too overpowering.

'I've known Arthur a long time,' she said weakly.

'That's it. They are all so ridiculously loyal to you. Jim suggested to Kellett he could find a better job. That's a joke. Kellett's your man, like all the rest of the staff.'

'Why do you resent their loyalty? To me the staff, as you call them, are my friends. I am concerned for them.'

'Why can't you be more business-like? They work for us, and that's it.'

'No, it isn't,' Sarah said. 'That's only the beginning. I can't explain now, I'm tired. I want a cup of tea. I'm going over to the cottage, and I won't bother coming back tonight.' She stood up a little shakily.

Claire put a hand on her arm. 'I'm sorry, Mother. I lose my temper so easily these days. Perhaps I ought to go away.'

'You need a break,' Sarah said firmly. 'You and Jim can take a little holiday.'

'No. Just me.'

'Why don't you go and stay with Margaret in London? You see so little of her.'

'And so do you. Meanwhile, your two beloved grand-children have turned up looking like down-and-outs. They are over at the cottage.'

Sarah's face lit up. 'I have three beloved grandchildren,' she said with dignity. 'Margaret means as much to me as the others. I've changed my mind, Claire. We'll all three be over for dinner with you and Jim. A family gathering,' she said.

CHAPTER 7

The lone horseman galloped along the ridged sand left by the receding tide.

'My God, he can ride.' Fleur wriggled into a more comfortable position in a depression in the sand dunes. She was moved by the poetry of motion. The man and horse were welded into one perfect whole.

'He's not bad.' Michael focused his binoculars. 'Good Lord, Fleur, it's Ramiro. You know him, he's a commis in the hotel kitchen. He's a Spaniard.'

'That accounts for it.' She was under the impression that all Spaniards were superb horsemen.

'It doesn't account for it at all.'

'Give me the glasses please, Mick.' She focused them on the fast moving rider. She was stirred by an emotion which hurt deep down; a satisfaction as if this was one of the great moments in her life. Ridiculous, of course. A Spaniard on horseback couldn't mean anything to her.

'How much longer do we have to hang about looking for the orchids? I don't believe they grow round here at all,' Michael said irritably.

'Of course they do. And I'm determined to find them. If we look properly we should find them in the patches of creeping willow. They are gorgeous, some white and some purple. We have to look on both the slacks and the slopes of the dunes.'

'Well, I'm not in the mood for orchid hunting. I'm hungry. I'm going back to the hotel for breakfast. Coming?'

Fleur hesitated. 'Okay. If you promise to come back with me later.'

'We can't. Claire is taking us to the shops in Liverpool to fit us out with some smart clothes for the dance tonight.'

'She can fit *you* up.' Fleur stood up. 'I choose my own.'

'If what you are wearing is your choice, you won't get across the doorstep.' Michael's scathing tone brought no response from Fleur. She was immune from criticism except where her cooking was concerned; then she accepted it, but only from someone with superior knowledge like the Renton's Royal Hotel's chef. She had renewed her friendship with him, and was convinced she would learn more from him than any of the classes she was expected to attend.

Claire protested at having to take Fleur and Michael into Liverpool. But Sarah was determined her grandchildren should do her credit at their first public appearance, and she had confidence in Claire's good taste.

Claire bundled them into the car and drove into the city and parked the car. 'We'll go to the tailor's first,' Claire said.

'Don't bother about me.' Fleur was already out of the car. 'I prefer to choose my own clothes.'

'Can I trust you to buy a respectable dress?' Claire asked doubtfully.

'I think I can just about manage that,' Fleur replied as she accepted the proffered notes.

'I shall make you change it if it isn't suitable,' Claire warned. 'Be back here in an hour.' She grabbed Michael's arm and dragged him away.

Fleur laughed, and headed for the nearest bookshop. She was determined to buy a newly published book on the wild flowers to be found on the north-west coast. She was in luck. The book was on display in Smith's, and after she'd bought it she wasted some time browsing.

She also bought a dress and shoes with time to spare and was back at the car before the others.

Claire's eyes widened in horror when she saw the name of the store printed on the bag Fleur carried.

'You didn't – ' Claire began.

'Oh don't be stuffy, Claire. I've money left over, can I keep it?' Fleur flung her shopping onto the back seat and climbed in beside it. 'I bought that super flower book, Michael.'

Claire, settling herself in the driving seat turned round. 'Do you mean you bought a book with the money your grandmother gave you for clothes? Really, Fleur – '

Fleur laughed and Michael joined in.

'Fleur looks good in rags. In fact, better. We can see more of her.'

Lightheartedly she cuffed him. 'Come on, Claire, let's go home. Chef has promised I can help in the kitchen with the buffet.'

Claire pretended to be annoyed that the arrangements for the dance had been dictatorially passed on to Fleur and Michael.

Sarah, as usual, put her finger on the truth. 'It bores you, Claire, and it will give the kids something to think about.'

Claire didn't admit the dances bored her. Once, she'd enjoyed dancing, but not now. Jiving about like lunatics wasn't her style. Nevertheless, she intended to keep control, and also to observe how Fleur and Michael shaped up.

The Young Farmers were a boisterous lot, and Claire had a couple of the porters on hand to keep things civilized. She already knew the names of the trouble makers, and they were quietly removed at the first sign of bad behaviour, before they could spoil the others' enjoyment.

She dressed with her usual care, and made her way to the ballroom. Her first inspection was the buffet laid out in the anteroom, and the waitresses lined up to serve it. When she entered the ballroom, the five-piece band was warming up, and Michael was talking to the leader, who was a pianist of great virtuosity. A pale middle-aged man, he stood up to greet Claire.

She didn't like him. His glance was too speculative, and his straight shoulder-length hair offended her. She admitted the band was good. Why else would she continue to employ them?

'Your nephew is certainly with it. He knows all the latest hits.' His slightly malicious tone brought a faint flush to Claire's cheeks. They were old adversaries; Claire always ignored his advice, choosing the tunes she thought suitable. She glanced round the players; she felt their tight black trousers and their long-sleeved blouses in brilliant colours were highly unsuitable. However, 'The Sandgrounders' were the best players in the district.

And where was Fleur? She came dancing into the room at that moment, and Claire stared at her in amazement. The thigh-length white silk shift with bands of glittering embroidery at neck and hem was so absolutely right. Her long shapely legs were encased in silver tights, and bracelets graced her bare arms.

Michael gasped, and a ripple of approval shook the players.

'Wow! You look terrific.' Michael pulled Fleur onto the floor. 'Come on, let's give it a whirl,' he enthused as the band struck up 'The Wonder of You'.

Claire watched them despondently; she envied their youth, their easy comradeship, and most of all that they were the favoured ones. She and Jim would be superseded unless they did something drastic.

She turned away, surprised to see Sarah standing quietly in the doorway.

'I'm not wrong, Claire. They'll be okay.'

'No experience. They know nothing, how can they match up to us?'

'Of course they can't, yet,' Sarah said sharply.

'And suppose they decide this isn't for them? Where does that leave us? You can't expect Jim and me to hang about and see if they make it. You are being very unfair, Mother. I think it is time we came to some proper arrangement. We do have our rights.'

'Of course you do, Claire. And I shall see you get them.'

Sarah didn't believe in rights, and had certainly never expected any. She had never understood what her rights were, but she understood Claire's insistence that she and Jim should be the inheritors. Her dilemma was clear-cut. If she encouraged Michael and Fleur to make careers of hotel-keeping, was she in reality intending they should inevitably have more responsibility than Claire and Jim?

She was uncomplicated in her reasoning. She did not trust Jim, and she believed that Claire would side with him. But could she trust her grandchildren to carry on the tradition which was so dear to her, and so much a part of her love for Gerald?

Her love for her husband had never dimmed. It had sparked into flame at the moment Gerald had carried her down the stairs in the early morning of the day the Renton house had burnt down forty-three years ago.

She had loved the little attic room at the top of the house, and she had made it her own. She didn't notice the poverty of its furnishings simply because it was so like the room she'd slept in over her father's café.

Although when she had lived there, no matter how frantically she had polished the rickety dressing table, the dresser and the washstand, the smell of frying had still permeated the walls. Whenever she had opened the window at night, the constant clip-clop of the great horses stumbling on the cobbles, dragging their loads from the docks, had pained her with the unfairness of life. She had loved those patient horses, and had lain in wait with a carrot or an apple taken from the store room. The dray drivers knew her. And never once in her presence dared they raise a whip or shout obscenities.

The quiet outside her window at Renton House had at first frightened her. The quality of the silence was broken only by the mewing of seabirds, and when the wind was in the west the rush and sigh of the waves advancing over the sand slowly began to fill a deep need.

The scar left by her father's death, killed by one of the same dray horses she so loved, had so far not healed. She had raged against his death as an outrage against herself. He shouldn't have got drunk. He must have seen and heard the pair of horses lumbering over the cobbles. And yet he had still died.

The removal of herself and her few treasures to the Convent of the Sacred Heart had given her some breathing space. She learnt to hide her feelings, her thoughts, and had gratefully taken the job at Renton House.

She hadn't minded the work, but she had minded Mrs Renton's constant complaints, and Mr Renton's surliness. Gerald's infrequent visits, however, lifted the household to another plane. Cook prepared delicacies, and Sarah sang at her work, and when she could she collected wild flowers, growing in profusion on the dunes. Especially she looked for Hound's tongue and Heartsease pansies, arranging them in jam jars round her room.

The blue vase she'd bought in Paddy's Market for

sixpence she reserved for blooms from the garden, pinched when the gardener was elsewhere, and treasured along with the photograph of herself, aged five, and her parents, snapped on Blackpool promenade. No one ever entered her little room, until the moment Gerald came racing up the narrow, uncarpeted back stairs, calling her name, and shaking her into wakefulness.

'Fire. For God's sake wake up, Sarah!'

She was frozen with fear. She lay stiff as a corpse in her white cotton nightgown, holding the covers tightly about her. Gerald wrenched them back, wrapped her in her old coat snatched from behind the door, and carried her down the stairs and out onto the lawn. They stood in a forlorn little group; Mr Renton supporting his sobbing wife, the cook who had discovered the fire, the gardener and his wife, and Gerald Renton holding Sarah against his heart.

It was the sight of her son comforting the girl that restored Mrs Renton to her vitriolic self.

'Put that girl down,' she shouted. 'Are we to stand here all day?'

She turned away from the burning building. 'My house is being destroyed and you are doing nothing.'

Helmeted firemen were spraying the building. Jets of water, rosy in the light of the rising sun, were directed here and there, tracking each new outbreak.

Gerald put Sarah down. The gardener's wife offered the shelter of her cottage, and she took one of Mrs Renton's arms, motioning to her husband to take the other, and together they part-carried her to the cottage.

Gerald put his arm round his father's shoulders and guided his faltering steps in the same direction. The cook, not knowing what else to do, followed on.

Sarah's sense of the ridiculous came to the rescue. 'What a pathetic lot we look,' she whispered to the cook. 'I'm off.'

Her bare feet left prints on the lawn. Neat little prints barely disturbing the dew as she ran lightly towards the rose garden. Sunken beds, roses in flower, a high surrounding wall. Here she felt a measure of safety. She leapt onto her favourite bench, and peering in the direction of the house, she saw the black smoke still rising. She sat down, folding her legs beneath her and wrapping her cold feet in the hem of her nightgown.

Tears of rage trickled down her cheeks. What now? Where could she go? She dropped her head down between her arms, oblivious to the sounds which, muted, could not penetrate her despair.

'Sarah.'

She lifted her head. Gerald came striding towards her. The sun now risen above the wall slanted onto the paths. Immediately all her senses functioned. She heard a robin singing, she saw a blackbird pulling at a worm, and the sun-warmed scent of the first roses wafted around her.

Gerald sat down beside her. 'What's the matter, Sarah?'

She held up her tear-stained face to meet his glance. She could not know then that that was the moment when Gerald fell totally in love with her.

Did he see the love and longing in her eyes? Perhaps? He took her cold hand in his.

'Don't be afraid. I am here.'

Brave words, comforting words. But Mrs Renton was also here, complaining more bitterly than ever. And Mr Renton, grey-faced with worry and fatigue was also here; and Gerald belonged to them.

'I'll have to go away,' she said. 'And I haven't anywhere to go. I mean my job – '

'Don't be silly, Sarah. You aren't going anywhere except to wherever we land up. It isn't the end of the world, you know. We shall rebuild Renton House when we've assessed the damage. So no more tears.'

She didn't want to be comforted, not yet. 'Your mother doesn't like me. She'll get rid of me.'

He shook his head.

'It's so awful for you. Your fine house burning down. You must be angry.'

'Not angry. Sad. Renton House was built over a hundred years ago. The Renton of that time also founded the tea importing business. He used to stand over there on that little rise, and watch his clippers sailing over the bar. And the cargo wasn't just tea. He imported treasures from China or from whatever other places the ships put into port. I hope some of them have been saved for my father's sake. Shall we go and look?'

There was no smoke now staining the pale blue summer sky and the firemen were rolling up their hoses.

The officer spoke to Gerald. 'It's safe enough now, Sir. I'll leave one of my men to help you clear up. The drawing room hasn't been touched. Luckily that massive door kept the flames out. I think you'll be able to salvage a lot of your stuff.'

'That will buck up my father.'

The officer laughed. 'The older generation get so attached to their heirlooms. We see it all the time.'

'Can we go in?'

'I wouldn't for a while. Wait until my men have made absolutely sure the fire isn't smouldering somewhere.'

Sarah listened in silence. She closed her mind to a discussion about insurance and fire assessors. She concentrated on her own treasures.

It was much later in the day before she was allowed to enter the house. She ran up the back stairs. The raging fire had sliced the house in half. But Sarah's room was untouched. Her treasures were exactly in the places she'd left them. She picked up the photograph and the empty blue vase and held them to her heart.

CHAPTER 8

The friendship between Fleur and Michael deepened imperceptibly. There was nothing sexual about it; more a fusing of ideas, hopes and ambitions. And most of all a love for their grandmother.

'She needs us,' Michael said.

'Don't be an idiot, Mick. She's stronger than all of us put together. Don't you understand, it isn't actually us she needs; we are part of her dream, her ambition, her pledge to the past.'

'Sometimes Fleur, I think you are potty.'

'Sometimes Mick, I fear you are too simple. Be careful people don't take advantage of you.'

His swift denial amused Fleur.

Mick needed protection; he was still vulnerable – as she had been, until she'd outgrown that difficult stage with the help of her mother.

She hoped her decision to stay on at the hotel wouldn't hurt Rachel, and with this thought in mind she telephoned her.

As always Rachel was slow to lift the receiver. In her mind's eye Fleur saw her mother putting down her book, looking at the clock, sighing, standing up, hoping the ringing would stop.

Rachel's voice announcing her number was soft and uncertain.

'Mum, it's me.'

'Hullo, darling.' Rachel's voice gained vigour.

'Are you all right?'

'Of course.'

'Mum, I want to stay.'

'Good. That will please my mother.'

'You don't mind?'

'I shall miss you.'

'Shall I come back?'

'Certainly not. It's your life. If learning to be a good cook is what you want, then follow the dictates of your heart and mind. I believe in you.'

'Are you lonely?'

Rachel hesitated. 'A little.'

'Oh Mum.' Fleur's love overflowed.

'I have plenty to do,' Rachel said firmly. 'The shop, and the garden, and the Flower Club. No need to worry about me at all. Give Mother my love,' she said and rang off.

Fleur did worry a little, usually when she was alone slouching on the sands, or messing about in the dunes looking for the elusive orchids. She blamed her father. If he and her mother had stuck out their marriage, she, Fleur, would not be weighed down by a sense of responsibility and duty.

She confided in Michael. 'Mum is kind of helpless.'

'She is not. She's as tough as the rest of the Rentons. My guess is she adopted that role because your father was so dictatorial. Now it's just a habit,' Michael told her reassuringly.

Fleur needed to believe Michael. She wanted her independence with no strings, but the tie between her and her mother was proving to be very difficult to loosen.

But gradually, as the days passed, and she became wholly immersed in her work, her concern for her mother lost prominence. And there was Ramiro too.

At first she had ignored him. And then when she realized he was completely indifferent to her she made the first advances.

His place in the kitchen was defined. Hers was not. Chef treated her with the kind of deference he thought was due to a member of Mrs Renton's family. That is, until Fleur spoke out.

'I'm here to learn the same as any of your commis. I don't care what job I do, but I mean to be as good a chef as you one day.'

She found working with Ramiro disturbing. If they stood side by side chopping vegetables or cleaning salads, and their hands accidently touched, she withdrew hers quickly.

'What do you make of Ramiro?' she asked Michael one afternoon.

'Make of him? What do you mean? He's a good-looking bloke. I don't know him though. Fleur, is he pestering you?'

'Don't be an idiot, Mick. It's just – ' She sighed.

'You can't trust foreigners,' he said decisively. 'Take Fortunata – ' His dislike of his stepmother had in no way abated.

'What's wrong with her?'

Discussing Fortunata took Fleur's mind off the enigma of Ramiro. He avoided her when possible, yet now and again she was aware of his admiring glance, and his seeming coldness intrigued her.

Fleur found no difficulty in settling down into the work of the hotel kitchen. She insisted on taking her turn on the roster, which meant split duties.

She and Michael continued to live at the cottage, because she knew this gave pleasure to her grandmother.

Fleur also enjoyed the strict routine to which she was now subjected. She discovered that the variation in her working hours lent an interest to her day. Her leisure hours were all the more precious. When she and Michael were free at the same time, they cycled along the coast, and Michael once again reminded Sarah she had promised he could learn to drive a car. Fleur had an elementary knowledge, having persuaded her mother to give her a few lessons, and she too wanted to pass her driving test.

Swimming was becoming their real passion of the moment however and the hotel's indoor heated swimming pool was the main attraction of each day.

The pool was the last building designed by Gerald before his death. It was reached by a covered pathway from a side door in the hotel. Gerald had conceived the building on a grand scale. He had envisaged a kind of modern Roman bath; the glassed-in walkway round the pool was wide and supported by tall white columns. A profusion of water-loving plants gave an impression of verdant greenness, and the tiny fountains throwing up clear jets of water among the foliage pattered back into stone basins.

Sarah loved the place, and often joined the guests for a drink from the bar on a balcony above the pool.

It was one of the duties of the night porter to open the doors and make sure the water was clear and free of rubbish.

Often in the early morning, Fleur had the pool to herself.

However, one morning she was nonplussed to find a swimmer already in the pool. She tossed off her robe, and dived into the water from the highest board. She rose to the surface to find Ramiro close by.

'I didn't know it was you,' she said as she shook back her wet hair.

'Good dive,' he said admiringly. 'You will teach me, no?'

'Yes, sure. Do you swim at home?'

'In the sea. No place to learn to dive. I like this pool. Especially when there is no other person here. Except you,' he conceded.

She laughed. 'I wouldn't have thought of you as a loner.' She studied the shape of his head, visible beneath his flattened black hair. His wet, deep-tanned face shone smoothly beneath the lambent lights, and the same lights were reflected in his dark brown eyes.

'A loner,' he repeated. 'Sometimes I seek a time away from others. I belong to a large family. Our house is full of girls. I have six sisters, and they are all musical. My family's needs are very demanding.' He sighed and his expression changed. 'They depend on me.'

He swam away from her with fierce strokes. Uneasily she followed him. He climbed out of the pool, revealing the long tawny length of him, chest and back and powerful things subtly ridged with muscle. Picking up his towel, he rubbed his face and hair.

'Next time,' he said, 'you show me the dive.'

When he had gone, the quiet in the pool seemed almost sinister. Fleur swam on her back, for a while kicking up spray. She was relieved to see Michael hurtling through the doorway.

'Why didn't you wake me, you miserable little worm?' He dived in and, grabbing her legs, pulled her down below the surface. They rose together, and swam several lengths side by side.

She did not tell Michael about her encounter with Ramiro. She sensed an antipathy between them, unaware she was the cause.

Ramiro's changed attitude towards Fleur did not go unnoticed by Chef who was totally aware of the ebb and flow of friendships among his staff. He saw no harm in it. The Spanish boy was lonely. He was proving to be an inspired cook, and Chef had no intention of letting him go. He was well aware also that eventually Ramiro might go back to his own country, but if for any reason he didn't, nothing would suit Chef better.

It didn't, however, take Claire long to note the ripening friendship between Fleur and Ramiro. She immediately made it her business to put a stop to it, unmindful of the fact that a similar kind of interference had driven a rift between herself and her own daughter. Perhaps subconsciously she remembered the quarrel that had driven Margaret away from home, and this influenced her now. Would Fleur take the same course?

Fleur hesitated about accepting her aunt's invitation to a cup of coffee in the apartment. She presumed Sarah would also be present, but when she arrived late, she found only Claire, tight-lipped, pouring coffee from a silver pot, a Renton heirloom. Nervously Fleur helped herself to the biscuits.

'I hope I won't have to trouble Mother, but I think you are getting too friendly with that Spanish boy working in the kitchen.'

Fleur took another biscuit and crunched it loudly.

'He's only an employee. You are family.'

'Honestly, Claire, I don't understand you. Why should you even think of bothering Gran with such a ridiculous matter?'

'He might be getting ideas.'

'Explain.'

'You are being deliberately stupid.'

'Perhaps you think history repeats itself.'

Claire flushed. 'Now you are being insolent.'

Fleur shook her head. 'Oh come on, Claire. You know family affairs are discussed by the family. Both your marriage and Mum's have been well and truly aired. Gran doesn't pretend. She says what she thinks.'

'I suppose you think she judges from a perfect marriage,' Claire sneered. 'How do you know whether she and my father always agreed?'

'Of course I don't. But you know in your heart that they were very happy. Perhaps you are envious?'

Claire's hands clenched, and she stiffened.

'I think you'll be sorry for those words, my girl. In case you've forgotten I hire and sack staff.'

'Are you threatening me?' Fleur said indignantly.

'Certainly not. I am merely pointing out that you can't do as you like now. You are family, and must behave accordingly.'

'What rubbish. Honestly, Claire, some of your ideas come out of the ark.'

'Do you realize Jim and I manage this hotel?'

'Gran – '

'Is the figurehead.'

'I don't believe you. She has her finger on the pulse all the time.'

'Certainly at the moment she has the final say,' Claire conceded. 'But her retirement is under consideration.' Claire's eyes glittered; she thrust out her chin, and a little niggle of fear sent a shiver down Fleur's back.

'I think you and Uncle Jim are the only ones considering it. Wishful thinking, I call it.'

'You can call it anything you like. But I assure you when Mother hands over to us, things will be different.'

Fleur's spirit was deflated. She realized that neither she nor Michael had a future in the hotel if Claire and Jim had their way. She began to reconsider her position. She tried to recall conversations she'd had with her grandmother, and on no occasion had Sarah intimated there was anything other than a bright future for herself and Michael if they applied themselves to learning their jobs.

Nevertheless the uncertainty Claire had raised troubled

Fleur so much she lost concentration later when she was working in the kitchen.

'I've shown you twice how to make Béchamel sauce,' Chef said crossly when she suddenly found herself at a loss with her efforts. 'Is something wrong? Are you changing your mind about being the greatest chef?'

She shook her head.

'Well, pull up your socks or I'll have a word with Mrs Renton.'

'You won't speak to Claire – Mrs O'Hara?' Fleur said urgently.

'Why in hell should I?'

'I thought . . .'

'Sit down, girl.' He indicated the empty table in the staff dining room, and called for a strong pot of tea. He remained silent until the tea was put on the table, and then he poured it out into the waiting mugs.

'What's on your mind?' he asked.

'Nothing,' Fleur said miserably.

'Have you been listening to gossip? Plenty of gossip in a place like this. We live in each others' pockets. Mrs O'Hara – ' He went on thoughtfully. 'A discouraging whisper in your ear perhaps? Take no notice, lass. I've worked here for more than twenty years, and there's been plenty of untruths bandied about. Truth has a shining face.' He liked the phrase so much he repeated it. 'I came here in '47 when Mr Gerald and his partner Mr Sefton Taylor were running the show. At least Mr Sefton was, and he knew his onions all right. Before he joined Mr Gerald he managed his father's high-class restaurant in the city. Old Mr Taylor died about this time, and Sefton sold up and came here. I expect you know all this.'

'Some of it,' Fleur conceded.

'You couldn't find a nicer man than Mr Gerald, but he

wasn't cut out for this kind of life. He did fine at the front of the house, but Mr Sefton was the driving force, and he taught Mrs Renton all he knew. Did you ever meet Mr Sefton?'

'No. I was at boarding school and spent my holidays at the cottage in the Lake District. My father didn't allow Mother and me to visit.'

Chef's expression registered extreme distaste.

'Mr Sefton retired for family reasons a few months after your grandfather died. That would be in '62. We all thought the place would fold up, but not so. Mrs Renton stepped in and took charge although Mr and Mrs O'Hara were already managers.'

Chef stood up. 'There's only one boss in this outfit, and that's your grandmother. And don't you forget it.'

Chef's words were reassuring up to a point. Claire might not be able to drive Michael or herself away, but what about Ramiro?

She mulled over the situation for a day or two before consulting Michael. They were enjoying their afternoon off. The hot May sunshine had brought families to the beach, and Michael and Fleur retreated to the dunes out of sight and sound.

'It's a desert,' Fleur said as she gazed at the long stretch of sand glazed by sunshine. 'Even the sand is hot.' She sifted it through her fingers.

Michael took off his shirt, and threw himself down beside her. 'I'm going home,' he announced.

Fleur stiffened. 'Home? Do your mean Spain and your father and that Fortunata?'

Michael closed his eyes against the intense light. 'We aren't wanted here.'

'Mick,' she said, shaking his arm, 'has Gran – ?'

'Of course not, silly. It's that ape, Jim. He keeps on about how different things will be when Gran retires.'

'She isn't – she isn't.' Fleur couldn't conceal her agitation.

Michael sat up. 'How do you know?'

'I do know she won't give up. This place means too much to her, and she wouldn't have suggested we learn the business if she was intending to abandon us.'

'Suppose Jim and Claire are too strong for her? And there's that character in the background, Charlie Mullins. I'd like to know which side he is on.'

Fleur interlaced her fingers together so tightly they showed white at the knuckles. 'It's up to us to protect her.'

'You say the daftest things, Fleur. We can't even protect ourselves.'

'I know. Claire threatened me.'

Michael grabbed her hands. 'She did what?' he shouted.

'Shush!' Fleur looked round. 'She doesn't approve of us being friendly with Ramiro. She said she was the one who did the hiring and the firing.'

'I don't believe it. She can't get rid of us, and if she starts on Ramiro, we'll make a stink.'

'You mean that, Mick?'

'Sure I do. Talk of the devil – '

Ramiro was walking rapidly along the sand. The water had the sheen of glass, there was scarcely a ripple, and yet it advanced insidiously as if driven by an unseen force.

Michael stood up, and called. The boy froze, turned, and then came to life. He ran towards them.

He was clutching a crumpled letter in his hand, and seemed very agitated. He sat down beside Fleur. She noticed his hand was shaking as he bundled the airmail letter into his jeans pocket.

'Are you all right?' she asked gently. 'Have you had bad news from home?'

Visibly Ramiro pulled himself together. 'It is nothing. Just a little upset, it will pass. Excuse me please. I have to write a letter to my father before I go on duty.' He regained the sands, and began to run until he was lost to sight.

'I wonder – ' Michael said. 'He doesn't usually behave so oddly.'

'Is it possible Claire has upset him?'

'Someone or something has. I think he would have told us if Claire had done her threatening act.'

'We must find out,' Fleur said. 'We are his only friends here and if he's in any trouble it's up to us to look out for him.'

'You like the bloke, don't you, Fleur? Perhaps Claire was right to warn you off. We don't want any more foreigners in the family.'

'You are ridiculous, Mick. Just because you can't stand Fortunata doesn't mean all foreigners are like her.' She sat up and clasped her arms round her knees. 'I do like Ramiro,' she said defiantly.

'Well, for God's sake, don't fall in love with him.'

'Why not? There aren't any rules about falling in love.'

'Of course there aren't, stupid. It's just – well – ' He fished around for words to convey his feelings. 'I guess lots of girls fancy Ramiro. He looks like a film star, he's kind and amusing. But the fact is, Fleur, I don't trust him.'

'Why ever not?' she said indignantly.

'It's just a feeling – '

'You are stupid, Mick. He's a loner. Homesick, perhaps.'

'All I'm saying, my sweet cousin, is watch it. And that includes our Aunt Claire.' He glanced at his wristwatch. 'Gosh, is that the time? Terry promised to let me drive the hotel car into Southport. He says I need lots of practice.'

'I expect I shall pass the driving test before you,' Fleur said, dodging his raised arm.

She watched him bobbing up and down the dunes until he reached the hotel gate, and turned to wave.

She sat on, the brilliant sun burning the skin on her exposed arms and head. She watched the long stretch of sand shimmering in the heat, and the sea, now a milky blue and frilled at the edge with a line of surf.

The beach was filling up with holiday-makers; children shrieking, digging in the firm sand, building romantic castles, filling moats with buckets of water. Deck chairs and wind breaks appeared as if by magic.

She was exhilarated by the movement and colour, and longed to be a part of it. She wished that she and Ramiro were paddling in the sea, arms entwined like the young couple she was watching, so oblivious to everything but themselves.

She sighed, and decided it was time to go. Mick had upset her. Of course she wasn't in love with Ramiro. Nevertheless she realized her liking was trembling on the brink of a deeper feeling, and this was the moment when she must make a decision. By the time she had run back to the hotel, her decision was already made.

CHAPTER 9

Claire boarded the Euston-bound train in Lime Street Station with two missions in mind. First and foremost she must talk to Margaret. Her second reason for the trip to London was nebulous, a formless idea she might or might not pursue.

Settled in a corner of a first-class carriage, she stared out of the window, seeing nothing of the changing face of England flashing by as she wrestled with her problems.

Margaret was, as always, being difficult. It upset Sarah, who defended the closeness of the family even though she was aware it was strongly divided; and in her estimation a divided house fell.

The subject of Margaret's twenty-first birthday had arisen. Sarah was determined to make it an occasion for celebration, and was, in effect, forcing Claire to take action.

'I've written to her,' Claire said. 'She doesn't bother to answer and so she doesn't care.'

'Of course she does. She's working hard,' Sarah declared in the slight tone of envy she adopted when she thought of the chances girls had of getting university education today, chances which were denied her when she was young.

'Well, I don't see why I should run after her.'

Sarah's expression deterred Claire from uttering the further outburst simmering in her thoughts.

'It's ages since you visited Margaret. Why don't you take a day off and go to London?' Sarah suggested.

And so the other mission, born out of desperation, took possession of Claire's mind.

Euston Station was busy with Saturday holiday-makers, but Claire had no difficulty in obtaining a taxi outside the station.

She instructed the driver to take her to Margaret's flat in Tavley Street, Pimlico. Claire paid the fare, and stood on the pavement a moment before ascending the two steps up to the front door. She noted the outside of the house urgently needed painting, and determined to tackle the landlord. She'd tried to persuade Margaret to rent a flat nearer to the university, but she had to admit that the flat in this converted Victorian house had character, retaining the high corniced ceilings, long sash windows and marble fireplaces so typical of the time. It also met exactly Margaret's requirements.

She answered Claire's ring almost immediately. She was wearing a Chinese housecoat embroidered with dragons and Claire had the feeling that she wasn't expected.

'Hi Mum.' Margaret drew her into the entrance hall.

'Did you get my letter? Were you expecting me? I do wish you'd have the telephone installed. It's so inconvenient.'

Margaret, taller than Claire, brown-haired, and dark-eyed, smiled. 'Yes, I was expecting you, and please, don't bring up the battle of the telephone now. Come on in.' She bent to kiss Claire's cheek. 'Coffee is ready.'

The rooms opened out of the square hall. Claire followed Margaret to the sitting room, but proceeded no further than the doorway. She was totally nonplussed by the presence of the young man standing by the window.

'I expected you to be alone,' Claire said peevishly.

'Oh, Peter dropped in unexpectedly,' Margaret said carelessly.

He turned round and came towards Claire, holding out his hand. 'I'm Peter Lovell,' he said, grasping Claire's hand firmly, 'It's a pleasure to meet you, Mrs O'Hara.'

Claire sat down, putting her large black leather handbag beside her and, carefully rolling her gloves into a ball, fitted them into a pocket of her black loose coat.

'Be a love, Peter, and bring in the coffee, it's all ready.'

Claire refused to relax. 'I do think you should have arranged for us to be alone. There are family matters I want to discuss with you. Do you realize we hardly ever see each other?'

'Oh I do. But Peter . . .'

'Does he live here?' Claire interrupted.

'Would it bother you if he did?'

'Really Margaret, I've only been here a few minutes and you are picking a quarrel already.'

'Sorry, Mother. As a matter of fact he doesn't live here. We are just good friends, and have the same interests.'

Claire's relief was obvious. 'Your father was against your living here alone.'

'Doesn't he trust me?'

'Of course he does. Perhaps he's over-protective.'

'You're joking. He resents me being independent, and attending university, and having to pay the rent of this flat.'

'That's not true. He isn't small-minded. I do wish you'd try and see his point of view.'

'I do. And I don't like it.'

Peter pushed open the door, carrying a tray. 'You need a new percolator, Mag. That old thing is temperamental.' He placed a mug of coffee on a table beside Claire and offered her a biscuit from a tin.

'Am I interrupting something?' Peter asked, glancing from mother to daughter.

'Nothing at all,' Margaret smiled sweetly, and turned back to her mother.

'Gran sent me postcards from Spain. Is she home yet?'

'She cut short her holiday. She imagines your father and I are incapable of running the hotel in her absence. She sent her love, and this.' Claire pulled an envelope out of her handbag.

Margaret tore it open and a cheque fluttered to the floor. Peter picked it up and whistled.

'Some grandmother!' He handed it to Margaret. 'Mine believes in austerity, saving, and sticking to what you've got. She's a tight old girl, and won't part with anything.'

'Not totally true, Pete. She does contribute to your living expenses.'

'And how do I live? Flat-broke most of the time, and dependent on the kindness of my friends.'

Claire's speculative glance rested on Peter. She supposed he was good-looking in a rangy, wild way. His thick fair hair needed cutting, and she thought his incipient beard off-putting.

'Pete exaggerates. It's his own fault he's impecunious. He's a big spender,' Margaret said.

Claire wondered why Margaret always attracted unsuitable boyfriends. She was so level-headed about other matters. She was reading Mathematics and her chosen career was in accountancy.

Sarah still hoped that Margaret would eventually decide to put her talent for figures at the disposal of Renton's Royal. Claire doubted it though. She was still not forgiven for breaking up Margaret's affair with Lewis – a man fifteen years Margaret's senior, and awaiting a divorce.

Sarah, surprisingly, had remained on the sidelines, and Claire had resented her unusual lack of involvement, feeling she favoured Margaret.

'Don't interfere,' Sarah had counselled, and now Claire was unable to stop herself falling into the same trap again.

'Are you intending to go into accountancy like Margaret?' she asked Peter.

'No. Languages are my speciality. I intend to work in Europe.'

Claire sighed with relief. That should put him out of Margaret's reach. But in the meantime . . .

'Will your family mind?'

'Not on your life. My parents have split up. I don't belong anywhere.'

Margaret stood up and familiarly ruffled his hair. 'Of course you do. Second home here, and besides, a cry for sympathy won't get you anywhere with Mother.'

He caught hold of her hand, and with a sinking feeling Claire observed the close bond between them.

'You are very lucky to have such a kind and generous daughter, Mrs O'Hara.'

'Oh, Mother doesn't think so. Gran thinks I'm okay. Is she better? I do miss her,' Margaret said wistfully.

'She overworks as usual. She won't listen to me. She's brought Michael back from Spain, and he and Fleur are staying at the cottage with her.'

'Oh great. She'll love that.'

'They are both working in the hotel.'

'You won't want that, will you, Mother? Upset your future plans.'

'I don't know what you mean,' Claire protested and glanced meaningfully in Peter's direction.

'Don't mind him. He's banking on you inviting him to the hotel in the vac. He'll probably get round Gran to give him a holiday job. He thinks it's exciting and romantic. He won't believe me when I tell him working in a hotel is hard graft.'

'Nonsense. Your father and I . . .'

'Are bosses. Well, invite him, and prove it's a life of ease and pleasure.'

Claire's irritation was rapidly turning to anger. She didn't know why Margaret had this capacity for arousing the worst in her.

'If Peter would like to come with you in the holidays,' she said stiffly, 'he's welcome.'

'Your dream come true, Pete.'

'That's very kind of you, Mrs O'Hara. It will be super.'

Claire saw her chance and took it. 'We must fit in his visit to coincide with your twenty-first birthday party.'

'What!' Margaret sprang up, thrusting her fingers through her closely curling hair. 'No party,' she said.

'My dear Margaret . . .' Claire's voice was measured and cool. 'You profess to think the world of your grandmother, and this is her dearest wish. A family party in your honour.'

'I don't want it,' Margaret wailed. 'I hate parties.'

'Sometimes one has to sacrifice one's own desires.'

'I can't stand family parties. We always end up quarrelling.'

'Not in your grandmother's presence. She suggested I come here specially to make arrangements with you, and I'm not leaving until we have drawn up an invitation list.' Claire's patience was ebbing fast. 'Your grandmother suggests a dinner party. Who do you wish to invite other than the family?'

'No one except Pete, and you've already issued an invitation to him.'

'You must have friends – '

'I'll think about it. But I hate the idea and I shall tell Gran so.'

Claire laughed. 'If you imagine you'll get the better of my mother, forget it.'

Margaret said, 'We'll see.'

Having won a small victory, Claire could now afford to be magnanimous. 'How about lunch?' She glanced at her watch. 'I have a few commissions to do in the West End. Would you like to join me?'

Peter smiled, and Claire realized she had underestimated his attractiveness.

'Me too?'

'Of course.'

'Come on, Mag. Get dressed and let's go.'

Margaret's lack of enthusiasm hurt, but, Claire reflected, she was used to both her husband and daughter's moodiness. And as always she ignored it. Peter's apologetic look did nothing to help matters. He collected the coffee mugs and went into the kitchen. Margaret flounced off to the bedroom, and Claire heaved a loud sigh. She cast a despairing glance round the room. The air of neglect annoyed her. The rent of the flat was high enough to cause Jim to grumble, and although the furniture was adequate, Claire had still had to supplement it.

She longed for a drink, and decided they would go to the little Italian restaurant where she was known, and where a tolerable red house wine was available.

'Well,' Margaret said, returning, 'how do I look?'

The red mini-skirted dress suited her. Her long legs were bare, and she wore red sandals.

Claire's approval was more restrained than Peter's, and Claire cut him short by suggesting he tried to get a taxi.

'What's wrong with the Underground?' Margaret said.

'You know I avoid using it. I have very unpleasant childhood memories of lurking on draughty platforms during air raids.'

They moved out onto the sunny pavement. Peter picked up a cruising taxi, and Claire found herself reluctantly liking him. He was enthusiastic, chatting about his studies, his hopes and ambitions. Perhaps after all, he might be good for Margaret, although glancing at her daughter, Claire recognized boredom.

'We thought of going to a film, Mrs O'Hara. Would you care to see Glenda Jackson in "Women in Love"?'

Claire was touched by Peter's invitation. She didn't feel like dragging round the shops and so she accepted on the condition that she paid for the tickets.

Seated in the darkened auditorium, Claire let her mind range over and clarify to her own satisfaction her pressing reason for seeing Charlie Mullins. She came to no clear-cut decision, but nevertheless was determined she wouldn't return home without making an effort to contact him.

Because of the uncertainty which was afflicting her mind, Claire was unable to concentrate on the problems besetting Gudrun and her sister. She was glad when the film ended, and they came out of the cinema.

She offered tea, but both Margaret and Peter seemed to be eager to be away. Peter waylaid a passing taxi, and directed the driver to take Claire to Euston. But as soon as she was out of their sight she redirected the driver to take her to the Westwood Hotel, situated in a short side street off Park Lane.

Charlie Mullins owned it exclusively. It was now part of his large limited company, and was his official residence. The penthouse suite on the fourth floor suited him perfectly. He was proud of it, and he boasted he'd come a long way to be there, and so he had – from a back street in Liverpool's dockland, to the Westwood Hotel, almost in Park Lane.

The uniformed hall porter swung open the glass doors and she crossed the thickly carpeted foyer to the reception desk. Now the actual moment had arrived, she was conscious of the fact that she could still pull back, and the events that might be set in motion by this meeting could be aborted.

She thought, I can pretend it is a social visit, nothing more, and nothing will be changed. She vaguely hoped that Charlie was away, but her enquiry brought an immediate response. Charlie was available and delighted to see her.

She rode up in the private lift to the fourth floor where Charlie opened the gates.

'There you are, my dear Claire.' He took hold of her hand and, drawing her close, kissed her cheek. He guided her to the spacious lounge, and once again she stopped short in the doorway.

The woman dispensing tea rose and held out her hand. 'Charlie tells me you are Sarah Renton's daughter. I knew your father, and Sefton Taylor is a great friend of mine. I'm Lydia Bouchier.'

'Sit down, Claire. Will you have tea?' Charlie said.

Lydia didn't wait for her answer, and was already pouring tea, and offering milk and sugar.

'Lydia is on my board of directors,' Charlie explained as he resumed his seat. 'Her father was a well-known hotelier in Paris.' He laughed. 'It's in her blood.'

Claire was not interested in Lydia's background, but she was impressed by her appearance. Not a hair of her carefully coiffured white hair was out of place. Her make-up accentuated her pink and white complexion, and her blue eyes were deep-set beneath straight brows. She wore a perfectly cut black suit, and she fingered a matched string of pearls.

Lydia took charge of the conversation, chatting about Claire's family with a familiarity which she found infuriating.

'Sefton has a great admiration for your mother. He says she is a remarkable woman. I would so like to meet her.'

Claire thought, If she is expecting me to invite her to Renton's Royal she's unlucky.

'I've recently been staying with Sefton in France. His brother is in poor health, and all the work of the vineyard has fallen on Sefton. He is, of course, an expert on wines. I understand your mother takes his advice on buying wines for your hotel, and you have built up an excellent reputation.'

Claire was beginning to dislike Lydia, and a glance at Charlie confirmed her opinion that he was not pleased with the turn of the conversation. Claire wished Lydia would leave. The longer she stayed the less chance she had for a private talk with Charlie.

At length Lydia glanced at the ormolu clock, exclaimed she was late for an appointment, and made an unhurried departure.

'The trouble with Lydia,' Charlie said, returning from seeing his guest into the lift, 'is she has an extraordinary memory, and too great an interest in other people's affairs, which she turns to good account.'

'I don't like her,' Claire said.

'Neither does your mother. Lydia fancied Gerald, but there was only one woman for him – Sarah.' He opened the drinks cabinet, stocked with a variety of bottles. 'We deserve a drink. Usual?' He poured a generous measure of gin and topped it with tonic and a twist of lemon.

'You remember?' Claire said.

'The mark of a good hotelier.' He put the glass beside her, and sat down with his whisky. 'What's brought you to town; I presume Jim isn't with you?'

She explained about her visit to Margaret, and Sarah's eagerness to hold a family party for her eldest grand-daughter's twenty-first birthday.

'Am I invited?'

'I'm sure Mother will invite you.' She showed no enthusiasm.

'What's on your mind, Claire?' Charlie asked abruptly.

She weighed up her answer carefully. It seemed to her that the future rested on this moment.

'I want a change,' she said.

'A flightless bird,' Charlie said softly.

She looked up sharply. 'What do you mean?'

'I see you, my dear Claire, twixt the devil and the deep

102

blue sea. But I must be honest, if you are looking for help from me, forget it.'

'Why?'

'Obvious, isn't it?' He moved about the room restlessly, and eventually returned to the cabinet to refill their glasses.

'The fight between me and Sarah began a long time ago. In fact from the moment when I asked her to stow away with me on one of the liners sailing from Liverpool. She thought it a daft idea. We were both aged fifteen. God, how I hated our life. I knew there had to be something better, and I wanted it for us. Sarah had romantic ideas of love, and a poor boy from the Pool didn't fit her bill.'

Claire had never before heard him speak so bitterly. It surprised and frightened her; there were dark depths in Charlie Mullins which were beyond her comprehension.

'Don't tell me you love Sarah,' she said. 'More likely you hate her.'

'Hate is akin to love. You should know.'

'Me?' Claire was indignant.

'Haven't you a love-hate relationship with your mother? Why are you here, Claire?'

His direct question cut at the core of her unhappiness. Why *was* she here? What did she want from Charlie Mullins? She'd been so sure of the answers before she faced him. She'd kept the purpose of her visit in the forefront of her mind all during the time Lydia Bouchier was asking her inquisitive questions but now, she was no longer sure of exactly what she wanted.

Charlie was standing at the window, looking down into the street. She cast a sly glance at him, and the thought she had wilfully suppressed was aching to be said: *I want him.*

He turned to look at her. 'What's your problem, Claire? You've never before visited me alone.' His voice held the same tone and timbre as her mother's, the unmistakable

103

Liverpool accent she hated, and before that sound she crumbled.

'I want – a job.'

'My dear Claire – ' the kindliness in his voice angered her – 'you have a job – and a good one. You have helped your mother make Renton's Royal a first-class hotel.'

'No – oh no, Charlie. I have carried out my mother's orders. I have stood by Jim. But now there's no future in it.'

He sat beside her on the sofa, and put an arm round her shoulders, drawing her close, his attitude fatherly. 'Will working for me change anything?'

She felt his lips brush her forehead. She had the wild idea of throwing herself in his arms, forcing him to make love to her, and extracting from him extravagant promises. She pulsed with a desire so strong, she was certain she had communicated it to him.

Almost violently he drew away and stood up.

'I can't give you a job, Claire, now or ever.'

'Why? Are you saying I'm not capable?'

'I don't mean that at all. You are capable of managing a hotel. Sarah has taught you well. But, you see, employing you alone without Jim would cause trouble between Sarah and me. Apart from anything else she would suspect me of using you as a bargaining point.'

'I don't understand,' she floundered. 'Surely I could make it easier for you to force Sarah to sell you our blasted hotel, if that's what you want?'

'You misunderstand me. I need Sarah too.'

Her desire coalesced into a bitter hate. She had to hurt him, take away hope. She stood up. 'My mother would never look at you.'

'You are hardly a judge. However, the offer I made to you and Jim still stands. The hotel in Barbados will be ready for occupation in three months.'

'Don't you understand,' she screamed, 'I want to get away from both of them.'

She picked up her handbag and swept out of the room. She kept her finger on the lift button until it rose to her level, and she clanged the gates closed, then rode down, seething with anger.

She crossed the brightly lit foyer, but paused in consternation in the covered porch. The sky was louring with dark purple clouds, and large drops of rain spotted the pavement. The porter offered to get her a taxi, but she brushed him aside and began to walk in the direction of Park Lane. A crack of thunder heralded a violent downpour, and Claire dodged into the public house on the corner. She felt disorientated; the strong drinks Charlie had given her and the burning anger combined with the storm was having a devastating effect on her.

She shoved aside the press of city men, rolled umbrellas, briefcases and a whiff of expensive after-shave, to reach the counter. There, she squeezed in and ordered a drink, heaved a sigh, and, unable to retreat, remained where she was. After a moment a two she became aware of the man standing alongside her. He was tall, thin, and had the well-used face she associated with adventurers. He was unexpected in this place, and therefore interested her.

'No briefcase,' she said, draining her glass.

'Not my line.'

'Care for a drink?' She opened her handbag, took out her wallet stuffed with notes, and noticing the chap's empty beer glass ordered another gin and tonic for herself and a beer for him.

He did not thank her, but his glance was speculative, and slightly unnerving. She could feel his shoulder pressing against hers, and a slight movement lodged his thigh too close for her liking.

In a gust of self-pity she realized Charlie had failed her,

simply because she had misjudged his intentions. She hadn't realized how deep the bond was between him and Sarah, and her humiliation became almost unbearable. She finished her drink, and pushed her way to the Ladies room. She washed her hands and face in cold water, and applied fresh make-up. But her morale was so shaken, the drinks she'd consumed began to cloud her judgement.

She left the pub by a side door, and stood on the pavement debating whether to return to the Westwood Hotel, and talk again to Charlie. She couldn't bear the thought of returning home with nothing achieved.

The rain was easing off, but the louring clouds made an early dusk of the May evening. Unexpectedly her pride asserted itself. To hell with Charlie, she thought, and crossed the road to the taxi rank. Annoyed that none were parked there, she began to walk along the road in the direction of Oxford Street.

She passed several narrow mews. Gloomy open mouths devoid of life. She quickened her pace, aware that footsteps behind her were drawing closer. She dared not look back. She was excited by fear. It lodged in the pit of her stomach and she felt an ungovernable driving desire to break into a run.

She was grabbed from behind, and frogmarched into the nearest garage entry. Her handbag was wrenched off her arm and a vicious punch sent her reeling against a closed garage door, hitting her head. She slid to the ground. She screamed, and afterwards, as the pain in her head intensified, she was convinced she went on screaming for a long time.

CHAPTER 10

'Gran, have you the seating plan for the golden wedding anniversary lunch?' Michael asked as he breezed into Sarah's office.

'Claire will have it.'

'Her office is locked up, and I've been up to the apartment, and neither she nor Uncle Jim are in.'

Sarah frowned. The Sunday golden wedding anniversary lunch was special. The Fergusens were good customers; and Sarah was pleased they had entrusted her with the arrangements for their big day.

She picked up her bunch of keys, led the way to Claire's office, and opened the door. The desk was neat, and in Sunday's In-tray was the required plan. She handed it to Michael, instructing him to give it to Mrs Lee, the catering manageress.

Prominently placed on the desk was a note in Jim's handwriting. It read: 'Golf match. Back late.'

Sarah studied the week's roster displayed on a notice board. Jim's name was deleted, and the under-manager Clive Booth's name substituted. Sarah felt again, as she had done on many occasions previously, that Jim was taking advantage of his position. She was annoyed because, having discussed the arrangements for this particular event, both Claire and Jim were aware of the importance of the occasion. Mr Fergusen was director of a flourishing store, and because of a long-standing friendship with the Renton family had put a lot of business Sarah's way. She felt both Claire and Jim should have notified her of their intentions, so that she could take charge.

She thought it possible that Jim's absence was intentional, but checking the staff roster once again, she realized that Claire was expecting to oversee the arrangements alone.

So where was she? Surely she'd returned from visiting Margaret, and if not, and she'd stayed overnight, she must have phoned.

Thoughtfully Sarah locked up the office. In Reception she asked to see the list of incoming calls for the past twenty-four hours.

'Something wrong?' Mavis Blair asked.

'Has Mrs O'Hara phoned?'

'If she has, it would be on the list.'

Sarah shook her head. 'If she calls put her straight through to me. I'm going to the Nealey Room now.'

Sarah loved celebrations. She remembered an occasion many years previously when she and Charlie Mullins had been on the outside, onlookers standing in front of one of the Victorian terraced houses in a street off the Dock Road. The christening party was local news. The cake and two bottles of wine were displayed in the front-room window several days before the event. The returning sailor father was heralded by a band, and lots of the kids were given balloons.

In the darkening winter's day she and Charlie had stood in the shadows holding hands, and looking in. Their unspoken thoughts were expressed by their drawing closer together. They never reminded each other of that moment, but they hadn't needed to; some memories remain to hurt for ever.

The Nealey Room was Sarah's tribute to her father, and she would have given much to have him standing beside her at this moment. How he would have loved to be one of the party, laughing, joking, but always watchful that no one was left on the sidelines. She thought how generous his praise would have been for Sarah's flair – the flower arrangements; yellow freesias and white roses, and a centrepiece of fruit decorated with golden ribbons.

Mrs Lee hurried across the room to Sarah's side. Her anxious expression cleared as Sarah approved everything she saw around her.

'Excellent, my dear.'

'I can't find Mrs O'Hara. Chef doesn't know about the cake.'

'One of the party is bringing it,' Sarah said, inspecting the place settings. 'You have the champagne on ice?' she asked the head waiter.

'I have,' he reassured her. 'Will you inspect the wines? Mrs O'Hara left the choice to me.' He led her to a side table. 'I thought a '66 burgundy, and the same year for a white wine. If you remember Mr Taylor particularly recommended that year, and saw we were well stocked.'

Sarah felt a glow of satisfaction. Her well-trained staff were knowledgeable and reliable.

'I couldn't have chosen better myself,' she said.

She was secretly pleased that Claire wasn't here. She loved these moments, which she felt were a kind of triumph, a culmination of hard work and competent preparation which brought the arrangements to perfection.

Michael joined her and together they returned to the foyer. Her consultation with Chef had been early that morning, and she had every confidence in him.

'I ordered a bouquet, Michael. Will you present it to Mrs Fergusen on her arrival.'

He flushed with pleasure. 'Will you be there?'

She nodded. 'You can do it.'

He smiled. And pride filled her heart. He looked so handsome in his dark suit and jaunty bow-tie.

She was called to the restaurant to sort out some bookings, but returned to the foyer just as the Fergusen party arrived.

Michael charmed; Sarah offered her congratulations. Mrs Fergusen insisted on Sarah joining them when the cake, now borne in by one of the family, was cut, and champagne served.

I haven't lost my touch, Sarah thought, and she certainly wasn't ready to retire. She had learnt the hard way. Sefton Taylor's careful tuition had given her confidence and knowledge. But her learning had started much earlier. Her father used to say, 'Serve 'em fish and chips with a smile, lass. Make the customers feel wanted, especially the foreigners.' She hadn't felt like smiling in those days.

She enjoyed a glass of champagne with the Fergusens, and sat down to a late luncheon alone. All morning she'd been hyped up with excitement, but now it was all successfully concluded she felt flat, and her thoughts centred on Claire's extraordinary behaviour. She was glad when Michael joined her.

'Gosh! I'm hungry, Gran.' He sat down. 'Well!'

'You'll do,' she said. Her heart and mind were weightless; Renton's would survive. And if she taught her grandson as well as she'd been taught she could cease to worry.

She had no sooner returned to her office when Clive Booth tapped on the door and entered. She had chosen him from a number of applicants for the job, because he had impressed her with his efficiency and his willingness to fit in. He had been trained in one of the large Blackpool hotels, and had a thorough knowledge of what was required.

'Ah, Clive. Sit down. Is something wrong?'

'The supper in the Nealey Room tonight. Mr O'Hara is due to take over from me. He isn't about, and no one seems to know where he is. I don't like complaining, Mrs Renton, but he is very unfair.'

Sarah pursed her lips. Damn Jim, she thought. His arrogance was increasing, almost as if he was trying to prove to Sarah that he was the boss.

'Fill me in on the details, Clive, please.'

'It's a buffet supper for thirty persons from the golf club. It's a regular booking. They serve themselves, but I need a couple of waitresses for the coffee, and Mr O'Hara or whoever is on duty looks after the drinks. It's been a busy day, Mrs Renton, and I don't think we can ask anyone else to take over.'

She hated being put in the position of asking favours. But Booth knew he had passed the buck from Jim to her.

'Will you do the extra duty?' she asked in the direct manner she always used with the staff. 'I'll ask Michael to give you a hand.'

He smiled, and she thought what a personable young man he was. 'I hope you won't have to cancel a date,' she said. He shook his head.

'You know I don't mind working extra time, but I am finding it very hard to get on with Mr O'Hara. If you could speak to him it might help.'

'Thank you, Clive. I will.' She realized his dissatisfaction might lead to his resignation, and this she must prevent. He was too good a manager to loose.

Her anger against both Claire and Jim was mounting. In a horrible intuitive flash she saw the slow disintegration of Renton's Royal. She felt quite sick at the thought, as if in some mysterious way she had failed Gerald.

She poured herself a drink, and carried it to the open window. The long day was ending in a flashing sunset,

111

reflected brilliantly on the calm sea. She stood there for a while, thoughts turned inward to successive pictures of Gerald, until the ringing of the telephone forced her back to the present.

She picked up the receiver, and Margaret's clear precise voice reached her.

'Gran, how are you? Mum said you are working too hard. I sent a note with her to thank you for the cheque, but I needed to speak to you.'

'Isn't your mother staying with you?'

'Good Lord, no. We put her in a taxi in the West End for Euston.'

'When?' Sarah asked uneasily.

'About six yesterday afternoon. Gran,' Margaret's voice quavered. 'Hasn't she arrived?'

Sarah's heart missed a beat. 'No.'

'She must be home. Are you sure?'

'Don't be silly. Of course I'm sure. Did she mention meeting a friend, Margaret?'

'No, she didn't. Gran, do you think she's had an accident or something?'

Sarah sat down. She felt weak, drained. It was the way Margaret said 'something' that was worrying.

'Oh Gran,' Margaret wailed. 'What shall we do?'

Sarah gathered her wits together. As always in emergencies she was at her best.

'She may have had an accident. Now listen, Margaret. To save you phoning the hospitals ring Inspector Willis at Scotland Yard. He is an old friend of mine. Explain the situation. He'll help, and phone me back as soon as you have any news. Don't panic, love. It will be all right.'

For a few minutes after she'd hung up Sarah sat still. Her heart was thumping, and in spite of her calm instructions to Margaret, she felt an overwhelming desire to scream. Suppose Claire was lying injured somewhere?

No one to help her, and no one to share this with me, she thought grimly.

She telephoned the golf club. It was a few minutes before Jim's voice reached her, and the waiting made her speak more sharply than she intended. She ordered him to come home immediately. He demurred.

'You fool,' she shouted. 'Can't you understand Claire is missing? Anything could have happened to her!'

'Don't be daft, Sarah.' His blurred speech incensed her further. 'Of course she isn't missing. She's probably staying with Margaret.'

Sarah made a great effort to speak calmly. 'Margaret has just telephoned me. She hasn't the faintest idea where Claire is.'

Jim slammed down the receiver. Sarah sat at her desk staring into space. And in an avalanche of memories all the arguments and quarrels rose up to confront her. In this moment, she was convinced that she had failed Claire. She hadn't understood her, and she had never forgiven her for insisting on marrying Jim.

Silently she cried out to Gerald, blaming herself because she had never given Claire the wholehearted love and support she deserved. Her loneliness was like a clamp, she was immobile with terror.

And that was how Fleur found her. 'Gran, for God's sake, what's the matter? Are you ill?'

Fleur's arrival was like the answer to a prayer. Sarah struggled to regain her self-control, but first, momentarily, she allowed herself the luxury and warmth of Fleur's concern, resting in the girl's strong arms.

'I'm not ill, love, just upset. Claire seems to be missing.'

'Missing?' Fleur's incredulous tone brought the relief of tears to Sarah's eyes.

'How do you know?'

'Margaret has just phoned. She thought her mother was

here. She says she put her into a taxi yesterday afternoon in the West End, and instructed the driver to take her to Euston.'

Sarah dabbed her eyes. 'Silly, I know, but I feel it is my fault. I suggested Claire went to visit Margaret.'

'What absolute nonsense,' Fleur said forcefully. 'But I don't understand, even if Claire has had an accident she could have let you know.'

'You don't think she is staying quiet on purpose, or . . .' Sarah couldn't go on. Nightmarish visions of Claire being attacked or kidnapped seemed to stretch like newspaper headlines before her eyes.

'She's more likely trying to bring Jim to heel. They were quarrelling like maniacs the night before she went to London,' Fleur said softly.

Sarah sighed. Perhaps Fleur was right. She gathered her courage and wits, ready for an attack on Jim.

He turned up a few moments later, drunk.

Sarah's anger was finely honed, and contemptuous, but it was Fleur who let fly.

'How dare you worry Gran?' she shouted. 'I heard you quarrelling and I suppose Claire is paying you out.'

'Miss Temper.' Jim grinned fatuously. 'My dear wife is able to look after herself without all this fuss. Honestly, there are times when I wish she'd walk out for good.'

Sarah drew a quick breath, and closing her eyes leant back in her chair. She thought, I hate him, I always have, but until this moment I haven't dared to put the thought into words.

Fleur glared up at Jim. 'She'd be a lot better off if she *did* leave you. I wonder she's put up with you for so long, and that goes for the rest of us too.'

Jim's face contorted with anger. He grabbed hold of Fleur's arm, twisting it behind her back. She screamed. The door flew open and Michael barged in. He pulled

Fleur free, and with a blow to Jim's chin knocked him to the floor. He turned to Sarah. 'For God's sake, what's going on?'

Fleur burst into tears and clung to Michael. He held her tightly, and looked over her head at Sarah. 'Gran?'

Her face was grey, and for the first time, Michael thought with dismay, she looked old. He let go of Fleur, and kneeling by Sarah's side put his arms around her.

'What's the matter, Gran?'

She put a hand on his cheek. The pain in her chest was slowly subsiding.

Fleur answered for her. 'Claire is missing. She hasn't come back from London. Gran is upset and worried.'

'I don't get it. If she's had an accident, surely the hospital would let us know? Doesn't *he* know anything?'

Jim stirred, and hauled himself into a chair.

Sarah said, 'Margaret is trying to find out. I told her to contact Inspector Willis. He'll make a search. If there has been an accident, or . . .' She couldn't continue.

The silence was breathless with conjecture. Time was an enemy, concealing from them the truth. Jim sat with his head in his hands and groaned. Their helplessness bound them together, until the ringing of the telephone tore them apart.

Michael grabbed the receiver. 'Hello, Margaret. What's happened?'

He listened, his glance fixed on first one and then the other of them. No one attempted to take the receiver from him. 'I'll tell her,' he said at last.

He cradled the receiver, and breathed a sigh of relief. 'It's all right, Gran. Claire is in hospital. Apparently she was robbed and knocked unconscious. She's coming round now. Margaret is at the hospital, and she'll phone early tomorrow.'

The colour seeped back into Sarah's cheeks. She didn't try to check the tears running down her cheeks, and it was Fleur who gently wiped them away.

'She's safe, Jim,' Sarah said.

'What in hell was she doing to get attacked?' he asked angrily. 'She's stupid. I thought Margaret would have put her on the train.' He sighed. 'A fuss about nothing,' he muttered.

The Rentons didn't answer; they drew together, as if to protect each other from the outsider.

Sarah stood up shakily. 'Let's go home.' She put a hand on Michael's and Fleur's arms for support.

At the door she paused. 'Are you coming with us, Jim?'

'No thanks.' He heaved himself out of the chair. 'I've had just about as much of the Rentons as I can take for one day. You're all alike – selfish to the core. I don't want to know. Hear me? *I don't want to know.*'

CHAPTER 11

Claire's convalescence was slow. She was kept in hospital for a few days, and then she and Margaret went to Brighton. Jim visited her. At least, he travelled to London and didn't return, and inexplicably and subtly the atmosphere in the hotel changed.

Fleur, ever sensitive, thought it felt like the lifting of a pall. It was as if her aunt and uncle created an aura of fear that fell upon all the members of staff indiscriminately. She tried to put her thoughts into words for Michael, but he scoffed at her probing.

'The truth is they are bloody-minded, and make everyone suffer,' he pronounced.

Ramiro, however, was closely tuned to Fleur's line of thinking. He and Fleur now enjoyed an undisturbed early morning swim in the pool almost every day.

Teaching him to dive gave Fleur pleasure, and she encouraged him to match her own skill. She didn't share Michael's distrust of him, and yet even she felt Ramiro was withholding from her the special part of himself, and that this was responsible for his unpredictable behaviour. Sometimes, as she sat close beside him in the car, seeing his gaze fixed intently on the road ahead, the light but firm control of his sinewy hands upon the wheel, she found herself imagining what it would be like if he turned to her

117

and fixed that gaze, those hands, his fierce, plundering mouth, on her. It always made her shiver. They shared so much, and more importantly, their ambitions were the same. Both were determined to become master chefs, and Fleur secretly imagined them one day working together in their own restaurant, when their long apprenticeship was finished.

She did not speak of this dream to Michael, knowing his allegiance to Renton's Royal was all-pervading. And he was becoming more deeply involved in the running of the hotel in Jim's absence. He liked Clive Booth, who was generously and unobtrusively teaching him the finer points of hotel management.

Sarah approved of the close working relations between Michael and Clive. Relieved of Jim's criticism, Michael was learning voraciously and was happy with the present arrangement.

Fleur remarked to Ramiro on Michael's new-found enthusiasm and keen pleasure in the job.

Ramiro touched Fleur's bare arm. 'For him, it is so. For me, I am happy with you.'

Fleur didn't quite believe him, nor did she think happiness was a part of her own feelings. She feared his moments of remoteness, moments when his eyes glazed with a kind of fear, and she couldn't reach him. That hurt, and she discovered to her dismay that she needed him in a way she had never before experienced.

Meanwhile she was becoming more and more involved with the kitchen staff. Apart from Chef and Ramiro she had an easy working relationship with the commis chefs, and the kitchen hands. She was always willing to help with the preparation of salads and vegetables and even to operate the dishwasher.

There was however one exception, a kitchen porter. Paddy fancied his chances with all the female staff. He was a massive black-haired Irishman, tolerated because of his smile and twinkling blue eyes. He liked to show off his strength, humping around sacks of potatoes and cartons of dry goods with surprising ease; and as he always wore a sleeveless jerkin he made sure his fellow workers were aware of his bulging muscles.

Fleur avoided him; she wasn't afraid of him, but his obvious masculinity was distasteful to her. She had persuaded Chef to let her take over the store-keeping while a replacement was being sought. The stores had an odd fascination for her, she found the shelves of stacked goods satisfying, and took pleasure in keeping a meticulous check on them, and arranging them in date sequence.

It wasn't long before she discovered that there was a pilferer at work; and this, she thought, reflected on her integrity as well, and so she reported her finding to Chef.

The last store-keeper had been careless and too easygoing, and there had been general access to the store rooms, but now Chef ordered the rooms to be locked, and withdrawal dockets given directly to Fleur, who would issue the daily requirements.

Paddy didn't like the new order. He considered the stores his domain, and resented having to ask Fleur for the keys, and disliked her constant checking of the goods as they were delivered.

'You aiming to change things, Miss,' he grumbled while he emptied a sack of potatoes into a bin, and stood, arms akimbo in front of her.

Fleur retreated. 'If you mean am I keeping a stricter check on the goods, yes.'

'Making more money for your grandmother, I suppose. There's them that have it, and them that hasn't.'

Fleur ignored this remark, and said, 'Will you please empty the old carrots out of the bin before you put in the new ones.'

'Perhaps I will, and perhaps I won't. It depends – ' He stepped closer, forcing her back against the wall.

'Kindly do as I ask, Paddy.'

'You ain't the boss – yet. I takes my orders from Chef.'

'Very well, I'll fetch him.'

'Not so fast, Miss. If you ask nice, and give Paddy a big kiss – ' He lurched closer and his hands encircled her arms.

Fleur tried to wriggle out of his grasp, but he grinned and just tightened his grip.

'Let go at once or I'll scream.'

'Scream away, Miss. No one will bother.'

Frustration and anger lent strength to Fleur's vicious kick at Paddy's shins. The grin on his face changed to a look of fury. His lips narrowed, and his brilliant blue eyes glinted in the glare of the electric light. Fleur was aware of the closeness of his face to hers, and an overwhelming unsavoury smell. As he let go of one of her arms, he forced back her head, and his mouth clamped down on hers. She felt nausea and a terrible fear of suffocation, and then as he lifted his head, she drew a quick breath and screamed.

'Shut up, Miss, or I'll shut you up good and proper.'

With her free arm she swept a pyramid of tins off the shelf, and screamed again and again. The door was flung open, and Ramiro was across the room in a flash. He punched Paddy on the chin, shouting, 'Let go of her or I'll break your neck.'

'You and who else?' Paddy sneered as he loosened his hold on Fleur and, catching hold of Ramiro, pinned him back against the wall.

Fleur screamed, and tried to move, but Paddy's bulk and one hand were blocking the way to the door.

'What the hell is going on?' Chef barged into the room. 'Take your dirty hands off Miss Fleur. At once!'

Paddy released Fleur and Ramiro. 'I didn't mean no

harm. A bit of fun; girls like a bit of fun.'

'How dare you put your filthy hands on Miss Fleur? Are you all right, my dear?' Chef put a protective arm round Fleur's shoulders.

Fleur was shivering. 'He kissed me – oh, Chef.'

'Right! You're sacked, *now*.'

'You can't do that,' Paddy exploded. 'I'll get the union – what about my wife and kids?'

'Out – now.'

'I'll speak to the boss. She'll listen.'

'I'm the boss in my kitchen, and you're fired this instant.'

Paddy's defiance hardened. 'You think you're Mr Big. Never fear, I'll get even with you. No one sacks Paddy and gets away with it.'

He kicked a pile of tins out of his way, and slunk out of the room, closely followed by Chef.

Fleur reached out to Ramiro. 'Are you hurt? Oh Ramiro, hold me, hold me.'

His arms pulled her close, so close it seemed that their two hearts were beating as one.

Chef reported the incident to Sarah the next day. His own anger had cooled; nevertheless he hoped Paddy's threats were without foundation.

'I hope I did right, Mrs Renton. I feel as if I was to blame for employing the man in the first place, and allowing him anywhere near Miss Fleur.'

'You did absolutely right sacking him. He's a trouble-maker, isn't he?'

Chef, remembering the furious expression on Paddy's face, nodded.

'Is Fleur all right?'

'She was being comforted by Ramiro.' He looked expectantly at Sarah. 'You do know . . .?'

'Have you any complaints about him?'

'Certainly not. He's a hard worker, a quick learner and determined to succeed. I hope he'll remain with us. He has only a few more months to finish his apprenticeship. I understand his father has a high-class restaurant in Spain.'

'That's so. I've met Señor Rodriguez a number of times, and he is keen for Ramiro to get the proper training.'

'Perhaps it will be for the best if he goes back to Spain when he's finished his training. I mean . . .'

Sarah sighed. 'Thank you, Bert, for coming to me. I trust you to see all's well in the kitchen.'

Some time later, Fleur was still troubled about being the cause of Paddy's instant dismissal.

'I don't think he meant any harm, Gran. He thinks girls can't resist him, and some of the staff do let him take liberties.' She shuddered.

'Chef did the right thing, darling. If he hadn't sacked him, I would have done so.'

'He has a poor down-trodden wife and a gaggle of children – they'll be the ones to suffer.'

'He should have thought of that before he laid a finger on my granddaughter.'

'But,' Fleur protested, 'I was just another girl to him.'

'I know it seems severe, but you can't run a hotel like this without strict discipline. You'll learn that, Fleur. Did it upset you very much?'

Fleur considered. 'I was angry, and then his kiss disgusted me, and I wanted to hit out, and at the moment I was glad Chef told him to leave. Claire is awfully angry about it. She says Chef had no right to interfere.'

'Leave Claire to me,' Sarah said.

Chef's temerity at sacking Paddy without consulting any of the family at last stirred Claire out of the lethargy which had possessed her since the attack.

'He'd no right,' she stormed. 'It's always the same, I get passed over all the time. First by you, and now Chef.'

'That's not true, Claire,' Sarah said mildly.

'Chef should have consulted me. I am the personnel manager, and all staff problems should come to me. But I'm flouted all the time. No one wants or needs me,' she added forlornly and sniffed.

'Don't be silly, Claire. We work as a team, and I'm sure you would have dismissed the man on the spot if you'd found him pestering Fleur.'

'You only think about Fleur and Michael. We don't count any more. I'm sick to death of it.'

'Do try and pull yourself together, Claire. I know you've had a nasty experience, but put it behind you. Neither you nor Jim are pulling your weight, and you keep on about me being overworked. Where is he, by the way?'

'On the golf course. Where else? Driven there by you.'

Claire's animosity hurt Sarah so much, she retreated into herself. She knew her father would have understood. Once when she'd come home from school crying, he'd said, 'Take no notice, lass, what others say. If it's right in your heart, then it's right.'

But this time it was not quite right after all. She felt she had in some way failed Claire, especially when it was clear to all that the mugging was having a deeper effect on Claire than could have been foreseen.

Claire's experience troubled Sarah deeply. And as Claire's despondency increased Sarah tackled Jim about a second opinion.

'Rubbish,' he said. 'You should know what Claire is like if she can't get her own way.'

'I don't understand. No one is putting obstacles in her way here.'

'Not us,' he said impatiently. 'Someone else.'

He refused to be more explicit, and Sarah had no

123

intention of forcing him to tell her. She did, however, take the opportunity to express her disappointment in his slipshod managership.

He was totally unrepentant. 'You keep the reins in your hands. Why should I bother? I advise you to leave Claire alone, she'll come round in time.'

Sarah was angry. She felt as if both Jim and Claire were deliberately making difficulties for her, and, after giving the matter a lot of thought, she decided on action. She was beginning to rely more than ever on Clive Booth. After several weeks of this unsatisfactory stalemate she called Clive into her office, offered him a substantial rise in his salary and a joint managership with Jim. Elated, he accepted, and also agreed to spend more time with Michael who was proving such an apt pupil.

Sarah waited for Jim's fury at her decision. He said nothing, and kept out of her way. She was pleased with the turn of events; the one flaw was the fact that no improvement seemed to be taking place in Claire's condition.

There was no more talk of Sarah's retirement, and for the moment Charlie Mullins was not pressing his offer to buy the hotel.

Sarah's present elation was reminiscent of the first time she realized Renton's Royal was hers. It was not until some time after Gerald's death that she had tried to set aside her grief and take charge. How she'd loved that first moment when, passing through the public rooms, treading the long corridors, taking possession of the office, she'd felt a completion, a pride which she had forced herself to hide and control. All the years before that moment had been a preparation; and she had accepted the responsibility without demur.

Sefton's departure had been a set-back, certainly. 'Sell now,' he'd advised. 'Enjoy life.'

'I do. I'll never sell, this is my way of life.'

'Watch out for the Rentons.'

'What Rentons?' she'd demanded. 'They are all dead. I am the head of the house, and my children will benefit. I will keep it the great hotel it is – for them. You'll see.'

Her son Paul's lack of interest had upset her although in the earlier days Gerald had been philosophical, and had said to her, 'He may turn to the hotel one of these days, but in the meantime we must give him his head.'

'And Rachel?' Sarah had asked.

Sadly Gerald had shaken his head. 'Not a chance, love. She's too shy, too uncertain. Perhaps marrying Mark is right for her. He is strong enough for her to lean on.'

So they had pinned their hopes on Claire, and for the first few years had never been disappointed. Her marriage to Jim consolidated her position, but it was only after Gerald's death that Sarah realized the strength and intensity of Claire's ambition. Sarah didn't delude herself and hide from it; she set about fighting it.

Although Sefton had admitted that the Renton family's influence was still potent, after Gerald's death he had suggested a change of name for the hotel.

'How can you think such a thing? Renton's Royal Hotel it is – for always.' And never once had Sarah regretted that decision.

Recently she'd asked Fleur if she thought another name for the hotel was a good idea.

'Lordy, Gran, you can't even think it. Renton's Royal is right, and there are still a few of us left to carry on.'

Too few, Sarah thought grimly.

As if reading Sarah's thoughts, Fleur said, 'You have Michael and me, and the best is yet to come.'

125

CHAPTER 12

Rachel's arrival at Renton's Royal passed without notice. She parked her car among the others ranged on the tarmac front, walked across the lawn, pausing only to admire the peacocks, and opened the cottage door with her key.

Ricki ambled out to greet her. She loved the old dog. She and her father had shared a passionate regard for animals, and it had been one of the unspoken but understood ties between them.

She had hidden her grief over his death, unable even to share it with Sarah, knowing their aspects of love were different.

Now she was glad of a few peaceful moments alone. It had been hot in the car, and the traffic on the motorway so fast that she had felt she was being carried along against her will. She was relieved to turn off on to the quieter secondary roads and drive at a slower pace.

She decided not to telephone through to the hotel until she'd washed her hands and face and made a cup of coffee and collected her thoughts which had randomly plagued her during the journey. Time enough to talk to Sarah later.

The evidence of Fleur's and Michael's occupation gave her a warm family feeling. Here she felt safe, and this was of paramount importance to her at the moment. She could set aside the misery of the past few days, and gain strength from her mother and daughter.

On impulse she entered Fleur's room, and smiled at the characteristic chaos Fleur appeared to enjoy. Books were spread open on the table; jam jars of specimen flowers were placed on every conceivable space except on the bedside table where a photograph held pride of place.

Idly Rachel picked it up, and stiffened. It was no more than an enlarged snapshot, and yet she suspected the pictured youth meant a lot to Fleur. Who was he? Fleur had always been open about her boyfriends, casually dropping them when she was bored.

Rachel replaced the photo and went down to the kitchen. She made coffee and raided the cake tin, and tried to fit this new development into the situation which was causing her so much heartache. Now she was impatient for her mother to come home.

Sarah was tired. She opened the cottage door, bent down to pat Ricki, and walked into the kitchen.

'Mummy!' Rachel threw her arms round Sarah, and kissed her.

'Hello, darling. What a lovely surprise. Why didn't you let us know you were coming?'

'I just made up my mind this morning. Mummy, are you well? Come and sit down. Have you eaten?'

Sarah smiled at the breathless questions and led the way into the sitting room. 'A cup of tea would be nice. Why didn't you come over to the hotel?'

'It's nicer here. Quiet. I'll make tea.'

When she carried in the tray, they sat silently for a moment or two, smiling, and adjusting to the pleasure of each other's company.

'I needed you, darling,' Sarah said, sipping her tea.

Rachel held back the words she had rehearsed on the

journey. She thought that for once her mother's need might be greater than her own.

'Is something wrong? Claire is home, isn't she?'

Sarah nodded. 'I'm afraid for her. She won't talk to me or Jim or anyone else. I thought perhaps you with your gentle ways could gain her confidence.'

'Claire has never had anything to say to me.'

'But this is different, she's changed. It's as if she's lost faith in herself. Perhaps I'm being foolish, Rachel, but I don't think the shock of having been attacked is the only reason. Something else happened.'

'I'll talk to her, Mummy, if you think it will do any good.'

Sarah sighed, 'Tell me your news.'

Rachel hesitated. She didn't want to burden Sarah further, but she would have to speak of the fear that was with her night and day. The very fact of its unexpectedness and her inability to cope with it had brought her here in desperation today.

'Bobby Brooks phoned me,' Sarah continued. 'He says there is no trouble in transferring the shop to you. He is a very astute solicitor.'

'He wrote to me. You know Mr Glover offered me the house, but I told him I preferred to stay on in the cottage. I want the shop desperately, but . . .' Her voice trailed away.

'What's troubling you, my dearest?'

'Mark.'

Sarah sat up.

'He wants me back. He came to the cottage . . .' Rachel's voice faltered. 'Oh Mummy, just when things seemed to be getting better for me at last. I'd made the break, thought I'd stopped missing him . . . He says I never will. Maybe he's right. I don't know what to do.'

For a moment Sarah was speechless with anger. 'How

dare he? I've never trusted him, or liked any of the Ashton family. You must come here.'

'I can't.'

'Then Fleur must go back with you.'

'No. I won't let him spoil Fleur's life. I thought our quarrels passed over her head, until the day she stood up to him on my behalf. He went off after that. Picked up this woman in a bar he frequents. That shocked me.'

'I knew we shouldn't have let you marry him,' Sarah raged.

'I loved him then,' Rachel said. 'I suppose I still do in a way. He came to tell me his mother is ill, Mark's father is taking her to America for special treatment. He needs me, Mummy.'

'He's no right . . .'

Rachel interrupted. 'But he has. We are still married – no legal separation or divorce. He pointed that out very carefully. He wants Fleur to live with us at Ashton Hall. He was furious when he found out she was working in the hotel.'

Rachel's face was colourless; her brilliant eyes suddenly glazed over with tears.

'He says I'm presuming on your kindness by living in your cottage. I'm depriving you of it. Am I?'

'Of course you aren't.'

'He told me Claire had spoken to him about your retirement.'

Sarah's face flushed. 'How dare she?'

'And he's going to stop the sale of the bookshop.'

Sarah stood up. The adrenalin was flowing; she was itching for a fight.

'I shall phone Bobby Brooks for advice now.'

'You can't. It's Sunday, his office will be closed. Let's wait, Mummy.'

129

Sarah reached for the telephone, flicked over the pages of her private book and dialled a number.

'Bobby,' she queried. 'Sarah here. I must see you urgently.'

She paused. 'No. It won't wait until tomorrow. Fine. We'll expect you.'

Rachel relaxed. 'Do all men do your bidding?' she asked wistfully.

'Not all.'

'I wish I was more like you.'

'I don't. You are gentle and loving like your father.'

Their glances met. 'Don't say it,' Sarah said. 'Don't say the words,' she repeated. 'I've always known his death hurt you as much as it hurt me. But I had to be strong, so much depended on me.'

'It isn't fair,' Rachel cried as she flung her arms round her mother and laid her cheek against Sarah's.

'Of course it isn't fair,' Sarah said vigorously. 'Life isn't fair. And why should it be? We have to do the best we can with what we have, for the family.'

'The family matters so much to you. Have we all failed you?'

'Oh no, it is I who have failed you. You and Claire are so unhappy. If I could have foreseen so much, and if Gerald had lived . . .'

'Don't,' Rachel said, taking hold of Sarah's hands. 'The family has been built out of your devotion. We are nothing without you.'

Before Sarah could answer, the front door was flung open, Ricki scrambled to his feet, and Fleur blew in with all the exuberance of youth.

'Mum,' she shouted, and flung herself into Rachel's arms. 'What an absolutely super surprise. Did you know she was coming, Gran? Can you stay? You must. It will be heaven to have you here.'

Rachel disentangled herself and wrinkled her nose. 'What have you been cooking?'

'I stink,' Fleur laughed. 'Don't either of you move one inch while I shower. Gran, what do you think? Chef is going to put the new sweet I've created on the special menu. I've called it Bransfell Delight, and it's really gooey. You'll adore it, Gran.' She whisked out of the room, Ricki following. They heard her voice on the stairs urging the old boy up.

'He sleeps on her bed,' Sarah said. 'I haven't the heart to forbid it.'

'Be thankful it isn't an injured hedgehog or an abandoned fox cub. We even had a family of rabbits, seven of them, and she was heartbroken when they ate their way out of the hutch.'

'I feel I'm cheating you, Rachel. She gives me so much pleasure.'

'She's happy and that's everything. Mummy, who's the boy?'

'What boy?'

'She has his photograph on the bedside table. It's signed, to Fleur from Ramiro.'

'Ah yes, Ramiro. Another of her protégés, so she says. He's a Spaniard. I've met his father; he keeps a restaurant, and begged me to take the boy to work under my chef. Fleur says he's lonely, and they are just friends.'

'He's very handsome. Do you believe her?'

'Come, Rachel. What seventeen-year-old girl is going to admit she's madly in love?'

Rachel smiled, remembering.

'Chef thinks very highly of him. Apparently he has a flair for cookery. Chef says Ramiro is troubled by the siege of Gibraltar, and is afraid the boy may decide to go home.'

Rachel sighed.

'Don't worry, she's a sensible girl, Rachel. And be sure I

keep an eye on her and all the young girls in my charge.'

Once more the front door opened and Claire called from the hall. She walked into the sitting room, hesitating when she saw Rachel.

She frowned, and her voice was aggressive. 'What's brought you here? Run out of cash?'

'Claire,' Sarah said sharply. 'I won't have you speak to your sister like that.'

'Rachel is a prize scrounger, and you fall for it all the time.'

Rachel faced her sister, her face flushing. 'I don't scrounge. I have no need; Mummy is always generous. Perhaps you don't count the perks you get living here.'

'Please,' Sarah said, 'don't quarrel. Rachel, give me my handbag. Claire, fetch me a glass of water.'

Rachel knelt down beside her mother, shook the pills out of the bottle, and when Claire brought the water she held the glass to her lips.

'It's nothing. Blood pressure just a little too high. It passes immediately.'

'I wish you'd rest more,' Claire said irritably. 'She won't let up, and she's determined to drive Jim and me away, now she's got her precious grandchildren.'

'I don't believe you,' Rachel said. 'You upset her, and she's worried about you. Are you feeling better?'

'I have a headache all the time. But who cares?'

'Don't be silly, Claire. Of course we care.'

Fleur burst into the room. 'I've used masses of bath salts. Smell me now, Mum.' She looked from one to the other. 'Is something wrong?'

'Claire thinks we don't care she's still suffering from her horrible experience. Of course we care. Will it help to talk about it?' Rachel said diffidently.

'There's nothing to talk about. I was robbed, attacked and knocked unconscious. That's it.'

'Are you sure?' Sarah said. 'Perhaps there is something else you can't remember.'

'I remember everything and I don't want to talk about it any more. Is that understood?'

'You must remember your talk with Charlie Mullins before you were attacked. He phoned to speak to you, Gran, and you weren't here so I took the call,' Fleur said suddenly.

'Why can't you mind your own business?' Claire snapped.

'He didn't say it was private. He wanted to know how you were, and hoped you weren't too upset about his refusal.'

Anger flushed Claire's cheeks, and she narrowed her eyes. 'That'll be the day when that obnoxious man upsets me.'

'Refusal,' Sarah lingered over the word. 'Kindly explain, Claire.'

'Why should I? It's between Charlie and me.'

'I don't see why you want another job. I thought you were determined to stay here and get rid of Michael and me,' Fleur piped in.

'Another job,' Sarah repeated. 'Why?'

'Because, Mother, you're making it obvious you find Jim and I no longer fit.'

'Why wouldn't Charlie play?' Fleur asked.

'Because, my dear inquisitive niece, Charlie won't decide on anything without consulting Sarah, except to get his hands on Renton's Royal.'

'He'll never do that,' Fleur said with conviction.

CHAPTER 13

'What do you think, Rachel?'

'I like it.' Rachel toured the almost finished octagonal conservatory. She frowned. 'The design – it seems familiar.'

Sarah laughed. 'Clever lass. It is basically one of your father's designs. Do you think he would have approved?'

Rachel nodded. 'The fountain? I'm not sure . . .'

'My little embellishment. When I was a girl I thought that to own a fountain – a real one – was something I'd never achieve. Charlie used to tease me about it. Fountains aren't for the likes of us, he'd say. And he was right then. I can't wait to show it to him.'

'But he isn't right now,' Rachel said. She leant over the basin to examine the sculptured figure. 'It isn't a dolphin or a mermaid; surely that's not one of my father's designs?'

Sarah laughed. 'Mine,' she said, and she couldn't keep the pride out of her voice. 'I spent hours and hours drawing it, until I thought I had it right. Don't you like it?' she asked anxiously.

Rachel drew back. 'I'm afraid of it. I don't understand what it is supposed to represent. Mummy, don't you think a fish would be more suitable?'

Sarah reached over the empty basin to touch the figure. The stone was cold; its contours were smooth, flowing from a central craggy head, not quite human, not quite animal. The feet were unformed, disappearing into a cavity, from which jets of water would shoot up into the air, and, falling in a kind of veil, transform the stone she'd chosen, aware of the subtle colours it contained.

Sarah put an arm round Rachel. 'Don't let it trouble you. It is a creature of imagination. It has meaning for me.'

Rachel looked surprised. 'Did you mean it for a talking point? An interesting puzzle for the guests? Perhaps when the fountain is playing it will look less fearsome.'

Sarah had expected Rachel, her sensitive and imaginative daughter, to understand what the figure might represent.

Fleur had. 'Your struggle, Gran. Crawling out of the pit and gaining strength and wisdom all the way up to that head raised to look at the stars. I like it. Gran, can I fill the place with plants? I have a plan of the kind I want. I like your idea of upright love-seats, and low tables. We want people to look around and be moved.'

Sarah didn't tell Rachel how completely Fleur's ideas coincided with her own; she said merely that Fleur was thrilled to be able to choose the plants.

'Mind she doesn't introduce frogs into the fountain. A change from coins,' Rachel said.

Sarah laughed. 'Rachel, darling – why should she?'

'She introduced a monster toad into the pool in the Ashton Hall gardens. She was seven at the time. Mark demanded its removal. She refused, and told him that ugliness was in the eye of the beholder.' Rachel's face softened at the memory.

'What did Mark say to that?'

'Took it surprisingly well. Called her an awkward, cussed, contrary little madam – and said she must take after his side of the family.'

'She has an original mind,' Sarah said.

'Like you, Mummy,' Rachel said wistfully.

'Rubbish, darling. Have you thought what you want Bobby Brooks to do about Mark? Please don't dither; either you want a separation or you go back to him.'

Bobby Brooks always acceded to Sarah's demands, partly because of his devotion to the Renton family, and partly because he admired her business acumen, but mostly because she was his friend Gerald's widow.

Reluctantly he left the golf club without his customary pre-dinner drink, and drove to Renton's Royal in his Rolls. He parked it in the spaces Sarah kept for her friends and herself, and locked the doors.

He had two enthusiasms; superb cars and beautiful women. He could still indulge in the former; but the latter had ended with his marriage to Vita Redwood, the youngest of the famous Redwood sisters.

He never entered Renton's Royal without stopping to admire the hotel's façade, one of the best examples of Gerald's work. He'd been present on the momentous day when the hotel had first opened its doors, and had engineered the party, inviting as many useful contacts as he could.

Gerald had managed to contain his excitement until he and Bobby were alone. 'You must tell me the truth, Bobby. Is it right?'

'Perfect, my dear chap.'

And so it was. Now the stones and bricks had weathered; the wistaria smothered the south wall, but in no way obscured the perfectly proportioned windows and arches.

He still missed Gerald, and felt an odd twinge of regret as he walked across the foyer to the reception desk. His tall thin figure, saturnine tanned face and characteristic walk were familiar to the staff. He nodded to Mavis and made his way to Sarah's office.

Entering, he was aware of her charisma; her wayward charm.

'Sarah, my dear.'

'Good of you to come so quickly. Do sit down.'

'How are you?' he asked. He chose an upright chair opposite to Sarah. 'I spoke to Jim at the golf club. He seemed to think you were ill, and was babbling on about retirement. Have I enough influence over you to make you see sense?'

Sarah frowned and narrowed her lips. 'I haven't the slightest intention of retiring,' she said forcefully.

'Good.'

'You think I'm right to stay on?'

'I do. You *are* Renton's Royal. You have fulfilled all Gerald's hopes and dreams.'

She smiled, and he was aware of her attractiveness, which had increased with maturity.

'Bobby, I'm troubled. Since Gerald's death I've always come to you for advice, and been glad to take it. I've often wanted to say how much your loyalty meant to me.'

'Tell me, my dear Sarah, what is wrong?'

'Rachel. She'll be here in a moment, but I wanted to speak to you alone first.'

'There's no hitch in the transfer of the bookshop. I advised her to steer clear of the house, too many problems.'

'It isn't that. It's Mark. You know how I feel about the Ashtons. I have never forgiven myself for allowing Rachel to marry into that family.'

'You couldn't have stopped her.' Bobby had never forgotten the intense joy on Rachel's face when walking up the aisle on Gerald's arm to stand by her future husband.

'Perhaps not. I didn't like the break-up of their marriage, but thought it was the best thing for Rachel. Now he wants her back.'

Startled, Bobby reached for his pack of cigarettes, and offering one to Sarah, they smoked in silence for a few moments.

'Any reason?' he asked at last.

'You can bet on that. Mark's parents are going abroad. Mrs Ashton is ill and is seeking treatment in America. Mr Ashton wants Mark to manage the estate in his absence, but he won't hand over control unless Rachel and Mark patch up their marriage. No doubt he doesn't want the Hall full of the kind of tarts Mark picks up nowadays. His other condition is that Fleur should live with her parents until she decides to marry. I'm appalled at such blatant interference in other people's lives.'

'I see. How has Rachel taken this?'

'Dithering as usual. Mark's always been a powerful influence over her.'

The door opened and Rachel hesitated before coming into the room.

'Come in, darling, and shut the door.'

She did so, and as Bobby rose to greet her, he thought she had hardly changed, except her likeness to Gerald was more marked. She wore the same gentle expression, and her unlined face had retained its youthful contours.

'My dear Rachel.' He drew her close and kissed her on both cheeks. 'You look younger than ever, and prettier.'

She blushed. 'Old flatterer.'

He didn't like being called old, but it certainly put him in his place.

Rachel sat down. Her short pink linen dress barely covered her knees, and she stretched out her bare suntanned legs.

'Has Mummy told you about Mark? I don't know what to do,' she said directly, 'but please don't let him take Fleur away from me, or interfere with her life.'

Her belief in his power touched him. He thrust aside his

cynicism; and considered her problem.

'Mummy says I must make up my mind, and I have. I want to be independent. I'm happy in the bookshop, and I'm working on a biography of Samuel Verne, and I won't give up Fleur.' Her head drooped, and she would not meet his gaze. Her voice was barely audible. 'Mark came to the cottage. He was very angry when I wouldn't agree to go back to him at once.' She shivered, and looking up saw Bobby's eyes narrow as he drew his mouth into a thin, hard line. 'Do you want a divorce?'

'I'm not sure. I want what is best for Fleur.'

'Would she go with you to Ashton Hall?'

'Never,' Rachel said.

'What do you want me to do, Rachel?'

She sighed. 'I can't make up my mind.'

'I think you should wait a while before you make a definite decision,' Bobby said gently.

'Yes,' she said eagerly, 'that's what I'll do. Thank you, Bobby.' She smiled. 'I expect you have business with Mummy.' She jumped up. 'Goodbye, and thank you. I knew you'd have the right suggestion.' She stood uncertainly in the doorway a moment, and then carefully shut the door behind her.

Sarah frowned. 'Is that wise? Waiting, I mean. Mark is much more determined than Rachel.'

Bobby said, 'Rachel will work things out in her own good time. Don't press her, Sarah. She's like Gerald. He saw all the way round a problem and my guess is she still cares for Mark.'

'That's all very well, but I won't have him make a convenience of my daughter.'

'Oh Sarah, my dear, you'll never change.' He stood up and bent to kiss her lightly on the cheek. 'You are like an arrow shot straight to the heart.'

'And Rachel?'

'She has the soft touch. And sometimes it works.'

'You think I'm wrong?'

'No, I think your heart is too big. You have too much love to give, and too much caring.'

'In fact, Bobby, I interfere.'

'You wouldn't be you if you didn't.'

CHAPTER 14

'Mrs Renton, there's been a mix-up about bookings.' Clive Booth's anxiety was obvious in the nervous way he flicked over the papers he was carrying. 'It isn't Mavis' fault,' he defended, 'bookings were taken when she was off duty.'

'Let's have a look.'

If Sarah sounded calm and in charge, she didn't feel it. Her training took over on occasions like this. Sefton had taught her never, ever to panic.

'Give me the details please,' she said.

'The British Golf Open is being held next week at Lytham St Annes, and we are over-booked by about twenty persons.'

'Have you tried the other hotels to see if they have any vacancies to offload some of our bookings?'

'Not yet. I wasn't sure what I should do.'

'Does Mr O'Hara know?'

'He's out, and Mrs O'Hara is in the apartment but won't answer the door.'

'Damn,' Sarah said. It was the first time a disaster of this nature had occurred. 'Ring round the other hotels now, and if you get no joy try the small private hotels and guest houses, anything in the district, and report back to me. In the meantime ask Mavis to come here with the booking sheets.'

Mavis was apologetic. 'I'm always so careful, Mrs Renton.'

'I know that. So who took the extra bookings? Were the sheets available?'

'Yes. You insist the sheets are always by the telephone on the reception desk, and that's exactly where they were.'

'But surely anyone taking bookings could see the rooms were taken. Who was it, Mavis?'

'The sheets weren't used. The bookings were scribbled down on a bit of paper, and when Clive came to sort them out he realized we were already full.'

'Mavis. I want to know who took those bookings.'

'Well, as a matter of fact, it was Mrs O'Hara.'

'I don't understand. She's usually so efficient. Why was she in Reception?'

'It was my day off, and Val was off sick, and the girls in Accounts were busy.'

'Leave the sheets with me, and give Clive a hand in phoning round.'

Sarah was angry. Over-booking was unforgivable; the staff knew her views on the matter, and so did Claire. She picked up her bunch of keys and took the lift to the apartment. Her knock brought no response, so she unlocked the door and walked in.

In spite of the comfort of the cottage she regretted moving out of the spacious rooms. Gerald had loved them too. Together they had made a home, shutting out the bustle of the hotel, a place for them to relax; a place to bring up their children.

'Claire,' she called, walking slowly round the sitting room, noting the changes. The bedrooms opened off a short corridor, and at the door of the master room she stopped and knocked. Receiving no answer she opened the door and went in. Claire lay on the bed, her face turned to the wall, her body humped under the duvet.

'Claire. Are you ill?'

Claire didn't move or speak. Sarah sat down on the bed and pulled the cover away from Claire's face.

'Leave me alone. What do you want? Is there no privacy in this place?'

'Claire, don't shut me out. I want to help, to understand.'

Claire rolled over and sat up. Sarah was struck by her haggard appearance; she seemed to have aged years since her scary episode in London.

'I shall send for the doctor,' Sarah stood up. 'I think it would be a good idea for you to go away. I'll see if Willowdene has a vacant room.'

'I refuse to go there and be fussed over. It's full of nosy old ladies.'

'Claire, have you told me the truth? Did that attacker *touch* you?'

Claire laughed. 'If you mean did he try to rape me, he did not. He was only interested in robbing me.'

'I know you had a rotten experience, love, but pull yourself together, we have a business to run.'

'You mean *you* have a business to run. Jim and I have outlived our usefulness.'

'I wouldn't say that.' Sarah's voice was dangerously quiet. 'It seems to me you are the ones opting out. Jim spends most of the time at the golf club, and the staff are doing the extra work.'

'I suppose Clive Booth has been complaining?'

'He has not. But he is in the position of having to rectify your mistakes.'

'What are you talking about?' Claire asked wearily.

'The over-booking for next week. The sheets were to hand, why didn't you consult them?'

'I had other problems on my mind.'

'In that case you are no use to me until you resolve them, or let me help.'

'You see,' Claire said triumphantly. 'You are just waiting for an opportunity to get rid of us. Well, it suits me.'

'And Jim?'

'I don't care what he does.'

'I see.'

'You only see what you want to see. You like to think Jim and I are cosily married. No hassle, no problems. But in your heart you know this isn't true. I think it would be better if we had separate jobs – ' She hesitated.

'And does Jim agree?'

'I have no idea.'

'Well!' Sarah was losing patience. 'I suggest you find out, unless you'd like me to talk to him?'

'I would not. Just leave us alone. You can't run our lives now.'

Before Sarah could answer, the telephone rang. Claire didn't move, so Sarah picked up the receiver. She listened intently, and then cradling the receiver said, 'I have a visitor, I must go.'

Claire sprang up. 'If it's Charlie Mullins don't you dare bring him up here.'

'Don't be silly, Claire. I've got the message, you don't want to see him. Anyway, it isn't Charlie.'

Was Charlie Mullins the key to Claire's unhappiness? It seemed so unlikely. Sarah dismissed the idea immediately, and yet, why Claire's sudden hostility?

Thoughtfully, she rode down in the lift and entering her office greeted Chief Inspector Graham Willis with an exclamation of pleasure.

'My God, Sarah, you don't change. You look as young as ever.' He grasped her hand, and a smile lit up his grey eyes, enhancing his handsome features. Sarah was in no doubt that he was, as she termed it, a fine figure of a man.

'The hotel looks flourishing. All those up-market cars in

144

the car park. Gerald built a beautiful place and you've obviously kept up the standard. You've travelled a long way from Joe's café in the Dock Road when you and Charlie Mullins teased me unmercifully.'

'You were years younger and always tagging on. You were so serious. We couldn't believe a Stick Street School lad would join the police force. I suppose we were envious of your smart uniform.'

She had a mental picture of the red-cheeked young man strutting up and down the Dock Road on the beat, and even more clearly the day he had kissed her in the backyard and Charlie had knocked him down.

'That's a long time ago.'

'I don't believe you've been here since Gerald's funeral.'

'More's the pity. I can only plead pressure of work, but don't think I haven't kept an eye on you. I get a report every now and then from your local inspector. I understand he brings his wife here for dinner on special occasions.'

'That's true, and as a matter of fact he delights in telling me of your progress. Well, how about a drink? Toast our past and our future.'

'Great idea. I'm on duty but I have a driver so no problems.'

Sarah opened her drinks cabinet. 'What will you have?'

'A small whisky and soda please, Sarah. Must keep a steady head. I have a meeting with the Chief Constable later.'

'Sit down, Graham. I insist on you having lunch with me. I'm so glad to be able to thank you properly for finding Claire.' She handed him a glass, and sat down. She thought maturity suited him, his silver wings of hair and his well-cut suit gave the impression of a distinguished diplomat rather than a senior police officer.

'My pleasure. Young Margaret was very worried, and it was good to be able to put her mind at rest.' He raised his glass to her, and continued. 'I'm still in touch with Charlie Mullins. He called in at the Yard very concerned about Claire. I gathered that you are still friends.'

'Dear enemies actually.'

Willis said sharply, 'That wasn't my impression. He offered to put up a large reward for information leading to the arrest of Claire's attacker.'

Sarah sipped her drink, warm thoughts of Charlie cut short by Graham's next words.

'Mullins was implying that you and he were more than friends.'

'That's what he thinks. Actually he wants Renton's Royal.'

'What!' Graham said.

'Don't get me wrong. His aspirations are legitimate, but his methods – well – you know Charlie from the old days.'

'Do you mean he wants to buy your hotel?'

She nodded. 'If he can't get it any other way.' She laughed delightedly at Graham's expression. 'It's all right. He'll have to be good to fool me.'

She felt light-hearted; Graham had so many of her father's qualities. He was like granite, strong, and smooth, but underneath raged the fires of his dedication to justice.

'Let's eat.' She led the way to the family table in the dining room, and was aware of Graham's appreciative glance round.

He studied the menu, and she suggested he chose the wine, but he shook his head. Without looking at the list she ordered. The waiter brought the bottle for her approval, and poured a little in her glass. 'Graham, you remember Sefton Taylor?'

'Of course.'

'He keeps us supplied with wine, most of it from his brother's vineyard. This is,' she held up the glass to catch the light, 'an excellent white wine. 1965, one of the good years.'

'Wasn't he Gerald's partner?'

'That's right, and he still has a financial interest in the hotel. It is because of his expertise that we have built up such a good reputation for wine.'

Graham refused starters, and ordered steak. He sent a message to his driver to return for him later, and settled down to enjoy his meal.

'Is Claire here?'

'Yes. She still seems very shocked, Graham. I've questioned her, but she swears her attacker only robbed her and knocked her down.'

'Delayed reaction, perhaps. I thought she was coping. I talked to her in hospital. She couldn't give us a description of her attacker, because she was grabbed from behind and it was dark.'

'Will you catch him?'

Willis shrugged. 'We have nothing to work on, and we haven't found her handbag.'

'Perhaps the injury to her head has affected her?' Sarah suggested.

'You needn't worry about that. I had a word with the consultant and he assured me there was no lasting damage.'

'But I do worry, Graham. Why was she in an alley off Park Lane when she should have been in a taxi heading for Euston?'

'Ask her?'

'I have. Repeatedly.'

'Could she have been visiting Charlie Mullins? You know the hotel he uses as his headquarters is very near. She would pass the corner pub if she was making for the taxi rank. And there was a thunderstorm at the time.'

'I don't understand her.' Sarah's voice held a note of despair.

Graham was becoming concerned about her. She seemed vulnerable in spite of her command of the business, and he guessed that she was having trouble with her personal relationships. To entertain her he launched into a description of the Prince of Wales investiture at which he'd been detailed to attend. He knew Sarah was keenly interested in the Royal Family.

Wistfully she said she would have enjoyed the ceremony, it was never the same watching it on television, but she had too many problems with running the hotel to jaunt off.

'You shouldn't be so hard on yourself,' he chided. 'All work and no play . . . not that the fascinating Sarah Renton could *ever* be dull.'

'Thank you for that, Graham. You always did know how to sweet-talk a girl.'

She leaned across to touch his hand and he surprised her momentarily by catching hold of her fingers in his.

To defuse an awkward situation, Sarah deliberately let her gaze wander and then fix on a point just beyond Graham's left shoulder.

'Good heavens! What on earth is Charlie doing here?'

Graham let go of her hand as if it was red hot but had the grace to laugh when he realized the trick she had played on him. The rest of the meal passed pleasantly but as she waved off her distinctly red-faced guest afterwards, Sarah reflected ruefully that once again Charlie Mullins had saved the day for her. Was there to be no escape from the man?

As she stepped back into the foyer, Clive Booth hurried up to her.

'I'm sorry to disturb you, Mrs Renton, but I thought

you should know. One of the guests is accusing a chamber-maid of stealing a valuable ring. Mrs Humphries is going berserk, she won't have any of her girls accused of stealing. Do you think you could have a chat with the guest? She's in her room.'

'All right, Clive, but please bring Mrs Humphries and the guest to my office. What's the guest's name?'

'Mrs Elwood-Price.'

'Oh, I see.' Sarah thought she knew the guest, having noticed her and her jewellery around the hotel.

'Would you also send Michael to me? I think this might be an interesting experience for him,' she said cryptically.

In her office, she sat down at her desk. She had a superstitious theory that troubles always attacked in threes, and so often had been proved right. She was grateful when Michael appeared first, and told him to stand next to her behind the desk and take careful note of everything she did and said.

Mrs Elwood-Price's attitude was immediately recognized by Sarah the moment she entered the office. Sarah had dealt successfully with other trouble-makers in the past. She had long ago fine-tuned a course of action that had been devised by Sefton Taylor.

'Do sit down, Mrs Elwood-Price.' Her tone was firm. This one, Sarah thought, is a wily bird. Perhaps too clever by half. She motioned Mrs Humphries, flushed and dishevelled, to a chair beside her. Clive Booth preferred to stand.

'I understand you have mislaid a ring, Mrs Elwood-Price.' Sarah's opening remark was brisk. 'You know we do not take responsibility for jewellery unless it is deposited in the safe?'

Mrs Elwood-Price's look of scorn was meant to wither Sarah. It didn't. She was as unruffled as a pond on a summer's day.

Mrs Elwood-Price edged forward in her chair, and crossed her legs. Her short black skirt rode up above her knees. She patted her dyed blonde, and tightly-waved hair, and her sharp features matched the sharpness of her voice.

'I left my diamond ring on the dressing table while I went down to the bar for a drink. When I realized I'd forgotten to wear it, I returned immediately to my room. It was gone, but there was a chambermaid working in the corridor. I asked if she'd been in my room, and she admitted she had been in to change the towels.'

'The chambermaids usually change the towels at the same time. Madam would know this as she has been staying here a few days. Vera is absolutely trustworthy,' Mrs Humphries put in.

'I guess the situation hasn't arisen before. What girl wouldn't be tempted by a magnificent diamond and ruby ring? My husband gave it me before he went away. He'll be livid when he finds out it has been stolen in a first-class hotel. He will certainly demand compensation, and if it isn't forthcoming he'll sue.'

'Isn't your ring insured?'

'I don't see what that has to do with it. The girl stole the ring.'

'She did not.' Mrs Humphries couldn't contain her agitation any longer. 'You have no right to accuse an innocent girl. There she is in floods of tears. She says she didn't go anywhere near the dressing table. She went straight through to the bathroom with the clean towels.'

'A likely story! As her employer, Mrs Renton, I hold you responsible.'

'Mrs Humphries, has a proper search of the room been made?'

'No, Mrs Renton. Madam wouldn't allow it.'

Michael stirred slightly and Sarah gestured for him to

150

leave this to her. 'Kindly describe the ring. We need to know exactly what we are looking for.'

Mrs Elwood-Price shrugged her shoulders. 'If you insist. It's a complete waste of time, the girl pinched it. It is a large diamond set round with slightly smaller diamonds and rubies. I am going abroad tomorrow, and I want this matter settled now.'

'There's no question of any settlement.' Sarah was getting angry. 'I want the room thoroughly searched.'

'I refuse to allow it.'

'In that case, that's an end to the matter.'

'Well . . .' Mrs Elwood-Price wavered. 'You're welcome to search so long as I'm present. Or we could come to some arrangement – '

'I'm sure that will not be necessary,' Sarah said in a glacial tone. 'If you will kindly return to your room with us, Mrs Elwood-Price, we shall see if our search has a happier result. Mrs Humphries, wait for us here, please. I take it you will allow Mr Booth, Mr Renton and myself to conduct a thorough search of the room while you are present?' she said to the guest.

In the face of such splendid self-assurance she could only agree. 'Naturally I have every confidence in you, Mrs Renton.'

Sarah gestured her from the room.

'We shall, of course, also need to check your personal belongings,' she told Mrs Elwood-Price, who was now looking distinctly uncomfortable. 'But since you have such confidence in me, I take it you will have no problem with that?'

'None at all, but I'm sure it won't come to that,' blurted the woman.

Michael, bringing up the rear with Clive, silently raised one eyebrow.

As Sarah and her companion turned a corner of the

corridor, Clive murmured out of the side of his mouth, 'When we get inside, keep your eyes off Mrs E-P – let her do her stuff! Your grandmother's got her rattled.'

Mystified, Michael did as Clive had suggested, keeping his eyes fixed firmly to the floor at the far side of the room; Clive made straight for the bathroom while his grandmother chose to begin inspecting the night tables to either side of the bed. Why was no one investigating the dressing table where Mrs Elwood-Price said she had left the ring?

All was soon made clear.

'Oh, goodness! Oh, silly me,' the guest exclaimed, bending down with her back to them and apparently picking something up. She turned to face them, displaying a showy ruby and diamond ring in the palm of her hand. 'What must you think of me?' she ran on. 'I can't think how it can have happened . . .'

Sarah raised one eyebrow. 'Can't you, Mrs Elwood-Price – if that really is your name – despite having pulled off the same stunt at The Majestic in Lytham and The Crown in Morecambe? Without losing your nerve on those occasions I might add.'

'I don't know what you mean,' blustered the guest, though her face looked pale and drawn and her eyes were darting wildly. 'If you mean to insinuate that I . . .'

Sarah remained perfectly calm as she crossed the room and turned her master key in the lock. 'I'm not insinuating anything. I am merely asking you to remain in this room until you can be interviewed by the local police in connection with a series of frauds. We were notified by our local force to be on the lookout for a fraudster who works just like you. Apparently some hotels have made large settlements with a guest who claimed jewellery had disappeared from their room, so as to avoid bad publicity. I'm afraid Renton's Royal won't be joining them.'

Sarah gestured to the phone. 'Michael, please call Mrs

Humphries in my office. Tell her to contact Inspector Collins and ask him to come here right away. She is to meet him downstairs, brief him and bring him here as unobtrusively as possible. I prefer to keep this sordid incident from the notice of our legitimate guests.'

Mrs Elwood-Price sank onto the stool before the dressing table and remained there, her back hunched defensively and turned to them. Michael was surprised to find himself actually feeling sorry for her. She did not say a single word, even when Inspector Collins, shown in by a grimly smiling Mrs Humphries, greeted her by name.

'Now then, Rosie. Been a naughty girl again, have we?'

'He cautioned her formally then nodded to the uniformed constable accompanying him who took the prisoner's arm and led her away.

'I'll need a formal statement, Sarah,' said the plain-clothes CID man in charge of liaison with local hoteliers.

'Can it wait till this evening, Jim? I can pop down about six if that suits you? Only I've got an engagement party and the Chamber of Commerce dinner to supervise first.'

'That should boost my overtime,' he said with a smile. 'All right then. Be seeing you.'

As Clive saw him out, Michael turned to his grandmother, admiration plain in every line of his open young face.

'Gran, you were fantastic! I've never seen you like that before. She properly took me in, I'm afraid. I thought we'd have to pay out on the insurance but you were suspicious right from the start. Why?'

Sarah shrugged. 'Jim Collins had been in touch about several similar incidents in the north-west, as I said, but basically I had a feeling she wasn't on the level. I've noticed her about the place the last few days and there's been something about the way she's been flaunting her jewellery . . . always preening herself, twiddling her rings and adjusting her necklaces. You get an instinct for these things after so many years in the business. She just looked a right 'un, if you know what I mean.'

He caught her hand and squeezed it. 'She was no match for you, Gran. Wait till I tell Fleur. She'll be wild that she missed all the excitement.'

'Well, when you do, do you think you could ask her to bring me some tea in my office? What with Claire, then Graham, and now all this, it's been quite a day – and I have to go down to the station this evening. Tell me, Michael, do you still want to be a hotelier?'

He nodded his head vehemently and she winced at the length of his wild dark hair – though warmed to the light of enthusiasm in his eyes.

'Oh, yes, Gran. More than ever now. I never realized it could be so much fun!'

CHAPTER 15

Clive returned to Sarah's office ten minutes later with the news that Inspector Collins was considering recommending her for a civil commendation for her prompt action in apprehending Mrs Elwood-Price.

Clive was impressed by Sarah's coolness, and said so. She shrugged aside the compliment.

'Now what about the bookings?'

'All fixed. Mavis is sorting out the casuals from our regulars and will bring in the lists later.'

'Good. When do you go off duty?'

Clive hesitated. 'Can Michael take over for a short while until Mr O'Hara is back? I have a dental appointment. Michael knows what to do, and any difficulty, he'll come to you. He's really good, Mrs Renton.'

She glanced at the clock. A quiet time between tea and dinner; she didn't foresee any more problems, and it would give Michael confidence to feel he was in charge. A visit to the bar later, and she could check then that nothing was amiss.

She settled down to drafting out some important advertisements she wished to insert in the local papers, but after a few minutes Jim blustered in.

'What the hell is going on, Sarah? Claire says Willis has been badgering her, and he has arrested one of the guests.'

'I think, Jim, it is time we had a serious talk.'

She observed him with dislike. He sat down heavily, and she suspected most of his time at the golf club was spent in the bar. His eyes were red-rimmed, and his skin blotchy.

'About what?' he said truculently.

'First about your wife. You do realize that Claire is still suffering from shock. She also has some problem on her mind. Do you know what it is?'

He scowled. 'You should have kept that damned policeman away from her.'

'So you aren't grateful he was able to locate her in hospital? It didn't trouble you that she was missing and maybe injured or dead? He did us a favour.'

'He did *you* a favour, Sarah. You have 'em eating out of your hand.'

She ignored his rudeness. 'Secondly, Jim, I am not pleased with the way you are running my hotel. Clive Booth is excellent, but he is doing your work as well as his own, and I won't tolerate it. Mistakes have been made, and I won't have the staff covering up for you and Claire. Just because you are family doesn't mean you have licence to do as you please.'

'Your hotel – that's all we ever hear. Well, keep your hotel and count us out. If you are thinking of sacking me, forget it. I resign.'

Sarah didn't take Jim's resignation seriously; it was the trump card he'd played too often in the past. Now it fell flat – a non-starter – and too late he realized his mistake.

'I think you should discuss such a serious matter as your resignation with Claire before I accept it.'

He seized on the loophole he was being offered, believing it to be a sign of weakness. He couldn't have been more wrong. Sarah's strength was in her compassionate understanding, and she was aware that her decision to bring Michael into the hotel had set off a chain reaction, the result of which she was beginning to see.

But she stood by this decision. Michael was of the generation which ensured the continuity of Renton's Royal Hotel. She believed she owed this to Gerald, and in a lesser degree to Sefton Taylor, and she intended it to be a lasting memorial to the Renton name. Clearly this decision influenced all her actions; there was no way she was willing to retire, and no way she would sell out to Charlie Mullins.

Michael was off-duty the following morning, and joined Rachel at the breakfast table in the cottage.

'This is super, Rachel. I'm glad you are here. It's like home and much better than going over to the hotel for breakfast.'

Rachel put the plate of bacon and eggs on the table in front of him.

'Are you busy this morning?' he asked. 'It's my driving test tomorrow, and I could do with a bit more practice. I can use one of the hotel cars.'

They set off later, driving inland. Rachel enjoyed the driving sessions with Michael. Fleur had passed her test, and Michael was determined to gain his certificate at the first attempt. She directed him along the narrow roads, flanked by the flat potato fields which edged down to the road. She let her glance wander over the white and purple expanse of flowers, broken only by copses, and here and there a ditch.

Michael practised his three-point turns in a field gateway, reversing into a narrow lane until Rachel pronounced that she thought he was ready for his test.

They returned by a different route, and pulled up at a wayside café. Tables and chairs were set out on a rain-green lawn, now sparkling in the sunshine.

Michael fetched coffee, and sat down, contentedly

stretching his legs. He felt closer to Rachel than any other person since his mother's death.

She dribbled cream out of a little pot into her coffee, and stirred it. The lawn was surrounded by a trellis of climbing roses, a private place, and for the moment their own.

'Michael, I'm concerned about Fleur's friendship with the Spanish boy. She is making sure I don't meet him. Why?'

'He's crazy about Fleur, and she is about him. Don't you approve?'

'It depends. I mean if it is just an affair of the moment, it will end naturally. But if it is a deeper relationship . . .?' She looked expectantly at him.

'Fleur hasn't said how she feels.' It was a little lie but he felt loyalty to Fleur, and in an odd way to Ramiro.

'That's why I'm concerned. Fleur shouts about her loves and hates from the roof tops. But not this one, and I wonder why?'

'I think she feels a need to protect Ramiro. She says he's lonely, dependent on her. He's a decent bloke, Rachel. It's just – well,' he continued lamely, 'Spaniards are different. Fleur says I should try and understand my stepmother. She says I'm jealous.'

'Are you?' Rachel asked.

'I suppose I am – in a kind of way. It seems disloyal to like her. Fleur says if Fortunata is making Dad happy that should be enough. Do you think that's right?'

'I don't know.' Rachel thought for a moment, 'Yes, I do know how you feel.' She put her elbows on the table and supported her chin. 'Fortunata isn't replacing your mother – no one can do that. Your mother is special to you and and your father. Paul and I have never been close, because of the age gap, but he and Claire are twins, so I'm much younger. It was always Paul and Claire ganged up together. I guess they are on the same wavelength.'

'You're different,' Michael said. 'Both you and Fleur really care about people.'

'Do you care about Fleur?'

Michael said vehemently, 'I do. She's very, very special.'

'I don't want to interfere – '

'Don't,' he said forcefully.

'Oh dear, it's worrying. Fleur's father is already objecting to her working in the hotel, and this won't help.'

'What difference will it make?'

She sighed. 'He thinks she isn't meeting the right people.'

'I suppose he means rich layabouts,' he said scornfully. 'Hey, wait a minute, Rachel. Fleur told me you and he are parted, and that suits her.'

'That might change. I haven't decided yet.'

'Does Fleur know?'

Rachel shook her head. 'I don't know how to tell her. He wants us to go back and live at Ashton Hall with him.'

'She won't do it. Good Lord, Rachel, you aren't expecting her to give up her career? She's mad on catering, and Chef thinks she's the tops. And Gran has high hopes for both of us.'

'I know. It isn't easy – '

'Tell him to get lost. You can't bust up things for Fleur now.'

'Please don't tell her anything, Michael.'

'I won't if you say so. But you've got to make up your mind not to let anything spoil it for her.'

Making up one's mind seemed easy for some people, Rachel thought. Sarah never had any difficulty. She never wavered; and Rachel knew wavering was her downfall. This time, however, she'd stick to her decision, when she made it.

Michael's outburst merely confirmed the line of Rachel's thoughts. Whatever was to be done must be for Fleur's sake. But Mark could be so persuasive sometimes and she still found him powerfully attractive.

True, she had Sarah's strength to lean on, and to a lesser degree Bobby Brooks', but the ultimate decision had to be made by herself, regardless of the cost.

So once more she dithered. Fate would settle her problem; she had great faith in the power of an unseen hand guiding her. As usual, Rachel touchingly put off till tomorrow what she should have done today, consigning thoughts of Mark to a dark uninhabited part of her mind. When she received a letter from Mr Glover warning her there might have to be a change of plans, and he was not yet in a position to sign the contract for the sale of the shop, she heaved a sigh of relief.

Now there was no urgency, Rachel drifted. She let several days slip by, spending the hours in the cottage or working in Sarah's garden, or walking Ricki along the beach. She avoided the hotel, waiting expectantly for the evening and the return of the family.

Dream-like existences don't last – events move forward inexorably; and even a dreamer like Rachel had to face reality sooner or later.

Saturday evenings were busy in the hotel. Fleur and Michael organized the dinner-dance, and Sarah rarely returned to the cottage until late. Rachel chose the peaceful afternoon to finish another chapter of her biography of Samuel Verne. Her mind was attuned to his life and times; she felt an affinity with him which she was beginning to fear.

She covered the typewriter, gathered up the loose sheets and went into the kitchen to make a cup of tea. She felt a need for exercise, and glancing at the clock reckoned the guests would be having a pre-dinner drink in the bar or already be in the dining room.

She changed into her bathing suit, and tying the belt of her bathrobe round her, picked up a large towel and a cap and meandered across the lawn to the outside entrance to the pool.

Only the gentle splash of the waterfalls cascading in from the sides broke the peculiar silence, and happily she dodged into a cubicle and disrobed.

She mounted the steep steps up to the top diving board, and stood poised, waiting until her usual feeling of trepidation passed. Suppose this time her dive wasn't straight and clean?

It was. The water was colder than she'd expected, and she struck out for the shallow end, swimming strongly. She touched the rail, and started back, exulting in the power of cleaving through the water. After several lengths she began to tire, and headed for the steps out of the pool. Before she could reach them, she was struck with an attack of cramp. She gasped, and cried out with the agonizing pain, and helplessly slid below the surface. As she rose, she threw up her arms and tried to shout before she sank again. Vaguely she thought she heard a loud splash, and then someone was grasping her, and pulling her up to the surface.

From a long distance she heard a voice, and gasping and retching she allowed herself to be towed to the steps. She clung to the rail, unable to make a further effort.

Her rescuer part-dragged and part-carried her to the top. At last the cramp pains relaxed, and the young man fetched a chair and gently lowered her into it. He wrapped her robe round her, and draped her towel round her shoulders.

At last she stopped shivering, pulled off her cap and dried her face. The man had tactfully moved to the edge of the pool and was now dangling his legs over the side, giving her time to recover her poise. She thought the back of his head looked familiar, and bending forward touched his shoulder. 'I don't know how to thank you,' she said. 'You saved my life. I was very foolish to swim alone. I've had bouts of cramp ever since I was a kid.'

He turned to smile, and now she recognized him. Inconsequently she thought: he is even better looking than his photograph.

'There is a notice asking people not to swim alone,' he said. 'The hotel management will not be responsible for accidents.'

Rachel smiled. How like her mother to issue a disclaimer.

'Lucky for me you turned up. I hope I haven't spoilt your swim.' She hesitated. 'You are Ramiro?'

He smiled again, his eyes sparkled and he held out his hand, and took hers in a strong grasp. 'Fleur has been promising we should meet, Mrs Ashton, but not when you nearly drowned. I have a confession. I followed you here. I thought, this time we shall meet.'

Rachel stood up, and Ramiro sprang forward to support her. 'Will you come across to the cottage with me please, Ramiro? May I use your name?'

'Oh yes.'

'All the family are out,' she said. 'I'll be glad of your company.'

Leaning on his arm they made a slow progression across the lawns.

'I long for a hot cup of tea,' Rachel said, opening the door. 'I feel very shivery.'

'I'll make it,' Ramiro said eagerly. 'Fleur showed me how to make proper English tea.' He laughed. 'I teach her how to make good coffee.'

Rachel switched on the electric fire, and settled herself in front of it, and was soon sipping the hot sweet tea Ramiro handed her.

162

'Excellent,' she smiled. 'Please sit down, and tell me how you come to be at Renton's Royal.'

Ramiro cradled the mug of coffee he'd made for himself, sat down on a stool at Rachel's feet, and in a moment Ricki had laid his head on the boy's knee.

'We have two dogs at home, but not like Ricki. They are guard dogs in my father's restaurant. Michael's father comes to the restaurant, and one day he brings Mrs Renton. That is nearly three years ago. My father asks her if she will take me on in her kitchen, and she agrees. So I come. My father wishes to add English dishes to our menu. We have a lot of English tourists, and sometimes they want roast beef and Yorkshire pudding. So I learn.'

'When your training is finished will you go back?'

'I wish to stay here, but my father will not allow. I am his only son, and the restaurant is for me. You understand it is a family duty.' He sighed, and taking Rachel's cup refilled it.

'Don't you miss your family and friends?' she asked, and was surprised to see hs expression change. Why is he sad, she thought, and spontaneously put out her hand to touch him.

Immediately he smiled. 'My friends are here. I do not wish to leave them.'

'And I'm sure they will miss you.'

'For a little while, then they will forget. It is better so.'

'No,' she said sharply. 'Fleur and Michael do not desert their friends. You can be sure of that. Does my mother know that you will be going back at the end of your training?'

He nodded.

'I understand Chef thinks very highly of you. If you are offered a permanent job – ?'

He stopped her. 'No, please you do not understand. It cannot be.' He jumped up. 'I must go. Shall I send Fleur to you?'

163

'No. I am fine, thanks to you. Please, Ramiro, let my foolishness in swimming alone be our secret. I don't want to worry Fleur or my mother.'

'Of course. But you promise not to swim alone?'

'I promise.'

After he'd left, she wondered if it was wise to have a secret with Ramiro. Secrets were a kind of bond, and in the circumstances she thought it might spell danger.

CHAPTER 16

On Monday, 21st July 1969 at 3.56 B.S.T. Apollo 11 landed on the moon. Neil Armstrong, the commander, was the first man to step on the moon. He planted the American flag.

The staff dining room was full. It seemed to Chef that all the shining faces turned towards the television screen were bright with expectation. A new millennium, perhaps. Well, at least the moon didn't appear to be peopled by little green men, and looked like a barren volcanic desert.

I'm getting old and cynical, he thought, organising the wine Mrs Renton had provided for the occasion. Arthur Kellett sat down next to him.

'Grand achievement,' he said without any enthusiasm. 'Will it change anything?'

'I doubt it.' Chef filled up Arthur's glass. 'The young think it will, and that's what matters.'

'Always the young,' Arthur said. 'Does the world belong to them?'

'Likely so, Arthur. You have a stake in it. Your boy is doing well I hear.'

Arthur's face was illuminated. 'The doctors say he's cured. The boy is back to normal. He lives with my sister. She has a youngster the same age as mine. They go everywhere together. I visit on my days off.'

'I'm glad it's turned out well for you, Arthur.'

Chef glanced round. Ramiro stood on the fringe – never quite integrated.

'Ramiro,' he called. 'Over here. Your glass is empty. Well, what do you think?'

The slightest shrug. 'The Americans are very clever. They fly to the moon, and they fight in Vietnam. My friend – he is killed.'

Chef was startled. 'How come your friend was fighting in Vietnam?'

'His father is American. He came to Spain on holiday, you understand, and married my mother's cousin. Wayne did not like living in New York. He came often to stay with us. My mother's cousin, she has come home.'

The pain in the boy's eyes touched Arthur. 'That's bad, Ramiro,' he said.

'Yes. Very bad. I do not forgive.' He turned back to the screen, finished his wine and left.

The Rentons sat round the television in the cottage sitting room. Michael's excitement infected them all. 'It's absolutely fantastic. I wish . . .'

'Don't be daft, Mick. I imagine you'd hate it. Trapped in that capsule. Suppose you never got back to earth, and went circling round the moon for ever until you were all skeletons?'

'Fleur!' Rachel shuddered. 'How can you imagine such a horrible fate!'

Michael expertly opened another bottle of champagne and filled up their glasses. 'She reads Science Fiction. Isaac Asimov is her hero.'

Sarah laughed. 'Watch it, Fleur. We don't want you dabbling in the unknown, and experimenting in the hotel kitchen.'

'As if I would, Gran.'

166

Sarah stood up. 'I'm off to bed. Too much excitement doesn't suit me.'

'Fleur, if I go away will you come with me?'

'Go away, Ramiro? I don't get it. Do you mean back to Spain?'

'No. Never there.'

'Well then?'

'Another hotel. London perhaps.'

'You are being as daft as Mick. I can't leave here, you know that.'

They sat close together on the diving board, legs just touching as they dangled over the pool. Fleur felt if they sat any closer she would melt in the heat from his skin. She gazed down at the unruffled water, magnifying the green tiles below.

'Aren't you happy here?' she asked.

'Yes, but . . .'

She waited, and reaching out touched his hand. He grasped it tightly in his own. His wet skin gleamed in the frosted light penetrating the glass roof. His unruly hair was sleeked tight to his skull and water dripped in tiny rivulets down his neck and chest. She couldn't see the expression in his eyes; his lids were lowered and his black eyelashes fanned onto his cheeks. She longed to press her mouth to his strong cheekbones and pulsing eyelids; the satin smooth column of his throat. She bit her lip, suddenly conscious that if she made a wrong move now she could jeopardize their precious closeness.

'But what?' she said at last. 'Is something wrong? Is Chef or Claire picking on you?'

'No. It is family trouble. I cannot say. I cannot go away without you. I cannot live without you.'

Fleur looked up. Happiness bubbled up, and as quickly burst. 'Don't go.'

'I must. It is better I go now before – '

'What are you talking about, Ramiro? Before what?'

'My father needs me.'

'What's changed?'

He didn't answer, and standing up dived cleanly into the water.

Fleur followed him. They swam several lengths side by side. Fleur thought, I will never let him go. Her loyalty was incorruptible. She wanted to shout out defiance, and yet she was powerless until she knew why his father was demanding his return.

That same day there were three personal letters in the sack of mail delivered to the hotel, two for Sarah, and one for Rachel. Sarah set them aside until she had dealt with the business letters, sorting them out for distribution either to Reception, or Accounts. From the beginning she'd always insisted on reading the mail. It was a technique Sefton had used, believing the life blood of the hotel poured in through the letter box.

It was late morning before she had time to open her own letters. Rachel's she set aside to take over to the cottage. She slit open the envelope with the Westwood Hotel name printed across the top.

Charlie Mullins wrote: 'Sorry Sarah, my dear, but I will have to postpone my visit. My wife is very ill, and I have to be near the hospital. I'll keep in touch.'

Sarah sighed with relief. Perhaps now Claire would respond, though what Charlie Mullins had to do with her strange behaviour Sarah couldn't figure out. With the letter in her hand, she made her way up to the apartment and knocked on the door.

Claire opened it.

'How are you, my dear?' Sarah didn't wait to be invited in.

Claire shut the door. She was dressed in a linen suit, bag and gloves on the table.

'Am I stopping you going somewhere?' Sarah sat down. 'You look very nice. I always think you should wear green. Perfect on you.'

'I'm in a hurry. I'm meeting a friend for lunch at The Adelphi.'

'That's good,' Sarah said warmly. 'Take you out of yourself. I won't keep you. I've had a letter from Charlie Mullins. He is postponing his visit. His wife is very ill.'

'That settles it.'

'Settles what, Claire? I don't understand your reluctance to meet Charlie. Has he offended you?'

'That wouldn't be hard for him. A man who speaks his mind, regardless of who he hurts. A hard-headed business man who bludgeons his way to success.'

'Am I right in thinking that you've changed your mind about Charlie buying Renton's Royal. Why?'

She picked up her bag, fiddling with the catch. 'He isn't right for a hotel of this class.'

Sarah let that pass. 'In that case you are not pressing me to retire.'

'I don't see the connection.'

'I do. Charlie plays fair with me. Your plan was to take over the hotel, sell to Charlie, on condition you and Jim remained to manage it.'

'Mother! How can you think such a thing?'

'It wouldn't work. Even if I retired from the actual running of the hotel, my capital remains, and in case you didn't know, Sefton Taylor has a big stake.'

'It was Charlie's idea,' she said sullenly.

Sarah put the letter down on the table and walked out of the room. She was angry. So angry she had to sit down on a chair by the lift until the rush of blood to her neck and face subsided. She found it incomprehensible that she should be plotted against, and by her daughter and her friend.

However, when she calmed down, and was sitting at her desk, she laughed at herself. Ridiculous, of course it isn't a plot. I've brought this on myself, by encouraging Michael and Fleur. It's only natural Claire and Jim feel outraged.

She helped herself to a drink and picked up the other letter bearing the Spanish postmark. She read it through, and then, completely puzzled, returned to the beginning. The signature was, she supposed, that of Ramiro's father. 'Please send Ramiro home. He is needed. I write to him, he does not answer. Tell him to come home at once.'

It was perhaps fortunate for Mr Rodriguez that his letter arrived at the same time as Charlie Mullins'. If Sarah hadn't been so incensed by Claire's shiftiness, she might have ignored it.

She did not. With an exclamation of annoyance she threw the letter on the desk and sent for Ramiro.

While she was waiting, conflicting thoughts warred in her head. Perhaps it would be safer – and she wasn't sure why the word safer came to mind – to let Ramiro go in spite of his contract. Her anxiety was, of course, for Fleur. Love affairs come and go when a girl is seventeen, but if Fleur was going to get hurt over this one, better now than later.

Ramiro's knock on the door interrupted her thoughts. He was still wearing his white high-necked jacket and his hat was set at a jaunty angle. Sarah had always been susceptible to good looks in men, and Ramiro had the same classical features and deep-set eyes which had so attracted Sarah to Gerald. The faint resemblance cooled her temper.

'Sit down, Ramiro. I've had a letter from your father. He wants you to go home, and he says you do not answer his letters. Why?'

Ramiro's head drooped.

'Is something wrong?' Sarah persisted.

After a moment or two, Ramiro said, 'Family trouble. It will pass. I do not wish to go.' He looked up and she saw hope illuminating his eyes. 'Will you tell my father I am necessary here?'

'Do you know why your father wants you so urgently? Is someone ill?'

'No. I think his partner is making difficulties.'

'What kind? Do you mean financial?'

'I do not know.' Ramiro gave a despairing sigh.

'Then I suggest you take two weeks' leave and help sort out your father's problems.'

He hesitated. 'Can I come back?'

'Of course, Ramiro.'

'But if I am not allowed – you will tell him you need me here?'

'Ramiro, what has changed your father? He wants you to be a good chef. You have already passed the first part of your diploma. I think you should come back and finish your training and I will certainly point out to your father it would be a pity not to do that.'

'I wish to stay here always,' Ramiro's eyes flashed, 'but my father will not allow. He works to make the restaurant good – for me.'

'That's only natural, Ramiro. We all work for our families.'

'You work for Michael and,' he added softly, 'Fleur.'

She had a presentiment that perhaps both she and Señor Rodriguez were trying to influence the lives of their beloved ones. I must hold back, she thought. They must not be tied to family out of ioyalty.

'Go home, Ramiro. Sort out your problems, and your job will be waiting for you.'

He thanked her without enthusiasm, and rejected her offer to arrange a flight to Spain.

I hope I haven't thrown him to the wolves, she thought, and then chided herself for such a ridiculous fancy. She dictated a reply to Señor Rodriguez informing him that she had given his son two weeks' leave, but expected him back at the end of that time.

She was troubled for the rest of that day, and it wasn't until she was ready to go over to the cottage that she realized Rachel's letter was still lying on her desk.

It was a great joy to her to return home and find Rachel there. She remembered the loneliness of her return to the cottage before the advent of Michael, Fleur and Rachel.

Ricki was lying on the mat waiting for her. She patted him. 'You've been for a walk, you old fraud. Hasn't he?' she asked Rachel who was coming down the stairs to meet her.

'We walked as far as Collie's Farm. I bought strawberries and peas.'

'Oh lovely, darling. Let's have a quiet drink.'

When they were seated, Sarah handed over the letter.

Rachel tore open the envelope, and unfolded the single sheet inside. 'From Mark. He's coming here. He says he wants to have this out once and for all. Oh, Mummy!'

'Do you want to go?'

'No. Not yet. I'm not ready.'

'Right. He can hardly carry you out screaming, and I don't see him having much luck with Fleur – when is he coming?'

'At the weekend.'

'I've had such a good idea. Why don't you and Fleur spend the weekend at the Westwood Hotel? I have an open invitation from Charlie. And perhaps you could meet Margaret, and pin her down about the party.'

'No. I can't leave you to cope. It wouldn't be fair.'

'Darling Rachel. I think I'm a match for Mark Ashton. And I shall have Bobby Brooks to back me up.'

Mummy, you won't – I mean, suppose he won't listen?'

'He'll listen,' Sarah said grimly. 'How about supper?'

It wasn't until later in the evening that Sarah mentioned the letter she'd received from Ramiro's father. 'I've questioned Ramiro about the family troubles, but he was very cagey, so I've given him two weeks' leave and sent him home. Tell me, has Fleur confided in you? I have the impression they are very close indeed.'

'I think that's possible. Oh dear, what will Mark say? He's so particular about Fleur's friends.'

'Fleur will always choose her own friends, and I don't think her father will influence her, and I hope he isn't going to influence you against your will. You know you have a home here, dear Rachel. All I want is your happiness.'

That's all I want for all of them, Sarah thought. But I can't give it them, it must come from within themselves.

CHAPTER 17

Next morning Claire presented herself in Sarah's office at precisely nine o'clock. She wore a navy blue cotton two-piece and a white blouse, and her hair was meticulously styled in a long bob. She always avoided the Renton Royal uniform colours, maroon and cream. Sarah remembered the arguments she'd had with Gerald and Sefton over the choice of these colours, and she'd had her way.

Claire handed Sarah a note. Sarah read the single sheet and flung it down on the desk with an exclamation of annoyance.

'Hasn't Jim the guts to hand in his resignation himself?' she asked angrily.

'He's gone – until there is a change here.'

'There are going to be changes, Claire. But I doubt if they will be to Jim's liking.'

'Are you angry, Mother?' Claire's smile was deliberately provocative. 'The first crack in the unity of the family.'

Sarah's direct gaze settled on Claire's face. 'No, I'm not angry, and not surprised. Jim has threatened to resign on several occasions. His screwy idea of blackmail. I am not dependent on Jim or anyone else. We work as a team, Claire, and Jim has always resented that. If he thought he was capable of filling my chair, he's proved he's not.'

'Jim fill your chair?' Claire took a seat at her mother's

right hand. 'I never thought or intended he should. I'm your natural successor, my dear mother, and perfectly capable of running this hotel alone as you have done since Father died and Sefton opted out. You've taught me well. But you see my position is now threatened, and I don't like it one little bit.'

'I have never promised – '

'Perhaps not actually promised, but implied, and the implication is that I should take your place on your retirement. Jim understands, and he isn't interested. His ambition to step into your shoes died a long time ago, but mine has been fed on expectation and hope.'

For the first time in their relationship Sarah felt at a disadvantage. She hadn't envisaged Claire to be a rival, presuming that Jim was the dominant partner. She still didn't believe that Jim had given up hope, and was probably biding his time, and no doubt trying to drum up support from Charlie.

She saw too late that she had let sentiment blind her to the truth, and that Claire's determination was rock hard.

'I expect you will be joining Jim,' she said.

'You don't expect that at all, Mother. I've no intention of joining him in the sleasy little club in Soho where he stays, and waits for Charlie to implement his promises.'

'What promises?'

'Come, Mother. You are well aware that Charlie has offered us the joint managership of the new hotel he is building in Barbados.'

'I see. He wants you two out of the way. Doesn't he need you any more to help him to get Renton's Royal? Why has he changed his mind? And why are you avoiding him?'

'You aren't likely to sell the hotel to him or anyone else. So Jim can go to Barbados alone, and I intend to stay here as heir apparent. I like the sound of that, and I intend to make it plain to my nephew and niece that I have prior

175

claim, and there isn't any way you'd sack your eldest daughter.'

'Of course I wouldn't dream of sacking you. You are being stupid. Your place is here. I've given the matter a lot of thought, and I intend making the changes Jim hoped for.' She picked up her pen and doodled thoughtfully on her blotter for a moment. 'I have decided you will make an excellent personal assistant, a kind of deputy.'

'Personal assistant?' Claire's voice rose, 'that's a nonsense. Now that Jim has resigned, I can fill his place as manager.'

'It won't do, Claire. I can't rely on you. Jim will whistle and off you'll go, or you'll plan something else with Charlie.'

'Are you telling me I'm not a fit person – '

'Think back to the agreement. Jim was appointed manager and you naturally fell into place as the manager's wife.'

'Second class. How dare you relegate me to a second-class position? Jim may have been manager in name, but I made the decisions. Jim knew his place, and you went along with it. The truth is, you're jealous. You're afraid I'll be as good as you or better.'

'That has to be proved.' Sarah checked her anger with great difficulty. 'And I don't intend you shall prove it here. Perhaps Charlie will offer you the kind of position you want.'

'You've fixed it between you,' Claire stammered as colour flooded her cheeks, and to Sarah's surprise tears filled Claire's eyes.

'What's the matter, love? Fixed what? I don't know what you are talking about.'

Claire sprang up, and moved over to the window, her back to Sarah.

Sarah longed to put her arms round her, but she knew from past experiences that Claire hated to be touched.

Sarah sat still, waiting. She remembered Claire's child-ish tantrums, often without reason, and that it had been Gerald who had always calmed her.

After a few minutes Sarah said, 'Perhaps you'd rather not attend the staff meeting, the others are due now.'

Claire returned to her chair. Her face was set in the hard expression Sarah dreaded, and her heart sank at the thought of the disturbance Claire might make.

Michael was the first to arrive. He breezed in, kissed his grandmother and greeted Claire. He was closely followed by Clive Booth, Mrs Humphries, and lastly Chef. They took their usual places round the desk, shuffling notebooks and papers.

Sarah's supreme confidence returned. As she had said to Claire, this was a team she could rely on, and she was determined that it should remain so.

She greeted than all by name, and putting a tentative hand on Claire's arm welcomed her. 'I have offered Claire the post of personal assistant to me. She hasn't made up her mind whether it is to her liking yet.'

Claire moved her arm out of her mother's reach, and didn't answer.

Sarah waited a moment, and then continued. 'I set great store by this weekly meeting. Working together as we do, most of our problems get ironed out. To begin with, you may be surprised to hear that Mr O'Hara has resigned, so that leaves the post of manager vacant. I am offering it to you, Clive. You have worked very well in difficult cir-cumstances, and I know you have the good of Renton's Royal at heart.'

Clive's face flushed with pleasure. 'Thank you, thank you very much, Mrs Renton. I'll be pleased to accept.'

'Good. I'll ask Mr Brooks to draw up the usual contract. That leaves the position of under-manager vacant. I'd like *you* to fill it, Michael.'

Claire thumped the desk. 'Are you mad, Mother! Michael has hardly any experience. You are being spiteful.'

Sarah compressed her lips. 'I'm sure you don't mean that, Claire.'

'Now you've got rid of Jim – '

'Just a moment, Claire. Jim resigned without any pressure from me. I have his letter in front of me. You have just expressed a desire to follow in my footsteps. Well, so you shall as my personal assistant. If you care to accept the offer.' She smiled at Michael. 'It's a challenge, love. But you have me and Clive to help. I guess you'll do well, and we'll see about college in the autumn.'

Michael had no need to answer, pleasure and excitement were obvious in his smile. 'I'll do my best, Gran. Clive, isn't this absolutely fab?'

Sarah was reassured. She was pinning her colours to the young, and when the time came she believed Renton's Royal would be safe with them.

'Now to business. Any problems, Clive?'

'No. There've been one or two room cancellations, but we have a waiting list. The organiser of the golfing party phoned. He wants a special dinner on Saturday night to celebrate Tony Jacklin winning the British Open. I've passed on his suggestions to Chef. I think we will have to open up the two dining rooms.'

'Can you handle the usual dance in the ballroom as well?'

'Michael and Fleur don't need any help with that.'

'I was thinking, Gran, would it be possible to lay out another tennis court on the west lawn? There's always a waiting list of people wanting to use the existing ones.'

'Excellent idea, Michael. I'll talk to the gardener.'

Sarah quickly dealt with Mrs Humphries' complaints about the laundry. Clive said Mrs Lee, the catering manageress, was short of waitresses for the weekends, and perhaps they could apply to the agency for part-timers.

Claire sat in stubborn silence through the proceedings, and when Michael, Clive and Mrs Humphries rose to leave, she made no move to follow them.

Chef too, had remained silent; now he stood up, and passed his sheaf of menus for the coming week to Sarah for her inspection. As a rule, Sarah agreed to them, and it was only minor details that needed discussion.

'I'd like to speak to you alone, Mrs Renton,' Chef said while he gathered up the menu sheets. 'Perhaps Mrs O'Hara will excuse us.'

Reluctantly Claire rose. 'Surely as *personal assistant* I should be present?'

Chef said, 'I'll come back another time.'

'No. Kindly leave us, Claire.'

Chef waited until the door closed behind her. 'She's trouble, always has been, always will be.'

Sarah sighed. 'I know, but she is my daughter. She's disappointed I didn't appoint her manager.'

'If you had, you'd have lost the best part of your staff. I've been here since the first day the hotel was opened, and as you know, I've never been afraid to express my opinion. No offence, I hope.'

Sarah smiled, 'None taken, Bert. I don't need to tell you how much I've relied on you.'

He nodded. Their relationship was an established fact. Chef never presumed, but on the other hand Sarah trusted his forthright opinions.

He sat down again. 'I understand the Spanish boy has family troubles, and you have given him two weeks' leave. Are you intending having him back?'

'Of course, why not? Is there any reason – '

Chef frowned, and undid the top button of his white jacket.

179

'What's on your mind, Bert?'

'Firstly, I'll need a temp.'

'Go ahead and contact the agency.' She looked at him expectantly. 'Aren't you satisfied with Ramiro? Does he cause trouble in your kitchens?'

'He's very good, and heading to be a top chef if he sticks at it. The staff like him; in fact, he is too well liked by some.'

'For heaven's sake, Bert, stop talking in riddles. What are you getting at?'

'I know this is none of my business, but the well-being of my staff is very important, and they all like Fleur.'

'Ah, I see.'

'You know?'

'Rumours reach me.'

'This isn't a rumour, Mrs Renton. It's a fact. Fleur and the Spanish boy are in love. I know the signs. I've watched them. The smiles, the touches, the secret communication of love.' He sighed. 'Once I knew it.'

'Me too,' Sarah said softly.

'But the fact is, Mrs Renton,' Chef said, 'I don't want this Romeo and Juliet carry-on in my kitchen. As you know, a kitchen can be a dangerous place, and I want my staff to concentrate on their work. Accidents happen, tempers get short in the heat and pressure, but most accidents are caused by carelessness and lack of attention.'

Sarah felt she was on shaky ground. Chef wouldn't sort this problem out because of Fleur's relationship to herself.

Chef was gazing at her expectantly. Together they had a long history of trial, errors and upsets, but this time there must be no mistake.

'Perhaps,' Chef's tone of voice was conciliatory, 'you could have a word with Fleur.'

What word, Sarah thought despondently, as Chef heaved himself up, picked up his sheaf of menus and walked, so it seemed to Sarah, with a lighter step towards the door.

'There's one other thing – ' he paused with his hand on the door handle – 'there is talk of change.'

'No change,' she said firmly. 'My family think that my sixtieth birthday would be a good time for me to retire.' She shook her head. 'It is too soon. I must make all safe.'

He sighed with satisfaction.

'Anything else?'

'It's rumoured that the Mullins Group are eager to buy you out. Is that true?'

'Certainly it's true. Charlie Mullins says Renton's Royal would be the jewel in his crown.' She chuckled. 'Renton's Royal is what we've all made it. One of the best hotels in the north. Can you see me parting with such a jewel?'

Chef laughed, a deep rumble which shook his pouch of a stomach and crinkled up the lines on his face. 'Not likely. It would have to be a better man than Charlie Mullins to take this place from the Rentons.'

'I don't know what to say to her, Rachel.' The cottage was alive with music from the record player in Fleur's room. 'It's a Wonderful World . . .' Sarah sighed. Was it?

Rachel's face looked bleak. There were dark shadows beneath her grey eyes; her face was thinner, giving her an air of fragility.

'Does Fleur know Ramiro has gone on leave?'

'I haven't told her. Maybe he has. Let's have a cup of coffee and then call her down.'

Putting off difficult moments wasn't Sarah's style. If anyone grasped the nettle, she did. While Rachel was making coffee she thought of a dozen gentle openings. Upstairs Fleur changed the record, and they could hear her singing along with the words of 'Those Were the Days My Friend'.

Sarah couldn't bear it any longer, and going to the bottom of the stairs called Fleur down.

The music abruptly stopped, and Fleur raced down the stairs just as Rachel carried a tray of coffee into the sitting room.

'Gran, what are you doing here? Are you ill? Is something wrong?' Fleur flung open the French windows and stepped out onto the terrace. She arranged the chairs and table and picking up the tray of coffee carried it outside.

'No biscuits? Honestly, Mum, you know I'm always hungry.' She fetched the tin, offered it round and helped herself.

'You two look awfully solemn. Has something grotty happened?'

An incomprehensible silence bound Sarah and Rachel together. Their faces were turned to the sun, their glances followed the peacocks strutting on the hotel lawn.

'Fleur – ' Sarah shaded her eyes from the brightness – 'did Ramiro tell you I have given him a fortnight's leave to go home?'

'Yes, he did. And he didn't want to go. He said his father was being difficult. He's gone because he thought his father might come over here and fetch him.'

'Did he say how serious his family problems were?'

'He kind of glossed over them. Said he'd fix things when he got to Spain.'

'Suppose he doesn't come back?'

'Gran, you must get him back. It isn't fair, he's nearly finished his training, and when he gets his diploma he can get a job anywhere.'

'But I thought the reason his father is having him trained here is so that he can take over their restaurant when he retires?'

'He doesn't want to do that now. He wants to be free to choose.'

'Fleur, are you sure Ramiro is telling you the truth?'

'Of course he is,' Fleur said indignantly. 'Gran, please get him back. I might never see him again.' Her voice quavered, and big tears formed in her eyes and slowly ran down her cheeks.

Sarah's heart sank. 'I can't go against his father.'

'Why not? I thought you had an agreement with the old man to allow Ramiro to stay here until he has finished his training. At least, that's what Ramiro says. If he doesn't come back I shall follow him to Spain.'

'Fleur!' Rachel's horrified tone brought a flicker of smile to Fleur's lips. 'Your father – he just won't allow it.'

Fleur threw back her head in defiance. 'Well, he'll just have to lump it.'

'That's no way to talk,' Sarah said. 'And it doesn't solve my problem.'

'What do you mean, Gran?'

'Chef is objecting to the two of you working in the kitchen. And I tell you frankly, Fleur, Chef is absolutely necessary to me and the success of the hotel. Highly as he thinks of Ramiro, he would prefer not to have him back.'

'Of all the rotten things! Gran, you're the boss, tell Chef to get lost. He knows we both do our work well, and he hasn't any right to blight our lives. He's as bad as Aunt Claire, although she's *always* making snide remarks.'

'Darling, you must be reasonable,' Rachel said.

'Reasonable,' Fleur shouted. 'How can I be reasonable when my whole life is being ruined? Don't you understand, I love Ramiro, and he loves me. We belong to each other, and no one will ever make me give him up. He's promised to come back. Gran, you've got to help me.'

Sarah was shattered. Her love for Fleur was deeper than she cared to admit, but this grandchild mirrored herself in so many ways. And her passionate support for the man she'd chosen was no less than her own remembered burning love for Gerald. She and Fleur were two of a kind.

'Gran!' Fleur flung her arms round Sarah, pressing her soft cheek against Sarah's.

Rachel said, 'You are behaving like a spoilt child. Don't think you can get round Mother. No one does.'

But Rachel was wrong.

Fleur was the exception. And Sarah was willing to disrupt as many lives as may be, to give Fleur her heart's desire.

CHAPTER 18

During the next few days the four Renton women drew closer together. Adversity, at least, had the effect of bonding their interests. Proud as the peacocks patrolling the lawns they showed no outward signs of the strain they were living under.

Jim's telephone call to Claire sent her tight-lipped in search of Sarah. 'He asked Charlie Mullins for his old job back, and Charlie refused. He told Jim he isn't doing anything until he's consulted you. Why? What has Charlie hiring staff to do with you?'

'Perhaps Jim didn't tell the truth about his departure from here.'

'Are you accusing Jim of lying? You've never liked him,' Claire whined. 'And you are going to stand in the way of him getting a decent managership.'

'Have sense, Claire. If I am asked for a reference I will naturally do the best I can for him.'

Claire's fury against Charlie redoubled. It was one thing to refuse her the kind of job she fancied – it was well known that he always favoured men – but to refuse Jim was a downright insult.

'Is he withdrawing his resignation?' Sarah asked.

'No. A bit late. You've already appointed another manager, and I may say I'm deeply disappointed. All

185

your fine talk about this being a family hotel doesn't apply to me.'

'I think we need some new blood, new ideas. We don't want to get into a rut.'

'If you think Clive Booth and Michael – '

Sarah cut her short. 'I do. Now, shall we let the matter drop.'

But thoughts of revenge festered in Claire's brain. She would bide her time and, when she was ready, she would strike.

The matter was not dropped by the staff however. During break times it was discussed with gusto, and the general consensus of opinion was they were well rid of Jim. He was a trouble-maker. Mrs Renton's choice of Clive Booth as the new manager met with general approval. He was one of them. He'd reached the top through hard work.

Michael's appointment aroused some controversy although it was agreed that as he was the boss's grandson, he had some right to the position he now enjoyed. The staff prided themselves on their loyalty to the family. Jim had always been excluded; he was not a Renton.

Meanwhile Michael's attitude toward Fleur was changing. At first he'd dubbed her his kid cousin, although there was only a few months' difference in their ages, but now when he looked at her he saw a woman, vulnerable and desirable, and he was troubled.

With Ramiro away the cousins spent all their free time together, either in the swimming pool or on the tennis courts. Michael was supervising the construction of the new courts, and Sarah suggested he purchase the nets and the surrounding netting.

They avoided the beach in the hot July days. Family parties enjoyed picnics on the dunes, children paddled in the shallow water, and rafts and dinghies rocked in on the incoming tide.

Few people ventured inland, much to Fleur's relief. Preserving the plants peculiar to this particular stretch of land had become desperately important to her.

She didn't mention Ramiro, although he was constantly in her thoughts, and she secretly hoped he would write to her from Spain. Michael, however, seethed with anger over a letter he'd received from his stepmother.

'She says she's persuaded Dad to bring her over next month,' Michael reported. 'Do you think I can get Gran to put them off? I don't want her here. She's only curious to see the hotel.'

'Well, you can understand that. I rather fancy meeting her myself. You make her sound an absolute bitch.'

'She is,' Michael defended his opinion. 'Dad has never visited here since Grandfather died.'

Sarah was, however, pleased. She'd always longed for Paul to decide to join the family team, but had to admit that Fortunata was a drawback. She hoped to dissuade him from joining his father-in-law in business, a man to whom she had taken an immediate dislike, and hadn't been afraid to tell him that she thought arms dealing immoral.

She'd put thoughts of Ramiro out of her mind, and was surprised to receive a telephone call from Señor Rodriguez enquiring why Ramiro hadn't arrived. Quoting from Sarah's letter, he'd expected his son to be home more than a week ago.

Sarah was momentarily thrown. Recovering, she saw no point in explaining that Ramiro had left for Spain ten days ago. 'There has been a delay, Señor. I will notify you when to expect him.'

Where the hell is he, she thought, sending for Fleur and Chef.

It was mid-morning, and Chef was annoyed to be dragged away from his kitchen.

'Is is important, Mrs Renton?' he shouted into the telephone above the kitchen noise.

'Yes, it is. And please bring Fleur with you.'

Chef marched into Sarah's office and refused to sit down. 'It's a busy time.'

'I know that, so I'll get straight to the point. Ramiro's father has just telephoned. The boy has not arrived in Spain. What do you know about it?'

She immediately regretted her angry tone, as Fleur uttered a sharp cry, and would have fallen if Chef hadn't caught hold of her and lowered her into a chair.

'Fleur darling.' Sarah was beside her. 'I didn't mean to frighten you. I thought one of you must know something.'

'I don't.' Chef was annoyed. 'He had a lift in one of the hotel cars to the station. The chauffeur reported the boy had boarded a train for London. He watched him, because he was waiting for a passenger.'

'Have you heard from him, Fleur?'

She shook her head. Tears slid down her cheeks, and she clung to Sarah.

'It's all right, darling. He must have changed his mind – met a friend in London perhaps.'

'He didn't want to go, Gran. He thought his father wouldn't allow him back.'

'That won't do,' Chef said gruffly. 'The boy is due to sit for his diploma. I won't have all that tuition and hard work wasted.'

'Fleur, do you know why his father was so anxious Ramiro should go home?'

'He wouldn't tell me. Oh Gran, what are we to do? He might be ill or murdered. We must find him.'

'My guess is he'll turn up on the day he's due back here, and not let on he hasn't been to Spain. Did he know you'd written to his father, Mrs Renton?'

188

'I don't think so.'

'There. He won't think his father will be expecting him, and is playing for time.'

'But why. I mean couldn't he just tell his father he was staying here?' Fleur asked.

'He's a bright lad, and I'm sure he won't have come to any harm. Buck up, Fleur,' Chef said, putting a fatherly arm round her shoulders. 'He told me that Spanish family ties are very strong, that's why he had such great admiration for your grandmother. You'll see, he'll turn up as if nothing has happened. If you'd rather not come back to the kitchen, Fleur, we can manage.'

'Of course I'm coming back.' She threw her arms round Sarah and hugged her. 'Chef is right. I know Ramiro will come back – for me,' she added softly.

'They faced each other in the cottage sitting room. It was raining, tempestuous rain laced with blue flashes of lightning, and crashing thunder.

'Where have you been?' Fleur's joy at Ramiro's return was soured with anger. 'I've nearly gone mad with worry. I thought – Oh God – I thought something terrible had happened to you.' She shuddered.

He took off his yellow rain cape. She snatched it from him, and hung it up on the stand in the hall.

He said, 'Fleur, I didn't mean to upset you.'

'You did, frightfully.' He moved a step nearer, but she backed away.

'Please, Fleur, I cannot bear your anger. Have you changed?'

'Changed? Do you mean have I stopped loving you. How could I? If I didn't care so much do you think I'd cry myself to sleep at nights – hating everything because you are not around to share it with me.'

'Oh Fleur.' He wouldn't be denied and pulled her into

189

his arms. His face was wet and cold. His kiss was kindling to her icy heart, which now throbbed with desire.

'Forgive me, beloved,' he said, at last drawing away to look at her face. 'I would give my life for you.'

'And I would give mine for you.'

Her arms were round his neck, and he held her so close their hearts seem to beat together. Time dissolved, there was only the hunger, the warmth, this being together.

They were oblivious to the noise of the front door opening, and only drew apart when they heard Sarah calling for Ricki.

She walked into the room, and stopped short. 'So you're back.' Her quick glance registered their flushed faces, their shining eyes. She took off her coat and untied her rainhood. 'I hate storms. The hall porter walked here with me, holding up one of those enormous golf umbrellas. Hang up my coat, Fleur, please.'

She sat down in an armchair with her back to the window. 'Now young man, where the hell have you been these last two weeks? I gave you leave to go home, so why didn't you?'

'How do you know – ?'

'I'll tell you how I know. I wrote to your father telling him I'd given you special leave to go home because of family problems. Three days ago he telephoned to ask when he could expect you. I didn't tell him I'd no idea where you were. No point in upsetting him too. So, where have you been?'

Ricki howled as a severe crash of thunder seemed to shake the house. Fleur flew to comfort the dog, lugging him into the sitting room.

Sarah's face paled. She was on edge; storms roused in her incomprehensible fears.

'I'm waiting, Ramiro,' she said.

'I stayed with my friend Luis. He has a restaurant in

London. He is Spanish, he understands how it is with families. My father is determined I stay home. I cannot.'

'I don't understand. Your father practically begged me to take you on here. Surely he realizes your training is nearly finished. What are these family problems?'

'It is complicated – the restaurant, and other things. The family need me. It is my duty to return.' His glance was despairing. 'I will go, but not yet. There are matters to sort out first.'

'I suggest you sort them out. I am very displeased. We have all worried about you since we knew you were not in Spain. I hope you won't give me any further cause for such alarm, or I shall have to ask you to go.'

'If he goes, I go,' Fleur declared.

'No, you don't, my dear child. You stay here where you belong, and I don't want to hear any more nonsense.'

Subdued, they left. Ricki pressed his shivering body against Sarah's knee. She was overwhelmed by a sadness, the old feeling of inadequacy, and as always, a compassion which brought tears to her eyes.

Ramiro's return preceded Mark's delayed visit by a few days. Ever since Rachel had received his letter, she had been on edge and had constantly put off telling Fleur of the imminent arrival of her father. The moment came when she couldn't wait any longer.

'I have to face him sometime,' she said to Sarah. 'I'm not running away, so I'll be here, and I must make sure Fleur is here too.'

Fleur was in her room. The radio was turned on, musical hits of yesteryear. She lay on the bed fully clothed, eyes closed. Rachel sat down beside her, but she restrained herself from touching.

'Fleur, your father is visiting us on Sunday.'

Fleur opened her eyes and sat up. 'Why?'

Rachel turned down the sound on the radio.

'I thought you and he were washed up?'

Rachel said defensively, 'We have had problems, it's true, that's why we have to talk to him.'

'Count me out.'

'I can't. He particularly wants to talk to you.'

'Why? What does he want?'

'He wants us to live with him at Ashton Hall.'

'What!' Fleur sprang off the bed. 'Is he mad or are you? I'll never go back to live in that grotty Dower House.'

'Not the Dower House, the Hall.'

Fleur stared at her mother, wild-eyed. 'You can't have agreed? Have you?' she asked suspiciously.

'No, of course I haven't. That's why I said I would see him here. I thought we could talk it over quietly.'

'Honestly, Mum, I despair of you. Have you forgotten the last quiet talk? You only just avoided a nervous breakdown, and then only because Gran intervened. Well, he isn't going to rant and rage at me.'

'Calm down, darling. He is your father.'

'That doesn't give him the right to dictate to us. I'm staying here, and that's final.'

'You must listen,' Rachel said, breathless with agitation. 'You see our decision has far-reaching results.' She sat down and covered her face with her hands. She had to think, present Mark's case fairly.

After a moment or two Fleur knelt down beside her, and took her hands away from her face.

'Go on, Mum.' She listened to Rachel's garbled account of the need for Mark's mother to go to America for medical treatment, leaving him to run the estate, and his father's hope that Rachel and Fleur would support him.

'Why should we? What's happened to the tart he picked up?'

'I don't know. I think he's changed,' she said defensively.

192

'He says he'd like to try again, the three of us living as a family.'

'So he can boss and control and ride roughshod over us again?' Fleur's anguished voice cracked as she continued: 'You have to stand up to him.'

'I do try.' Rachel sounded so hopeless, Fleur hugged her. 'It's easy for you, I end up being sorry for him. And in a way I still care for him.'

Fleur's delight at Ramiro's return was tempered by his refusal to discuss his family problems, and her frustration was mounting. Therefore it was not surprising she was far from sympathetic to her father's problems. To please Rachel she hung about the car park at the appointed time, waiting for the Ashton Daimler to drive in.

Mark was driving himself. Fleur observed him critically as he alighted, carefully locking the car doors. He wore a perfectly-cut suit, silk shirt and matching tie. He owed his slim figure to the hours spent on the golf course and the tennis court. Fleur's new adult impression of him was worrying. Rachel was no match for such a self-assured man.

She slouched across to the car. 'Hullo!'

He turned sharply, and was unable to hide an expression of disapproval. One look registered Fleur's stained white overall, her hair held back by an elastic band, and her scuffed and dirty white plimsolls.

'Darling!' He made a tentative movement towards her, but she neatly sidestepped out of his reach.

'Mum is over at the cottage. Come on.'

He walked quickly across the lawn, trying to match his stride to hers. Rachel stood in the doorway watching them.

Mark's greeting was brief but warm as he followed her into the sitting room. It was to be a charm offensive then, rather than all-out war. Fleur fled up the stairs, and into the bathroom. After a quick shower, clean underwear, and her newest mini cotton dress, feet strapped into her high-heeled sandals, she felt more able to cope.

She descended the stairs slowly, listening for their voices. They sat facing each other and turned to the door as she entered. As a child she'd wished passionately that her parents were more like those of her school friends, strolling around the grounds arm in arm on Speech Days. Rachel had often come alone, and Fleur had deeply resented it.

'That's better.' Mark half-rose. 'I recognize my daughter now.'

'That's a surprise.' Fleur dropped into an chair, one leg crossed over the other, foot negligently swinging. 'I guess it's two – no three years since you last set eyes on me.'

Mark frowned.

Fleur regarded him dispassionately. His good looks were so obvious; straight nose, deep-set blue eyes marked by well-defined brows.

Her school friends had envied her such a handsome and debonair father, but never once had she betrayed her true opinion of him.

'Hardly my fault,' he said. 'Your mother – '

She interrupted him. 'You walked out on us with the fancy barmaid from the Crown.'

He flushed with annoyance. 'How dare you speak to me like that!'

Fleur was jolted out of her own problems. She had found a target at which to shoot, and she wasn't going to let up. She had suffered too many hurts in the past, principally on her mother's behalf.

But as always he retreated and instead attacked the weaker of the two – Rachel.

'If this is how you've brought up our daughter, I'll soon alter her behaviour.'

'Don't pick on Mum. She's put up with enough from you.'

'Fleur, please,' Rachel pleaded.

'All right, I'm being bitchy.' She moved over to the arm of her mother's chair, and put a comforting arm round her shoulder, kissing her on the cheek. 'Wouldn't it be better if I left you two alone? I can go into the kitchen and make tea.'

Mark latched on the word 'kitchen'.

'Your mother tells me you are working in the hotel kitchen. Hardly a suitable job for an Ashton.' Rachel's warning fingers on her arm kept Fleur momentarily silent. She had a frightening picture of the future her father was planning for her. She rebelled in her heart, mind and soul.

'If you really want to work, Fleur, why not help me out with the administration of the Estate?'

'Nothing doing. I'm staying here. I'm happy in my job. I love living with Gran. Renton's Royal is in my blood, and no way am I deserting. It's a fantastic hotel. Michael and I are completely involved.'

'Michael?' he questioned.

'My brother's son,' Rachel said.

'Is he a kitchen hand too? Cheap labour, I presume.' He raised one eyebrow disdainfully. 'Look, darling, if this cookery thing is really so important to you, we could always send you on a cordon bleu course. God knows your mother could have done with one before we married!'

His attempt at humour failed dismally. Fleur bristled with rage to hear him denigrating Rachel once more. Whatever he said, nothing had changed.

Both of them were standing now. Fleur was as tall as her father, her eyes on a level with his. He reached out and grasped her arm. She shook him off. 'The time is past when you can intimidate Mother. She has me to fight for her.' He was too angry to reply. He walked out of the cottage and they watched him cross the lawn. Fleur grasped Rachel's hand. 'Oh Lordy, Mum. What have I done?'

195

CHAPTER 19

Charlie Mullins' wife died on the first of August. He telephoned Sarah a couple of days later. She was surprised by the regret in his voice, and promised to attend the funeral, and to meet the family afterwards.

The service was attended by a great number of people, none of whom Sarah knew, and she was glad Michael had opted to accompany her. She had tentatively mentioned the funeral to Claire, who had shuddered away, but not to Rachel, who seemed so sunk in gloom that it would have been unkind to worsen her misery.

Terry, the hotel chauffeur, drove them to the church, and afterwards to the tall Victorian house in Seaforth. It stood among houses built in the great sea days, when captains abounded, and the ships sailed over the bar in view of the house windows.

Sarah hadn't seen Charlie's sister-in-law since the days when she was a snivelling youngster being dragged to Stick Street School. She greeted Sarah and Michael effusively and led them into the front room which was crowded. Ettie Coxon took Sarah's arm, moved a youth out of a chair, and brought a glass of warm sweet sherry to her. Ettie's husband was a seafarer and evidence of his travels was visible on tables, shelves, a piano and the crowded mantelpiece.

'Alice didn't have much of a life,' Ettie said as she leaned confidentially over Sarah and cast a malicious look in Charlie's direction. 'Never enjoyed his money, she didn't. Or much of his company for that matter. The poor woman wasted away. I hear you and Charlie are in the same business. My *family* keeps me busy.' She puffed out her generous chest, and her sharp eyes disappeared momentarily behind flesh which rolled up from her scarlet cheeks. 'This lot is mostly mine. Three sons and three girls, all married with kids.'

Sarah felt overwhelmed. Had she ever enjoyed wedding and burial feasts? She supposed they had made for a break in the monotony of working long hours in her father's café, and looking round she caught Charlie's glance. He pushed his way to her.

'Sarah. Good to see you.'

'And you,' she said thankfully.

He shook hands with Michael, and beckoning to a young girl presented her to Sarah. 'My Betsy,' he said. 'My one and only grandchild. Her mother is in California. Betsy is at a catering college. Runs in our families, I guess.'

Betsy grinned at Michael. 'Can you drive a car?'

Yes,' Michael said casually, omitting to say his driving licence was only three weeks old.

'Like to see the sports car my darling Charlie has given me?' She put an affectionate arm round her grandfather and kissed him. 'It's absolutely fab. I passed the test first time,' she added proudly.

Charlie found a chair and placed it next to Sarah. 'What do you think of her?'

'She's a beauty, Charlie.'

'A blondie like her mother,' he said fondly, 'and the Mullins eyes. Sarah, I need to talk to you. Not here, with this crowd. I've got my car. Let's have tea at The Adelphi.'

Sarah instructed Terry to wait for Michael, and joined

197

Charlie. He drove a Jaguar. He laughed as he gave her a hand in and said, 'Remember the old tin lizzie I bought when I was seventeen. Ten quid, and a good runner.'

'You taught me to drive, and Dad was furious. He said I shouldn't trust myself to you.'

'He was right.' Charlie set the car in motion, and headed for the city. 'He thought I was no good. You know, Sarah, I set out to prove him wrong. Pity he didn't live to see what we've made of our lives.' He touched her knee. 'We'd have done all right together, lass.'

Sarah didn't doubt it. Nor did she doubt her father's early assessment of Charlie's character. In spite of all his success he hadn't really changed. Easy come, easy go, Joe Nealey had said. Not the lad for my lass.

The Adelphi Hotel impressed. Sarah noted the atmosphere of stability, the well-trained staff, a kind of sepulchral hush that must have seemed intimidating to the not-so-rich.

Charlie ordered tea in the lounge. 'Old-fashioned, but I like it. That's where you score. Afternoon Tea at Renton's Royal is becoming the "in" meal, I understand.'

They chatted amicably for an hour or so and then moved to the bar. Charlie ordered a gin and tonic with ice for Sarah and a whisky mac for himself, and then quite suddenly the atmosphere changed.

'I expect you know, Sarah, that Jim asked me for his old job back.'

She nodded.

'Did you give him the push?'

'No.'

'Rumours get around. I heard he was becoming a golf-club johnny.'

Sarah ignored the implication of Jim's fondness for drink. 'I'm afraid he resented Michael joining my staff. He thought it would injure his prospects.'

198

'I suppose you know that Claire asked me for a managership on the day she was assaulted. I had to refuse her, and I've felt guilty ever since.'

Sarah looked at him in amazement.

'She didn't tell you?' he said.

'So that was it,' she said softly.

'You mean I was to blame.'

'No. She can't bear rejection. Why did you refuse her?'

'I don't ever cheat on you. I needed to know the lie of the land. Has she split up with Jim?'

'I fear they might part. I suppose that is why she wanted you to take her on. Their marriage seemed to work while they were secure in their positions in the hotel. But the thread was wearing thin, and it snapped when I changed the scenario.'

'What do you want me to do?'

'Don't ask me. You never take anybody's advice. You'll do what suits you, and I guess it won't be taking on Claire and Jim.'

'Why not?' He was belligerent.

'Because you think of them as a lever to oust me. I retire, and what happens? Jim and Claire think they will inherit Renton's Royal. So, they sell to you on condition they retain their managerships.'

'Sarah, you can't think that?'

'I do. But it won't work. If and when I retire from active management it won't make the slightest difference. I'm not selling the hotel, Charlie.'

'I can wait. I'm a patient man.'

'You'll need patience, my dear Charlie,' she promised.

'You know that I've offered Jim and Claire the management of my new hotel in Barbados.'

'Oh that,' she said impatiently. 'As a matter of fact Claire has opted to stay on. She considers herself heir apparent.' Sarah smiled. 'She will not believe that if

Michael makes the grade he will eventually be in control.'

He sighed with relief. 'To be honest, Sarah, Claire was the stumbling block. Her ambition blinds her to the fact that alone she isn't capable of a top job.'

Sarah didn't say she endorsed his opinion. Her loyalty to the family was too strong for that. Had she on the other hand treated Jim shabbily?

As if reading her thoughts, Charlie said, 'Jim has always resented that when he married Claire he was not considered a full member of your family. He confided in me years ago. I counselled him to give it time, but now it's too late. I guess I can find a place for him.'

'Thanks, Charlie.'

'And if Claire wants to join him any time, she's welcome.'

'I hope she will. It makes me sad to see her marriage falling apart. I wonder where I failed?'

He took hold of her hand. Instantly she remembered the comfort of his grasp on the unhappy day when he had delivered her to the convent. She'd needed him then, but did she need him now? 'Nothing to do with you, they were unlucky, like me.' He sighed.

She withdrew her hand. 'I was so lucky, wasn't I? Gerald was all I asked of life. I should have known such happiness couldn't last.'

'He was right for you when you were seventeen. I remember your dream of romantic love. A rough ragged boy from Dockland didn't fit the picture. I loved you then, and I love you now.'

'Charlie – '

'I had to let you go. I was no match for the Rentons.' He sighed gustily. 'Gerald had it all going for him. Looks, money, education and the kind of romantic nature that fulfilled your dream. And now you've made it to the top.'

'And so have you.'

But *had* they fulfilled their ambitious expectations? Weren't they still striving for more?

They finished their drinks and returned to the car. Charlie drove with his usual élan along the busy city streets, heading towards the coastal road.

This city was peculiarly their own; both had been proud to defend it in the war days. Sarah never failed to notice its new face, new buildings covering the scars and craters, new roads, churches, schools. But in her mind's eye she still saw the burning city as it had been during that shocking weekend in early May 1941. She hadn't forgotten the feel of the bucking ambulance as she steered it along roads made hazardous by ever more craters and potholes. Dark nights, the buzz of aircraft, the crump of falling bombs; fires springing up around her; and always the hard lump in her heart as she imagined the dangers Gerald was facing in France.

Faces often returned to haunt her. A turn of a head, a smile, a voice, and she was reminded of another time, another place, another anger and fear.

Gerald had been called up at the beginning of the war. The O.T.C. at public school and the territorial army had ensured that. Sefton Taylor had taken over complete control of the hotel, perpetually filled with high-ranking civil servants and wounded officers.

Sarah lived from day to day, or rather from one terrible and frightening night to the next. Volunteering for the ambulance service was her choice. The children's schools were evacuated to considered safe areas, and only in the holidays in the security of the cottage in Bransfell did Sarah let the peace of the country heal some of the hurt, readying her for the next onslaught.

Gerald was wounded at Dunkirk, and was eventually posted to the War Office, although his main worry was still for Sarah.

Charlie's service career had been more spectacular. He joined the Navy, and two of the ships in which he served were torpedoed, but he came through unscathed.

At the end of the war he applied for a job to Harold Stavely, head of the Stavely group of hotels. Charlie's friendship with Harold's only son was the link, and when the boy was killed, Mr Stavely saw in Charlie his successor. Charlie's training was comprehensive, and Mr Stavely, when he died, had been content to pass on his vast business to Charlie, believing it would continue to prosper under his management. Perhaps it had all been too easy, and Charlie now saw the acquisition of Renton's Royal as his final challenge.

'Well, here we are,' said Charlie, parking on the forecourt.

Sarah thought Renton's Royal always looked its best in the summer evening sunshine.

Charlie obviously agreed with her. 'I like it. I like it very much. I can raise my offer.' Charlie alighted and stood looking at the building glowing in the suffused warm light. He came round the car and opened the door for her.

'Don't bother, I am not selling.'

'Sarah, would you consider a partnership?'

'I have a partner. Sefton Taylor.'

'I didn't know.'

'I'm surprised. Claire and Jim have slipped up.'

He laughed. 'It wouldn't have been difficult for me to find out. That changes the situation. I mean, Taylor would have to want to sell too.'

'Sefton does not. Renton's Royal means a lot to him, so don't go sneaking behind my back and contacting him.'

'As if I would!'

Sarah made a mental note to write to Sefton and appraise him of the situation. In the meantime she suggested a visit to her new conservatory.

'You have class, Sarah.' He walked round, taking a close look at the design, the plants, and stood in front of the fountain for a few minutes.

'I get it,' he said at last. 'Struggle. Our struggle. The force of our determination, it's there. Who designed it?'

'I did. And its copyright.'

He laughed. 'Remember that grotty little fountain in the wall in the Dock Road? I think it was a drinking trough for the horses really, but we used to get unsuspecting passers-by to throw in pennies for luck and then shared our ill-gotten gains. Looking at all that water makes me thirsty – how about a drink?'

It was unfortunate that Claire was already in the bar. She tried to push past Charlie, but he took her arm and piloted her to a table.

'Sit down, Claire. I want to talk to you.'

She turned on Sarah. 'I told you to keep him away from me.'

'He has a right to refuse you a job, Claire.'

'How dare you tell her?' she stormed at Charlie.

Sarah sat down, and asked Kellett to bring drinks to their table. 'What makes you think he wouldn't? He isn't going to run the risk of being accused of pitching in on my preserve.'

'You needn't worry. I wouldn't take a job with him if he went down on his bended knees.'

'Fine. We can be friends again.'

'No Charlie, we can't. You are never friends with women. You desire them or you don't. You're so arrogant you think no woman can resist you or run a business as well as you. *Mother* can.'

His eyes narrowed. 'You have a knight in shining armour to defend you, Sarah. Odd how people change. You asked me for a job, Claire, because you wanted to get away from your mother. I think you said she stifled you.

And now you've clarified the difference between you; Sarah is strong and single-minded, you aren't.'

'I suppose you'd give Sarah a job without a quibble.'

'Too true. I'd trust Sarah with the whole of my business, and I'd know it would prosper.'

He finished his drink, kissed Sarah, and for a moment put his arms round her. 'Thank you, my dear, for attending Alice's funeral. It meant a lot to me.'

Sarah watched him walk away. 'He's lonely,' she said softly.

'He's putting on a damn good act for your benefit, Mother. I hope you won't be stupid enough to fall for it.'

Dear Charlie. Poor Charlie. Why did the image of him so many years earlier still haunt her – a thin pale boy, in a cast-off jacket with bony wrists protruding from frayed sleeves.

Claire was right though. Charlie had no need of pity or compassion now. He was a success.

CHAPTER 20

In spite of Margaret's reluctance, plans for her coming-of-age dinner went ahead. Invitations were issued, and Sarah was looking forward to the occasion. It was her hope that the event would give Claire the opportunity to try and patch up her marriage, and with this end in mind she was determined Jim should be present.

Rachel's marriage was a different matter; she envisaged no reconciliation between her daughter and Mark Ashton.

Her deep disappointment over the apparent failure of both her daughters' marriages filled her with a sense of guilt. Her thoughts turned constantly to the long years, as she dubbed them; the war years and her separation from Gerald and her children, during school term-time; and the hard slog after the war to bring the hotel back to the standard they had set for themselves.

Had Renton's Royal occupied too much of her time to the detriment of her children's happiness? School holidays at the cottage in Bransfell had been ecstatic. The communicative silence of the mountains brought a kind of peace and she allowed evocative thoughts to possess her mind.

She and Gerald had been in agreement about encouraging the children to do their own thing; but she had never understood Paul's and Rachel's turning away from the hotel. They had been thankful that Claire had opted for hotel management; less thankful when she had announced her engagement to Jim O'Hara, then the under-manager.

Jim had served his apprenticeship with the Stavely group of hotels, and had come to Renton's Royal on Charlie Mullins' recommendation, and in the early years had proved his worth. His ambition had become fully fledged on his marriage to Claire, and after Gerald's death, the glittering prize of ownership of the hotel seemed to be within his grasp. He had two options; to work for the early removal of Sarah or to co-operate with Charlie Mullins.

His resignation and flight from the hotel had been a spur-of-the-moment decision, and one which he was already regretting, especially as Charlie was up north and unlikely to return to London for a time.

Resigned at having to wait about in London, it was only natural for him to try and improve his relationship with Margaret. He needed one member of the family to be on his side.

Margaret was not pleased to find her father on her doorstep. She greeted him warily.

'I have to be in London for a few days. Can you do with me?' He entered the hall, put his arms round her, and kissed her. 'I won't be any trouble.'

Reluctantly she agreed.

He dumped his holdall and followed her into the kitchen. 'I'm just making coffee,' she said.

'You've made the place look nice.'

'Yes.'

She poured coffee into mugs and handed one to her father. He sat down.

'Are you here on business? I mean, wouldn't you be more comfortable in a hotel?'

He smiled. 'I expect I would, but it isn't convenient.'

'What is this, Dad?'

'I need a bolt-hole, and this will do nicely, especially as I'm paying the piper.'

She refused to be lured into that argument. 'What's happened this time?'

He narrowed his eyes, and carefully lit one of the black cigars he affected.

'I've resigned.'

Startled, she looked at him and with dismay observed the complacent expression in his eyes.

'You can't. I mean, you're family.'

'My dear Margaret, you know very well that I have never been or ever will be family in your grandmother's eyes. I am your mother's husband, and as such tolerated.'

'That's nonsense. You are the manager of the hotel.'

'I was,' he corrected her. 'Sarah manages Renton's Royal. She *is* Renton's Royal, the rest of us do her bidding. Surely you know that. I've had enough.'

'But what about Mother?'

'Oh you needn't worry about her. Claire is a Renton, and she's keeping her place at the front of the queue.'

Bewildered, Margaret said, 'What on earth are you talking about?'

'We now have other contenders for Sarah's place, that is if she ever retires. Michael is being groomed to head the team, and young Fleur runs him a good second.'

'They're family.'

'Exactly.'

'Jealousy,' Margaret said softly.

She looked at him closely, and was concerned to see the coarsening of his skin, his greying hair, and his recent weight gain.

'Dad, are you ill?'

'Sick in spirit, my dear daughter. You, on the other hand, are looking very beautiful.' His voice softened, and she felt the transient glow which he'd always raised in her with his fulsome praises during her childhood. He knew how to draw out her sympathy. He had won her over as he intended. He had always dallied with her affection, playing it off against Claire's waning love.

'The flat is all yours,' she said. 'We are going to Bransfell tomorrow.'

'We?' he questioned.

'Gran has lent the cottage to me and my boyfriend. Apparently Rachel isn't there. Then we have to be at Renton's Royal for the 20th – my birthday dinner. Dad, you will be there, won't you?' she cajoled, putting her arms round him.

He pushed her aside. 'First I've heard of a boyfriend. Who is he?'

'Didn't Mother tell you? She met him when she was last here. His name is Peter Lovell, and he is a student like me.'

'I don't approve of you going off alone with this boy.'

She laughed. 'Oh don't be stuffy, Dad.'

'Does your mother know?'

'It doesn't bother her.'

'I suppose I can't stop you – '

'No.'

'Then I shall come with you. I need a holiday and my business can wait,' he said. 'Margaret, I can't stay here alone. I want your company.'

'You'll hate it,' she said sullenly. 'You've always said the mountains depress you, and the country bores you.'

'I was brought up in the country.'

'But you said – '

'I know what I said. My parents lived in a village in Southern Ireland. My mother died when I was fourteen, and I ran away from home. I thought Liverpool was Mecca. My first job was as a page boy in a hotel.'

'Does Mother know?'

He shrugged his shoulders.

'You must have spoken of your childhood to her,' Margaret persisted.

'Would you tell anyone, even your wife, you were the youngest of ten children, always hungry, wearing cast-offs, practically begging for a living?'

'Why are you telling me? Dad, is this the truth?'

'I couldn't tell anyone else. I always intended to tell you one day.'

She was moved by the love she'd always felt for him, recognizing his weakness, and at last able to give of her strength.

A glance at Margaret's softened expression and Jim congratulated himself that he had chosen the right moment to divulge the past. Margaret was now on his side. He didn't care that compassion or pity had changed her, he needed her loyalty, and a way back to the other side, which only Margaret could make possible.

'Will your boyfriend mind me coming with you?'

Peter was philosophical and cynical. 'If the old boy wants to guard his ewe lamb, let him. I guess he won't bother us, Mag.'

'I guess he will. He'll want to run our holiday. We'll have to stand firm.'

Jim wasn't prepared to like Peter. And he intended to establish his superiority before they even began their journey. He was shocked to find that Margaret and Peter were proposing to hitch-hike north.

'We must have a car. I am not relying on a driver's charity, or travelling in the back of a lorry.' He was all energy now. He hired a car. He visited Fortnum and Mason's to buy luxury food and a selection of decent wines, first cashing a large cheque on his and Claire's joint account.

The car was delivered to the flat with all the requisite

papers, and Jim familiarized himself with the controls. He invited Peter to sit in the passenger seat next to him, leaving Margaret to climb in the back. He hadn't driven far when he realized Margaret was the prototype back-seat driver, and he was getting ruffled by her comments.

'Isn't this better than hitch-hiking?' he asked Peter.

'I guess so.'

'I won't spoil any of your plans.'

'We don't have any plans.'

'How do you propose to spend the holiday?'

'Walking, rock climbing, lazing as the mood takes us.'

'Rock climbing? Once I was a champion. Have you the right gear?'

'We hire it.'

They left London by the M1. Jim concentrated on the traffic, weaving in and out, taking risks. Hadn't he always taken risks? The uncomfortable thought persisted that the time he and his brother had risked climbing the rocks near their home, his brother had been killed. The family had blamed him; when he thought about the dead boy lying at the bottom of the rocks he broke out in a cold sweat, like now, and automatically he pressed harder on the accelerator, cutting in to the blaring of horns of outraged drivers.

'For God's sake,' Margaret shouted. 'Do you want to kill us. Stop the car. At once.'

Claire's voice; Claire's child too.

Jim had turned off the M1, and was cruising along the A5 in readiness to join the M6. He ignored Margaret, gathering speed.

Peter, aware of Margaret's agitation, said, 'Look, Sir, you are upsetting Margaret, please slow down.'

With bad grace Jim drew into the verge, and reluctantly allowed Margaret to take the wheel.

Margaret drove a car in the way she did most things,

carefully and with complete control. The M6 stretched ahead, mile after mile, and she confidently kept the car going at a steady pace.

Jim sat in the back, mortified. His daughter had dared to criticize his ability to drive with care. He knew without doubt that Claire would have been just as critical, and he maintained a sullen silence.

Margaret slackened speed as the motorway ended, and turned off onto a secondary road.

'Look, Pete – ' She dug a finger into his knee – 'the mountains at last, not far now.' She wound down the window and breathed deeply. 'Fresh, clean air, can you smell the fells? It's heaven to be back.'

Eventually she turned into a narrow lane, just wide enough for a car, but with frequent passing places cut into the hedges. The lane dipped gently into the village nestling in the bottom of the valley and bounded by the river. Verne Cottage was the last one in the row before the lane rose steeply, and opened out to fells, dotted with conifer plantations, and the still, small tarn below the jagged rocks of Bransfell.

As always Margaret felt a coming together of all her senses; sight, smell, and strangely, taste, aromatic and wind-wafted from the conifers. She braked in the lane in front of the cottage, and elated to be back, sprang out of the car. 'What do you think, Pete?'

He grinned. 'Now I understand.'

'What?' she demanded, opening the double gates in preparation to drive to the doors of a ramshackle garage. 'You.'

She leant on the gate demanding an explanation. He was out of the car and put his arms round her.

'I'm talking about that little part you don't care to reveal to others. The softness in your nature I knew was there, but could never reach.'

Jim alighted. 'Nothing changes. Dull as hell.'

She rounded on him. 'You knew what it is like here. Why did you come?'

'Better the devil you know than the one you don't.'

She unlocked the boot, and helped Peter to unload their personal luggage, and the hamper and wine from Fortnum and Mason's. Rachel's next-door neighbour was looking out for them. She kept Verne Cottage aired and dusted and held the key.

Margaret had telephoned her to expect them, and tea was laid in readiness for their arrival.

'I miss Rachel and Fleur,' Mrs Hawkins said, making tea and cutting slices of her home-made cake. 'Not that I'm lonely,' she added, a smile on her round plump face. Fleur called her Mrs Dumpling, wholesome on the outside, and full of delicious surprises inside. 'There's milk, eggs and home-cured bacon in the fridge, so you'll manage.'

'How kind of you to look out for us, Mrs Hawkins.'

'I'm just being neighbourly. I'll leave you to enjoy your tea. I've made up the beds in all the rooms. Anything you're short of, Margaret, give me a call.'

'Old busybody,' Jim said sourly, cutting himself another slice of cake.

'I hope,' Margaret said sharply, 'you aren't going to offend her. She's kind, and that's more than can be said about some people.'

During the following days Jim tried to hide his misery, for such it was. He'd hoped to build up a better relationship with Margaret, but his ill-humour only led him into further criticism of her methods. He objected strongly to being organised by his daughter, thought Peter was a fool to go along with her, failing to recognize their compatibility.

More and more he sought the solace offered at the pub

in the village of Shalington, half a mile away. Although Margaret and Peter always invited him to join them in their walks or sightseeing, he declined, and so they left him to his own resources.

The Triple Crown was originally built in the seventeenth century, and not a lot had been done to modernise it, which appealed to the few villagers who patronised it on Saturday nights, and the travellers seeking quiet, strong beer and home cooking.

Jim toyed with the idea of moving into one of the two letting rooms. He was beginning to feel an unwanted third in the cottage. He had struck up an acquaintanceship with the guest occupying the larger of the two rooms, who was full of praise for the comfort and excellent meals.

Jim found Denby Tripp's company exhilarating. Apart from a fund of amusing stories, he had a sympathetic nature; just what Jim relished.

'I've visited Verne Cottage at the invitation of Rachel Ashton. Are you related to her?'

'My sister-in-law,' Jim admitted.

'I thought her charming,' Denby enthused. 'I'm a lecturer at the city university, and I was able to hunt up some papers relating to the death of Samuel Verne. You know, of course, she is writing a book about his life. Is she staying at the cottage now?'

'No. Just my daughter and her boyfriend. I'm finding them very tedious. All this enthusiasm about dead poets, and following in their footsteps.'

Tripp laughed. 'Not your line. Are you interested in fishing? The river is full of trout. And of course there is some excellent rock climbing. Have you managed to climb Brant Crags?'

'Not yet. But I'd certainly like to have a stab at it.' Immediately he uttered the words, he regretted them.

'Done much climbing?'

Jim nodded, unwilling to admit that the only rocks he'd ever climbed had ended in disaster.

'I was thinking of making an assault on Brant tomorrow, if the weather holds. Would you like to join me?'

Trapped, Jim said he'd left his boots at home.

'No problem. You can buy a pair in Kendal. A pity not to make the most of it while you are here.'

To Jim's relief the weather did not hold. Fat-bellied clouds squatted on the top of Brant all day, and rain brightened the green fields at the back of Verne Cottage, and spattered into the river.

'Postponed,' Tripp said when Jim met him in the bar at lunchtime. 'Gives us a chance to get you a decent pair of boots.'

Jim had no intention of informing Margaret of his proposed climb with Tripp. Her objections would be succinct, and too reminiscent of Claire. He had to climb Brant, not only to prove his prowess, but to submerge that old memory for ever. He believed that a successful climb of Brant Crags would exorcize the ghost of his dead brother, and prove to himself that the fault had not been his.

On the third day the weather was perfect. The rocks thrust upward, untroubled with veils and wreathes of mist, and in the intense clarity Jim fancied he could already see the hand- and foot-holds.

It wasn't until Jim met Tripp at the base of the rocks that his confidence wavered. He wanted to shout 'no, no,' but instead allowed Tripp to tie the rope round him, and instruct him to make use of the crampons, though as leader he would indicate the best holds.

Their ascent was slow and painful, at least for Jim. Tripp, in spite of his sedentary occupation, was in better nick, and shouted instructions to Jim, trailing on the end of the rope.

Jim forced himself to concentrate. With appalling

214

clarity he realized that this was a different proposition from the easy climb near his home, one which had had such terrible consequences. And yet as they made the careful ascent, his spirits rose. He wished that Claire and Sarah, particularly Sarah, were watching. It would revolutionize their opinion of him.

Now he was totally aware of the physical effort. His hands reached for the holds, his feet lodged in the crevices Tripp indicated. He swung his body upward, the wind teased and tugged at him. But he was strong, he was a conqueror.

Tripp reached the narrow ridge on the summit, and guided Jim up beside him.

'Well done! Worth the effort.' Tripp flung out an arm, encompassing the bird's-eye expanse of fields and fells, the blue streak of the river, the half-hidden roofs of villages, and above and beyond, the range of mountains, blue-grey merging with the sky.

Jim was breathing quickly. The exertion had tired him, but he felt something else; suddenly his horizon was widened; he swelled with the knowledge of his achievement.

'Princes of all we survey,' Tripp said.

'Okay. Don't quote Wordsworth. I've had a bellyful of him.'

'I wasn't going to,' Tripp said in a hurt voice. He enjoyed making literary allusions.

'Shall we make the descent by the north face? It's more difficult, but we can abseil part of the way.'

'Forget it. We'll go down the way we came up.'

'I realize you haven't done much climbing.'

'That about wraps it up. One climb in my whole life and that was on the miserable little hill near my home in Southern Ireland.' He caught hold of Tripp's arm. 'And that climb killed my brother.'

He felt Tripp stiffen, and glancing at him saw his lips tighten and anger flash in his eyes.

'How dare you risk my life as well as your own?'

'I guessed you had enough confidence for two or more.' Jim laughed. The sound reverberated like faint thunder in the hills.

'Why?' Tripp asked softly.

Up here, suspended in space almost, it was better than any dark and secret confessional. Here, sitting on the ridge with the sun hot on his head, and the wind whining persistently, he could speak to this man, whom he might never meet again.

'It's like this,' Jim said carefully. 'I've had my brother's death on my conscience for a long time. It wasn't my fault he fell. He was stupid and stubborn. But my family blamed me, so I left home and stowed away on a fishing boat landing in Liverpool. I can tell you, because you aren't interested and you don't care and we can part as strangers. You see, my life changed, ended and began at that moment. Everything that has happened to me since is because I ran away. I'm still running. Oh, not from that accident, but from the life which I thought was settled, and has turned sour. I am at the crossroads, my friend. And the uncertainty is killing me.'

Tripp's anger exploded. 'How dare you use me? First to risk my life, and secondly to unload your bad conscience on me. It's unpardonable.'

Jim laughed. 'I was thinking you were the kind of man to give a fellow creature absolution. But no bother. I suppose you have in a way. You showed me how small I am in the scheme of things. All this, and heaven too.'

Tripp stood up. 'I'm going down.'

He hitched the rope to a pinnacle, and began to descend. After a few feet he stopped. 'Come on,' he shouted, 'or I'll have *you* on my conscience.'

216

'Leave me be.'

Tripp made light work of the descent. He reached the base, and walked rapidly away. When he was out of sight Jim stood up. He felt no fear, only a driving desire to prove to himself, his family, the world, he was invincible.

He began the slow descent, making use of the rope. He felt for each hold and exulted when he found it. His confidence became overpowering. Twenty-five yards from the base he missed his footing, hung on for a moment by his hands and stretched arms, and then with an agonizing cry he let go and fell.

CHAPTER 21

Sarah received the news of Jim's accident and injuries with an outward calm she wasn't feeling. She comforted Claire.

'I must go to him,' Claire declared, subduing any doubts that were perhaps in her own and her mother's mind.

'Of course you must,' Sarah soothed, 'and stay as long as necessary.'

Could this be the catharsis which would bring about a reconciliation and reunite them? Regretfully, Sarah doubted it.

After Claire's departure, Sarah telephoned Margaret. 'What exactly happened, love?' she asked.

Margaret had recovered from the shock of returning to the cottage to find Mrs Hawkins hovering, afraid to break the news that Jim was in hospital suffering from injuries received in an accident.

'He picked up with a bloke in the pub,' Margaret said. 'Apparently Dad boasted he was an expert climber, and this chap took him up on it, and they tackled Brant Crags. You know Dad, they had a quarrel on the summit, and this man came down without him. Eventually Dad made the descent but fell when he was near the base. Luckily the chap felt uneasy, returned and found Dad and got him to hospital. He's broken a leg and arm and was concussed. The bones have been set, and the surgeon doesn't anticipate any complications.' Margaret's concise description of events reassured Sarah.

'Don't worry about my birthday party, Gran. Peter and I will be with you for sure, and more than likely bring Mother back with us.'

The three of them duly arrived on the day before Margaret's birthday. It was obvious to Sarah that there was a contentious undercurrent between Claire and Margaret, and only Peter was unaffected by Jim's accident.

Claire was pale and tight-lipped.

'Margaret won't mind I'm sure, if you want to postpone her party?' Sarah said.

'Jim had no intention of being present anyway. Margaret actually begged him to come; that is, before he had this stupid accident. She doesn't say anything, but I can tell she's hurt.'

Privately Sarah doubted it. 'Right. We'll go ahead. Don't upset yourself, Claire. At least Jim's accident is a legitimate excuse for him not being present. You are welcome to use the Bransfell cottage when he comes out of the hospital.'

'He insists on coming back here.'

'It's your home,' Sarah said, her gaze encompassing the apartment sitting room, changed and yet completely familiar since the days she and Gerald had enjoyed such happiness. Why hadn't it rubbed off? Impregnated the walls; brought contentment to their daughter?

'Have I any choice?'

'None,' Sarah said firmly.

'Reconciliation – and then what?'

'For heaven's sake, Claire, take each day as it comes.'

'But I have no future,' she wailed, walking about the

room with small steps, as if the walls had, like a concertina, compressed inward.

'Don't be silly, Claire. You have a home, a loving daughter, and Jim – '

Claire interrupted her. 'There is no place for him here, once he is recovered.'

Sarah said, 'You may feel that way but don't try and corner me into making decisions now. Let's just get him home and better, and then we'll see.'

'Don't procrastinate, Mother. Tomorrow the sun will shine – '

'You can hardly accuse me of deferring action. Nevertheless, I will not be pushed into any decision regarding you and Jim and Renton's Royal. I shall make up my mind when the time comes.'

'I can't believe that. You are bedevilled by your emotions. You think you should like Jim, because he's your son-in-law, and worked for you all these years. You certainly owe him some consideration, but I know you *don't* like him, and so you'll put off any decision.'

'I can't pretend, Claire; we don't get on. He's been a big disappointment. He started off so well. Energetic, keen, full of ideas, and both your father and I stifled any doubts we had about your marriage.'

'If my father was alive he wouldn't allow us to be cast aside.'

'Oh Claire,' Sarah sighed. 'Can't you understand how deeply I care for the future of Renton's Royal? You must understand,' she continued vigorously, 'your father and I created it; we fleshed out our dream, it is our contribution to the future of our family. It was never just a business; although Sefton considered it so.'

'Sefton had the right idea,' Claire said. 'Renton's Royal is a commodity. We make money out of it. A commodity to sell to the highest bidder.'

'No, never.' Sarah stood up. 'I think I'd rather burn the place down than allow it to fall into other hands.'

'You're mad,' Claire shouted. 'Here we are sitting on a gold mine, and you're too stubborn to take advantage of it. Your pal Charlie can straighten out your ideas. He isn't sentimental, he sees things exactly as they are. Wake up, Mother. Sell up. Let go. Give us all our freedom.'

Sarah was too hurt to answer. Claire's outburst encapsulated Sarah's own doubts. Was she denying the family she loved so deeply the freedom of choice?

She walked unsteadily to the lift, and rode down to the ground floor. She couldn't face the activity in the foyer, and entered the garden through the side door. Her heart was bumping, and she breathed deeply as she walked slowly down the narrow path only used by the family. Once or twice she stopped to lean against the trunk of a tree. And only by exerting her strong will-power could she conquer the complete devastation she felt.

At the end of the narrow, tree-shaded path, she crossed part of the lawn in the direction of the rose garden.

She had recovered enough to regard with wry humour her desire to sit on the bench which she and Gerald had made their own.

The place had become something in the nature of a shrine. A place to remember their love; the place she always chose to face up to her difficulties. She passed beneath the archway. The sun was shining directly in her eyes, and it wasn't until she reached the bench she realized it was already occupied. For a bewildered moment she thought it was Gerald, and then as her gaze focused, she realized it was Peter Lovell, Margaret's friend.

He stood up and held out his hand. 'Are you all right, Mrs Renton? You look a bit rough.'

He guided her to the bench and she sat down.

'Am I intruding? Is this your private preserve?'

She shook her head.

He made a move to leave, but she laid a hand on his arm. 'Please stay.'

'Do you mind?' he indicated a half-smoked cigarette.

'Of course not.'

'Will you?' He offered the packet.

She took one, he flicked his lighter, and she drew deeply.

'I needed that.' She didn't explain further, just leant against the hard wooden back, and relaxed.

'Was this retreat your idea?' he asked.

'No. The first Renton to live here planted it. He was a seafarer. His clippers sailed into Liverpool with full cargoes. He founded the importing business, and his warehouses were crammed with tea from India, China and Ceylon. He left diaries written on the long voyages which make riveting reading. He was quite a romantic, and when he came home to stay he planted this garden for the girl he loved and lost.'

'Nothing changes,' Peter added dispassionately.

She looked at him closely. She liked the shape of his face, his clear grey eyes beneath slightly shaggy brows, and his brown curly hair. He looked dependable. She felt they had immediately established a basis for friendship.

'I'm afraid it does. Values change most of all.'

'I was thinking of lost loves,' he said.

I too, she thought. She wondered if her longing for Gerald would ever grow less. There were times when she felt him near, and unbidden thoughts and decisions seemed to rise out of her desperate longing for him.

'You are too young and handsome to have a lost love,' she said brusquely 'You have Margaret.'

'We are good friends,' he said flatly. 'That's the way she wants it.'

'And you?'

'I go along with that, for now. Mag worries about you.

222

And now I've met you I understand why. She sees you as beleaguered.'

She looked at him in surprise.

'This is a great place. You won't be persuaded to give it up, will you?'

'No, I won't.'

'Mag was afraid you might. She sees life in black and white, right and wrong. There are no grey areas in Mag's philosophy. She's a campaigner. I get frightened for her sometimes. She flies too high, and falls too low.'

'I'm glad she has a friend in you.'

'At last I understand why she ran away. This place offered her too much. Like you, she wants to make it to the top her way.'

'You've done it again, Sarah.' Charlie, sitting at Sarah's right hand, smiled warmly.

Sarah's glance swept round the table. She was deeply content. They were all here, her family. But as always she ached to have Gerald at her side.

Charlie stood up to propose a toast to Margaret. 'As Sarah's oldest friend . . .' She didn't listen to his words, only the sound of his familiar voice which carried her back over the years to the day her father had arranged a treat for her. Charlie had been there sitting on her right hand, as now. He had toasted her thirteenth birthday in lemonade, and had bought her a necklace of blue beads to match her eyes. She still had them.

When had Charlie changed? When had he become her dear enemy? Why should Renton's Royal mean so much to him? He had never envied her success in their young days. She had always been top of the class at school. She had learnt to paint, and he'd thought her amateurish landscapes of Dockland wonderful.

She sipped her champagne and then applauded

223

Margaret's graceful little speech of thanks. Gerald would have been so proud and happy today. Her heart cried out for him. She glanced round the table, set in the best Renton's Royal tradition, even to the Renton silver bowl filled with white roses and freesias.

Her gaze lingered on each of the eager young faces. Margaret was wearing a long white dress, low-cut to show off the Renton amethyst necklace, Sarah's gift. She wore white rosebuds in her brown hair, for this occasion dressed high on her head and falling in curls on her neck.

Fleur's sea-green dress down to her ankles fitted her slender boyish figure perfectly. Like Claire, shades of green complemented her bobbed bronze-gold hair. Bangles on both arms clashed as she moved, and her long string of bronze and gold beads glittered.

Sarah observed Betsy, Charlie's granddaughter, with growing interest. She had a sophistication which was missing in the other two girls. She wore a short black embroidered dress high in the neck, Chinese fashion, but leaving her arms and back bare. Her styled lint-fair hair was shaped in a way that gave added piquancy to her face.

Michael responded to Margaret's shy speech of thanks. How handsome he looked in his dress suit, carnation in his buttonhole. Peter, leaning close to Margaret, wore his finery self-consciously. Andy Fergusen, on the other hand, looked as if he'd been poured into his. He was sitting next to Fleur and whispering intimately in her ear.

Sarah smiled. She had high hopes for all of them, even for Claire who had thrown off her despondency and was in animated conversation with Bobby Brooks.

Charlie's suggestion that the celebration be continued at The Cocked Hat, a popular nightclub, was greeted rapturously by the younger members of the party, especially as the fabulous Beatles sometimes put in an appearance.

The nightclub was packed. It was hot and noisy, and

Sarah hated it. She danced with Charlie, and the boys.

Tiredness overcame her. 'Do you mind if we go, Charlie?'

He grinned. 'Not exactly our scene. The young ones don't need us.'

Silworthy drove them to the cottage. He would return to the club later for the rest of the party.

'What do you think of the place?' Charlie questioned her a little later.

'Why?' she asked suspiciously.

'I was thinking of buying it.'

'Haven't you enough?'

'All except the golden egg. And you are sticking tight to that, Sarah. Well, what did you think?'

'Awful. Garish, bad taste, and terrible champagne.'

He roared with laughter. 'Sarah, my darling. You are wonderful.'

Over cups of coffee in the peace of the cottage sitting room they sat quietly. She was aware of Charlie's change of mood. Hadn't she always been? Hadn't she known in her heart the bitter disappointment Charlie suffered when she told him she was going to marry Gerald?

Six months later he'd married Alice. Poor Alice, she'd had a rotten deal from the start and Charlie knew it.

'Once, long ago,' he said, 'I dreamed that it would be like this between us. Harmony, no conflicting interests. I couldn't bear the thought of you being Gerald Renton's wife. It had nothing to do with his money or his superior education, or the fact that he looked down on chaps like me. I believed that you were mine, always had been since the first day we went to that miserable school, and you were scared and hung onto my hand. And when I lost you, I had to prove to you that I was as good as any Renton. I'll tell you why I want this hotel. I want to erase his name. I've never stopped loving you, Sarah, and I never will.'

She was deeply moved. 'Erasing Gerald's name from

the hotel means nothing. You can't erase him from my heart, my mind, my being.'

'Let me try. I want you so much, Sarah.'

'Oh Charlie, it's too late.'

'I won't believe that.'

'You must.'

Now she could pinpoint the moment when it had become too late. It had nothing to do with her falling in love with Gerald, but with a sinister event which occurred when she was a twelve-year-old girl, and which had lain on her conscience all these years because she believed that inadvertently she had been the cause.

And she had never overcome her fear of fog as a result, though now she could close windows, draw curtains, turn on the light. But then it had been different. November was the month for fogs, Liverpool pea soupers. That November day the mist rose up from the river, thickened, and as dusk fell it obscured the darkened warehouses. The Dock Road became strange territory. Circles of feeble light preceded the few cars, and from the river came the sound of the ships' foghorns, constant, an odd warning of doom.

Sarah was late leaving school. Earlier the teacher had sent her on an errand, and she'd been delayed. The other kids had been sent home. She collected her satchel crammed with books, and set off fearfully. If only Charlie had waited! And then she remembered he hadn't been in school that day.

She crept along cautiously, hugging the walls of the warehouse's unfamiliar shapes, face averted as she passed dark alleys. A car crawled by. She longed to hear footsteps, and when she did, and saw the flickering light from a torch, she called out.

The footsteps stopped abruptly. The faint light was focused on her face, and then lingered for a split second on the man confronting her. She recognized him. He was a regular in the café and for a moment she was reassured. He was called Pedro. He was thick-set, walking with the rolling gait of a sailor, black-haired and bearded. He peered at her, narrowing his small sly eyes.

''Ello, girlie.' She shrank back against the wall. His rum-smelling breath mingled with the vile stench of the fog. He reached out and caught hold of her arm. She struggled, but he pressed her back against the wall, his fingers fumbling at the buttons of her coat. She screamed, and he put a hand over her mouth. She bit him. He let go for a second and she took her chance. In desperation she swung her heavy satchel at him, and caught him a blow in the groin. With a yell he keeled over.

She ran. The Dock Road was endless; it spooled away from her, stretching to eternity. Her feet in thin-soled second-hand shoes clattered on the cobbles. The stench of the fog was in her nostrils, closing up her throat and she drew great rasping breaths. She dropped her satchel, but ran on blindly, bumping into obstacles; twice she fell, cutting her knees, tearing her black wool stockings.

She barely recognized her father's café, and would have passed it, but for the pungent smell of fish and chips. She flung herself against the closed door, shrieking their names. Dad. Charlie. She was aware of their startled looks. Hard salty tears blurred her eyes, dragged up from the depths of her new knowledge.

She sobbed out her story. Joe Nealey's anger was deadly. It seemed to the young Sarah his red hair bristled, and his eyes were pinpoints of blue flames. She turned to Charlie. He led her into the back room. He made sweet hot tea, and held the cup while she drank. He promised to find her satchel, and held her hand until her father carried her up to bed.

Pedro didn't come back to the café, ever.

His body was recovered from the river. The thin blade of a kitchen knife had pierced his heart. The police reckoned he'd had a fight. He could have fallen off a ship, or been the victim of a vendetta. He carried no papers. No one claimed him. No one mourned him.

But Sarah remembered.

He had changed the relationship between the three of them. Joe Nealey, his daughter Sarah, and Charlie Mullins. She perceived a new bond between her father and Charlie. It seemed to her the three of them were drawn closer together by some secret Sarah couldn't comprehend.

'Charlie, do you remember the night of that dreadful fog, when I was twelve years old? It lasted for days. There was a man called Pedro. He was found dead in the river. How did he get there?'

Charlie puffed out a cloud of smoke.

'Can't say.'

'Yes you can. You and Dad went after him. I know.'

'Don't be daft, Sarah.'

'Until I know the truth his death will always haunt me. It changed us. I am afraid to trust you.'

'Good God, Sarah, that's nearly fifty years ago. How can it make any difference between you and me, *now*?'

He was right, perhaps. And yet that episode had tainted the years. Charlie's values were not hers; he had never been able to distinguish right from wrong.

'Your dad loved you more than life. He'd have swung for you.'

Her love for Joe Nealey eclipsed at this moment all the other loves of her life.

'He was a good man,' she said, hugging her arms round her body, holding on to the reality of that statement.

'Pedro's death was an accident. You can't hold that against us.'

But she did. She hadn't really faced her knowledge until this moment. And it was as clear and sharp as the knife which had pierced black Pedro's heart.

CHAPTER 22

In the dog days of early August Sarah was restless. She had instituted 'family weeks' during the early years to cover the first two or three weeks of this month. Gerald and Sefton had been against this innovation, believing it cheapened the prestige of the hotel, but Sarah had as always had her way.

'It pays off,' she declared. 'There are no business conferences in August, and it's better to have the hotel full of half-price children than empty rooms. Besides,' she added 'our business guests like the idea of bringing the wife and kids.'

The staff didn't share her enthusiasm, particularly Mrs Humphries who was in charge of erecting extra beds in the big rooms, and dusting off last year's cots and high chairs.

Chef opted out. He took two weeks of his holiday and headed for France, where he spent nostalgic days looking up old chef friends, drinking wine and looking for new menu ideas. He spent the last few days with Sefton Taylor, and brought back disturbing news of Sefton's brother's illness.

In earlier years a temporary chef had always been engaged, but this year Chef persuaded Sarah into letting Ramiro take over.

'It's too much responsibility,' she declared.

'I don't agree. The lad has to try out his wings sometime, and the catering for children's meals is much simpler.'

Sarah's anxiety drove her into the kitchen several times during the day. She was, however, impressed by Ramiro's handling of the meals and the staff. She revised her opinion of him. He had unaccountably matured, as if by refusing his father's commands he had become his own man.

And there was the problem.

Señor Rodriguez was not satisfied. His letters to Sarah were acrimonious, claiming his right to demand Ramiro's return immediately. Sarah's explanation that Ramiro was gaining valuable experience by being in charge of the hotel kitchen while Chef was on holiday was brushed aside. Sarah had no intention of making the same mistake as on the previous occasion when Ramiro travelled no further than London. No more leave, she thought, until I get to the bottom of Ramiro's reluctance to return to Spain. She believed the boy must have good reasons for not complying with his father's wishes.

Rodriguez's persistence only served to rouse Sarah's stubbornness. She, who, in her own mind believed herself to be the upholder of the family unity was being forced into a false position.

Fleur was amused.

'Gran, you are being weather-cockish. But I'm glad. You do like Ramiro, don't you?' she asked anxiously. 'As a person, I mean.'

Sarah did. She was as aware of his charisma as was Fleur, and she feared the consequences.

Claire's unhappiness hurt. And yet Sarah's questioning only skimmed the surface of her daughter's discontent. Jim had been brought back from Bransfell by ambulance

230

and was installed in the apartment. His demands were incessant, and Sarah feared another big row and Claire's departure. Rachel refused to help Claire out. At least she didn't waver over her dislike of her brother-in-law. In any case she was sunk in gloom over her own problems with Mark, and Fleur's defiance of him.

Sarah's love for Rachel intensified. She had long ago given up trying to put 'a bit of backbone' in the girl, and now she was beginning to realize she must let go.

I can't run their lives, she told herself grimly. I must move to the sidelines.

She set aside her worries and entered into the spirit of the entertainment for the children staying in the hotel. Fleur was in her element, and drew Michael and Clive into her projects. They organised games on the beach, junior tennis tournaments, cricket on the lawns, nature rambles, and visits to the fairground.

Sarah was relieved when Charlie arrived unexpectedly.

'What do you think of our 'family weeks'? she asked.

'Fine. Good for business.'

'It isn't just that – '

'Of course it is, Sarah. We're in business to be successful and make money.'

'Charlie, why do you take away the – the glamour?'

He laughed. 'What a darling romantic you are beneath that hard exterior. How can I reach your soft centre?'

Sarah had this capacity for fixing moments in her memory for ever. This one, standing with Charlie's hand in hers, admiring the majesty of her peacocks; feeling the hot sun on her head, and a vague distant chorus of children's joyous shouts, would remain.

Charlie's past and hers were threaded together. She was totally at ease with him. Now as his fingers entwined with hers, she thought that maybe she was foolish holding out against this man's devotion.

231

A weak moment, perhaps.

'Those birds have got it made,' Charlie said. 'Only you would think of having peacocks strutting all over the place, and there they are being fed and watered, and enjoying all this admiration.'

They strolled back to the hotel. 'Care for tea in the lounge?' Sarah said.

'Great. I shall pretend we are passing visitors. A couple on a day out which includes tea at Renton's Royal.'

Sarah laughed. 'You're crazy, but good for me. I needed someone of my generation to talk to.'

'I know the feeling,' Charlie said. 'Shall I order tea, my dear?'

Sarah poured, and Charlie ordered a second plate of cucumber sandwiches, a weakness of his.

'Fancy a trip to Barbados, Sarah love? I'm going on a quick business trip, and I'm afraid it's bad news for Claire and Jim. The new hotel building project has fallen through.'

For a moment she imagined she was a housewife with no other responsibilities except the care of her family.

'Oh dear. I think they will be disappointed, Jim especially.'

'Well, how about it? A sort of preliminary honeymoon in Barbados.'

'Charlie!'

He grinned, and taking hold of her hand raised it to his lips. 'You can't blame me for trying. But I'm serious, if you fancy a few days' break and no strings.'

'I can't,' she said briefly.

'If you really wanted – '

'Then say I don't. There's a time – '

'And this isn't it.'

'No.'

He sighed. 'What's holding us back now?'

232

'Us,' she said softly, 'us.'

'I can wait. For you and Renton's Royal.'

'It'll be a long wait. And in the meantime hadn't you better tell Claire and Jim the bad news.'

Charlie refused to go alone to the apartment. 'I know you think I do deals behind your back. Not true.'

Jim was alone in the apartment. He reclined on the settee, newspapers scattered round him. His injured leg supported by cushions.

'Hi, Charlie. Good to see you.'

'You won't say that when I give you the bad news. The hotel in Barbados has fallen through. Impossible restrictions and labour trouble. I've abandoned it.'

'What about me?' Jim said.

'I'm sorry, but that's the way it is.'

'You promised.'

'I don't like breaking promises, but it can't be helped.'

'That's not good enough. We want compensation.'

Charlie's face set in an angry expression. 'Compensation – nothing. I offered you and Claire a job in good faith. Now there's no job, and that's the end of it. Come, Sarah.'

They travelled down in the lift in silence, and in her office Sarah mixed Charlie a strong whisky.

'How in hell do you put up with them!' He flung himself into a chair. 'And what's up with Claire? I phoned the other day and she refused to speak to me.'

'You tell me.'

'She still hasn't forgiven me because I had to reject her as a suitable manageress. She came to see me. It was the day she was attacked. I've felt guilty about that ever since, Sarah.'

'That's it. Rejection. She can't bear to be rejected, Charlie, and I haven't helped. She insists it is her right to be manager here but – '

'I know. She isn't reliable. Tell you the truth, Sarah, I

233

was beginning to have doubts about the Barbados job. Jim was a hell of a good manager at one time but he seems to have been losing it lately.'

'My fault,' Sarah sighed. 'He wants me out. And I'm not ready to go.'

'Come away with me, love. Let's forget all this.'

'You can't forget what's in your blood. As Jim so often says, I *am* Renton's Royal Hotel.'

Charlie stayed overnight, and the next morning accompanied Sarah to the fortieth Southport Flower Show. They arrived in time for the opening ceremony by the Belgian ambassador to the court of St James, who happened to be an acquaintance of Charlie's.

Sarah's gardener had entered an exhibit in the amateur class of a hybrid rose he had perfected. Sarah had high hopes that this dark red rose named 'Renton's Royal' might win first prize.

Charlie teased her. 'Unfair advertising,' he said. 'I would have named it "Sarah".'

They passed through the turnstile, Charlie paying sixteen shillings and sixpence each entrance fee, and bought two half-crown programmes.

Sarah adored the atmosphere of expectation. Even the smell of the trodden grass mingling with a sea breeze heightened her excitement.

'Where first?' Charlie asked as soon as the ceremony was over.

'Roses, of course.'

Entering the tent, Sarah stood transfixed, her glance encompassing the riot of colour.

'Oh Charlie.' She clutched his arm. 'The scent and the colours, what heaven. Roses are so special.'

'A red rose called "Renton's Royal" is special. It looks as if it's won first prize in its class.'

Tears of happiness blurred her sight. Charlie drew her closer. 'You've done it again, lass.'

'Not me. Dan, my gardener. He's besotted with roses too. Can you see him? I must congratulate him on his success.'

From the rose tent they moved into the Grand Marquee to view the superb Begonia Carpet, a tribute paid by the Belgian government to the Southport Show. Here, Charlie caught up with the ambassador who explained to Sarah that there were close and friendly links between the horticulturists in both countries.

After lunch they watched the horse-jumping, listened to the band of the Coldstream Guards, and took a quick look at the rock gardens, complete with waterfalls.

'That's it.' Sarah sighed happily. 'Thank you for a lovely day, Charlie.' He drove her back to Renton's Royal well satisfied that he and Sarah through their shared interests were slowly drawing closer.

'Gran, I've got three days off and so has Ramiro. Can I borrow one of the cars and take him to Bransfell? Margaret phoned. She is fed up being there by herself.'

'Of course. You both deserve a break. The family weeks have been the best ever because of your splendid efforts.'

Rachel objected. 'Your father will be furious if he finds out.'

'He isn't going to, so long as you don't tell him.'

'I don't think this is wise,' Rachel complained to Sarah. 'It's encouraging them, and you know what Mark will say.'

'I don't care a fig what Mark says. I like that boy and he's going to make something of himself. You're Fleur's mother. You stop her.'

Rachel didn't. She wavered this way and that, and only the fact that Margaret was at the cottage decided her; she would go with them.

To Fleur's surprise, Ramiro demurred.

'Why? You are always saying it would be heaven for us to be alone, and now when we have the opportunity, you don't want to take it.'

'I do. But you see in Spain it is different. We would not be allowed to go away alone.'

'Well, we're not in Spain, we're in good old England, and in any case Margaret is there, and Mother is thinking about coming too. Do you or don't you want to come?' As always Fleur was direct.

'Yes I do. I want to be with you more than anything in the world.'

'Then what are you dithering about? You're getting as bad as Mother.'

'Please, not to say that. Your mother is too sweet and kind.'

They arrived at the cottage in time for lunch the following day.

Margaret was watching out for them.

'That's my first long run. I love driving. I did well, didn't I, Ramiro?' Fleur said.

Ramiro agreed, unable to dash her enthusiasm, and not caring to remember the one or two close encounters which had brought him to the edge of his seat.

So began an idyll.

A time Ramiro would remember all his life. A time of such intense happiness, that every moment seemed too precious to spend. Nothing outside their pleasure in each other's company existed.

Rachel observed, and was afraid. She could see no future for them, and yet she could not imagine them ever parting.

Margaret's attitude was as matter-of-fact as her own relationship with Peter.

'What's going to happen when Ramiro has to go back to

Spain? You say his father is pressing for his return. Surely you won't allow Fleur to go with him? Her father will raise the roof.'

Rachel sighed. 'I don't know what to do, Margaret. Even Mother is on their side. In spite of her business head she is incurably romantic.'

Margaret hugged her. 'Don't worry so much, Rachel. Fleur is very sensible; I'm sure she'll make the right decision when the time comes. Would you like me to drive you over to Mr Glover's house tomorrow? I'm as interested as you in these old books he's discovered. I wonder if there are any first editions among them. Amazing how old people sit on valuable books and then go and die.'

'Thanks, Margaret. I'll be glad of your company. Where is Peter though? I expected him to be here.'

'He's paying a duty visit to his grandma. Actually he's very fond of her. He's her favourite grandchild, and she helps out with his college expenses.'

'The lake,' Fleur declared next morning. 'A perfect day to try out Gran's wee motor boat. If you two are going to see Mr Glover you can give us a lift to Shane's Landing.'

'The boat is all ready for action. Peter and I had a day out on the lake last week, and we filled her up afterwards,' Margaret reassured her.

Rachel said nervously, 'Fleur, please be careful. You haven't driven one before.'

'I have,' Ramiro volunteered. 'We have a motor boat at home. I'll take care of Fleur, Mrs Ashton. Please don't worry.'

Later that afternoon they were out on the river.

'Isn't this fab?' Fleur asked Ramiro happily as she trailed one hand in the water.

'It's a super boat,' Ramiro said, accelerating. 'Much better than ours at home.'

'I know a great place where we can stop and eat our lunch. It's a private landing stage belonging to one of Gran's friends. We can tie up the boat and picnic in a little bay.'

'Sounds perfect.' Ramiro carefully drew alongside a narrow wooden landing stage. He tied up the boat and carrying the basket followed Fleur up a narrow path above the water line. Where the path opened out into a plateau, Fleur said, 'How about here?'

Ramiro put down the basket, and touching Fleur's cheek, drew her into his arms. For long moments there was no time. Fleur was utterly lost in the feel of Ramiro's fingers stroking her arms, his lips on her brow, closing her eyes with his kisses.

He slid his hand beneath the hem of the skimpy tee shirt she wore hanging loose over a gauzy Indian print skirt. Fleur felt her heart jump beneath the gentle, tentative quest of his work-roughened fingertips.

She had always been half-ashamed of her narrow boyish figure and its lack of curves. When he started to slide the tee shirt higher she put her hands on his.

'No, don't.'

He was instantly remorseful. 'I'm sorry, Fleur, I didn't mean to frighten you.'

'But you didn't!' She almost laughed. For weeks now she had ached for Ramiro, longed for him to take her in his arms and do all the things she'd heard the younger members of the kitchen staff and the waitresses joking and sniggering about when Chef was out of earshot. She and Ramiro were old enough after all, and surely no two people had ever been so in love. Now her own stupid shyness had to go and spoil things.

Before she could think better of it, she slid the tee shirt up and over her head, and sat before him, eyes lowered.

'Not very voluptuous, as you can see,' she murmured.

238

When there was no reply she raised her eyes and saw him gazing at her with an expression of such tenderness on his face that tears pricked her eyes.

Slowly, with infinite gentleness, he traced a line of little kisses from her mouth to the sweet hollow of her throat and down to the two rosebud breasts below.

Fleur shuddered and clutched him tightly to her. 'Don't stop!' she moaned. 'Ramiro, I'm not afraid. Please don't stop.'

But he did. Eyes cloudy with desire he told her, '*Querida*, enough. That is far enough for us until we can be married.' Tenderly he dressed her again and smoothed the hair away from her brow with hands that still shook slightly.

'Let's eat,' he said. 'I'll open the wine.'

He popped the cork, and poured the sparkling wine into the glasses. He raised his glass to her. '*Mi amor*,' he said.

'My love.' Fleur reached across to touch him. 'For always.'

'For always,' he repeated. '*Mi amor*, I need you.'

She smiled. She felt such utter contentment, she was almost afraid. Happiness, she thought, is made up of little things; like the quiet, the pair of swans flying low over the water, Ramiro lifting his face to the sun.

'Gosh, I'm hungry,' she said. She had to break the intensity of her feelings. 'Have a sandwich.'

Ramiro laughed. 'I made your favourites. And I chose the peaches.'

'Clever you. I'll always let you fill the picnic basket.'

'And I will let you choose the wine.'

'I didn't,' she admitted. 'Gran did.'

'We will finish it. She will not like us to waste one drop.'

They ate and drank with enjoyment. 'Food always tastes better outside,' Fleur declared.

Ramiro emptied the last of the wine into their glasses,

and Fleur packed away the remains of the food. 'If we walk up that path through the pine wood, we come to a kind of look-out place above the trees. It's been here for years, and no one remembers who built it, but someone secretly keeps it in repair.'

The woods were summer-scented, the path strewn with pine needles crunching beneath their feet, and wide enough for them to walk close together, hand in hand.

The little hut had been newly painted, and a new bench stood outside the door.

'What do you think?' Fleur sat down. 'Look over that way, and you can see Brant Crags and that's Brant Fell.'

'I wish we could stay here for ever.'

Fleur moved closer, into the circle of his arms. 'Wouldn't it be running away from life? I mean it's all going for us. Oh Ramiro, it's like a wonderful dream, us being together. We'll make it a reality, won't we? Promise?'

Later she wondered if his passionate kisses were his promise for the future. Now she clung to him, believing he was totally hers. When they drew apart, shaken by consuming desire, it was Ramiro who whispered, 'Wait.'

She didn't care how long she had to wait, but she knew this was a peak of happiness which might never be achieved again.

CHAPTER 23

Sefton Taylor's brother died during the last week in August, but it was ten days later before Sarah could book a flight to France.

Terry drove her to Manchester Airport and saw her safely onto the plane bound for Paris. Here she changed planes before continuing her journey to Bergerac Airport, where Sefton would meet her.

Her anticipation heightened the nearer she approached her destination. It was three years since she had last seen Sefton when he had made a flying visit to England, and managed to spend a few hours at Renton's Royal. Although it was seven years since he had joined his brother at Le Clos Rozelle, Sarah had never been able to spare the time to visit them.

The plane touched down, and taxied along the runway. Sarah, with nothing to declare, passed through customs quickly, collected her one small suitcase, and found Sefton beside her, holding her tightly to him.

'Sarah, thank the Lord you managed to get away. I was desperate to see you. Was it very difficult?'

'Of course not.'

She looked up at him, and was shocked and saddened by the dark circles beneath his eyes, and the fine lines round his mouth. But he was nothing if not disciplined. His thick white hair was brushed back as neatly as always; his painfully English clothes as well-kept and neatly pressed as ever. Only the sherry-brown eyes lacked their customary warmth and life.

He settled her in the passenger seat of his car, and drove out of the car park.

'You look as if you've had a rough time, Sefton.'

'It has been tough,' he said, concentrating on the traffic on the busy road.

Sarah knew he hated to talk when he was driving, so she was able to gaze around. The little town of Bergerac, glimpsed in the distance, looked inviting, as did the slow moving river which gave the Dordogne district its name.

There was no mistaking they were in wine country. Fields of vines swept away from the road and up to the hills. Occasionally a green field broke up the landscape, and trees grew on the slopes. After a few kilometres Sefton turned into a narrow road; they passed through a village, a cluster of houses, a church, and a restaurant, and a little further on he slowed down and turned into the driveway of Le Clos Rozelle.

'This is it.' He parked the car in the courtyard and helped Sarah out.

She was enchanted. The house was a warm yellowstone with a red-tiled pointed roof. It was two-storeys high, with one long window above the front door, and flanked on either side by additional buildings. Blue shutters protected all the windows.

On the other side of the courtyard were barn-like buildings, and she caught a glimpse of a rose garden, and a large vegetable patch.

'Come on in. I'll show you round later.'

They entered a long room directly through the front door. It was simply furnished with a large table, chairs and a dresser. The stairs rose up from the back of the room. It had not the feel of a family room, just a place to sit and eat, and yet it appealed to Sarah in an odd way. She liked the simplicity, and the uncluttered feeling of space.

'It's so peaceful, Sefton.'

He didn't answer, but looked at her strangely, as if she were aware of something he was not. He carried her case through a door in one of the wings, and ushered her into a bedroom.

'I have to go out for a short while. Maybe you'd like a rest and Marie will bring you a cup of coffee. If it suits you we'll eat about seven.'

She sat down on an easy chair by the window, and closed her eyes. A tap on the door, and Marie entered.

'Good evening, Madame.' She put the cup and saucer on a table by the side of Sarah's chair. 'Shall I unpack for you?'

'Thank you, no. I only have this small case.'

'I always unpacked for Madame Louise. When she died, God rest her soul, I come to live here to look after Mr Rafe and Mr Sefton.'

She was neat as a little brown bird. Her abundant brown hair was fastened back with a length of brown ribbon, and her large brown eyes had golden tints. Her smile redeemed the ordinariness of her features.

Sarah warmed to her immediately.

'I am glad for Mr Sefton's sake you are here. He is unhappy and lonely,' Marie said.

'His brother's death must have been a great shock.'

Marie's typical Gallic shrug of her shoulders surprised Sarah.

'Shall I run you a bath, Madame?' Marie asked rather formally, indicating the bathroom.

Sarah relaxed in a hot bath and, much revived, returned to the bedroom and lay down on the high double bed, first removing the embroidered counterpane.

243

She closed her eyes and felt a lightness of spirit; a drifting away from reality giving her a strange feeling of being unrestricted. She had nothing to organise, no keeping a watchful eye on this and that, no decisions to make, and the freedom from the constant burden of the hotel was intoxicating. I am not, at this moment, Sarah Renton, proprietress of a large and prosperous hotel; I am Sarah Renton, a guest in the house of an old friend. I am just me.

She was pleased with this humble image of herself and, sliding off the bed, considered her wardrobe, eventually choosing to wear a silk patterned dress. She took care with her make-up, and brushed her hair until it shone.

She descended the stairs and found her way into the courtyard through the open door in the living room. Heat seemed to rise from the paving stones, the sunshine was fierce, and shade minimal. She walked towards a strip of greeny-brown grass, beyond which was a stone-walled garden.

Here roses grew in random profusion. The scent lingering on the hot air was almost overwhelming. In the shade of a cherry tree she noticed a bench, and thankfully sat down. Immediately her attention was caught by the small plaque screwed into the back. She turned to read the inscription, and for a moment her sight blurred. 'In memory of Gerald. 1901–1962.'

She realized how strong Sefton's ties were with England, and how deeply he'd felt his exile. She felt a surge of compassion, and an overwhelming desire to comfort him.

'You found my bolt-hole?' Sefton sat down beside her. 'I hoped you would come here one day, and all that was begun could be finished. My brother called me a sentimental old fool to make this rose garden, but he couldn't know how much closer it brought me to you and Renton's Royal and your friendship.'

'Perhaps he didn't understand the nature of friendship.'

'Do you, Sarah, my very dear?'

She smiled up at him confidently. 'Help, comfort and understanding. Not always easy.'

It took Sarah a day or two to realize that Sefton's attitude had changed. Buoyed up by their reunion, she thought their spontaneous pleasure in each other was as it had always been. But slowly she sensed that he was holding back, that their conversations only touched on matters which were of no great concern.

Maybe the shock of Rafe's death was still paramount in Sefton's thoughts, and he was putting off any decisions as to his future. She tried to await patiently the return to their formerly intimate understanding, and in the meantime she enjoyed unaccustomed leisure and Marie's pampering, which included breakfast in bed.

'Such luxury. You are spoiling me.' Sarah arranged the bed table across her knees and sniffed the delicious aroma of coffee appreciatively.

'It is no trouble. Monsieur Sefton says not to hurry. He has gone into Bergerac on business.'

Marie arranged the pillows behind Sarah's back, plumping them up vigorously. She carefully filled her cup and put the warm croissants and a dish of cherry jam within reach.

'It is like old times,' Marie sighed as she fastened back the shutters and opened wide the window. 'Always I bring Madame Louise her coffee, and we speak of household tasks for the day.'

'Did you live here then?'

'*Mais non.* I come up from the village on my bicycle. If it was rain, Monsieur Sefton fetch me in the car. He is never too busy to look after his workers.'

'I thought Monsieur Rafe managed the vineyard.'

'He not know how.' Marie's voice registered indignation, and glancing at her Sarah detected a contemptuous twist to her full lips.

'But surely he managed it before Monsieur Sefton joined him seven years ago?'

'My husband was manager. He work here since he was a boy of fourteen. He knew how to bring the bloom to the grapes. He made good wine. His *vin rouge* was always the best in the district. He died, and Monsieur Rafe send for his brother.'

Sefton didn't return in time for lunch, and Sarah ate bread and cheese and drank red wine sitting under the fig tree in the courtyard.

She was still sitting there when he drove into the courtyard in a van.

'It's so good to find you here waiting for me, Sarah.'

He sat down, and Marie brought him food and wine.

'What do you think of this?' He held his glass up to the sun. 'Such wonderful colour. 1966, one of the really good years. We did well that year. '67 and '68 were not so good, but this year is going to be the best.' His glance rested on the vines stretching away to a blue distance.

'Are you content here?' Sarah asked. 'I mean, do you prefer wine growing to hotel keeping?'

'The question doesn't arise.' He refilled his glass. 'I have always been interested in wines as well you know. My father was an expert, and he taught both Rafe and me to appreciate a good wine at an early age.'

'Then you were pleased when Rafe asked you to join him?'

'Of course.'

She persisted. 'I needed you too.'

'Oh no, Sarah my dear. You didn't need me or anyone else. You knew exactly where you were going. You outstripped both Gerald and myself. Your hotel is a splendid achievement.'

246

'You forget, Sefton. It is not wholly mine. You have a financial stake in it. If you remember, I have not taken any important decisions without consulting you; and our reputation for an excellent cellar is due to your guidance.'

'Thank you, Sarah. Sometimes I wondered if you resented my interference.'

'I did not,' she said indignantly. 'That day you left, so soon after Gerald's death, was one of the worst days of my life. I had to come to terms with life without Gerald, but your going was different. I was jealous, resentful, I wanted to lean on you. I did not want to have to carry on alone.'

'But you did.'

'Oh yes I did. My dad used to say he hated quitters worse than liars or cheats. He made me promise that whatever disaster befell me I'd never quit.'

'And you never have.'

'That's all in the past. What about the future, Sefton?'

He stood up. 'Come and look at my beautiful vines,' he said.

There was no mistaking his enthusiasm and his knowledge. Sarah found it difficult to summon interest as they walked up and down the avenues between the vines, already heavy with bunches of grapes.

She began to tire in the hot sun and was glad when he suggested a return to the house and tea.

'I guess you brought a packet of tea,' Sefton joked. 'Show Marie how to make a decent cup.'

Sitting in the chair by the window in her room, she could not rid herself of the feeling that Sefton was deeply troubled. His explanation of the art of viniculture had struck Sarah as being automatic, he'd said it all before many times. She decided that a frontal attack was necessary, and having made up her mind she sipped her tea with pleasure, and then settled back in her chair for a doze.

However when she joined Sefton at the dinner table, he

247

once again talked at some length about the work of a vineyard. In spring and summer he worked from dawn to dusk, until the grapes were harvested in late September or early October.

'What was Rafe doing while you were working all hours?'

He refilled their glasses before answering. 'Does it matter?'

'Yes it does. Okay, you have all the know-how at your fingertips, but where did Rafe fit in?'

'I don't think it is any of your business, Sarah.'

'Sefton, why did you ask me to come here? You sounded distraught on the phone, I feared all sorts of terrible things. And now I'm here, and wanting only to help, you hold me at a distance.' She reached across the table and took his hand in a firm grip.

'Sarah, do you mind if we go and sit in the rose garden. I feel stifled by this house.'

She stood up at once and draped her stole round her shoulders. A faint mist was seeping up from the direction of the river, and with the setting of the sun, dusk was blurring the vines, the outlines of the house, and the sheds.

They sat down on the bench dedicated to Gerald.

'Rafe committed suicide,' Sefton said.

'Oh no! Why?' She took hold of Sefton's hands, squeezing them tightly. 'How?'

'In the river. He couldn't swim. His father-in-law's estate has a river frontage. It was a humid day, and then late in the evening there was a thunderstorm. His body was found next day.'

'I'm so sorry, Sefton. It must have been a dreadful shock for you. Could it have been an accident?'

'That's what I allowed everyone to believe. But Sarah, he left me a letter telling me what he was going to do. I was away that night, and I didn't find it until the next day.'

'Was he so unhappy? Did he miss Louise so much?'

'Louise died three years ago. Their marriage was a mistake, they were always quarrelling. I couldn't stand living here with them. I lodged in the village with Marie's family. After Louise's death, Rafe begged me to come and live here.'

'If you've always managed the estate, Rafe's death won't make any difference, will it?'

'It certainly will. Rafe didn't own the vineyard. It belongs to Louise's family.'

'Does that mean you have to leave?' Sarah said indignantly.

'Not necessarily. Old Villiard is a decent bloke, and we haven't discussed the future yet.'

'Sefton, why didn't you tell me all this before? I imagined you were happy. I thought you and Rafe were close.'

'It was a duty. Rafe needed me. He felt overpowered by the Villiards, and Louise was selfish and determined. She didn't want me here, but there wasn't any way I was going to desert Rafe. After she died his need was even greater. You see Sarah, Rafe was desperate for money. He was wily and secretive and he kept the accounts. I thought all was well, but I was wrong. There isn't any money at all.'

'But I thought you'd had some very productive years.'

'We have. Rafe paid the workers, and my salary, and there should have been a large bank balance.'

'And there isn't?'

'No, Sarah my dear, there isn't a franc. Apparently my brother was a compulsive gambler, and there are more debts than I care to think about.'

'Won't Louise's family – '

'Not a chance.'

'But Sefton, you can't make yourself responsible.'

'Debts of honour. I think so.'

'How much?'

He named a sum and she gasped in horror. She was stunned by Sefton's revelations. She'd thought Sefton's need for her was to console him over his brother's death, and perhaps do a little tentative planning for the future. Only Sefton had no future. He needed financial help and with a sinking feeling she saw exactly where his need lay.

'I understand now,' she said sharply. 'You want your capital stake in Renton's Royal repaid.'

He nodded miserably.

'All right. You are entitled to draw it out any time you like, that was our arrangement. I'll talk to our accountants.'

'Oh God, I hate doing this. My stake in Renton's Royal means more to me than words can say. While I have that, I have a part of you and Gerald and our dream.'

'Don't distress yourself, my dear Sefton. Nothing can change that. I promise it will be all right.'

She knew it wouldn't. Alone in her room that night she scribbled figures on a piece of paper, and then tore it up into tiny fragments. Her fertile imagination produced ways and means, but none were good enough.

She needed capital to draw on; one bad season, one disaster, and she was sunk. Where would she find a substitute for Sefton who had allowed his money to lie fallow all these years and asked for no interest.

Towards dawn she faced the inevitable. If Charlie was still willing – but of course he was. The thought of her humiliation at having to ask him for help forced her out of bed, into the dawn-cool morning. Like a child reaching out for comfort she ran to Gerald's seat in the rose garden.

Her failure was almost too bitter to bear.

CHAPTER 24

'Sefton thinks he is to blame for his brother's death. It's absolute rubbish, Bobby, but for the moment I can't make him believe otherwise.'

Immediately on her arrival home Sarah had telephoned Bobby Brooks. She felt there wasn't one member of her family in which she could confide. None of them knew Sefton except Claire.

Bobby turned up that same evening. He knew Sarah wouldn't beg him to visit her unless the matter was urgent.

'I see no reason why Sefton should blame himself. Rafe was always unstable. Too like his grandfather. The old boy drank himself to death.'

'I tried to point out to Sefton that he was working fourteen or fifteen hours a day in the vineyard, so how could he keep an eye on Rafe as well? I feel very angry about the situation. Here is Sefton having to fork out for Rafe's debts, because the rich Villiard family don't want to know.'

'I take it the marriage was not popular.'

'Exactly so. Villiard is a hard-headed business man, and he knew Rafe was a wastrel. But he couldn't deny Louise anything, and he allowed the marriage to go ahead.'

Sarah had found the flight home tiring. There had been a long delay in Paris, and it was late by the time she reached Manchester Airport. She'd had plenty of time to think over Sefton's dilemma, which in turn was creating trouble for herself.

Bobby was understanding. He sat comfortably in the cottage sitting room, which for once was peaceful, the young ones being elsewhere. Sarah refilled his glass and asked him to stay for dinner.

His acceptance pleased her. Bobby had long been acquainted with the Taylor family, they had all been his clients, and he had also met them socially. She felt she hadn't to explain more than necessary, and although revealing Sefton's private business was a kind of disloyalty, she had warned Sefton she would have to talk to Bobby.

'We'll enjoy our dinner,' Sarah said, rising, 'and try and find a solution to this wretched business afterwards.'

However the hotel finances were affected Sarah was determined to return Sefton's loan to him. She acknowledged gratefully that she'd had the use of the money for so long, and had always faced each year with equanimity knowing the reserve fund was sufficient to tide them over a poor season.

'I think you have two choices, Sarah. Either you get a bank loan and the consequent high interest, or you replace Sefton.'

'No, I will not. Sefton was different. He was a partner with Gerald and me from the beginning. But I will not have a stranger – '

'Wait a moment, Sarah. I have been approached several times by Charlie Mullins declaring his interest in not just a share but to buy the hotel. He isn't exactly a stranger – '

'Bobby, I can't bear to lose control. If I let Charlie in, he will override my decisions.'

Bobby said, 'Be careful, Sarah. I think you might be letting the power and glory cloud your good sense.'

'It isn't that, Bobby. I want Renton's Royal to go on belonging to a Renton. Sefton understands that.'

'Aren't you putting a heavy burden on young Michael? I think you should talk to him. He has a right to know the changed situation.'

Agreeing with Bobby was one thing, putting it into action was another matter. She was besieged by reasons why she should go it alone, even though she knew it was only fair to Michael to put him in the picture.

She waited a couple of days, perhaps with the faint hope that somehow the situation would resolve itself. A letter from Sefton outlining his plans forced her to take action.

When Michael dropped into Sarah's office for coffee the following morning she showed him Sefton's letter. She waited for Michael's reaction with curiosity.

'Why can't Mr Taylor go on managing the vineyard even though his brother is dead?'

'Not possible.' Sarah gave Michael a succinct report of the situation at Le Clos Rozelle. 'I have talked this over with Bobby Brooks, and he agrees with me; I have no option but to pay Sefton back the large amount he has invested in the hotel, and which is of course our reserve fund.'

'I don't agree,' Michael said stonily. 'Surely he can borrow – '

'He has no collateral other than his share in our hotel, and if he hasn't a job how will he pay the interest?'

'It isn't fair. We need that reserve fund. One disaster, and then what do we do? I think you should consult the rest of the family. We're all involved.'

Sarah made a great effort to control her rising temper. Certainly, the family were all involved, but only so far as she allowed it. She knew they hated her making autocratic decisions, and she perfectly understood Michael's fears. If he was to take over control of the hotel, then he needed the safety net of the reserve fund. Well, she didn't intend to hand over control yet, and God willing she'd have the finances on an even keel before she did.

'You realize that Sefton considers his brother's debts honourable ones.'

'He's a fool,' Michael said savagely. 'I suppose he wants to come back here.'

'I've made it clear he is welcome.'

'What are you doing to us, Gran? First you quarrel with Claire and Jim. Mind you, I don't blame you for that, but can't you see that if Sefton Taylor comes back he'll expect to have a share in running the hotel, even if he's taken out all his capital. And suppose he wants to sell? What then? I think it will be wrong to bring him back.'

'You don't understand, Michael. If it is a debt of honour for Sefton to pay his brother's debts, then I, too, have a debt to honour. All these years Sefton hasn't asked for a penny of his money, and was adamant that he wouldn't take any interest, allowing it all to accumulate in the reserve fund. He has in no way criticised the way that money has been spent, although I have always paid him the courtesy of consulting him. I thought of him as a sleeping partner, and it was his initial investment that helped us to build up the reputation of this hotel as one of the best. By all means, let us consult the family; let's fix a time for a meeting in my office.'

'Gran, I feel a bit of a heel about this. I suppose I think of Taylor as an outsider, and like you, I'm jealous of any interference in our family hotel.'

'I should indeed be worried if you didn't express your opinion, my dear boy. I have great hopes that you will be even more successful than I've been.'

Michael put his arms round her, and kissed her resoundingly on both cheeks. 'No one can touch you, Gran, and you know it.'

254

But that was just the point; she felt a slow loss of confidence as if she were being overtaken by youth, and all her experience counted for nothing. She didn't like it, and decided to remedy it forthwith. Renton's Royal was hers, and she intended it to remain so, until she chose the moment to pass on the power and glory, as Bobby Brooks so aptly stated.

Sarah was still in the same determined mood when the family eventually gathered to discuss the situation created by Sefton's need to withdraw his capital from the reserve fund. She wanted then all present and so they were.

Sarah had done her homework. She knew exactly the state of the hotel finances, and was supported by Bobby Brooks. She left them in no doubt she was in charge, and although she was doing them the courtesy of consulting them, the final decision was hers.

She knew where the opposition would arise. And it did.

'I don't think Sefton can possibly expect to take his money out at such short notice, and I think he should make Rafe's wife's family responsible,' Claire said.

Margaret disagreed. She was studying the figures Sarah had acquired from the hotel accountants. 'I don't think that comes into it. Sefton is entitled to withdraw his capital any time he likes. That was the agreement, wasn't it, Bobby?'

'Is there a properly drawn-up agreement? Or is this one just in Mother's head?' Claire asked.

Bobby looked uncomfortable. 'As a matter of fact I believe it was a gentleman's agreement.'

'There! I knew Mother was too sentimental to arrange a proper legal agreement,' Claire said triumphantly. 'We are under no obligation to pay out if it doesn't suit us.'

'You can't say that, Claire,' Rachel was roused to retort. 'If Mummy and Dad agreed with Sefton that he was at

255

liberty to take out his money when he required it, that settles it.'

'You are a fool, Rachel,' Claire said sharply. 'Do you realize that the loss of so much capital will cripple the running of the hotel unless we can get another backer, or sell.'

'How can you talk about selling!' Michael said. 'Renton's Royal is our future.'

'It's certainly yours as things are.' Claire didn't try to hide the bitterness in her voice. 'You don't care a toss for Jim and me. Jim won't be able to get a job for months. If we agree to sell we can take our share and buy our own hotel. Let me look at those figures, Margaret.' She studied them closely, and without comment passed the paper to Jim.

'I'm afraid you are under an illusion if you think any sale monies will be shared,' Bobby said. 'The entire proceeds will belong to Sarah.'

'That isn't fair,' Claire said.

'Of course it's fair,' Margaret said. 'Gran owns the hotel. But actually I don't see any great problems. Okay, if Sefton takes all his holding, that will leave an empty reserve fund; so what, I've been working in Accounts these last few weeks, and I know the takings will more than cover the expenses, and we can begin to build up a balance.'

Privately Sarah applauded Margaret's clear assessment of the situation, but she was determined to stay quiet until she heard out the others.

'Gran would be crackers to sell,' Fleur said. 'If we are short of cash, we, the family, can work for less, or for love if necessary.'

'That's right, Fleur,' Michael said. 'And we don't want any outsiders muscling in.'

'Gran has made a great job of running this place.' Margaret smiled at Sarah. 'I didn't realize how good until I helped in the Accounts office. And it's not just the money, it's the goodwill, and the appreciation of the guests. I agree with Fleur and Michael, come what may, we carry on.'

Sarah's joy filled all her being. Her faith in her grandchildren was completely vindicated, and the realization that the future of Gerald's dream was ensured was almost more than she could bear.

Claire turned to Bobby. 'How could a legal case affect all this euphoria?'

'I don't think I follow your reasoning. We don't have any legal cases pending.'

'Then you will have. Jim and I have decided to sue for the return of our positions as managers, or for a considerable sum in compensation.'

'Are you mad, Mother?' Margaret's anger spilled over. 'You shame me. Do you want to ruin Renton's Royal? You and Dad have had it good for long enough. You'd be surprised at the opinions flying round the staff about your inefficiency and overbearing behaviour.'

'Margaret, I won't have that. Claire and Jim have always served the hotel well, and I am grateful for their past services. I am sure, Claire, when we discuss this, we can come to an amicable arrangement.'

'Isn't it true, Bobby?' Claire ignored her mother's remarks. 'Charlie Mullins has made an astronomical offer for the hotel, and also offered to reinstate Jim and me as managers?'

Bobby narrowed his eyes. His anger was evident in the whitening of his face. 'Mr Mullins' offer is confidential.'

'I think not, Bobby. Mr Mullins informed us, and suggested we used our influence.'

'You have no influence,' Sarah was at last roused to say. 'I'll never accept any of Charlie's offers, and don't forget the decisions rest with me.'

'Why, I should like to know, did you bother to assemble the family here? We all know you will go your own way, and we know exactly what you intend to do. Pay out your dear friend Sefton, and screw the rest of us. Has he some hold over you? What, for instance, is your relationship with him?'

'Claire, how dare you speak to Mummy like that. You shame us all. How can you be so vindictive and selfish?' Rachel was flushed with the strength of her feelings.

Bobby Brooks stood up. 'I don't think anything further can be gained from this meeting. Kindly excuse me.'

One by one the family dispersed.

Sarah didn't move. She had won the day, but at what cost? She had secured the future of Renton's Royal, and the future of her grandchildren. Her thoughts drifted back to Gerald. 'He'd say I've done right, and so I have,' she added defiantly.

CHAPTER 25

The family meeting had been, as far as Claire was concerned, a fiasco. She saw her hopes for ownership of Renton's Royal slipping further away from her grasp. It was useless complaining to Jim. He certainly saw no future in the hotel for himself, and very little for Claire. He spent too much of his time in the hotel cocktail bar, and as he became more adept with his crutches, transferred his custom to the golf club bar.

Claire switched her attention to Margaret.

'Have you changed your mind about joining the family in the management of Renton's Royal? There isn't any reason why you can't share with Michael.'

'There's every reason. I don't see my future here.'

'Why not? Between us we are far more suited to take control from Mother.'

'Take control? I don't follow you. Gran isn't giving up.'

'She can't go on for ever, and you and I can be ready to take charge when she retires.'

'Count me out.'

'Don't be stupid, Margaret. Think, when I take over from Mother, you'll be next in line.'

Margaret laughed. 'What is this? A Renton's Royal succession. I'm enjoying working in Accounts. But it is temporary until I get my degree.'

'I hope you aren't going to throw yourself away on that impecunious student.'

'What have you got against Peter – apart from the fact he's poor, doesn't own any property, and is not madly ambitious.'

'Do I need to have any more reasons? And another thing, he and Rachel have their heads together too often. Supposedly over that ridiculous book she's writing.'

'If you are trying to make me jealous, forget it.'

Nevertheless a seed was planted.

And seeds watered by innuendos have a way of taking root.

Claire's next move was to write a letter to Charlie Mullins. She set aside her anger over his rejection of her until it suited her to renew it. Her motive was perfectly clear to Charlie. In effect, she was willing to part with inside information regarding the financial position of the hotel which would make it easier for him to strike a bargain with Sarah.

Charlie was angry. He read the letter a couple of times and then shredded it. There was no way he was going to cheat on Sarah. His desire to own Renton's Royal had started as a game; a pitting of wits, like a game of chess where each move was blocked by the other.

Now it had developed into something else for him; an obsession. He realized his obsession was to possess Sarah, and was far greater than his desire for ownership of Renton's Royal.

Even in Charlie's book games had rules.

Although he had ignored Claire's letter, it lay heavily on his mind. He wanted that information but not at the price Claire would exact from him.

Claire too, was obsessed, and Margaret was becoming afraid for her.

'I don't like it, Gran. I think that blow on Mother's head has affected her more than we realize.'

'The doctors assure me – '

'I know what the doctors say,' Margaret said. 'But she's obsessed with the idea we are all against her.'

'No, that isn't true.' Sarah felt the familiar flutter of her heart; the secret guilt that she was to blame for Claire's unreasonableness.

'I don't know what she's up to, but I'm warning you – look out.'

'Margaret, I won't believe that Claire would do anything to harm me. She is my daughter.'

'And I'm hers. She wants Renton's Royal more than anything in the world.'

Sarah sighed. 'I wish – '

'I know,' Margaret said gently. 'You wish Grandpa hadn't died. I guess we all wish that. But I doubt if he'd have made a better job of running the hotel. You're the tops.'

Margaret's faith in her was comforting, but she doubted the truth of it.

'Can I ask you a favour, Gran?' Margaret continued. 'Some friends have invited me to join them on a European trip. Will you mind if Peter stays on in the cottage?'

'Of course he's welcome. But shouldn't he be going too?'

'He can't afford it.'

'Can I help?'

'Thanks no, Gran. He has his pride. And in any case Rachel's Sam Verne book has really caught his interest. He's a historian, you know, and has offered to give her a hand with research in local archives. Rachel's thrilled.'

Before she left, Margaret gave Peter the keys to her flat. 'When you've had enough of the Rentons use my place.'

'Margaret, I wish I was coming with you.'

'No, you don't.' She was realistic. 'A break will do us good. I'll be back in time for Gran's birthday. Look after Rachel,' she added thoughtfully.

It was Margaret's realism which was at the root of Peter's doubts, but unlike Claire's it was based on common sense.

Claire, however, was past seeing sense. She was convinced the family were against her, and the obvious person on whom to vent her fears and anger was Jim. She brooded over his laziness and his refusal to take any responsibility, or even to set about looking for another job.

Sarah was determined that Claire, as personal assistant, should be involved in the day-to-day running of the hotel and delegated to her the sorting of the morning mail. Sarah loved her rounds, as she called them. It was as if she had to see for herself that nothing was amiss. A visit to the kitchens always reassured her, as did a little chat with Mrs Humphries in the housekeeper's room.

Claire secretly enjoyed the hour or two she spent alone in Sarah's office. If however, she allowed her imagination to project her into the future, Sarah's return did nothing to sustain it.

Nevertheless for a while she was in charge. She answered several telephone calls, and when the bell rang again and she picked up the receiver, she recognized Bobby Brooks' voice.

'Claire here,' she said.

'Oh good. I wanted to speak to you. There's a bit of trouble – '

'What?'

'I'm at the golf club. It seems there was trouble last evening and the secretary has asked me, in my capacity as a friend of the family, to tell Jim he is barred from the club for the time being.'

'What the hell are you talking about? They can't do that to Jim.'

'It's the rules.'

'To hell with the rules. Why pick on Jim?'

'I'm afraid he got into an argument with another member. Damage has been done.'

'Jim doesn't make trouble. He must have been provoked.'

'I'm sorry, Claire. Please make sure he doesn't come here. This is a friendly warning, the official one will be sent later.'

She slammed down the receiver.

How dare those stupid officials pick on Jim?

She stormed up to the apartment, and flung open the door. Jim was sitting comfortably, his leg up on a footstool, a glass and the telephone to hand, and the sheets of the racing paper scattered round him.

Rachel was sitting at the table sorting out library books, and both hers and Jim's heads were sharply raised at Claire's precipitous entrance.

'What have you to say about last evening?' Claire advanced on Jim. 'How dare you disgrace the Renton name?'

'I don't know what you are talking about.'

'Don't give me that! Bobby Brooks has been on the phone and says you wrecked the golf club bar, and the secretary is barring you from going there again.'

'Rubbish,' Jim yelled. 'I had a bit of an argument with some chap who was laying down the law about dicey hotel keepers. So I hit him.'

'Are you mad? You know the kind of people who are members of the club, and not only that, we get a lot of business through them.'

'Ah, now we reach the crux of the matter. Business. That little tin-pot god you and your mother worship.'

'And you live comfortably out of the profits.' Claire's voice was dangerously measured. 'I've just about had enough. Either you leave or I will. I'm sick to the back teeth of your behaviour.'

'By all means leave, my dear. Are you intending running to your friend Charlie Mullins? He's not very co-operative I must say, turning you down. But then perhaps he's waiting for you to offer him favours – '

Claire's hand shot out and caught Jim a resounding blow across the cheek. Instinctively he raised his hand to rub the place, and awkwardly got to his feet. They faced one another, eyes on a level, and as Claire raised her arm again, Jim caught hold. 'No you don't. No woman hits me twice.'

Claire tugged her arm free and stepped back.

Rachel said, 'Please, Claire. Jim . . .'

Claire rounded on her. 'Don't you dare interfere. This is between Jim and me. And don't you dare go running to Mother. I know you, my dear sister, only too well. Look to your own affairs. I must say you've made a fine mess of your marriage, and while we are about it, don't interfere between Margaret and that good-for-nothing student she fancies.'

'Lay off,' Jim said. 'Rachel's business is her own, and she won't want you poking your nose into it. Well, when are you moving out, Claire? Because I'm staying here.'

Rachel felt physically sick. She grabbed the library books and fled down the stairs, across the foyer, and pounded over the lawn to the cottage.

She flung open the door, dropping the books in the hall, and sank down on the nearest chair in the sitting room. She burst into tears.

Peter came through from the kitchen with a mug of coffee. 'Rachel, what's the matter? Are you hurt? Has there been an accident?'

She buried her head in her hands, bending forward, rocking and sobbing. Peter put down the mug, and knelt beside her.

'Rachel, dearest Rachel, don't. Please tell me what's happened. Is Margaret all right? Your mother?' He put his arms round her and held her shaking form close. She felt warm and comfortable in his embrace. Too comfortable perhaps. She pulled away slightly.

'Hanky,' she mumbled. He took a clean white one out of his shirt pocket, and she wiped her eyes and blew her nose.

'Oh Peter, it was awful. Claire and Jim quarrelling. She said terrible things.' She continued to sniff.

'Come, you mustn't let their quarrels upset you.'

'But Peter, she attacked me about Mark, and said I was interfering between you and Margaret. It's not true, is it?'

'Of course not.'

She lifted her head, and gazed at him with eyes glazed with tears.

'Oh, Peter . . .'

He smiled wryly. 'You haven't come between Margaret and me, I promise you. We're very good friends and once I hoped it would be more. Lately . . .' He gave her a long look from his kind, clear grey eyes then stood up. 'I'll make you some coffee. Just sit there.'

She crouched back in the chair, too drained to move. When he came back, she smiled. 'Sorry to weep all over you.'

'Any time. Rachel, don't ever change.'

'Change?' Puzzled she accepted the coffee mug and sipped the hot liquid gratefully. 'How can I change? I'm me.'

'Whatever others say to you never lose your confidence in yourself. Don't let them hurt you.'

She didn't say that the insensitiveness of her family often reduced her to a state when she found it difficult to make a decision. With Peter it was different. She was totally conscious of his compassion and tenderness. Margaret was a very lucky girl, did she but know it,

265

and yet there seemed to be a reluctance for these two to commit themselves wholly to each other.

'Let's cheer ourselves up,' Peter suggested as he collected their empty mugs. 'My Gran has had a win on the Pools and has shared her good luck with her favourite grandson. I'll treat you to lunch and I know just the place.'

She protested. He needed his money.

'I need to spend it on something which will give me pleasure. Treating you will do just that. May I drive your car?'

They set off half an hour later.

'Where to?' she asked.

'The moors,' he said decisively, 'and a little inn Margaret and I found. It's called The Moorhen – all oak beams and super grub. We'll gorge ourselves and then take a walk over the heather to the top of the fell. Even the weather is perfect.'

Rachel thought how completely a little kindness could change her outlook on life. She thrived on gentleness, pushing to the back of her mind Claire's harsh accusations.

Peter was her friend, and nothing Claire could say would change that. She repeated to herself the word 'friend'. But did friendship cover this feeling of gaiety, the flutter in her heart when their hands accidentally touched, the sweet contentment just to be sitting beside him in the car?

And Margaret – what of her? It was all very well for Peter to say he doubted they'd ever be more than just friends. Rachel's niece might secretly harbour quite different thoughts but lack the confidence to act on them. Rachel knew just what that felt like and her heart ached at the realization.

Peter was obviously enjoying himself. He chose a table by the window. 'We'll have grouse, it's their speciality,' he said confidently, and spent a long time over the wine list.

'This is fabulous,' he said, after tackling his grouse with gusto. 'I do so enjoy your company, Rachel.' He raised his glass to her and guilessly met her eyes. 'I've been wondering . . . we seem to have reached an impasse with our research round here. There's a very good local archive at Grange-Over-Sands which could be worth a look. I was wondering if we could go together – stay locally maybe?'

She knew exactly what he was suggesting, and her heart leapt. To be desired again, courted, pursued – it was heaven. But caution prompted her to tell him: 'I'm not sure, Peter. I'll give it some thought.'

Later, walking over the springy turf, holding his hand, she knew she would remember this day. The purple heather surged about them, the wind chased clouds across a blue sky, casting shadows which ran joyously ahead, changing the colours of grass and heather.

At the top they stood still to catch the view.

'It's so peaceful,' she said.

'Fine for an interlude, to strengthen us for the times when we need to remember moments like this.' It was a declaration and a proposal. He caught hold of her hands and drew her close.

'Rachel – I – ' He kissed her.

She was overwhelmed by a momentary longing for this never to end, and then the folly of her own imaginings was brought home to her. She was nearly twenty years older than this warm-hearted, impetuous young man, with a daughter almost his age and a niece who might well be in love with him. And she was married to a man who would never let her go.

'No, Peter, no.'

'Afraid?'

She turned and began to run down the fell. She understood with appalling clarity that this time she must not waver.

CHAPTER 26

'Sarah.'

Sarah inched the telephone receiver further away from her ear, recognizing Alida Ashton's penetrating tone.

'Hello Alida.'

'Ah, you recognize my voice. Most people do. I presume you know that my husband and I are travelling to the States. I want to see Fleur before I go.'

Sarah's heart sank.

'She is my only grandchild.' Mrs Ashton continued, 'I have spoken to Rachel, but I can't get a definite answer from her. You understand how I feel about Fleur, she is your grandchild too. My treatment is a last ditch chance . . .' Alida Ashton's voice softened so as to be almost unrecognizable.

A truce, Sarah thought, maybe in the face of death. 'I'm sorry,' she said inadequately.

'I hate to ask you favours, but will you explain to Fleur how much I want to see her?'

'Of course.'

'I know I can rely on you to arrange a meeting.'

Sarah waited until evening, mulling over various ways to approach Fleur and then rejecting them. She walked over to the cottage slowly, giving herself more time to decide on what she should say. She opened the door and listened. Ricki fussed round her legs, and for a moment Sarah thought Fleur wasn't in. There wasn't a sound from Fleur's room, and Sarah hesitated, wondering why Ricki was shut out too.

She knocked and waited. No answer. She opened the door. Fleur lay on the bed, her head buried in a pillow.

'Fleur, are you ill?'

A muttered 'no', caused Sarah to walk briskly across the room and sit down on the bed.

'Darling, what's the matter?'

'Nothing.'

'Of course there's something wrong.'

Ricki leapt onto the bed and snuggled down beside Fleur.

'A trouble shared is a trouble halved,' Sarah quoted one of her father's favourite proverbs.

Fleur sat up, and hugged Ricki. 'I wonder who thought up these ridiculous sayings.'

'I expect there's a grain of truth in them. So what's the matter?'

'It's Ramiro. His father has threatened to send someone to fetch him, if he doesn't go home.'

'I see. Has he told you why he is so reluctant to go?'

She shook her head. 'Only that if he goes, that's the end.' She pressed her face against the top of Ricki's head. 'Please Gran, will you talk to his father? Ramiro will be angry, but what else can we do?'

Sarah was in a dilemma. She'd no wish to face Señor Rodriguez's anger. But on the other hand she felt it was time that Ramiro came clean about the troubles at home.

'I'll think about it,' she said, promising herself she'd have a word with Ramiro before incurring his father's wrath. 'I came to tell you your grandmother phoned – '

'You're my gran – '

'Mrs Ashton is your grandmother too.'

269

'What did she want?'

'She wants to see you, Fleur – and she's right. She's worried that this treatment isn't going to cure her – '

'No. I won't go.'

'Fleur, that isn't you. She needs you. She cares very deeply for you. She spoke to your mother, but – '

'I know my Mum – yes, she will. No, she won't. Darling Mum, I feel awfully protective over her.'

'So do I.'

'Why does Grandmother want to see me? I don't trust her, Gran. And she is hurtful to Mum.'

'I know that. But I guess it cost her a lot to ask me to ask you.'

Fleur rolled off the bed, and flung herself against Sarah, nuzzling her face against hers.

'If you say I must go, OK.'

'No. That won't do. That's doing it for me – not her.'

Sarah felt breathless with love. Of them all Fleur was her dearest, the child of her heart.

Rachel was difficult. She faced Sarah across the breakfast table.

'She phoned me. I said – '

'Just what *did* you say, Rachel?'

'I said – I said I'd think about it. I think it's rotten of her to speak to you behind my back.'

'And what else?'

'I don't want to go to Ashton Hall, and I don't want Fleur to go, in case – '

'Aren't you being unreasonable? Mrs Ashton can hardly grab Fleur and lock her up in an ivory tower.'

Rachel laughed. 'Mummy, you are ridiculous. Do *you* think I should let Fleur visit her?'

'Yes.'

'Why?'

'Mrs Ashton fears she might die in America. She didn't say so, but – '

'Do you think I'm being stubborn – hard?'

'No. I think you have too much compassion. I feel the same way as you about the Ashtons. They've made you unhappy.'

'I hate her.'

'No. Hate is too strong a word, my darling. The truth is you're afraid of her, and the only way to conquer fear is to face it. My dad told me that long ago when I was a girl. Strange how I remember little incidents – '

'Tell me more. I want to know about you.'

'It was a silly, childish thing. I lost a book belonging to my teacher, and I was afraid to tell her.'

'Did you?'

'Yes. Do you know what she said. Thank you for telling me, my dear, it was brave of you.'

'Oh Mummy.' Rachel jumped up, and came round the table to hug Sarah.

'Right, we'll go. Mummy, I want to change my mind about the bookshop. I hope Mr Glover won't mind, but I don't want to live alone in the cottage any more. I love being here looking after this place, and helping out at the hotel when they are short-handed.'

'Rachel, that's wonderful news. I can't tell you how much I look forward to the evenings and coming back here to you.'

Rachel's sudden willingness to visit Ashton Hall baffled Sarah until she realized that in fact, Rachel had no intention of seeing her mother-in-law.

Fleur wasn't pleased and complained to Sarah.

'Mum says I can drop her off at Mr Glover's house. That's not fair.'

'Mrs Ashton wants to see you, and for heaven's sake put

271

some decent clothes on. I haven't forgotten your father's face when he saw you in your working gear.'

'OK, my beloved Gran, I'll dress up and behave myself. That's a promise.'

Sarah wasn't completely at ease about the visit however. She felt responsible, and was afraid there might be consequences. She'd interfered again, and each time she had done so she'd vowed it was the last time.

The following day Peter returned to London.

Rachel had protested, asking him anxiously if he planned to return.

'Don't worry, I'll be back in time for Mrs Renton's birthday. I have some research to do, and I can't get the books I want here.'

Still, Rachel was afraid that he had been lying. She felt guilty because she believed she'd allowed him to think there could be something more than friendship between them. And because she regretted that there wasn't.

Fleur drove the Marina. 'You look very smart,' Rachel told her, her heart swelling with pride.

'Gran's orders. My Ashton relations don't go for scruffiness. You look pretty good yourself,' Fleur conceded, dropping Rachel at Mr Glover's gate, and arranging to meet later in the Nag's Head in Bransfell.

Fleur drove into the grounds of the Hall with a flourish, brakes squealing as she brought the car to a standstill. Strangely, she had an unaccustomed feeling of pride as her gaze swept over the mature façade of the house, the lawns, a glint from the lake, and beyond, the pastures and woods. It was a different kind of pride from the one she felt for Renton's Royal. Here her father's ancestors had lived and farmed these acres, and filled the house with treasures garnered from their travels.

She'd hated being an Ashton, but now as she ran up the stone steps and pushed open the front door she felt a quirky pride, or was it a realization of belonging?

'Grandmother, where are you?'

'Here,' Mrs Ashton called from the drawing room. Fleur crossed the room and, bending, kissed her grandmother on the cheek.

'Lavender,' she said, sniffing appreciatively. 'I love it. Do you remember the time when I was little and I dabbed myself all over, and the dog as well. You were ever so cross.'

'I do remember being angry because you doused that great brown dog you rescued.'

'I adored Rascal. Some rotten person had abandoned him in the village. I thought you were going to make me take him to the police. Why didn't you?'

'Your father overruled me.'

'I didn't know. I thought he only liked dogs with impeccable pedigrees.'

'That is true, but he loves you,' Mrs Ashton said. 'Fleur, my dear, how nice you look. Sit down over there where I can see you.'

Fleur was shocked by the change in her grandmother. She seemed to have shrunk, and the high colour in her cheeks had faded to a waxy yellow.

'I'm sorry you are ill. Do you have to go to America for the treatment?'

'I'm afraid so. It isn't available here yet. I don't want to go. But your grandfather and your father insist.'

'It's worth a try,' Fleur said, glad that Gran had made her come. 'Are you afraid?'

'I don't want to die in a foreign country.'

'Of course you won't die!' Fleur was glad to be interrupted by the housekeeper bringing in a tray of coffee.

'Shall I pour, Grandmother?' Fleur said. She filled the

273

eggshell-thin cups and placed her grandmother's well within her reach.

'Are you happy, Fleur? Mark says you like your job. You know we don't think it's suitable.'

'I love it. I mean to be a great cook. I shall write cookery books and all that stuff.'

Mrs Ashton sighed. 'Do you not feel any pride in this place? I ask you this because of course you will inherit it after Mark.'

Fleur laughed. 'What in the world would I do with a whacking great place? It's awfully kind of you, Grandmother, but I don't want it.'

'You will, one day.'

Fleur glanced round. Everything seemed to be exactly the same as when she and Rachel had lived in the Dower House, and been summoned for tea on Sundays in this room. How reluctantly they had gone, and – was she merely imagining it in hindsight? – how disappointed her father had been that they were unable to share the love and pride he felt for Ashton Hall. Now she could appreciate the sense of permanence; each piece of furniture had a history. Only the flowers were changed, and today the tall Chinese vases held yellow and bronze chrysanthemums.

'I've been thinking, Fleur, and I've come to a decision. I want you to have these now.' Her grandmother took a red leather jewel box off the table beside her and handed it to Fleur. 'Open it.'

Fleur gasped. 'I can't take these.' She held up a gold chain and locket.

'I particularly want you to have that. Open it, dear. There, that's a picture of my mother, and opposite is one of my only brother. He was killed in the First World War. Come close, let me put it round your neck.' She fumbled for ages but at last managed the clasp. She nodded. 'I can

274

imagine you wearing it at parties.' She lifted out a bracelet, gold and inset with rubies. 'This was one of my twenty-first birthday presents, and this little ring was given to me by a dear friend. Try it on.'

Fleur slipped the ring onto her finger. The large diamond sparkled in the sunlight as Fleur twisted her hand this way and that. 'He also died towards the end of that same dreadful war. I was just seventeen. We were to have been married.'

'These are your treasures,' Fleur said, bewildered. 'Why give them to me?'

'You are my only grandchild.'

'I know. But won't Daddy object?'

'Hardly! You're his daughter, Fleur. Whatever the distance between you, Mark will never forget that. Family is all important to him. This diamond necklace belonged to my grandmother. She wore it at her coming-out ball. I want you to promise to keep them for the daughters you may have one day.'

'And if I don't – marry, I mean? Grandmother, thank you very much, but – '

'No buts. I want to make amends. We didn't welcome your mother in the right way, and I regret that now. Tell her, will you?'

Fleur nodded. 'Grandmother – '

'It's all right, my dear, dear granddaughter. I'm not afraid. Now off you go, and take care of yourself.'

'She can't buy my love.' Fleur put the red leather case on the table between them.

'No.' Rachel moved the beer mats to make a pattern. 'You can't buy love, only give and receive.'

'What am I to do? I don't want her jewellery, but she made it impossible for me to refuse. She said I was to keep it for my daughters – '

You could do just that. Put the box safely in your bag.'

'Mum, she was awfully sad. I felt sorry for her until I remembered how unkind she was to you.'

'We'll forget about that. It's ancient history.'

'Daddy isn't ancient history. He isn't going to let up, I guess.'

Rachel brushed aside any speculation. 'What shall we eat?' She picked up the menu. 'How about king prawns and chips? Sounds awful enough to be good.'

Fleur watched her mother weave her way to the bar counter to order the food and return with two glasses of lager. A man offered to carry them for her, but Rachel froze him with a look, and Fleur smiled.

'Oh damn everything,' Fleur said. 'My grandmother is going to die in the States and not where she belongs.'

'Rubbish. She'll come home and live to a ripe old age.'

Rachel sipped her lager and arranged the beer mats into a different pattern. 'Do you think I should see her? I mean – '

'She said giving me her family jewellery was a way of making amends to you.'

'I'll think about it. Our food is ready, please fetch it, darling.'

The same chap offered to carry the plates for Fleur. She grinned; you had to give him full marks for trying.

'How did you get on with Mr Glover?' Fleur asked, expertly spearing prawns onto her fork.

'You won't believe this, but he was wondering how to tell me he didn't want to sell the bookshop.'

'Why? I thought he was going abroad.'

'Not any more. He's in love.' Rachel giggled delightedly.

'Don't be daft, Mum.'

'Absolutely true. Mind, he didn't tell me, but I know the signs. And the house, I couldn't believe it. You remember how dreary it was. Now his lady friend has spruced it up. Fresh white paint, new curtains and covers.'

'Who is she?'

'She used to be the local librarian, now retired, and now she is going to marry Mr Glover and run the bookshop.'

'That's fantastic. I always liked the old boy. He used to buy me sweets when I visited you at the shop. Will we be invited to the wedding?'

'I don't think he'll want a splash, but you never know.'

'Why have you changed your mind about the bookshop? You were dead keen. Does Gran know?'

Rachel nodded. 'She's pleased. The truth is I'd forgotten what it was like to be part of the family. I was always on the outside – '

'Not true,' Fleur interrupted. 'Just because you lived in Bransfell, didn't mean you didn't belong. And what about the Sam Verne book? I thought you and Peter were besotted with it.'

Rachel shuddered inwardly at this choice of words. Besotted? Yes, she supposed she had been – until she came to her senses. 'I seem to have lost interest in the book,' she lied.

'I don't believe you. Has your change of heart anything to do with Peter?'

'Certainly not.'

'He's pretty moony about you.'

'Don't be ridiculous. He's gone back to London to work.'

'Was he getting fresh?'

'Fleur, how dare you suggest such a thing?'

'I don't blame him or you if you fancy him. I'm lucky to have such a darling mother.'

'Fleur,' Rachel said as her defences crumbled, 'I wish Mark – '

'I don't. Daddy is best where he is, and not interfering with our lives. Let's have coffee.'

Rachel's glance followed Fleur's progress to the bar counter. Maybe I have failed her, she thought. Perhaps I should have tried harder with Mark, maybe this break is my fault. Her thoughts returned to Peter's abrupt departure. It had hurt her more than it should have done but she was glad she had braved the pain. It had helped her resolve to sort out once and for all her feelings for Mark.

Fleur came back to the table balancing cups of coffee on a tray and sat down.

'Mum, am I spoiling things for you being so against Daddy and Ashton Hall and all that? Grandmother said that if anything happened to Daddy I would inherit Ashton Hall. Is that true?'

Startled, Rachel said, 'I suppose so. I've never thought about it.'

'If you and Daddy get a divorce, he might marry again and have a son. Where does that leave you?'

'I've no idea. In any case Mark won't consider a divorce.'

'And in your heart you don't want one. I think you still care for him. If I go and live in Spain it would be the best thing that could happen for you.'

'Fleur, what are you talking about?' Rachel reached across the table and grabbed Fleur's hand. 'Has Ramiro . . .'

Fleur's delighted laugh reassured Rachel slightly. 'He hasn't taken advantage of me, and he hasn't asked me to marry him.' Her expression saddened. 'He said, wait.'

Fleur disengaged her hand. 'I won't wait for ever, you know. Come on, let's go.' She led the way out of the pub. 'Where now?' she asked, unlocking the car doors, and blinking in the sunshine.

'Back to Ashton Hall.'

'Are you sure, Mum?'

Rachel nodded. 'Come on. I'll drive before I change my mind.'

'Is it because of Daddy?'

'I don't think so,' Rachel said seriously.

'As long as you understand I'll never go back.'

Rachel drove in silence, and turned in at the gates.

'I have to talk to her alone.'

'OK. I'll walk down to the lake.'

The rowing boat was still there. Fleur rowed into the centre of the lake, and rested on the oars.

She had forgotten what pleasure the lake had been during her childhood: swimming, and fishing for tadpoles with a green net the gardener had given her, begging empty jam jars from the cook.

She thought how it would be if Ramiro was with her now. She thought that their happiness was menaced by family ties and duties, and she was overcome by sadness.

CHAPTER 27

The white peacocks were dead. The staff were unbelieving. One by one they pilgrimaged to the aviary to view the corpses, and they grieved, wondering who was responsible for this outrage, for such it was, to destroy such magnificent and innocent birds.

Sarah was white-faced and tight-lipped. She, too, grieved for the despoliation of such beauty, but much worse, she was fearful of the consequences.

Michael tried to talk her out of her fears. But superstition was rooted in her nature, and no amount of reasoning made sense to her.

'How can the killing of the birds change our luck, Gran? Someone is trying to spite us, and it's cruel and senseless vandalism. I'll inform the police.'

'No. It won't do any good. We can't bring them to life again, poor, poor things. Michael, do you think someone close to us could have done it? I mean, someone who knows I am superstitious about the birds?'

'The thought crossed my mind. I'm sure we can rule out the family and the present staff. I expect other people know you are superstitious about the peacocks. I don't know why you let the idea build up. It's dangerous, and makes us vulnerable.'

'The peacocks died when Renton House burnt down,

and the day before Gerald died the new ones disappeared, never to return. I shall buy some more.'

'No, Gran. I don't think that's a good idea. The way I see it, only the peacocks that are born and bred at Renton's Royal can protect us as you so firmly believe.'

'Not so. The Renton who first introduced them to the grounds made it quite clear that a peacock was the symbol of good luck. He was very specific about this. He wrote in his diary, "If one or more or all should die, then efforts must be made to replace them."''

Later she walked across the lawns to the aviary. She forced herself to look at the birds lying where they had been killed. She went inside the aviary and gently touched the proud crowns, flattened for ever. Sorrow wasn't enough. Anger set her senses throbbing, her heart hammering. She would find the perpetrators of this outrage, and take her revenge. When she arrived back in her office, she sat at her desk, calming herself with the thought that maybe she was a foolish woman, but in her heart she knew she was not. After a moment she noticed the bunch of flowers laid on the side table. She got up, thinking there was some mistake. She searched for the card, it read: 'To Mrs Renton. From your staff.'

The white roses and carnations were fragrant with the scent of summers past. She was moved to tears and, unwrapping the cellophane, was enraptured by the purity of the flowers. Moreover she was comforted by the staff's caring. It was a barrier against the terror she'd endured ever since she'd knelt in the dust in the aviary and said goodbye to her beautiful birds.

Michael and Fleur buried the peacocks. They chose a site near the aviary, beneath a flowering cherry tree.

'Are we burying our luck, Mick?'

He rested on the spade. 'Of course not. Don't tell me you're superstitious too.'

'I think I am. I need signs and there aren't any.'

'We make our own luck.' Michael resumed digging.

Fleur didn't argue. She wrapped the birds up in old sheets begged from Mrs Humphries and laid them in the grave. While Michael was filling it in, she fetched the last of the summer roses, arranged them in a container, and stood it under the tree.

Later that morning she and Ramiro stood there holding hands.

'Today I have a letter from my father, I have to go home.'

'You mean just a visit – a holiday.'

'I don't know. There is much trouble between my father and his partner.'

'But what can you do?'

'My father says it is in my hands.'

'What do you mean, Ramiro? You've been here three years. How can it possibly concern you?'

'It is complicated. I cannot tell you all now.'

'Take me with you.'

'No, *mi amor*. I must talk to my father first.'

'Didn't you mean you wanted us to be together for always.' She broke away from him.

He caught hold of her and pulled her into the privacy of the shrubbery. His kisses reassured her momentarily. She clung to him, afraid if she let go he would disappear.

'I love you, Fleur,' he whispered. 'Remember that. Whatever happens, remember.'

'I don't want to remember,' she said rebelliously. 'I want to be with you every moment. I love you so much. Tell your father you are staying here with me. Tell him you love me.'

'I will tell him all these things.' He sighed. 'Tomorrow I

282

must go. I will speak to you on the telephone every day, I promise.'

'Your father is unreasonable, Ramiro. You've had your holidays for the year, and we are very busy. What is this urgent problem that needs you to be there?'

'I am sorry, Mrs Renton, to let you down, and also Chef. I do not wish to go. But I have this fear – '

'Fear?' she latched onto the word. 'What fear? Really, Ramiro, you owe me a proper explanation.'

'It is my father's partner. He is being difficult. He is rich, you understand. My father is building a new dining room. He needs – '

'Don't be silly, Ramiro. Your father can borrow money elsewhere. I'm sure his credit is good. I don't believe you are telling me all the truth,' she said.

'Please, I cannot say any more.'

'I can't stop you going. Have you spoken to Fleur? Have you told her the truth?'

She was moved by his conflicting expressions, his thoughts so clearly reflected in his brown eyes. 'I won't have Fleur hurt. Arrange with Chef to have your place filled, and Ramiro, please make your visit short.'

Claire was encroaching on Sarah's preserves. She was not obviously flagrant, but in little subtle ways needled Sarah like thorns in her flesh.

She objected to Ramiro having more time off to go to Spain. 'You'll regret not telling him to stay there. Best thing that could happen. In any case,' she accused Sarah, 'you favour him, just because your beloved granddaughter is crazy about him.'

Sarah was annoyed, but for the moment held her tongue. The killing of the peacocks had unsettled her. She continually dreamt about Gerald, and woke with wet cheeks.

283

Claire was really digging in. She opened the mail and sorted it. It wasn't until Claire opened a letter from Charlie, marked private, that Sarah let fly.

'You've no right to open my private letters.'

'Something to hide? What's Charlie getting at, wanting to talk to you about plans. I bet they don't include Jim and me.'

'You go too far, Claire.'

'But not far enough. You want Jim and me out, well, you'll be unlucky, I am staying. You can be sure I'm not going to let my kid relations put one over on me.'

Sarah was not the only one to whom Claire was a problem . . . Clive Booth was needled by Claire in little ways too.

'That woman follows me about like a guard dog,' he complained to Michael. 'And then she has the cheek to change my orders. If she doesn't get off my back . . .'

Michael reported the conversation to Sarah. He too was receiving a share of Claire's treatment, and he wasn't prepared to be silent, and intended bringing their complaints up at the next staff management meeting.

Claire spiked their guns however and was first to lay complaints against both Michael and Clive, charging them with inefficiency. Sarah brushed them aside, much to Claire's fury.

Clive reported that the hotel was fully booked for the next fortnight, and it was a pity the plans for the building of the extra bedrooms had not yet been passed.

'Just as well,' Claire said. 'Mother is being too lenient with Sefton Taylor, and if he withdraws his capital, it will be unlikely we can continue with the building. Now if I was running the business, I would make sure he didn't.'

'You aren't running the business, Mrs O'Hara,' Chef said. 'Nor likely to,' he added.

Claire glared at him. 'Don't you be too sure. You'll be sorry for remarks like that.'

Chef's eyes narrowed, and a faint flush coloured his sallow cheeks. 'Mrs Renton is our boss, and that's the way we want it. And don't think you'll ever put one over on Mr Sefton. He has his rights, isn't that so, Mrs Renton?'

Sarah nodded. 'There's no point in discussing the new buildings until we get the plans passed.'

'Why not ask Charlie Mullins for a loan, Mother? Naturally it would be conditional on me being restored to my rightful place,' Claire said.

'You should know places have to be earned,' Michael said. 'Gran has made it clear that she has no intention of asking Charlie Mullins or anyone else for a loan. And she certainly isn't selling, so why don't you let up about it.'

'Listen,' Sarah said. 'Michael is right. Charlie Mullins is a very old and trusted friend of mine, but I haven't the slightest intention of selling out to him, and there is no question of my retiring from active management of this hotel. Is that understood?'

She noted with satisfaction the expressions of approval on everyone's face except Claire's, but she didn't doubt that Claire would return to the fight despite her assurances that she intended to remain in control.

After the staff dispersed she sat on at her desk, knowing only too well that one dissenting voice was enough to cause trouble. She rose slowly, and going to the window flung it open. She breathed deeply. There was a stiff wind blowing, bending the tops of the pines. She listened for the mournful cry of the peacocks, forgetting for a second that they were dead.

Here Arthur Kellett found her. She turned at his tentative knock and invited him in. 'Sit down, Arthur. Is all well with your son?'

'He's fine. My sister has decided to move in with me, bringing Alan and her son.'

'That's great news.'

She sat down to wait, remembering Arthur always took his time, as if assembling words in his mind before speaking.

'I'm sorry to trouble you, Mrs Renton. But I cannot let this account run on without speaking to you.'

'What account?' Sarah was puzzled.

'Mr O'Hara's drink account. It's been much bigger since he was barred from the golf club.'

'You know about that?'

'It isn't a secret.' He handed over a bill and Sarah gasped.

'There must be some mistake, Arthur.'

'I have asked him several times to settle it, but he refuses. It isn't right or fair. He says he's family and you owe it to him.'

'Thank you for telling me, Arthur. Don't worry, I'll deal with it.'

The size of Jim's bill frightened Sarah. Was he becoming an alcoholic? Or was it just a sign of his complete dissatisfaction with his life?

She thought of tackling Claire, and then decided there was only one way to straighten out this matter, and that was to speak to Jim. She waited a while until her first hot rush of temper had cooled, and then she made her way up to the apartment.

Jim was watching television. He made a tentative effort to get up.

'Don't bother, Jim.'

Sarah sat down.

'What brings you here?' he asked indolently.

'This!' She thrust the bill into his hand.

He glanced at it. 'What about it? I told Kellett I'd pay some time.'

'That time is now.'

'Oh come on, Mother-in-law. I'm out of work, remember.'

'And likely to remain so if you carry on like this. It's time you pulled yourself together, and got a job.'

'Claire says when you find out how inefficient Booth is, you'll be glad to have us back.'

'Claire is wrong. I have every confidence in Clive.'

'And none in me. Is that it?'

'Exactly.'

'You owe it to us,' he whined, and turned to the door as Claire entered. 'Your mother is carrying on about a little bar bill.'

'Little?' Sarah snatched it out of his hand, and offered it to Claire.

She glanced at the total. 'Well. You owe it to him. Dismissing him without compensation.'

'Just a moment,' Sarah exploded. 'Jim resigned. And if you think I shall reinstate him, you are quite wrong. Please make arrangements to pay this bill, and stay out of my bar.'

'That won't be a problem. We are going to London in the morning. Jim has an appointment with a specialist. His leg is troubling him. He may have to enter a hospital. That will suit you, Mother.'

Sarah was tempted to agree. She didn't. 'Very wise to get a second opinion. Will you be staying with Margaret?'

'Probably.'

Sarah was relieved. At least for a short time she'd have a respite and so would the staff from Claire's constant interference.

Chef was meticulous in his choice of staff. He had retained the right to hire or fire, without deference to Claire, but always the matter was discussed with Sarah before his decision was made. Over the years he had developed small eccentricities, which Sarah found endearing. He had never believed that the luck of the Rentons was tied up with the peacocks, but he did believe that one small disaster always led to more.

The small disaster was a mistake of Fleur's. Any other member of his staff would have received the rough edge of his tongue, but with Fleur he was always gentle, as if in some way he perceived that harsh words would bite too deeply. It was a simple mistake, the wrong mixture for a special sweet, but there was no room for any mistakes in a busy kitchen, and it necessitated the changing of the menu.

He was tired and overworked, living on his nerves and his passion for perfection. He may have spoken more angrily than he intended, and the flush of colour flooding Fleur's face was an indication that she was indeed mortified.

He did not apologize, but the small incident brought on one of his bouts of insomnia. His room was adjacent to the staff room. It suited his simple needs. It faced east, and he always felt renewed by the sunrise, sometimes spectacular. When he tossed and turned restlessly he was compensated by flashes of inspiration. His famous dishes had always been conceived at such times.

This particular morning he woke early. He had an uneasy feeling that some little thing had been forgotten, and dressing in slacks and a sweater he pottered into the kitchen. As he opened the door, he stiffened. The smell of smoke was pronounced, and yet he could not see anything wrong. He crossed to the door leading to the various store rooms.

Smoke was puffing out from beneath the bottom of the ill-fitting door of the vegetable store room. His heart began to pound as he hurried along the passage and opened the door a chink. The smell of burning and a surge of smoke enveloped him. Eyes stinging, he rushed back to his office and dialled the emergency number for the fire brigade.

He ran back to the passage and opened the heavy service doors at the end, and then to his horror saw that smoke was filling the corridor from more than one store room.

He felt as if he was choking. His senses were reeling. The fresh air surging in through the open service doors blew the smoke in clouds so that he was no longer sure where the seat of the fire lay.

The fire engine swept up the back road, and squealed to a halt at the open doors. The firemen unrolled their hoses, familiar with the nearest hydrant, and to Chef's relief plunged into the corridor where flames were now visible.

Chef's thoughts were chaotic. At no moment did he think of phoning either Sarah or Booth. Nothing had changed; this was his domain and he'd deal with it in his own way.

It was some time before the fire chief pronounced that the fire was out. That crisis dealt with, Chef still had another one on his hands. The breakfast shift would be starting shortly, the hotel was full, and somehow breakfasts must be served.

Chef didn't panic. He had the situation in hand, but he was deeply disturbed when the fire chief told him that in his opinion it was clearly arson, and the police should be informed.

Chef was appalled. It was then he telephoned Sarah at the cottage and summoned Clive Booth. They both arrived quickly, and were followed by Fleur and Michael. Crowded into Chef's office, they dealt with their priorities. Breakfast first. Luckily there was sufficient bacon and eggs in the refrigerator in the kitchen for a number of meals, and frozen kippers and haddock could be used to eke out the fair, along with a discreet explanation of the circumstances. Bread was stacked in the cold room, and as soon as the staff arrived the breakfast cook was informed and took charge. Fleur took her place in the kitchen, and

Booth went off to Reception to have temporary menus printed.

Sarah, Chef and Michael assessed the damage. They had been warned not to touch anything, but there seemed little they could touch. Three of the store rooms were burnt out completely, but the fourth containing dry goods had suffered less damage.

'We shall have to restock quickly with enough for today and breakfast tomorrow, and then order comprehensively,' Sarah said. Chef agreed, and the three were hard at it when Detective Inspector Morris arrived.

'I've been talking to the fire chief,' he said. 'Our preliminary conclusion is that the fire was started from inside, but of course the insurance fire assessor will investigate.'

Sarah was aghast. 'Are you telling me that one of my staff – '

'Of course not, Mrs Renton. But it's possible an ex-employee had access.'

'I knew it,' Sarah declared. 'First my lovely peacocks are killed, and now this.'

'Are the staff supplied with keys to the side door, or is it left open?'

'I open the side door early each morning,' Chef said, 'and it is then left open until the late shift go off duty.'

'So someone could have sneaked in and hid until all was clear, and then started the fire?' Morris asked.

'I can't believe . . .' Sarah began.

'Perhaps someone was harbouring a grudge, Mrs Renton. An ex-employee maybe. Have you sacked anyone who might think it was unfair.'

'Well, there was that porter, Chef. He was very threatening both to you and me. What was his name?'

'Of course. Paddy Kelly. He swore to get even with me.'

'Well, well,' Morris said. 'It's possible Kelly is up to his old tricks. Don't worry, Mrs Renton, we know where to pick him up.'

Sarah made her way to her office, and sat down exhausted. Her heart was fluttering and she felt strangely light-headed; her mind kept slipping back to the time when Renton House had been burnt down. She'd felt lost and cheated. Her job had seemed swallowed up in the flames. Gerald had rescued her then; who would rescue her now?

Michael brought in a tray of tea and toast.

'I guess we both need this. Come on, Gran, I've even rescued some butter. Don't worry, our guests understand, and are being kind. It's going to cost a hell of a lot to rebuild the store rooms. Are we well covered by the insurance?'

Sarah said, 'Of course. Jim looked after the policies. Perhaps we'd better have them out before the company sends a representative round. They are in the safe in the manager's office.'

Michael fetched the bundle and laid them out on Sarah's desk.

'This can't be right,' Michael said. 'According to this we aren't covered for the loss of foodstuff, and the premium on the buildings seems low.'

'Of course it isn't right.' Sarah pointed at the date. 'It must have been updated. Have another look in the safe, Michael.'

'It's empty. This is the lot.' A quick scrabble through the remaining policies didn't help.

Angrily Sarah said, 'I trusted him. There must be some mistake. For God's sake, Michael, we can't afford to foot a large bill for rebuilding and re-stocking.'

'There's no mistake,' Michael said soberly. 'Look at this letter acknowledging the cancellation of the policy.'

'He must have changed companies without telling me,'

Sarah said wildly. 'He couldn't just have let the cover lapse.'

'He didn't.' Michael was sorting through the papers. 'He changed companies all right. Five years ago. I suppose you've never had to make a claim until now. The building and contents are insured for a minimum amount, and this policy hasn't been updated, even though there are letters suggesting a more realistic cover.'

'What the hell was Jim playing at?'

'Gran, why didn't you ask him?'

'Gerald trusted him,' she said slowly, 'and after his death I just supposed that Jim was a good enough manager to attend to basics by himself. I was wrong, Michael.' She sounded so forlorn, he put an arm round her shoulders for comfort.

'It's not your fault. You carry so much of the management. You have a right to trust your staff, especially family.'

'Of course it's my fault,' she said, 'and it's up to me to set it right.'

'We've still got the reserve fund.'

'Most of that will be needed to pay out Sefton. Get on to this insurance company, and say I want to see the manager personally right now. And telephone Mr Craig, the builder; he'll be here like a shot.'

She was in a situation where she was always at her best, rising to the challenge. 'Get going, Michael. We've no time to lose.'

CHAPTER 28

'I want the family together, Michael. I feel we are drifting apart. I suppose my sixtieth birthday is as good a time as any.'

'Great. I'll go ahead with the arrangements.'

Sarah's objective was simple. It was a declaration of intent to her family, close friends and rivals. She intended to make it clear beyond all doubt that she had no intention of giving up the management of the hotel, and the setbacks she was presently experiencing were of a temporary nature.

Michael issued invitations. A letter to his father brought the response that he and Fortunata would be on a protracted business trip in America, and sadly would have to miss his mother's birthday celebration. That suited Michael. His antipathy to his stepmother never wavered.

Claire was unresponsive, but Rachel was not, and Michael turned to her for help and guidance, and he knew he could count on his cousins.

As the date of her birthday drew nearer, Sarah found herself drifting back into the past, almost as if it had more reality than the present. Gerald figured largely in her thoughts. Little incidents lying fallow in the recess of her memory sprouted. She saw as in a glass darkly the joy on Gerald's face as he held his new-born son in his arms. When she entered the foyer, automatically she looked for him. He'd been so proud of the design of the foyer and staircase.

But mostly she recalled his tenderness; his loving tenderness which had given her the feeling she was a worthwhile person; a feeling that had persisted through the years without him right up to this moment.

And beyond Gerald lurked the figure of her father. He had given her so much, not only the knowledge that she was special to him, but that he had faith in her future. Even the young Charlie and Sefton were recreated in a burst of nostalgia. Both had shared their ambitions with her, encouraging her to wrest her own success from an indifferent world. Dear friends, both of them.

She thought of them as the men in her life, each contributing to the woman she'd become.

To reach retirement age may have been a milestone in other's people's lives; Sarah didn't think that way. It was just another birthday, indicating inexorably the passage of time. I don't feel older, she thought. Just a little slower than twenty years ago, she conceded, and at that moment she heard the screech of a peacock.

Out of bed, drawing back the curtains, the pre-dawn light held all the expectancy of a brilliant autumn day. Each second that the day advanced so did the morning sun rise above the horizon. The dun sands freshly washed by the sea were amber-gold; the pines black cut-outs against the clear sky. And again the screech of a peacock set the silence aquiver.

Sarah, dressed in slacks and a heavy-knit jersey, set out for the aviary. She had chosen the secret place, surrounded with flowering bushes, keeping it private. She reached the cage and stared in. Her heart leapt with excitement. There he stood, his head proudly lifted, his glorious fan stretched out for admiration, and near him the hen, dull and adoring.

A note was fastened to the cage wires. She detached it, and read with swelling heart. 'To Mother with love. Renton's luck is now.'

'Bless them,' she said aloud. 'Bless all my dear family.' She stood a while gazing at the birds, a lump in her throat. At last she turned away and returned to the cottage for breakfast.

Sefton Taylor arrived to find that Sarah had sneaked down to the aviary for another look at the peacocks, and he came striding across the lawn to her.

He kissed her. 'Sarah my dear, you look the youngest sixty I've ever seen. I think you're fooling us. Oh Sarah, Sarah, it's good to be with you.'

'You're being sentimental,' she accused him, and then holding him at arms' length studied his face. It had filled out, she saw, and he was tanned and fit-looking. A handsome man in fact. 'You're looking much better. That nice Marie is obviously looking after you.'

'Feeds me like a fighting cock, and anyway, hard work suits me. It is going to be a splendid wine season.'

His gaze fell on the birds. 'I thought you told me they'd all been killed.'

'They were, poor darlings. I was so angry. Innocent victims killed to hurt me. The family have given me these today.'

He took her hand, and smiled down at her. 'I hoped you'd grown out of that stupid superstition. I don't think Gerald really believed it.'

'He did,' she responded indignantly. 'At least – he tried not to believe that our luck was mixed up with these beautiful creatures. Oh Sefton, I miss him so much.'

'I know. But no sadness today,' he said as he kissed her again.

* * *

295

That evening the rest of Sarah's guests assembled in the cocktail bar waiting for her to make her entrance. She took more time than usual to dress, and when she was ready surveyed herself in front of the long mirror in her bedroom. She decided now that she'd reached the impressive age of sixty, black lace was suitable. But not me, she thought, changing to a deep blue ankle-length dress she'd bought on impulse. It had narrow diamanté shoulder straps and a silver belt, and was perfect with the Renton sapphire and diamond necklace and earrings. She slipped her feet into matching shoes, picked up her evening bag and, flinging a lacy stole round her shoulders, descended the stairs.

Michael was waiting in the hall. 'Gran, you look absolutely fab.'

His admiration was all she needed to boost her ego and, leaning on his arm, they walked the short distance to the hotel and entered the foyer, making their way to the cocktail bar. She never forgot the unbearable moment of expectation as her family and friends surged round her, offering congratulations and gifts. She was so overwhelmed she felt near to tears as she realized that these people cared for Sarah Renton for herself.

Dinner was served in the intimacy of the Nealey Room. Sarah wanted this, not because the room was a tribute to her father, but because she wished for a little while to shed the aura of her position, and appear as mother, grandmother, and friend.

And that's how it was. Michael had done a good job. All her loved ones were present except for Paul, and his early morning phone call had made up for the omission.

Chef had chosen the menu with care, as had the wine waiter, who had enlisted Sefton's approval. Sarah suggested a simple meal, but Chef's touches of genius lifted it into the cordon bleu class. Perhaps too, the wine helped, the best from Sefton's vineyard, and his superb champagne was in readiness for the toasts.

The talk ebbed and flowed about her. Laughter stimulated, and Sarah experienced a feeling of pure contentment, until Claire shattered it.

'Have you a surprise for us, Mother?' she asked.

'Surprise?' Sarah was momentarily taken offguard. Oh Sarah, my dear old fool, she told herself, why do you let yourself be lulled into false security?

'Surprise, Claire? I wonder what you have in mind? Perhaps I'll make a guess.' She rose to her feet. 'First I want to thank you all for this wonderful evening. It is a great joy to me to have my family and friends here to celebrate my sixtieth birthday. I'm well aware that this is considered retiring age for most, but I'm afraid I must disappoint you. I haven't the faintest intention of retiring.' She looked around the room and her voice strengthened. 'This is not the time for surprise decisions, and I assure you that when the time comes for me to step down it will not be a surprise, but a considered decision and discussed with all those concerned.' She sat down quickly and sipped her wine.

Michael jumped up and, coming to Sarah's side, put an arm round her. 'Renton's Royal would be just another ordinary hotel without you, Gran. We really need you.' He reached for his glass and raised it. 'To you, Gran, and Renton's Royal.'

Charlie said, 'I second that. To Sarah, with love.'

She felt their love and goodwill to be so tangible, she felt she could almost touch it.

Now it was Margaret's turn. Gracefully she rose, holding a large parcel in her arms. 'Gran, this is a present from your three grandchildren. We hope you will like it.'

She handed over a parcel artistically tied up with ribbons. Sarah tore open the wrappings, and gave a little

297

gasp of joy. She held in her hands a painting of Renton's Royal Hotel.

'It's painted by Marcus Smith. What do you think?' Margaret asked anxiously.

Tears blurred Sarah's eyes. She had thought of asking Marcus Smith, noted for his superb studies of buildings, but never quite had the courage. Now she held a Marcus Smith in her hands, she saw how perfect a choice he was. He had caught the essence of the building, the dream made reality. Set against the background of the sea, the pine woods, the spacious sky, the intimation of gardens, she looked upon a graciousness that seemed to belong to another age.

She was overcome with emotion.

Margaret smiled. 'You like it,' she stated.

The staff supper-dance was in full swing by the time Sarah put in an appearance. She had cut the cake, sipped champagne, chatted and laughed; her hazel eyes sparkled behind her spectacles, which she occasionally removed to wipe away emotional tears.

In the ballroom they were dancing to the tune of 'Some Enchanted Evening'. The Sandgrounders were churning out the notes in familiar style. Reg, the leader and vocalist, signalled a change, and the band swung into the strains of 'Happy Birthday, dear Sarah'.

Chef came forward to welcome her. The staff crowded round, and instinctively she felt the slight change of atmosphere; and in a way she was gratified. Her staff respected her; she was generous and fair. Why not? Hadn't she too, started on the bottom rung, and hadn't most of them achieved their ambitions under her guidance?

Fleur arrived, carrying the cake, already cut into pieces. Michael and Peter ferried in bottles of champagne and glasses were filled. Chef launched into his prepared speech. Perspiration glistened on his brow; speech-making wasn't up his street, he explained. Nevertheless his words touched Sarah's heart. He had taken possession of his kitchen on the day the hotel opened, and he'd loyally served the Rentons ever since.

Sarah was deeply moved. She felt that all the trials and traumas of the past seven years had by some magic been transformed into a glittering way, and the future was still in Renton hands.

Clive presented her with the staff gift. She tore off the wrapping with childish pleasure to reveal a hand-painted tea-set.

'Chef, Clive, all of you, it's beautiful.' She studied the twelve cups, saucers and plates, noting that a different wild flower was depicted on each matching setting. 'Thank you for a present I shall treasure for always, and only use on special occasions.'

She subsided into a chair. The band struck up 'For She's a Jolly Good Fellow,' and she was surrounded by a circle of dancers.

'That says it all,' Chef said and offered his arm as the music changed to a waltz. He led her sedately onto the floor. 'We've come a long way together, Mrs Renton.'

'And we still have a long way to travel.'

'Aye, that's so. Is Mr Sefton thinking of coming back now his brother is dead?'

'Do you think he should?'

'No. There's none can make a better job of running this hotel than you, and think on, there are the young ones to follow. Best to leave it like that.'

'I don't think Mr Taylor has come to a decision yet.'

'It's the other one we need to watch. He was snooping round in my kitchen. Tells me I'm the best chef in the north. Mr Charlie Mullins is up to no good, but I guess,

Mrs Renton, you're a match for him.'

Was she? She wondered. When at last she had dutifully danced with those members of the staff who were old friends, she slipped away and took the lift to the apartment where family and close friends were gathering.

Rachel was watching for her. Mark, immaculate in his dress suit, was hovering close by.

'There's tea and coffee, Mummy.' Rachel looked at her anxiously. 'Are you tired?'

Sarah smiled. 'Not yet, love, but I wouldn't say no to a cup of tea.'

'It all went off well, darling.' Rachel put the cup and saucer to hand, and sat down close to her.

'Perfect – except . . .'

'Daddy,' Rachel whispered. She took Sarah's free hand and held it tightly.

'He would so have enjoyed this. He loved social occasions, and was such a good host.'

'I know. Like you, he only thought of the family. We have to survive, Mummy, for his sake.'

'Yes, the family.' Her gaze rested on Mark, now in animated conversation with Sefton. She had always admired Mark's good looks, much improved now that there were threads of grey in his dark hair, and a fining-down of his strong Ashton features. She had understood the young Rachel's passionate love for him and even now had begun to hope that some event might draw them together again.

Sarah sighed, and her gaze shifted to Claire, in animated conversation with Charlie. He looked up suddenly, caught Sarah's glance, and with a quick word he turned away and threaded a route across the room to Sarah's side and sat down.

'Well, Sarah my dear, how excellently you arrange parties.'

'Not this one. Rachel and Michael fixed it, and Chef

cooked the dinner. You could almost say I'm a fellow traveller.'

Charlie laughed. 'Oh come on, Sarah. Nothing takes place at Renton's Royal without you.'

'And if I'm not here?' she began.

'But you will be, won't you?' The question held little doubt.

'I shall die in harness,' she said. 'My Dad always said that was the only way to go.'

'So he did. And he harnessed the pair of us. Oh God, those mountains of dishes,' he said, shuddering. 'And Joe, your father, on the bottle, singing bawdy songs. It's the smell I remember. I thought I'd never get the smell of fish and chips out of my nostrils.'

'We got used to it, but don't forget, Charlie, my dad gave value for money. I don't mean fresh fish from the market, or the gallons of strong tea; I mean he gave stability. The sailors needed that, they needed Joe's café. It was the first staging post on their return home. As soon as the ships docked they headed straight for us. If Joe was still singing, 'Pack up your troubles in your old kit bag', they were sure nothing had changed.'

'How right you are, Sarah. And you have the same knack of giving stability.'

'But you want to change that,' she said quietly.

'Be a part of it, Sarah. That's what I've always wanted.'

'Don't kid yourself. Our ambitions diverged long ago.'

'But now they are coming full circle.'

She shook her head, and turned to speak to Michael. Betsy Holroyd was hanging on his arm. Sarah felt a sudden misgiving. Was this one of Charlie's little ploys, encouraging the friendship between the two of them? But when she saw the girl's flushed face and shining eyes, and saw the loving look with which she regarded Michael, she was reassured.

301

'Do you mind if we go back to the ballroom?' Michael asked.

'Just where you should be, and take the others with you. And Michael, instruct the band leader to go on playing as long as you want, and I'll make it right with him.'

She was aware of the shift and change in the company the moment the young ones left. It was as if the vital heart had slithered away, and all that was left was the hard core whose lives were drafted on another plane.

Unexpectedly she felt desperately tired.

'I need my bed,' she said, standing up. 'Please stay as long as you like, and thank you for making this such a wonderful day.'

Charlie draped her stole round her shoulders, holding her for a moment. 'I'll see you home.'

They descended to the ground floor by the lift. The foyer was deserted, but music still flowed from the ballroom. Bill, the porter, opened the glass doors for them. 'It's been a grand night, Mrs Renton.'

Outside it was a grand night too. The sky was alive with points of light, and the moon-shadows flickered – now dim, now bright – on lawns, the sea, and added mystery to the pine woods. The air was sharp.

'A touch of frost,' Charlie said and took her arm. The lamps bordering the main drive were still lit, and only when they walked along the sandy path to the cottage was Sarah aware of her deep feelings for this place.

'Sarah and Charlie, mates from the Dock Road. Lovers?' he questioned.

This moment was important to her. She had a choice. It was only a fleeting hesitation, and yet she was convinced she would look back and for ever in her mind's eye see Charlie's serious expression, feel the warmth of his arm, breathe again the sharp clear air.

She had a moment of weakness, a longing to share as she

302

and Gerald had shared their hopes, ambitions, and most of all their living love.

In a whisper he repeated his query. 'Lovers?'

She caught a movement over by the hotel from the corner of her eye and realized that a white-haired man was standing in the shadows, smoking his pipe.

'I'm sorry, Charlie,' she said. But there was still enough vigorous youth in her veins to awaken desire and later make her regret the choice she had made, even though in her heart she knew it was the right one.

CHAPTER 29

'Tomorrow I go back to England,' Ramiro told his father as he hung up his white jacket and took a final look round the restaurant kitchen, a habit he'd caught from Chef.

'No, my son, you do not. You stay here. I need you. We have talked – ' Señor Rodriguez sat down wearily.

'I cannot stay. Please, I have listened to all you say. I will not marry Isabella Cortez. I love Fleur. I will not give her up.'

'An English girl. Bah! And a non-Catholic, and out of favour with her father, and no money to come with her. You see how it is here. Business is bad. I am tired,' he said. 'I need the Cortez money.'

'I do not love Isabella. I can never love her.'

'Love! We do not always marry for love in Spain. Love comes with the children. You are my only son. I have daughters, yes, but you will follow on as head of this family. You must make a good Catholic marriage to a Spanish girl. Isabella is well connected. She has rich relations.' Señor Rodriguez stood up. 'So you will stay here. Help me to build up the restaurant and marry Isabella. It is settled.'

Ramiro said, 'It is not settled. I cannot live without Fleur. If you could see her – '

His longing hurt. The pain in his heart spread to all his body, and he doubled up with the intensity. After a moment he straightened, aware of the implacable expression in his father's cold dark eyes. The thought of losing Fleur was unbearable, yet he understood his father. If he had never left Spain he thought, he would not now be torn by love and duty. And he realized his father would never understand him.

He sighed, 'Father, please.'

'Who will look after your mother and your sisters when I am gone. I am not young – '

Ramiro felt the jaws of a trap tightening round his body, his mind, his life.

'Let me go,' he whispered.

'No. You are a good son. Your place is here, you know your duty.'

'I will go,' Ramiro shouted. 'You can't keep me here against my will.'

'I can. We will not speak of this again, and tomorrow you set the date for your marriage to Isabella.' All kindness and compassion had fled from Rodriguez's expression.

The quiet in the kitchen was disturbing, gone were the chattering staff, the clatter of dishes, the shouted instructions, only the all-pervading smell of food remained, and lay like a sickness in Ramiro's belly.

'Tomorrow I tell Señora Renton that you are to stay here. She believes in the importance of families.'

'No.' Ramiro's strangled cry was as instinctive as the lunge he made towards his father. Señor Rodriguez moved so that his back was against a work table.

'Keep away,' Rodriguez shouted. He reached behind him for support; one hand closed over the shaft of a knife. He snatched it up and held it in front of him in an attitude of self-defence. 'Get back,' he cried.

In recoiling horror Ramiro stepped back. His foot slipped on a carelessly spilt patch of grease and although he flung out his arms to save himself, he keeled over, and crashed to the floor, banging his head. He felt a searing pain, and cried out in anguish. His father was down on the floor beside him. 'Son, son,' he moaned, lifting him into his arms. Now there was only the pain, and a darkness, and he lapsed into unconsciousness.

Fleur waited five long days for Ramiro's next telephone call. His last one promising to tell his father how matters stood between himself and Fleur had abruptly cut communication between them. Why? She fussed and worried, going over in her mind every word he'd said, and at last, unable to bear the uncertainty alone, she turned to Sarah.

'Gran, it's five days since Ramiro phoned me, and he promised to ring every evening. I'm frightened. I think it's all gone wrong. He said he'd tell his father about us. Oh Gran, what shall I do?'

Sarah was studying the plans for the new annexe laid out on the sitting-room table. She lifted her head sharply, and then seeing Fleur's distress rolled them up and stacked them away.

'Suppose you tell me what you and Ramiro are planning?'

Fleur hesitated. 'I think he was going to ask his father if we could marry. He wants to come back here, work in the hotel, but . . .'

'Difficulties, I presume,' Sarah said thoughtfully.

'Gran, I can't bear it if he doesn't come back and I never see him again.' Her voice rose to a wail.

Sarah held out her arms, and Fleur kneeling beside her was safely enfolded. 'Faint heart never won anything – much less a man. It's not like you to give up.' She kissed Fleur's upturned face. 'Here, blow.' Sarah wiped away the tears, and pressed the cologne-fragrant handkerchief into Fleur's hand. 'Now,' she said, when Fleur had stopped sniffing. 'We talk, we plan. There must be a reason why Ramiro doesn't phone.'

'Can we phone him?' Fleur asked eagerly.

'We? Fleur are you sure this is what you want?'

'Yes,' she nodded vigorously 'We want to be together always.'

'Then presumably his father has refused – '

'He can't,' Fleur wailed. 'Why should he?'

'Señor Rodriguez is a man concerned only with his family and business. He expects Ramiro to succeed him. He won't want interference with his plans, and he has a large family to support.'

'What has that to do with Ramiro and me?'

'Everything, darling. Ramiro will have to take on responsibilities. The reason his father asked me to take him was because he wants Ramiro to be a first-class chef, so that they can expand the business.' Sarah thought a moment, and then picked up the staff holiday rota. 'According to this Ramiro should have returned to work yesterday. I think that entitles us to make a telephone call to Señor Rodriguez.'

Sarah waited patiently for the connection to be made, conscious of Fleur's agitation and flushed face.

At last she heard Rodriguez's voice. 'Good evening, Señor,' she said. 'I was expecting Ramiro back on duty yesterday – '

'An accident. Oh no! Still unconscious. His head.' She listened carefully to the Señor's voluble explanation. 'That won't do. We have an agreement. I shall expect the boy back when he is better. Please keep us in touch.'

She replaced the receiver.

Fleur took hold of her arm. 'What's happened?'

'Ramiro has had an accident. He's hurt his head, and is still unconscious in hospital.'

Fleur moaned. 'Gran, he won't die – '

'Of course not. Concussion – '

'Oh my poor Ramiro. How soon will it be before he comes back?'

Sarah debated whether to withhold the rest of the bad news from Fleur. Rodriguez had made it plain Ramiro wouldn't be allowed to return. 'I'm not sure if he will be coming – '

Fleur clutched Sarah's arm. 'He must come back. Is he badly injured? Oh Gran, what shall I do? I must go to him.'

The front door opened and Rachel called, 'I'm home.'

She came into the sitting room, taking off her coat. Her face was flushed, and her eyes bright with excitement. 'It was the most wonderful concert, Mummy. I wish you'd been there. Afterwards Mark introduced me to the superb pianist.' Suddenly she was aware that neither Sarah or Fleur seemed to be listening. 'Is something wrong?'

Fleur flung herself in her mother's arms. 'Something dreadful has happened. Ramiro has had an accident, hurt his head and is still unconscious. And his father says he won't be coming back. I've made up my mind I shall go to him.'

Rachel held Fleur close, and looked across at Sarah. 'What happened?'

'We don't know all the details.'

Rachel's face paled. 'Fleur darling, you can't go off to Spain.'

'Of course I can. Who's to stop me?' she challenged.

'You must ask your father. He's just parking the car.'

'Ask me what?' Mark said. 'The front door was open so I walked in. Good evening, Sarah.' He bent to kiss her cheek. He made a move towards Fleur, but she side-stepped. He frowned, and repeated his question.

Fleur hesitated. 'I must go to Spain,' she said in a rush.

308

'My boyfriend has had an accident. He's unconscious in hospital.'

'He'll be brought home. Who is he?'

'He is home. He's Spanish.'

'Rachel, you didn't tell me.'

Rachel's face set in stubborn lines. 'Fleur is in love with a Spanish boy. He works in the kitchen here. He's had an accident, and Fleur wants to go to him.'

Sarah decided a little further explanation was called for. 'Ramiro is employed by me as a trainee chef. His father has a restaurant in Alicante, and wanted his son to gain experience under our chef. I have spoken to Señor Rodriguez and he tells me Ramiro has had an accident and is in hospital.'

'Well, I'm sorry to hear it but if you think I'm going to allow my daughter to go off to Spain, you are all very much mistaken. I told you, Rachel, I was against Fleur working in this hotel from the start.'

Rachel wilted under Mark's onslaught, but Sarah didn't. The Nealey temper simmered. Mark's snobbishness had always been distasteful to her, and now it came to a head.

'You are wrong, Mark. Fleur is learning a profession she has set her heart on. And our chef is one of the best in the country. Young people fall in love, as you did with my Rachel, and you married her in spite of the opposition of your family. So you'd better be careful what you say.'

'I won't have interference in my family affairs from you, Sarah!'

'Ramiro is very charming,' Rachel ventured. 'Perhaps we – ' She wavered, then in a rush she said, 'He saved my life.'

Mark turned on her, and took hold of her by the shoulders. 'What do you mean, saved your life?'

'I wasn't going to mention it, because I knew you'd all

309

be angry. I went swimming in the pool, and got cramp, and Ramiro pulled me out.'

'Oh God, Rachel, will you never learn sense?'

His arms tightened round her, but she tried to push him away.

He let go, flushing angrily. 'So you think we owe this Spaniard a favour? *Anyone* would have dragged you out of the pool.'

'Ramiro did.'

'Thank God for that,' Mark said. 'But it doesn't alter anything. I will not have Fleur rushing off to Spain to a man we know nothing about.'

'I've met his father,' Sarah said. 'Ramiro comes from a very good Spanish family. Fleur is in love. Ramiro is a decent honest boy.'

'All this is your fault, Sarah. You've ruined Fleur's chance of making a good marriage!'

Fleur was speechless with rage. If it wasn't so pompous her father's pronouncement would have been funny.

'How dare you speak to Mummy like that?' Rachel's face was scarlet, her hands tightly clenched. 'I think it is time I spoke up for myself. I've put up with a lot from you over the years – I did it for Fleur's sake. Now, after years of neglect, you're plotting to get her back. But you won't! I'll fight . . .' She crumpled into tears.

'There's absolutely no need, Mother,' said Fleur, her voice deadly calm. 'I'm more than capable of fighting my own battles.' She squared her chin defiantly at her father. 'Don't imagine for one second you can come swanning back into our lives and order us about like before. You left us! You left us flat for a cheap tart and we'll never forget that. Have you got that? You'll never let us down again because we won't let you. Now go away and leave us alone.'

'You don't understand!' he pleaded. 'You were just a child . . .'

'Well, I grew up pretty damn quickly when you walked out on us. Now you want things back the way they were, do you? Well, that doesn't suit us. We won't come crawling back to Ashton Hall, now or ever, and no one on this earth is going to stop me going to Ramiro, so I warn you not to push it.'

Sarah was shattered by the hard words, by the lack of understanding between them; like a lanced boil the pus of years was flooding out, and she saw no way of stemming it. She felt choked by an emotion stronger and more potent than anger, pity compassion and fear. She blindly reached for a chair, and sat down heavily. Fleur was beside her immediately.

'Gran, are you ill? Can I get you anything?'

Rachel took charge. 'Where are your pills? Get her a glass of water, Fleur.' She opened Sarah's handbag, and found the bottle. Obediently Sarah swallowed a pill and drank the water. 'I'm all right, love. Just a little hiccup, nothing more.'

She sat back in her chair and closed her eyes. In a moment the room would stop whirling round her, and the erratic beats of her heart would settle down to a steady rhythm.

Mark waited, a sullen expression marring his handsome features. 'I forbid you to go, Fleur. If you persist, I shall have you stopped at the airport,' he said. He stood up and left the cottage, banging all the doors as he went.

Rachel went to the phone, and dialled Reception. 'Mavis. Please book two seats on the first available flight to Spain. Alicante Airport. And book a double room in a hotel in Alicante. My daughter and I will be travelling to Spain together.'

'Mum!' Fleur flew across the room into her mother's open arms.

'Surely you didn't think I'd let you go alone?' Rachel

lifted her head and met Sarah's glance. She was rewarded with a vigorous nod of approval. 'Come on, we'd better get packed.' Rachel smiled at Sarah. 'Don't worry, Mummy. It will all work out fine. I promise you.'

CHAPTER 30

The rebuilding of the new store rooms was taking considerably longer than Sarah had anticipated. She didn't blame Craig, he had his troubles, but she was impatient for the job to be finished, and made her usual morning visit to note progress.

She was surprised to find Sefton in earnest conversation with Craig, and from their expressions she deduced that there was some argument.

'Good morning, Mrs Renton,' Craig greeted her with relief. 'Mr Taylor isn't satisfied with the materials we're using. I tell him they are the best we can do for the price.'

Craig was in one of his obstinate moods. His bushy eyebrows bristled, his bulldog stance and the ferocious puffs from his pipe indicated to Sarah he was not to be trifled with.

'Mr Taylor thinks we should have extended the wine store. I told him we can't do that, Mrs Renton. Chef has his rights and he won't give way over a smaller vegetable store. I take my orders from you, Madam, and no one else, or I chuck the job in.'

Sarah's heart sank. Not today, she thought, not while I'm worried sick over Rachel and Fleur in Spain, and the cost of this building keeps rising.

'I've a bit of bad news,' Craig continued. 'I've got a rush

job on and will have to take the men off this work for a few days. I'm sorry, Mrs Renton, because I know you are waiting to have the use of the stores.'

If Sefton expected her to protest, he was disappointed. Some things can be changed, and some are immutable. Craig was just that.

'I'm surprised you allow that man to do as he likes,' Sefton said as he followed Sarah through the kitchens to her office.

'And I'm surprised you see fit to interfere in my business,' she snapped and stumped ahead.

She opened the office door to find Michael waiting for her.

'Good news, Gran. The police have picked up Paddy Kelly trying to board a ferry for Belfast. He's confessed to killing the peacocks. Apparently he shares your superstitions.' Michael grinned and winked at Sefton as they all sat down. 'However, the instantaneous bad luck didn't follow, and as he admitted his grudge was more against Chef he liked the idea of burning up the kitchens.'

'How did he go about it?' Sefton asked.

'The inspector told me Paddy thoughtfully retained his key and sneaked in by the staff entrance. The rest was easy.'

'Do all the kitchen staff have keys?' Sefton asked.

'Only those who come in very early and unfortunately Paddy was one of them. It looks as if we may have to think of another system, Gran.'

'I don't like the idea that the staff think we don't trust them,' Sarah objected.

'I think Michael is right. You've always been too trusting, Sarah.'

She was a little resentful of Sefton's interference, searching in her mind for an ulterior motive, and as soon as Michael left, she tackled Sefton.

'Are your opinions general, or have you something else in mind?'

'I wondered if I would be of use to you here.'

She was so startled, she stared at him, as if his words hadn't registered.

'Don't look so surprised. It was always on the cards I might want to come back. Why else would I invest so heavily in the hotel?'

'I thought it was just an investment, no strings.'

'Of course there aren't any strings,' he said impatiently. 'It's just an idea. I have problems.'

'I know that, Sefton.'

'And I don't like the idea that Charlie Mullins might jump the gun. What exactly does he want?'

'Renton's Royal Hotel.'

'I don't follow. He took care to tell me he has a chain of hotels all over the country and on the continent.'

'That's right. But Renton's Royal is different. It isn't just professional jealousy. It stretches back to our youth, when we used to sweat in my father's café on the Dock Road, and we were two youngsters longing to conquer the world.'

'Haven't you?'

'He wants Renton's Royal so badly he's asked me to marry him to get it.'

'That's preposterous. How dare he!'

'Charlie and I understand each other. He wants what I have, but strangely I don't want to poke a finger in his pie. You know, Sefton, how much I wanted this to be a real family hotel. I'm old-fashioned in my belief in the unity of the family although it isn't working out that way.'

'Of course it is. You have Michael and Fleur, and possibly Margaret at some later date. I can understand your problem with Claire. Too ambitious, I'd say. I think, Sarah,' he continued, 'you need a man at your side. A helpmate.'

She didn't look at him. She picked up the silver-framed

photograph of Gerald, always close and within her view. She held it turned so that the light could not reflect or distort.

'He's gone,' Sefton said harshly. 'And I'm here. Sarah, how do you think of me?'

She put down the photograph, took off her spectacles, wiped her eyes and turned her myopic gaze on him. 'As a friend, Gerald's friend,' she said, as if surprised he should ask such an extraordinary question.

'No more?'

'Isn't friendship enough?'

'Not for me,' he said violently. 'I love you, Sarah. All these years I've waited. And when Gerald died I couldn't bring myself to tell you, because I feared your refusal. Oh God, I thought you were the loveliest girl I'd ever seen. And nothing has changed.'

'Don't be ridiculous, Sefton. Of course I've changed. I was silly and seventeen when I first met you.'

'And your hair was as fiery as your temper, and your eyes as brilliant as an autumn day. And you were in love with Gerald.'

'At least that hasn't changed, Sefton,' she said before she could stop herself, wondering for the first time if it were still true.

Sarah felt like a skater on thin ice. Any moment now she anticipated an ominous crash and the house of Renton would fall about her ears. Old certainties were foundering, leaving the ground shifting and unstable beneath her feet. Sefton loved her.

It was a shock, she told herself, and yet it was not. Subconsciously, somewhere deep inside, had she not always nurtured the warm unchanging certainty of his love for her? Had she truly been as surprised as she had always claimed that he had never married?

Sarah forced herself to examine her heart and was relieved when Bobby Brooks arrived to keep their appointment. He was closely followed by a waiter with his coffee.

Bobby's familiar jaunty walk and wide smile restored Sarah to her usual composure.

'A most enjoyable evening, Sarah.' He kissed her on both cheeks. His aftershave was subtle and reinforced her belief that he enjoyed female company. 'You're a great organiser.' He acknowledged Sefton's greeting and sat down.

'Getting a bit grey at the gills for the light fantastic,' he joked.

'Nonsense,' Sarah smiled. Bobby's dinners with clients who always happened to be young and pretty was a family joke.

'Will you stay to lunch, Bobby?'

Regretfully he refused. 'Another client,' he said, firmly putting the present meeting on a business footing. 'I expect you want to discuss the withdrawal of your capital from the hotel, Sefton,' he said. 'It's quite straightforward.'

'Not so fast, Bobby.'

Sarah was surprised by the firmness in Sefton's voice. She was impressed by his new image. Privately she dubbed it arty French. He sat confidently in his chair, legs crossed, one hand in the pocket of his velvet jacket, the other fingering his floppy bow-tie.

'My interest in Renton's Royal Hotel has never wavered. My investment in the business is a long-term insurance against just such a situation which has now arisen.'

'What *are* you talking about?' Sarah snapped. 'You insisted on me visiting you in Bergerac, and discussing Rafe's debts and the situation created by his death. Are you trying to tell me you don't now require the money?'

317

'As you know during the first week or so Monsieur Villiard, Rafe's father-in-law, absolutely refused to pay off Rafe's debts, but now he has changed his mind and offered to clear them completely. There is, of course, a condition.'

Sarah and Bobby exchanged glances. Sarah was wary; she felt she was being forced into a trap.

'What exactly is this condition?' Bobby asked.

'Simple, really. After Rafe's death the vineyard reverts back to the Villiard family. However, the old man suggests I carry on as manager on a hefty salary and a share of the profits.'

'Good.' Sarah heaved a sigh of relief. 'You enjoy living in France, and you are happy working in the vineyard.'

'I shall be much happier working in the hotel alongside you, Sarah my dear.'

'But,' Sarah said after a moment's thought, 'if you refuse Villiard's offer, surely you will be responsible for Rafe's debts?'

'Exactly so.'

'And in that case you will have to draw out your capital invested in the hotel.'

'Certainly.'

'Are you proposing to become a salaried employee?' Bobby said.

'What an extraordinary idea, Bobby. I was thinking along the lines of a working partnership.'

Sarah's expression hardened. 'I think we should face reality, Sefton. If you intend to pay Rafe's debts, your investment will be depleted.'

'I think that can be overcome, eh, Bobby?'

'And I think it can't,' Sarah said angrily. 'I won't pretend that I don't need your capital at the moment because I do. But that's not the point. I have to manage Renton's Royal my way and there isn't scope for two bosses. You know how grateful I've been for your advice and guidance about wines, and you have given us a reputation for a superb cellar, but you've been away seven years and out of touch.'

'I see,' he smiled ruefully. 'The old Sarah in action. Do it my way. Suppose I don't want to do it your way? Is there any reason why I can't draw out my money and buy myself a vineyard?'

'None at all,' Bobby said. 'It has always been understood you are free to withdraw your financial interest any time you like. But it seems to me, Sefton, you would do well to consider Monsieur Villiard's offer carefully.'

'Is that what you want, Sarah?'

'I want what is best for you.'

'And of course if I withdraw Charlie Mullins is waiting to take my place.'

'No.'

'But, my dear Sarah, you'll need capital, and Charlie has plenty of that.'

She felt like weeping with anger and frustration; she was well aware as a woman she was vulnerable.

Bobby came to her rescue. 'I don't see any future for you here, Sefton. As you know, Sarah is a superb manager, but she prefers to work alone. You must understand that the hotel, that is the buildings and contents, belong to her. Gerald secured that in his will. She has worked hard all these years so she has something worthwhile to hand over to her grandchildren when the time comes.'

'I'm under no illusion about her intentions.' Sefton turned to Sarah. 'Have you forgotten the day the three of us first walked into the foyer. It was quite an emotional moment I recall, but even then you did your best to exclude me.'

'That's not true,' she protested.

'Renton's Royal Hotel. No other name would do.'

'Don't let's be hasty,' Bobby said. 'I'm sure you, Sefton, and you, Sarah, want to consider the matter again.' He stood up. 'Perhaps when you have proposals in writing from Monsier Villiard, you'd like to consult me further, Sefton.'

After he left the silence was heavy. It was charged with emotions which Sarah felt to be tangible.

'Why?' she asked at last.

'A kind of revenge,' Sefton said. 'I doubt if you'd understand it. You persist in calling Gerald my friend. We were business partners, but you see he took the only thing I've ever wanted, hungered for all these years. You, my darling Sarah. I fell in love with you that first moment I saw you. Gerald brought you to my father's restaurant, a celebration he said. Your engagement. That was the moment I should have cut my losses. I should have put you both out of my mind. When Gerald suggested a partnership in the hotel I agreed. I had a wild idea I could win you from him.'

'I loved Gerald with all my heart and strength. I've never stopped loving him for one moment. I thought you understood that, Sefton?'

'After Gerald died I believed you might turn to me. But you made it plain you never gave me a thought.'

'That's not true! I valued your friendship,' she protested.

Sefton shook his head sadly. 'But you didn't need me, and Rafe did. You still don't need me, Sarah. I think on balance it's better I go back to France. I don't think I could bear to be with you every day, wanting you the way I do, and afraid to even hope.'

He stood up, and reaching for her hands, pulled her out of her chair, holding her close to him.

'Don't shut me out for ever, Sarah. I'm a patient man. I've waited so many years for you, I can wait some more. Remember, when you need me, I'll be there for you.'

He kissed her and she was filled with a mixture of sweetness and regret. Their friendship had entered a new phase, one she was not sure she could handle.

320

CHAPTER 31

Claire's hope of succeeding Sarah seemed to be getting more remote, but she was determined not to give up fighting. During the past years she'd carried on, putting up with Jim and, since her father's death, enduring Sarah's increasing stranglehold on the running of the hotel.

She returned to London with Margaret who was due back at college.

'I need a change, Margaret,' she explained, and asked Margaret if she may take possession of the small spare room.

'Do you good,' Margaret said immediately, her thoughts already concentrating on the term's work ahead. 'A few days in London will buck you up, and of course you'll be visiting Dad.'

The temporary change Margaret had in mind was not the change Claire was opting for. A permanent change, she told herself, sitting in the taxi the next day on her way to visit Jim.

Sarah had made it clear to Claire that Jim's appalling lapse over the insurances policies spelt the end. There was no possibility that his resignation could be anything but final.

The nursing home where Jim was recovering from his

fall was plush and expensive. She entered Jim's room noting the fresh flowers, and the general air of specialized treatment.

Jim was sitting in an armchair in front of the window. He half-rose as she entered, and then sank back. He held out a hand but she ignored it, and sat down in a fireside chair, throwing off her fur coat to reveal an emerald green jersey suit.

'How are you?' she asked perfunctorily.

'Much better thanks. My leg is at last responding to the treatment. The doctor says I can go home in a day or two.'

'We haven't got a home,' Claire said.

'You're joking of course.'

'Unfortunately not. Mother is determined that you won't go back to Renton's Royal. She's blazing mad over your stupidity in not updating the insurance policies, and now she's faced with horrendous costs.'

'Oh that,' he said. 'Too bad.'

'Yes it is. It's cost me my home, my job – '

'Wait a minute. You aren't serious. No room at the hotel for us?'

'No place for you,' Claire said. 'I'm leaving you, Jim.'

His face paled, and a nervous tic in his jaw distorted his mouth. After a moment his expression changed to the cunning look which always angered Claire.

'You can't leave me. I'm a sick and helpless man. Where will I go? And you know I'm hard up.'

'I don't care.'

'Why? What have I done?' There was enough of a whine in his voice to irritate Claire even further.

'It's what you haven't done! I've given you all the support I could in the job, ever since my father died, because we hoped Mother would pass on the hotel to us. She won't.'

'I'll change, Claire, I promise. If it's the drink – '

322

'It's everything,' she said stonily. 'Margaret will probably give you a bed until you find somewhere.' She stood up and drew her fur coat around her.

'Claire, you can't just walk out on me.'

She heard the desperation in his voice, but chose to ignore it.

'I can and will. I'm sorry, Jim, it has to end like this. But I can't see any future for us. We quarrel all the time and I've had enough.'

'I thought you cared,' he said.

For a second she was tempted to gloss over the past once more. She remembered how close they had been, but the temptation faded almost immediately. Her mother had made it alone, and so would she. 'I'll phone Margaret,' she said. 'The best thing you can do is go back to your family in Ireland. You told me that there's plenty of room in your father's house, and that members of the family live happily together.'

'Wait!' Jim's desperate voice halted her at the door. 'It isn't like that.'

'I never thought it was. But that's your problem.' She closed the door quietly behind her, and going outside hailed a taxi and directed the driver to take her to the Park Lane Hotel.

She thought, burning one's boat is traumatic in a way. But I'm free at last.

It began to rain. The wind gusted long slanting rivulets against the windows. 'Driver,' she called, 'I've changed my mind, make it the Westwood Hotel.'

She alighted, paid the fare, and a porter came out and held a large umbrella over her while she ascended the steps into the foyer.

She saw Charlie immediately. He was talking to Lydia Bouchier, and Claire's heart sank. Lydia was the last person she wanted to see now, especially as the woman was looking more elegant than usual. Her quick glance spotted Claire, and she rushed forward, holding out her hand.

'Claire, how nice to meet you again. You are looking well, isn't she, Charlie? I hear your mother has celebrated her sixtieth birthday, no doubt a signal for retirement. A pity I'm just leaving. I've just been talking to Charlie about you. A little proposition,' she said and smiled mysteriously. 'Charlie will reveal all.'

She laid a proprietary hand on his arm, and held up a smooth pink cheek for his kiss. 'Darling, ask someone to call my car. Now don't forget,' she continued roguishly, 'I expect you for dinner tomorrow, and Claire too, if she's free.'

Her chauffeur appeared in the doorway, and came forward to carry her parcels, and escort her beneath an umbrella to her car.

Charlie sighed with relief as the glass doors swung behind her.

'Is she always around?' Claire said peevishly.

'She keeps an eye on me, in case I stray perhaps. I'm pleased to see you, Claire. Come on up to the apartment.'

He opened the door, took her coat, and settled her comfortably, putting her usual gin and tonic on the small table beside her.

'Am I out of the doghouse?' He balanced his whisky glass on his knee with one hand. 'Has Jim got over his disappointment at not going to Barbados?'

'I've left him.'

Charlie finished his whisky and put down the glass. 'Does Sarah know?'

'No.'

'I see.'

'No you don't. You are thinking how will Claire's decision to leave Jim affect Sarah, how will it affect me? Well, will it bother you at all?'

'Why have you come here?'

'I've nowhere else to go. I pretend you don't matter to me, but you do.'

'As a friend.'

'If you say so.' She crossed her legs, gently swinging an elegantly-shod foot. She looked at him provocatively, smiling, breathing a little quicker than usual.

He stood up and crossing to the cabinet refilled his glass.

'Naturally we are friends. You are Sarah's girl.' His colour heightened. 'What do you want of me?' His voice was hoarse.

She laughed, and he heard a mocking echo of her mother. 'I want Renton's Royal too. I'm not giving up. I know you want to own it. Together – '

He interrupted. 'And how do you propose we do that?'

She heard the cynical note in his voice, but disregarded it. 'She's cheated me. Jim and I have worked for her believing that when she retired we'd take her place. I believed you too,' she went on passionately. 'You as good as promised that when you owned the hotel it would be a joint concern. You see, I've no intention of giving up my rights. But you are chicken, Charlie Mullins.'

His eyes narrowed, and he bit his lip. He would not admit to Claire he only wanted Renton's Royal if Sarah was part of the deal. There was no place for Claire in his calculations. The sexual desire which had once moved him in her favour, and had made her a challenge, was now dead.

'Have you thought carefully about the consequences of leaving Jim?'

'I have. Mother won't have him back at the hotel.'

'Does that place you in an awkward position?'

She shrugged her shoulders, drained her drink and held out the glass for more.

'Why should it? He can get on with ruining his own life without dragging me down any more.'

Charlie poured her a small second drink. The last thing he needed was Claire drunk and emotional – or even more emotional, he corrected himself. How had such a sensible, level-headed couple as Sarah and Gerald ever produced this hard-eyed and even harder-hearted young madam? If Claire returned to Renton's in her present ugly mood, he dreaded to think of the possible consequences for Sarah.

Sarah . . . funny how consciously or unconsciously he allowed her to dictate his every move. She informed his thoughts, dictated every decision he reached. Pleasing Sarah, looking out for her interests, had been the path he had trodden all his life. He wasn't going to change now.

Charlie had never particularly cared for Claire or the very blatant come-ons she had treated him to over the years, but her decision to leave Jim had been a pleasant surprise. O'Hara was a lame duck who'd drag down anyone weak enough to let him. Charlie respected Claire for cutting loose when she had.

Maybe, if he appealed to her vanity and her pride in equal measures, there'd be a way to cut her ties to Renton's Royal too. And that could only be a blessing for Sarah, however much she might feel obliged to deny it.

'You haven't asked me what Lydia Bouchier proposed?' he tempted Claire.

'I'm not interested,' she said flatly.

'You will be when I tell you all about it. It's a revolutionary new concept – really ground-breaking. Lydia's a sharp operator – the best. For a couple of years now she's been making plans to re-vamp the portfolio of European hotels her father left her. There are some fine examples among them and a couple of real white elephants but all the locations are prime, worth a fortune when she puts them on the market. She's negotiated three sales – they should hit the financial pages in the next few weeks.

'You see, Lydia reckons the days of the grand hotel, catering to five or six hundred residents and a variety of outside functions, are numbered. They're dinosaurs, eating into the profits faster than they turn them over. Her idea is to branch out into a chain of "boutique" hotel – quietly luxurious but low-key and relatively low-maintenance in terms of staffing levels anyway.

'They'll have no more than fifty rooms, all fitted out in top-quality furnishings, antiques maybe, and offering limited catering only – breakfast and light room service meals maybe. The sort of clientele she envisages will be well-to-do if not wealthy, confident and knowledgeable enough to make their own arrangements to eat out locally. They want the comfort, luxury even, of a grand hotel but on a smaller, more personal scale. Lydia thinks it's the way ahead in hotel-keeping. She's planning to open a pilot venture in St-Germain early next year.

'We were having a talk earlier about possible managers. I suggested Jim and you. I could just as easily call her and suggest you on your own – I think she'd take me up on it. It'd be tough, Claire, I can't pretend otherwise. New city, strange language, a boss who's forgotten more about hotel-keeping than most people ever learn – including you,' he told her sharply. 'She'll be a bitch to work for, but I'd lay odds you could handle it. So what do you say? Shall I tell her you're interested? Only she wants someone right away. It would mean leaving Sarah in the lurch . . .'

'In that case, why don't you make the call. You can tell her where to contact me if she wants to.' Claire got to her feet and picked up her handbag and gloves. 'Will you call me a taxi?'

'Where are you going?'

'Euston, of course.'

'I'll see you there,' he offered, remembering the last time she had visited him in this apartment.

She put one hand on his arm. 'No, Charlie. I'm a big girl now. If you trust me to manage your *friend*'s hotel – ' she could not resist the malicious emphasis – 'I think you can trust me to catch a train unattended. Don't you?'

And with a final cool wave of the hand she left him to his thoughts. Lydia would either bless him or curse him, he decided. There'd be no half measures with Claire.

And Sarah? He devoutly hoped that once she'd got over the initial shock she'd see this as the best thing that could possibly happen for Renton's Royal, and for her.

Sarah felt restless. She put on her coat and walked down to the aviary. It was dusk, and the birds were roosting.

Peter joined her. 'You look sad. No company?'

'Yours will do very nicely. Walk to the rose garden with me.'

He took her arm. 'I'm off tomorrow. Thank you for all your kindness to me.'

'Peter, are you and Margaret more than friends?'

'I guess not. She's a loner.'

'Will you look out for her?'

'I sure will.' He hesitated. 'Will you say goodbye to Rachel for me when she gets back from Spain. I'm sorry about the book. I guess we ran out of steam. She'll be all right, I mean . . .'

'I know. She's very much loved.'

'Will she and her husband get together?'

'I don't know, Peter. It would be best.'

'Yes,' he said.

'No regrets, lad. She thinks a lot of you.'

He kissed her on both cheeks and ran back to the hotel, whistling.

Sarah settled down on Gerald's bench. Half-turning,

328

she traced the letters of his name cut into the wood with sensitive fingers. It was almost dark and cold here, so cold compared to that other bench in another garden – a French garden basking in the golden sun of the Midi. The lamps along the drive glowed, and she wished she'd walked back to the cottage with Peter. Unaccountably she shivered, and pulled her coat more tightly round her. At this moment she saw lights springing up in the hotel windows. The carefully placed arc lights were switched on and bathed the front façade of the building with warm amber light. This was how she and Gerald had envisaged it, a place of light, of comfort, an oasis offering so much.

She heard Claire calling her and called back.

'What are you doing here, Mother? Sitting in the dark and cold.'

'Looking.'

Claire sat down. 'Ours. The Rentons. The way you want it.'

'Don't you? Or do you still think Charlie would be a good exchange?'

'Not on his terms,' she said defiantly. 'I won't let him stand in my way. You must see I'm perfectly capable of taking charge, now I'm free of Jim. I've left him. The truth is, Mother, I can't stand him any longer. You'll stick by me, won't you?'

'Of course, Claire. Are you sure you are doing the right thing?'

'Absolutely certain.'

'What will he do?'

'He'll get by. He always has, and he always will.'

'Claire, I didn't want it to end like this.'

'It's a beginning. I'm not giving up. Don't imagine I'll ever do that, Mother. Wherever I may be. Come on, you're starting to shiver.' She stood up, impatient to be gone.

'In a few minutes.'

Sarah watched Claire disappear into the gloom of the garden. She felt incapable of moving. Her thoughts were with Rachel and Fleur, and a terrible chill sent shivers down her back. She stood up, surprised at the sudden coldness of the wind, and walked quickly to the aviary. As she approached the peacock shrieked several times and then was silent. She looked in; he was turned away from her, and raising and lowering his fan of feathers as if agitated. Yet she couldn't see anything to disturb him. Then with a final shriek he strutted inside the wooden shelter.

She turned away and hurried back to the hotel.

The small private hospital run by nuns was in a tree-lined avenue. Fleur was conducted to Ramiro's room; she opened the door and went in. The window shades were pulled down, and the light in the room was so dim that it took Fleur a moment to adjust her sight.

Ramiro was propped up with pillows. His head was bandaged and his eyes closed. She said his name, and he opened his eyes and his unhappy expression changed to one of joy.

'Fleur, *mi amor*, Fleur.' He held out his arms, and a few steps brought her to the side of the bed. She kissed him gently, stilling the wild beating of her heart. 'I was dreaming of you, and it is a miracle, you are here. I feared I'd never see you again.' He stopped short and looked towards the darkest corner of the room.

Fleur directed her gaze in the same direction, and in onsternation saw a woman sitting on a wooden chair. In he poor light she could only make out a shadowy outline, but enough to curb the excitement of her reunion with Ramiro.

'Isabella,' Ramiro said nervously clinging to Fleur's hand, 'This is Fleur, my friend from Renton's Royal.'

Isabella Cortez rose, and adjusted the blinds, and a rich golden bar of light fell on the floor and illuminated Isabella's clear-cut patrician features and highlighted the smooth black hair drawn up and held by a comb on the top of her head.

'Ramiro has spoken of you. We did not expect you.' She approached the bed, and stood looking down at Ramiro, an accusing expression on her face.

Fleur eyed the tall, stately young woman in surprised annoyance.

'Isabella,' Ramiro said desperately, 'I wish to speak to Fleur alone.'

'I think not. I want to hear what lies you are going to tell the girl this time.'

'Lies – what's she talking about? Who is she?'

The silence between the three spun out like teased sugar. It should have been filled with explanations, words pouring forth in a torrent.

'Ramiro.' Fleur's voice was shrill with fear. 'Tell me at once.'

'Fleur, I cannot . . .'

'I can,' Isabella Cortez said.

'Isabella, please go away.' Ramiro's voice had an unusual authoritive ring. 'This has nothing to do with you.'

Isabella wavered. 'The doctors say you must not get excited. Kindly remember that, Señorita. I will wait a few moments outside.'

'*Mi amor*, I have not lied to you. I have tried to tell you many times, but the words would not come, and – and, Fleur, I was afraid of losing you.' Ramiro sighed, and pressed the palm of her hand against his lips.

Why did he speak of losing her?

'I have been so troubled. I had to speak to my father. Make him change his mind. Allow me to be free for you.'

331

'I don't understand, Ramiro. Please tell me who that woman is – she seemed so possessive.'

'Ah, it is so difficult. You see, in Spain, marriages are sometimes arranged.'

'Are you trying to tell me you are marrying that woman? You *can't*. You belong to me. Ramiro, say it isn't true.'

'Before I met you it didn't matter. I love you, Fleur, with all my heart.'

'You can't marry her.' Fleur's fears crystallized. 'You are mine. I won't give you up, ever. Tell her we belong to each other.'

'*Mi amor*, I have no choice.'

'You mean – ' Fleur's incredulous tone brought a flush to Ramiro's cheeks – 'You mean you're going to marry her. I won't let you,' she cried wildly. 'I'll kill her – '

'Hush.' He reached for her other hand, pulling her close. She snatched them away.

'Why – why?'

'My father needs her dowry – '

'Money!' Fleur spat out the word.

'We are a large family. Business is not good. We have been promised to each other for a long time.'

'I don't care. Come back to England with me. We have a great future.'

A little wind shook the blind, and lifting it, the light illuminated his face. She read all she needed to know in the agony of his expression. He would never come back.

She drew back from the bed, trembling and afraid. 'This can't be happening to us. I love you. I believed in you. You must fight your father. If you love me, fight.'

He shook his head. She felt the weight of the family, the circumstances arraigned against her. The pain of her loss overwhelmed her. She crossed her arms tightly over her breasts, and with a heart-rending cry staggered from the room.

Vaguely she was aware of Isabella Cortez standing in the corridor. The woman caught hold of Fleur's arm, digging vicious fingers into her flesh.

'It is arranged. You understand.'

Fleur turned on her, pulled her arm free and slapped Isabella's face hard. 'I hate you – I hate you.' She ran down the corridor, her sight blurred by the tears she had so far held back.

Outside the light was brilliant, merciless. Fleur narrowed her eyes against it and began to run along the crowded avenue, bumping into the people impeding her escape. Totally disorientated, she stepped into the road. Too late she heard the squeal of car brakes. Panic-stricken, she tried to move back, but her heel caught on the kerb. She had an instant vision of the bonnet of the limousine, the frightened face of the driver, and then the terrifying sensation of being tossed into the air over the bonnet. She flung out her arms, and crashed down onto the road.

'Mummy.' She saw Rachel's beloved face just as she lost consciousness. She died before the ambulance reached the hospital.

Meanwhile Rachel waited alone at their hotel. She wished she'd insisted on going to the hospital with Fleur to see Ramiro. But Fleur had made her mind up. 'I have to do this alone, Mum,' she'd said.

Rachel realized that Fleur was no longer a child. The bond between them was as strong as ever, only changed. She had held Fleur close in her arms and kissed her. 'Wish me luck,' Fleur said.

As time passed, Rachel's unease increased. She left the hotel, and walked along the Esplanada de Espana, faintly amused by the weirdly-tiled seafront, and sat down at one of the terrace cafés and ordered coffee. Suddenly she hated the burning sun, the moving fronds of the palm trees, the carefree tourists passing in front of her in a bizarre kaleidoscope of colour.

She closed her eyes for a moment, and thought she heard Fleur calling to her. She opened her eyes, jumped up, and looked round. Imagination, she thought, but the feeling was so strong, she thought, I must go to her. She set off at a sharp pace in the direction of the hospital, and as she neared the building her pace increased as if driven by an unreasonable urgency. She entered the hospital, gave her name to one of the nuns, and asked for Ramiro's room.

The nun asked her to wait a moment, and when she came back escorted her down a long corridor, and ushered her into a doctor's consulting room.

As she sat down at the doctor's suggestion, her first thought was that Ramiro was much worse.

'My daughter came to visit Señor Rodriguez. Is she still with him? Perhaps I could join them?'

'I am so sorry, Señora.'

'Is he worse?'

The doctor sat down, and Rachel felt a shiver of fear.

'I am so sorry to have to tell you there has been an accident. Your daughter – '

'Where is she? Take me to her at once. Oh God, what has happened to her?'

'She was knocked down by a car. I am afraid – '

She knew in that instant, and yet hope forced her to speak. 'Is she badly hurt?'

The doctor shook his head. 'I am sorry – we could not do anything for her.'

'You mean – no, no. There's some mistake. I won't believe . . .'

Rachel stared at the doctor's bearded face, which seemed to be dissolving in a kind of mist. She groaned, and reached out her arms. He was besides her, supporting

334

her.

'Come Señora, you must rest.' With his arms still round her, he led her to a room, and gave her into the care of two nuns. Gently they undressed her, helped her into bed. Obediently she drank the draught offered, and clung to the cool hand holding hers so comfortingly.

For a long time she drifted in and out of sleep. When she was awake she inhabited a terrible emptiness. And at these times she called for Mark, so that it was no surprise to find him by her bedside.

'Rachel, my darling. Rachel.' He gathered her into his arms, holding her close, safe.

'Mark – I – my fault.' She couldn't bring herself to speak Fleur's name.

'No,' he said, 'no. Not yours. You couldn't have stopped her and she needed you.'

'We came against your wishes.'

'You did right to come with her,' he sighed. He held her hand against his cheek. 'I was so wrong, my dearest Rachel, so wrong, so blind. Can you ever forgive me?'

She found his apology unbearable. Clinging to him, she wept. His arms tightened round her, he kissed her eyes, her wet cheeks, burying his lips in her soft hair. He whispered her name, and when she lifted her head she saw his tears were sliding unheeded down his face. Gently she wiped them away.

'Mark, can we go home?'

'Home,' he repeated. 'And I'll never let you out of my sight again.'

She kissed him. And the love which she'd stifled, flowed and crept into the empty places in her heart.

CHAPTER 32

Mark telephoned Renton's Royal before he left Spain. He asked for Michael. There was no way he could speak to Sarah.

Michael received the call in his office. At first he was too stunned to speak. Mark's voice seemed to come from an enormous distance, and the words weren't making any sense.

'She can't be, Mark. It's a mistake.'

'Try and break the news gently to your grandmother. I'll telephone you again when Rachel and I are back at Ashton Hall.' Michael sat with the receiver to his ear, hearing only the buzzing which denoted Mark had sharply severed the connection. In a while he cradled the receiver, and stared round his familiar office in a daze.

'Fleur. Little Flower. No. No. No.' The words were wrenched from his guts. He beat his fists on the desk. The screaming was inside him. How was he going to tell his grandmother? He began to shiver. His eyesight blurred, and then focused on the orchid in a pot in front of him. Fleur had planted it, instructed him to look after it. The flower lived. Fleur did not.

His howl of pain echoed round the room. He laid his head on the desk and wept.

Clive opened the door and stopped short. 'For God's sake, Michael, what's up?'

Michael lifted his head and stared at Clive as if he were a stranger. In a husky voice he said, 'She's dead. Fleur is dead.'

Spoken words changed everything. Out of chaotic thoughts came words. 'How can I tell her? How can I tell my grandmother?'

'You'll think of what to say.' Clive came round the desk and took a firm grip on Michael's arm. 'What happened? Was she suddenly taken ill?'

'An accident,' Michael said dully. 'A car accident. She was knocked down in the street.'

'Would you like me to come with you to tell Mrs Renton?'

'Thanks, no.' He stood up shakily. 'I'll just swill my face in cold water.' He squared his shoulders. 'Don't tell anyone yet.'

Sarah was in the conservatory. She spent more and more time there, as if sitting quietly she could solve her problems. The familiar assumed importance. She found strength from the continuous shooting up and cascading down of the jet of water in the fountain, splintering into points of light. Above her head rain hammered on the glass roof, beating out a recognizable rhythm. She thought of November as a month of increasing darkness; long dark nights, a sorrowful month.

She'd always hated November. Even though she recalled her father's words: 'It's over lass. The war is over today, the eleventh hour on the eleventh day of the eleventh month. Listen.' She'd listened to the sirens and the ships hooting on the river, but had found it hard to adjust her nine-year-old mind to the change from war to peace.

Michael's soft-footed arrival scarcely disturbed her until she looked up at him and saw his face. The marks of tears

337

were still visible, his eyelids were swollen, and there was about him an air of such dejection that automatically she held out her arms to him.

He sat down beside her on the narrow white-painted and scrolled seat facing the fountain.

'Tell me.'

After all it was easy to tell her gently. But his chosen words could not cushion the stark fact of Fleur's death and instinctively he knew Sarah at this moment would shy away from any diversion of the truth.

He held her hand, feeling her convulsive grip, seeing the colour recede from her face, and the blind movement as she took off her spectacles and closed her eyes. He was aware of the rocking movement of her body, as if keening inwardly could relieve the pain.

'I can't bear it,' he said.

He wondered if the screaming question blotting out all else was echoed in her mind. Why? Why Fleur?

In a moment he laid his head in her lap. Her cold thin fingers smoothed back his hair.

'Oh God, why?' she whispered.

Michael sat up. 'Mark said it was an accident.'

'Poor Rachel.' She stood up unsteadily, and reached for Michael's arm. 'I must talk to her.'

'Mark said he and Rachel were going straight to Ashton Hall as soon as they can get a flight.'

Two days passed before Sarah heard Rachel's voice on the telephone. 'I'm all right, Mummy,' she said. 'We're home.'

'We give thanks for her life.'

The family, friends, and members of the staff of Renton's Royal Hotel and the workers on the Ashton estate filled the pews in Ashton church.

Sarah sat between Rachel and Michael. Her crying, like Rachel's, was done.

'We give thanks for her life.'

But that wasn't enough. We question too. Fleur's body lying in the flower-covered coffin before the altar was a recrimination. She was made for life; for happiness and joy.

Sarah fixed her gaze on the mass of flowers, yellow, bronze and white chrysanthemums. Vibrant colours, and right for the girl whose life had made such an indelible mark on them all. She stood up, erect, as the organist touched the keys for the opening bars of 'All Things Bright and Beautiful.'

Fleur had been, no *was*, bright and beautiful. Nothing of her would be lost; she lived securely in their hearts and memories, for ever bright and beautiful.

Rachel reached for Sarah's hand, their fingers entwined. Courage and love, and much, much more was passed from one to the other.

Fleur's grave was dug beside those of her father's ancestors. The Ashtons dominated this quiet country churchyard. There they lay beneath plain headstones, crosses, and even a stone angel, wings outspread. So many Ashtons, old graves lichen-covered and awry. Who remembered them now?

They followed the vicar in procession to the graveside, stumbling on the uneven ground. Sarah was glad of Michael's strong arm. She felt light-headed, and only will-power forced her feet to step one before the other. She lifted her face up to the wind, driving ragged clouds across a dun-coloured sky. The wind tore off the last of the leaves; so bright and beautiful in death.

The family lingered at the graveside. Others moved silently away. A little group now, Sarah thought, her gaze lingering on each of their faces. Rachel and Mark, his arm supporting her. Claire and Margaret, hands linked. And Michael, giving freely of his young strength to Sarah. They stood as if reluctant to move away from each other, or leave the beloved one so alone now. Sarah held out her arms; her family was diminished, but not broken.

CHAPTER 33

Sefton stayed on at Renton's Royal until after Fleur's funeral. Unobtrusively he supported Sarah, and she accepted without comment. The builder, Craig, was harried. He never took advantage of Sarah because she was a woman – but the thought was there. He believed that women had their places, and one of them wasn't the successful proprietor of one of the best hotels in England.

Sefton was amused by Craig's attitude and carefully monitored his remarks. As time passed Sefton's admiration for Sarah's administration increased. She did not set aside Fleur's death, but mourned in secret. At last the rebuilding of the store rooms was finished, and Sefton supervised the storing of the wine. He checked the stock, and gave instructions to the head wine waiter, drawing on his vast knowledge of the wine of most countries, but particularly his region in France.

He had a batch of mature wine ready for dispatch, and he planned to return to his vineyard and have it crated and delivered in good time for the Christmas festivities. Unexpectedly he began to pine for his vineyard. He longed to return to the work governed by the seasons. He shivered in the damp and windy weather, and ached for the warm sun, and the wide vista of soldierly rows of vines beneath a high sky.

He took action when he received a letter from Monsieur Villiard confirming the proposal for his continued occupancy of Le Clos Rozelle, and made an appointment with Bobby Brooks for advice.

'Any snags, Bobby?' he asked, settling himself in the client's chair placed conveniently near the large mahogany desk which had belonged to Brooks Senior. No fly-by-night furniture in the Brooks office. It was all of solid crafted English manufacture.

'It looks like a fair deal,' Bobby said. Having carefully perused the letter, he laid it down to meet Sefton's quizzical gaze.

'Would you advise me to take it?'

'As a financial proposition it's sound, but – '

'I know,' Sefton said. 'Where does Sarah fit in?'

'Exactly.'

'She doesn't need me. When I was in trouble I needed her. But even though she's badly dented, and I care like hell about that, she'll survive, and she'll gain more strength from adversity. She has inner resources which Gerald recognized and drew on. I love that woman, and I have to learn to let go.'

Bobby smiled. Their early friendship re-emerged, mint-new.

'A waiting game?'

'Perhaps, as long as that wily devil Charlie Mullins doesn't gain an advantage on me in my absence. I've made up my mind to go back to France, I wanted your opinion on Monsieur Villiard's offer before I discuss it with him. Now that he is willing to pay off Rafe's gambling debts, it leaves me able to continue my financial arrangement with Sarah.'

'Will she agree?'

Sefton smiled. 'The awkward little madam has no choice. Have you seen the size of the bill for rebuilding the store rooms? I'm well aware that meeting that bill will leave her skint. But most importantly I want to keep a foot in the door of Renton's Royal Hotel, even if I never need to push it open.'

'I'm sure that is what Gerald had in mind.'

'Not so fast, Brooks. Gerald and I were business partners. We were never friends. How could we be, when he won the woman I adore, and have done so ever since the moment I first saw her. I want to do what's best for Sarah.'

He'd thought about Sarah constantly since the day she became widowed but he was no fool, and he knew that Sarah would take a long time to get over Gerald's death. Was seven years long enough? It was with a kind of despair he'd come to realize during the last weeks that Sarah might never put another man in Gerald's place.

Sarah showed no surprise at his decision to return immediately to France, and expressed great relief that he was willing to continue the existing financial arrangement with her.

'It means you will still have a stake in our hotel, and I can turn to you for advice and co-operation. I'll miss you,' she said wistfully.

'Enough maybe to visit me in the spring?'

'That will be nice, very nice, Sefton.' It sounded weak, she knew, but in the present circumstances he could hardly expect more.

She admitted that Sefton's generosity over the financial agreement had disposed of the most pressing of her commitments, namely the settling of Craig's account. His backing also freed her from Charlie's tiresome attentions and she was now in a position to fend him off.

She was able to settle back comfortably into her routine. Claire made no pretence of carrying on with her work as Sarah's personal assistant, and this too was a relief.

Claire's departure was not unexpected, though typically she shrouded it in secrecy.

343

'I'm off, Mother. I don't know when I'll be back, maybe not until you retire and I take your place.'

Sitting at her desk, Sarah frowned. Claire's constant harping on an event Sarah was determined wouldn't take place for many years, was unsettling. 'You'll keep in touch?'

'Naturally. No missed opportunities for me.'

'Claire, I do wish you'd confide in me. You set me aside.'

Claire threw back her head, one of her most theatrical gestures, and laughed.

'*I* set *you* aside? That's rich, Mother dearest, coming from you. You have *always* kept me very firmly at a distance. Because I wasn't soft and silly like darling Rachel. Because I wasn't a boy, an heir, to be pampered and indulged like Paul. Not that that got you anywhere – he couldn't flee the coop quick enough, could he?

'And why? Because of you, Sarah Renton, the Great I Am. Perfect wife, hotel-keeper of genius – and a truly lousy mother!'

Sarah's eyes were two dark pools of suffering in her pale face.

'You are my darling daughter, Claire. If I failed you – as I must have done for you to feel so bitterly towards me – please believe me when I say I have never stopped loving you, no matter how it may have seemed.'

'How much?' Claire demanded. 'Enough to retire in my favour? Enough to hand over Renton's Royal Hotel to me?'

Sarah said, 'If you are trying to measure love – '

'I'm not. I'm demanding, and you are refusing. No matter, my time will come.'

Sarah sighed. She was tired, and had slept badly since Fleur's death. She thought if one could ever measure love it was in the spontaneous giving, the joy she'd felt in Fleur's response.

Claire stood by the window, so elegant, so hard and untouchable. The sea-light, Sarah's term for the quivering light reflected off the sea, and only discernible when the tide broke against the defences surrounding the hotel garden, subtly changed the deeper green of Claire's wool suit. The pure silk scarf draped across her shoulders, and the pointed leather Italian shoes completed a fashion-plate ensemble. Sarah was certain that Claire could go far, if only she had the right attitude.

Sarah in a way had expected Claire's departure, noting the increasing dissatisfaction which affected her daughter. She did not, however, anticipate Margaret's sudden arrival – riding pillion on the back of Peter's borrowed motorbike.

'Gran.' She burst into Sarah's office, and flung her arms round Sarah. 'I had to come. I don't know what to do.'

Peter stood uncertainly in the doorway. 'Come in, Peter, shut the door and both of you sit down.'

Peter took off his helmet and leather jacket, and helped Margaret out of hers.

Sarah felt a flutter in her heart; the feeling that once again she must gather her wits and strength to deal with another crisis.

'It's Dad,' Margaret said. 'He's been arrested.'

'Oh my God no. Why? What's he done? I thought he was safe in that nursing home.'

Margaret shook her head. 'It's been awful, Gran. Hasn't it, Pete? Dad turned up one day saying he'd been thrown out of the nursing home because Mum refused to pay the fees. Where is she? I phoned here, and Mavis said she'd gone, and hadn't left a forwarding address. I didn't want to bother you, Gran, but . . .'

'You silly girl. You know I'm here to help.'

'Yes,' Margaret said. 'The one permanent being in my

life. We all turn to you.' She bit her lip, her face was ashen, and Sarah reached for her hands and held them tightly.

'Tell me about your father,' she said gently.

Peter said, 'He's made Mag's life a misery. She was forced to stay away from college to look after him, and he's scrounged enough money from her to go boozing at night. He got into a fight and was arrested. He was bailed, but we didn't have enough money – ' He shrugged his shoulders.

Sarah's heart sank. She'd hoped to be rid of Jim for ever.

'I don't want him back.' Margaret's voice wavered.

Sarah was deeply concerned for Margaret. She'd always thought of her as the strongest of her grandchildren, and able to cope with any situation. Claire is the damn limit, she thought. How dare she leave Margaret to deal with Jim at his worst? Her quick wits moved into top gear, and clearly she assessed what action it would be best to take.

'How much is the bail?' she asked.

'But don't you see,' Margaret cried,' if you pay his bail, and why should you, he'll be sent back to me.'

'I think not,' Sarah said with determination. 'I'll talk to Bobby Brooks, and see if he can fix the bail and have Jim brought here.'

'But you don't want him. That's not fair.'

'Don't worry, darling. I know just the place for him. Now, you must stay the night. I won't allow you to make that long journey until tomorrow.'

'Do you know where Mum is?'

'I don't. She went off into the blue without a word, and lots of mystery.'

'She really is the absolute end. She's no right to clear off – '

'Come, Margaret. You know your mother doesn't like anything unpleasant. And unfortunately your father is just that in her view. We can't expect help from her.'

346

'How dare she think of ever running this hotel. You won't let her have it, will you?'

'Don't worry, lass. I have you and Michael and – ' She stopped and her lips quivered, hot tears pricked the back of her eyes.

Peter put his arms round her and kissed her cheek. 'You did mention grub, didn't you?'

Arms about each other they headed for the dining room.

Jim was brought back to the hotel a few days later. In the meantime Sarah had made her arrangements. Jim was aggressive. He was unshaven, and there was a wild look in his eyes. He leant heavily on a walking stick.

'I won't have you here,' Sarah said. 'I've arranged for you to stay at a guest house nearby. It's run by an ex-policeman.'

Jim's expletives shook her for a moment. 'Take it or leave it. I'll pay for your keep there until your case comes up. After that, I suggest you go back to Ireland.'

'Where's my bitch of a wife? Is she here?'

'She is not.'

'If she is – '

'Don't be stupid, Jim. She's through with you, and so are the rest of the family. So lie low, and don't make any more trouble, because next time I swear, I'll not lift a finger to help you.'

'This is all your fault. If you'd treated us right – '

'Did you treat *me* right? Neglected your job, upset my good and faithful staff. I don't want to hear another word from you. So watch it.'

It took her a few minutes to recover from her anger, and strangely it persisted and turned against Claire who was so adept at avoiding trouble.

Her anger continued to simmer for some time. A picture postcard of the Eiffel Tower in Paris from Claire brought

347

her fury to a head. Claire wrote: Having a great time. Staying with Madame Bouchier at her super hotel. Claire.

Lydia Bouchier, Sarah thought, ripping up the postcard. She hadn't known that Claire and Lydia were acquainted, and what the devil was the name of her hotel?

Charlie would know. Lydia was a friend of his, a partner or something in his vast network. She dialled the Westwood Hotel, and asked for Charlie, giving her name. The manager took the call and apologized for Mr Mullins' absence. Mr Mullins was in Paris on business and wouldn't be back for a few days. Would she care to leave a message?

She would not.

Suddenly she felt old and frightened. What was Charlie doing in Paris with Claire and that objectionable Bouchier woman? What were they planning? She felt betrayed and she didn't like it.

Next day Rachel telephoned. 'Are you terribly busy, Mummy? Would you have time to come here?'

'I can make time. Why?'

'I've sprained my wrist and can't drive the car.'

'I'll come,' Sarah said.

She was pleased to have the chance of a day out, and the early December days were inviting. Sharp early morning frosts, and blue days filled with deceptive sunshine, a vague promise of spring.

She loved driving. The latent power of the Mercedes was a challenge, and the steady purr of the engine as she sped along the motorway restored her confidence in her capabilities. She hadn't visited Ashton Hall for some time, and when the house came into view in a bend in the drive she was again struck by the beauty of its proportions.

Rachel was thinner and paler. There was a haunted look in her eyes which troubled Sarah, although the bear-hug she gave her mother was as spontaneous as ever.

348

'Mummy, it's heaven to see you.'

Rachel led the way to the suite of rooms in the west wing, overlooking the sweep of lawns and the small gem of a lake.

'What do you think?' Rachel said, showing off the sitting room, the narrow galley of a kitchen, and the two bedrooms.

'I like it,' Sarah said,

But the thought was in both their minds that because Fleur had never stepped into these rooms, there was no continual reminder to distress Rachel.

'Mark arranged for the wing to be opened up, stripped of all the old furnishings and gave me a free hand to decorate and furnish it.'

'It's delightful. So restful,' Sarah said, admiring the plain wallpaper, sprigged curtains, and bookshelves sagging under the weight of Rachel's collection of books.

Rachel made coffee, and when they were comfortably seated she said, 'Tell me about Renton's Royal and everyone. Michael often phones, and so does Margaret. It's kind of them,' she added formally.

'They love you,' Sarah said. 'And how are you, my darling Rachel?'

'I get by. A day at a time.'

'Where's Mark?'

'He's out on the estate somewhere. One of the tenants sent for him.' She put a hand on Sarah's arm. 'It's all right really, Mummy. I help in the estate office. Lucky I learnt to type. We work together,' she said firmly.

Sarah nodded. Working together was a narrow bridge. It led somewhere eventually. It was just a question of sticking on, keeping the eye and mind fixed on the objective.

Sarah knew better than to ask Rachel about the state of

her marriage. She was content that there was a thin thread holding them together.

Mark came back to lunch. Sarah was at once struck by a difference; not only in his looks but in his gentleness and thought for Rachel. She had prepared the food in her own kitchen, and served it on a gateleg table placed in the bay window.

'I have all Fleur's recipes,' Rachel smiled. 'I guess they were wheedled out of your chef, Mummy.'

'He gave them to her willingly. He cared for her very deeply. What delicious soup, Rachel.'

'What do you think of this idea? I'm collecting all Fleur's notes on the wild flowers growing on the shore. Mark thinks we should get a little book published.'

Sarah was relieved they were able to talk naturally about Fleur.

'I expect that is what she had in mind. Have you given up the idea of the Sam Verne book?'

'Not at all. In fact – ' Rachel coloured softly – 'a small Lakeland press has made me an offer of publication. After Fleur died I could hardly bear to be alone with thoughts of her. I just sat down and worked solidly. Peter was a brick, did all sorts of research for me in London and locally.'

'He brought Margaret up to the hotel on a borrowed motorcycle. I haven't had chance to tell you the trouble Jim has made for her,' said Sarah.

Mark listened with keen interest to Sarah's report of Jim's arrest and the subsequent happenings. 'And to crown everything,' Sarah continued, 'Claire sent me a postcard from Paris with no address, saying she is working in one of Lydia Bouchier's hotels, and apparently having a marvellous time.'

'So you can't contact her,' Mark said.

Sarah hesitated. 'I did try. I phoned Charlie, but it seems he is in Paris too.'

'Well, well.' Mark jumped up and cleared away the dirty dishes and brought in coffee. Sarah couldn't remember ever seeing him do anything like that before.

'What is she up to, Mummy?' asked Rachel.

'I wish I knew,' Sarah said disconsolately.

'You won't weaken, Sarah, about keeping the hotel for the Rentons?'

Sarah looked at Mark in surprise, and he smiled. 'I'm interested in the fate of your hotel. I've come to see it in a different light.'

'Mark, I'm so glad. Your brother, Rachel, called it a devouring monster. I was afraid . . .'

'Don't be,' Mark said firmly, pouring coffee into egg-shell thin cups, and offering Sarah cream and sugar. 'I've always admired your guts. Fleur loved you so much. Two of a kind, I suppose you could say.'

Some of the agony of guilt Sarah had endured began to seep away. She'd thought Mark had blamed her for the defection of his wife and daughter, forgetting he too had a heritage to pass on.

He finished his coffee. 'Back to work.' He kissed Rachel lovingly, and Sarah on both cheeks. 'If you need me, darling, I'll be in the estate office.'

Rachel went to the window to wave to Mark, and on the way back picked up a letter out of a desk.

'From Ramiro.' She sat down on a deep divan and Sarah joined her. 'I wanted to talk to you about it before I show it to Mark.' She sighed. 'He's still terribly bitter.'

'I can understand that, I suppose I feel the same.'

'I know. Ramiro is asking our forgiveness. He is still in hospital, another minor operation to his head and a general relapse due to the shock of Fleur's death.'

'I don't want to know,' Sarah said.

'You used to say to us when we were children that every problem is two-sided. I believed you.'

'All right, tell me.'

Rachel spread out the two thin sheets of airmail paper. 'He loves Fleur with all his heart and she loved him. He was afraid – '

'Afraid?' Sarah questioned sharply.

'Yes. Afraid of losing her. He hoped to persuade his father to free him from the arranged marriage, and then he need not mention it to Fleur.'

'I didn't realize – '

'His father was adamant, they quarelled in the restaurant kitchen, and Ramiro's father picked up a knife and threatened him. Ramiro slipped.'

'So that's why Rodriguez phoned me. Making sure Ramiro couldn't come back.'

Rachel picked up the letter. 'Unfortunately Ramiro's fiancée was in the room when Fleur visited. She insisted on Ramiro telling Fleur the truth.'

Rachel sighed and put the letter down. Sarah's heart expanded with love and pity for her beloved grandchild. She was swamped with all kinds of guilt, sins of omission.

'So you see, Mummy, we must forgive him. He needs your forgiveness and understanding particularly. He says he learnt to love you.'

Sarah closed her eyes, and yet tears forced their way between her lids. 'You, Rachel, have you forgiveness in your heart?'

'I have thought about this night after night in the hours when I could not sleep. And I think it is no *one* person's fault that Fleur died. You could say it was a combination of circumstances.'

'But if I hadn't employed Ramiro in the first place . . .'

'Or Fleur hadn't been determined to learn her craft at Renton's Royal. Or Rodriguez hadn't arranged his son's marriage because he needed the girl's dowry. Or I had obeyed Mark.' She sighed and tears slid heedlessly down her cheeks. 'We can go on *ad infinitum* – '

They sat with their arms about each other, gaining comfort and courage.

At last Sarah stirred. 'I must go. It's getting dark, and it's a long way home.'

Rachel watched her mother drive out of the gates. She knew Sarah would not fail her.

CHAPTER 34

'Michael,' Sarah said, 'will you come down to the plantation with me to choose the Christmas tree?'

Sarah usually jealously guarded her right to choose the tree. She wasn't sure why she set such store by this simple act, but now she wished to share it with Michael, an admission that perhaps one day it would be his right.

The plantation was the head gardener's special delight. Wishing to exploit his knowledge of forestry he'd persuaded Sarah to invest in this plantation of young trees. 'A follow on' he'd called it.

The plantation was graded; small new trees on the outside rising to trees – firs and pines – fifteen or twenty feet high, which the gardener planned to introduce in the existing pine wood.

'This is the one,' Michael said enthusiastically.

Sarah surveyed the fir critically, and admitted his choice was right. It had enough side branches to give it a good shape, and was the right height to fit comfortably in the foyer near the staircase.

Michael twined a scarlet ribbon round the trunk for the gardener's guidance. The tree would be dug up, fitted into the tub, and replanted later.

With Ricki at their heels they followed the path through the pine wood to the shore. The tide was racing in, a blustery wind piling up the breakers.

As they clambered over the dunes, Sarah told Michael about Rachel's plan to have a small book published from Fleur's notes on the wild flowers to be found on the shore.

'Super idea. She'd like that. Sometimes I think if I look hard enough I'll find her bent over one of her old specimens. If only . . .'

He took hold of Sarah's hand, and they marched over the ridged sand to the gate.

'Let's go and sit in the rose garden for a few minutes. It's sheltered, and there's something I have to say to you.'

'Fire away,' Michael said, stretching his long legs out before him.

'It's about Ramiro. He's written to Rachel asking us to forgive him.'

Michael sat up straight. 'No. Never. He killed her.'

'No. We all did.' She explained Rachel's theory of collective responsibility. 'You like him, don't you, Michael?'

'Yes, but – '

'Fleur loved him. She wouldn't be able to bear our rejection.'

He was not convinced. He sat stiff and angry. Sarah did not know how to reach him.

'I miss her so dreadfully, Gran.'

'I know. So do I.'

It began to rain, and Michael jumped up, pulling Sarah to her feet, and hurrying back to the hotel.

It was a sad and quiet Christmas for the Renton's staff that year though on the face of it everything stayed the same. The Christmas tree that Michael and Sarah had picked out was erected in the foyer, hung with the glass baubles that Mrs Humphries carefully safeguarded in the house-keeper's office the rest of the year.

A florist transformed the public rooms with great swags of spruce and ivy and scarlet-berried holly. A local children's choir gave a carol concert on Christmas Eve, and on Christmas morning every guest at the hotel was given a small present and personally written Season's Greetings from Sarah.

No, there had been no falling off in the hotel's high standards of hospitality and housekeeping, she was pleased to see. But behind the scenes it was a different story. Lethargy prevailed; the seasonal jollity was forced. Sarah knew she could not allow things to continue this way. Her hardworking staff deserved to carry out their tasks in an atmosphere of cheerful professionalism and not one pervaded by gloom. It was up to her to restore things to the way they were before Fleur's death.

It was a tradition at Renton's that the staff Christmas dinner took place in the afternoon, after the guests had been served and before a buffet supper was laid out for them in the dining room.

In the past, Sarah and members of the family had eaten at the same time as the guests then called in at the staff dining room to join in the festivities there. This year Sarah decided to abandon the hotel dining room after being on hand to welcome the guests. Instead, places were laid for Michael and her, the only family members present this Christmas, at the long staff table.

Chef had done them all proud as usual with a succulent golden turkey and all the trimmings. He carved it himself, white toque replaced by a fur-trimmed Santa hat in honour of the occasion, and later he supervised the setting aflame of a spectacular plum pudding, served with brandy butter for the sophisticated, and custard for those who didn't see why they should have to be.

After everyone had eaten their fill, Sarah rapped on the table to attract their attention then got to her feet.

'If I could have your attention, please, just for a moment, there's something I'd like to say. First I'd like to thank each and every one of you for your expressions of sympathy and tireless support of myself and the family during the past few months. Your help and encouragement has meant more to me than I can put into words, and I know Michael has felt it too.'

She glanced at her grandson as she spoke. He sat, head bowed, before a plate he had barely touched. The next part of the speech was for him. She hoped he was listening.

'I needn't tell you how much my granddaughter has been missed at this special time of year when our families are so much in our thoughts. I know you've missed her too. But I've something else to say to you today and it's this: a life lived constantly looking back is a life wasted. Fleur wouldn't have approved of sighs and long faces. She was in favour of music and dancing, of laughter and living. She met life head-on, without sadness or fear. I think, in memory of her, we should do the same.

'Ladies and gentlemen, I would like you all to raise your glasses in a toast. I give you: the future!'

Chairs were pushed back around the table and the toast rang out. Michael was the last to rise to his feet. He mouthed the words and touched the glass to his lips but did not drink, Sarah noticed.

Nevertheless her Christmas Day speech had a good effect on the staff. There were no more sad-faced little huddles or hushed voices when Fleur's name came up in conversation. She was remembered often and fondly by those who had worked with her. Only Michael refrained from speaking openly of her – or of Ramiro when Sarah raised the subject of his letter once again.

'Leave it, Gran!' he warned her sharply one day in February when she wondered if perhaps it was time to let the Spanish boy have word from them. 'You write to

357

him if you want but send no message from me. I hope he
rots in hell for what he did!'

To take his mind off his preoccupation with Fleur's
death, Sarah consulted Clive and asked if they might give
her grandson some additional responsibilities.

'I thought personnel if you've no objection, Clive?
Michael's always been good with the staff and they seem
to like him. I thought he might handle recruitment for us,
at least at junior levels.'

'Why not?' Clive answered. 'I've every confidence he'll
do a good job.'

Michael advertised locally and in the trade press in
plenty of time for Easter when the hotel would fill up
once more and hopefully stay that way right through till
autumn. The chambermaids' and other housekeeping
posts were easily filled with local recruits, but trained
kitchen staff, or even unskilled youngsters keen to learn,
seemed to be thin on the ground.

Ramiro's old position eventually went to a young
commis from The Adelphi. When consulted, Chef grud-
gingly agreed that he seemed to know his *onglets* from his
oignons. Fleur's position was harder to fill. None of the
youngsters Michael interviewed seemed to share her
passion for cooking. *I expect I'm just prejudiced,* he
admitted to himself finally. *That girl from the Bear in
Chester wasn't so bad . . .*

He was about to dictate a letter offering her the position
when Marian, the secretary he shared with Sarah and
Clive, brought in the second post.

'Any more answers to my ad in *Caterers' Weekly*?' he
asked.

Marian, a plain but jolly woman in her late-thirties,
glanced at him, her eyes sparkling.

'There is one I think you'll find interesting.'

She detached it from the rest and handed it over.

Michael's eyes went straight to the signature at the bottom. 'Betsy Greenwood . . .? That's Charlie Mullins' granddaughter, isn't it? I've met her a couple of times. But why should she want to work for Renton's? She must be in a very cushy billet, working for her grandfather.'

Marian bit her lip and refrained from replying. Young Mr Michael was well liked by the staff but it didn't seem to occur to him that on very similar grounds he too could be said to occupy a cushy billet – not that he didn't work hard too, she added to herself.

'I expect you'll be wanting to interview her? Shall I ring her this morning and enter it in the diary?'

'Yes, I suppose so,' he said doubtfully.

It would be the first time he'd interviewed someone he'd met socially and he wasn't sure quite how he should handle it. Betsy Greenwood had made quite an impression the last few times he'd met her. What on earth could a girl like that want with a skivvy's job in the kitchens?

'A change, you see,' Betsy told him frankly. She crossed her shapely legs, displayed to advantage under a yellow and black striped mini-skirt. It made her look like a pretty little wasp, he thought, distracted. A pretty blonde baby-faced wasp . . .

'I mean, it can get a bit wearing, being constantly torn between family and your loyalty to your fellow staff members, can't it? You must have faced similar situations?'

'You could say that,' he replied, not adding that it was his own aunt and uncle who had given him the most trouble.

'It seems that your experience with Charlie – er, Mr Mullins, has been mainly confined to front-of-house jobs: reservations, reception, special events co-ordinator. Kitchen work is generally seen as a step down from the more glamorous work of dealing with guests.'

She levelled her dark brown eyes on him. 'Is that how you see the work – honestly? Trying to pretend that you've never seen Mr Smith before when he turns up with his second "wife" in a month, or persuading the local Rugby Club Supper that the Soroptimists in the meeting room next-door would rather not hear their entire bathtime repertoire?

'Let's face it, any glamour that a hotel possesses is an illusion created for the guest by a well-trained and dedicated staff. Culinary skills can play their part in creating that illusion, and I intend to master them. After all, if I'm to have charge of my own hotel one day, I want to be an expert in every aspect of its running.'

'Do you really want your own hotel?' Michael found himself asking.

'Oh, yes. Don't you? I mean, it's in my blood, it's a life I enjoy, but I don't want to keep on working to make other people rich all my life – even if they are family. Hence the break from Grandfather. He's a wonderfully generous man who's given me the best possible start in the industry. Now I want to step out on my own. If you'll have me, that is?'

Her gaze was as shrewd and direct as Charlie's, he realized, disconcerting when coupled with that white-blonde hair and soft husky voice. He found himself unable to meet it and looked instead at those mesmerising legs as he replied: 'Yes. That is . . . I suppose I should just mention this to my grandmother first. You being a Mullins and everything,' he added lamely.

Betsy coloured angrily. 'I'm a Greenwood – as you'd have noticed if you'd once taken your eyes off my legs and bothered to read my application properly!'

A wasp that knew how to sting, he thought, as she stood up hastily and made for the door.

'Well, as you obviously have me down as a spy, sent here

by my big bad grandfather to make trouble for Renton's, I take back my application. I wouldn't work here if you paid me!'

'That would be a poor do, lass.' Unnoticed by both of them, Sarah had opened the door to her grandson's office, alerted by Betsy's raised voice. 'I'm sure Michael doesn't expect you to work here for nothing.'

'He doesn't seem to want me to work here at all,' said Betsy with a scornful glance in his direction. 'Thinks I'm just a plant sent here by my grandfather.'

'Well, let's face it, love, it wouldn't be the first time, would it?' said Sarah calmly. 'Michael was right to be cautious. Now, why don't we sit down and go through your application again?'

She held out her hand for the letter and wordlessly Michael passed it over. He had never felt so humiliated in his life. First the girl had the cheek to accuse him of looking at her legs – which all right he had done, but only because she was practically *flaunting* them – and then she went over his head and tried to win his grandmother over. Worst of all, he knew exactly what Sarah was going to say.

'Very well, my dear. This all looks most impressive. If you're sure you'd like to take on a kitchen job, the trainee's position is yours. Live in or out?'

'Oh, out, I think. Grandfather bought me a little flat a few months ago and it's my pride and joy. I can't bear to think of leaving it.'

'Well, you won't be seeing much of it,' Sarah warned. 'Split shifts three days a week like the rest of the staff. Think you can manage?'

Betsy smiled widely. 'I'm sure I can, Mrs Renton. And thanks lot for giving me this chance when others weren't so keen.'

She flashed a mischievous smile at Michael. 'Sorry

for flying off the handle like that. I won't be any more trouble, I promise. From now on, you'll hardly know I'm here.'

In her first week in the kitchens Betsy incinerated the scones for afternoon tea, added sugar instead of salt to the Brown Windsor, and slammed shut the oven door, causing Chef's celebrated Yorkshires to fall flat for the first time in thirty years.

'Not a natural in the kitchen,' he told Sarah one afternoon as they both watched the girl industriously rolling out some flaky pastry she had made. A fellow trainee had caught the knack easily and his plump flour-dusted pastry cushion was steadily increasing in volume. Betsy's was limp and grey as an old dishcloth.

'You'll not use that for the guests?' Sarah asked.

Chef looked reproachful. 'You know me better than that. It would serve young Betsy right if I made her eat it, but once she's had enough of playing around with it, she can sling it in the pig bin.'

Sarah raised an eyebrow. 'That's very mild, coming from you. Is this the man who made Fleur chop onions for three solid hours till she could do it the correct way with her eyes closed?'

'Fleur was different. A natural. A great chef in the making. I was trying to give her the very best start by making her acquire the classical techniques. Betsy . . .' He shook his head. 'The lass will never be a chef, it's just not in her, but to be fair she works like ten and never a bad word from her. She's pretty reliable when it comes to the more routine tasks, and all the staff like her.'

All except Michael, thought Sarah. Though she had hoped the two youngsters would become friendly, coming as they did from similar backgrounds, so far they had had little to do with one another since Betsy had joined their staff, though on Betsy's side there had been several friendly overtures, she knew.

It seemed Michael resented seeing her in Fleur's old place, winning over Fleur's old friends. She grew daily more popular with fellow staff members. If there was a trip to a Liverpool club, a Sunday afternoon ramble or an impromptu party in the staff quarters, Betsy was always invited; Michael, with his gloomy face and lack of conversation, less and less often. He was a different lad from the lively, ebullient youngster of a year ago, his grandmother thought with concern.

Someone else had noted Michael's preoccupation and thought it was a pity. Shirley Hodges, a young waitress, had befriended Betsy in the first week and filled her in on all the gossip.

'That young Mr Michael's lovely looking. Wouldn't kick him out of my sleeping bag, if you know what I mean?'

She nudged Betsy as they sat side by side in the staff dining room one morning. Betsy always chose late-meal break if she could. Having to eat early, before the guests were served, meant breakfast at seven sharp and lunch at an unbelievable eleven-thirty.

'I suppose he is,' she said now, studying Michael where he sat on his own, reading a newspaper, while at the other end of the long table a rowdy gang of kitchen porters swapped jokes and winked at any female member of staff unwise enough to look their way. 'If only he wasn't always so cold and supercilious,' Betsy pronounced.

'He didn't use to be,' said Shirley in his defence. 'When Fleur was here he was a different lad, always game for a laugh. It's a real shame, the way he's changed.'

Betsy agreed, remembering what fun he had been at Margaret's birthday and later at Sarah's sixtieth celebrations. She said nothing more until they'd finished breakfast and were stacking their plates on a kitchen trolley.

'I've been thinking,' she said suddenly. 'Michael doesn't get out much, does he? I think we should ask him to that concert next Saturday.'

A group of young workers from Renton's had clubbed together to organise a mini-bus that was to take them into Liverpool where Johnny Kidd and The Pirates were playing at The Jacaranda.

'Do you reckon he'd come if I asked him?'

Shirley looked her friend up and down. Even in food-spotted kitchen whites, and with her hair scraped back under a severe little cap, Betsy was a sight for sore eyes.

'He'd be mad not to,' said Shirley loyally. 'Go get him!'

With Shirley looking on, Betsy crossed the room, neatly avoiding the kitchen porters who clamoured for her attention, and stood beside Michael.

'Is that interesting?'

'Sorry?' He made a show of having been absorbed in his paper.

'Only you haven't turned a page for nearly ten minutes. Shirley and I were watching.'

'Really? Has neither of you anything better to do? You know, like work, doing what we pay you to.'

'That's a cheap shot!' she exclaimed. 'You know damn well I pull my weight.'

Michael instantly regretted his words. Why did this girl have the knack of always catching him on the raw?

'I'm sorry,' he muttered. 'That was uncalled for. Did you want me for something?'

Betsy took a deep breath. 'You, me, Johnny Kidd and The Pirates. A date on Saturday night. What do you say? There's a busload going from here so transport's no problem. Come on, Mike, it'll be a blast.'

'I don't think so.' He quickly folded his paper and got to his feet. 'Thanks for the invitation but I don't think it would be a good idea.'

'What – with me being staff and you management?' she taunted.

He looked at her levelly.

'That's nonsense. If you must know it's because you're too pushy and I'm just not interested.'

He brushed past her, leaving her standing, red in the face, with everyone looking on.

'Well, if he's not, love, I am!' one of the kitchen boys shouted. 'Daft devil. He doesn't know when he's well off.'

The sad truth was that Michael *did* know. He'd got off on the wrong foot with Betsy, and time and again since then he'd opened his mouth and the words had come out wrong. He hated himself for being so graceless and maybe hurting a girl who'd never shown him anything but friendship. Was it because she had taken Fleur's place in the affections of the staff? Could he really be as petty and small-minded as that?

There were times when Michael could clearly see the changes in himself since his cousin had died, and what he saw appalled him. He wanted to change back, for things to be as they once had been, but after Fleur's death he had lost his way. All the joy and colour and excitement had faded from his life, and he was not sure he would ever experience them again.

Betsy was not a girl to give up easily. She hadn't given up on learning to cook, for instance, even though it was painfully obvious she was not another Fanny Craddock, and she wasn't about to turn her back on Michael, even though he'd made it brutally plain he wasn't interested.

Betsy didn't believe him. It wasn't that she was vain – she knew there were others as pretty as her – but she had recognized something in Michael's expression, a deep loneliness and sense of bewilderment, which had stuck in her mind and would give her no peace. She bided her time and chose her moment well.

One afternoon a few days later, when she was on a split shift, with no time to return to her flat before the evening stint, she decided to go for a walk on the beach.

It was warm weather for May and Betsy was looking her best in a pale pink linen shift worn with a matching floppy-brimmed hat and a long chiffon scarf in pastel colours trailing from her throat.

She almost passed Michael by without seeing him. He was sitting among the dunes, a little way off the main path. She held up her hand to shield her eyes from the sun. Yes, it was him, sitting among the wild flowers, eyes closed, face tilted into the breeze from the sea.

Betsy walked as quietly as she could over the cushions of marram grass. She didn't want him running away today.

'Hi,' she said, dropping down beside him. 'Mind if I join you?'

Michael opened his mouth to speak, obviously thought better of what he'd been about to say, and answered instead, 'No, I don't mind. Finished for today?'

She pulled a face. 'No, worse luck. Split shift. I'm on again from six to eleven. What about you?'

'Same. Waste of a glorious day, isn't it?'

Betsy screwed up her eyes against the sun which dazzled her when she tried to look him in the face.

'That doesn't sound like the hard-working, dedicated Michael Renton we usually see.'

He smiled wryly. 'Is that how people see me? Dedicated to the hotel? If only they knew . . . This place means far more to me.' He gestured at the carpet of rough grass and frail flowers, the blue dazzle of sunlight on water beyond.

366

'It was Fleur's favourite place too, wasn't it?' Betsy prompted.

She'd heard so much about the dead girl that she sometimes felt as though she'd known Fleur herself. They'd met briefly at various parties and from those occasions, and from all she'd subsequently heard, Betsy felt strangely convinced they could have been friends.

Michael looked at her, surprised. 'Yes, it was. How did you know?'

'Oh, just picked it up. People talk about these things.'

'Don't they just?' he said raggedly. 'What else have they said about Fleur and me?'

'That you both came to work here at the same time and became very close, the best of friends. And then she met Ramiro and fell desperately in love with him.'

She saw the pain in his eyes and couldn't stop herself from taking his hand in hers.

'It's all right, Mike. No one realizes – except me, and maybe your grandmother.'

He started. 'Realizes what? I really don't know what – '

'There's no need to pretend with me. You see, I've been there too. I loved somebody who didn't love me.' Betsy's voice was so low he had to strain to hear it against the crash of the surf on the wet silver sand.

'I was eighteen and had just started my first job at Charlie's Liverpool hotel. There was an under-manager there. Sean . . . Sean Jeffries. He was kind to me, helped me out when the teasing about Charlie got a bit too pointed. We went out together a few times but he was out of my league, really. A couple of months after I started work he got this really fantastic offer from the Savoy Group. Naturally he accepted.

'We had a night on the town to celebrate. Roses, champagne, dinner at The Adelphi. Afterwards, I . . . we went back to his room and I spent the night.

367

'In the morning I woke up and lay there feeling so happy. I really thought he'd say it then. After all, we'd slept together. I thought he'd have to ask me to marry him, or at least go with him to London.'

'And did he?' Michael did not sound judgemental, merely sympathetic.

'He asked me to make him a cup of tea, and when I did, he said: "Thanks, doll. That was fantastic. All of it." Me, and a used tea bag – equally fantastic!

'I was broken-hearted. For months afterwards I crept around, convinced everyone knew and thought I was cheap, or else plain stupid.

'So you see, Mike, I meant what I said. I know all about loving someone, and the pain when that love isn't returned. At least Fleur didn't lead you on. You always knew what she felt for Ramiro.'

'Do you really think that made it any easier?' he ground out. 'Having to be with them all the time, seeing the way they looked only at each other, heard only each other? Never me.

'But I got through all that, the pain and the jealousy, because I could see how happy he made her. Fleur loved him – and then the bastard betrayed her, led her on in the worst possible way until he broke her heart and she died. I'll never forgive him for that! He was my friend but I can't forget what he did to her.

'And do you know the worst thing of all? Because they were a couple, because she loved him even if he didn't love her, people pitied him when she died – well, the ones who didn't know it all – said how awful it was for him, losing her like that. And he never loved her! Not the way I did. He can't have done. He was going to marry another girl all along.'

'I don't think it was quite as simple as that,' Betsy said gently. 'From what I've heard, the engagement was forced on him by his family. I think he really did . . .'

'Shut up, damn you! What do you know about it anyway? You weren't even here.'

Michael scrambled to his feet and stood over her, glaring down into her shocked face.

'Oh, God,' he said, and passed a hand wearily over his face. 'There I go again. You really are the most infuriating girl. I don't know what it is about you – you always seem to bring out the worst in me.'

Betsy stood up too and stepped closer to him – as close as she could be without touching him.

'I expect you're attracted to me,' she said matter-of-factly. 'I know I am to you.'

He was six inches taller than her. She had to stand up on her toes before she could slide her arms around his neck and start to kiss him, gently at first, then more eagerly as his passion matched hers.

Eventually he held her away from him but continued to caress her smooth bare arms as he spoke.

'Look, we shouldn't be doing this.'

'Why? What's to stop us? You've got to let go, Mike. Fleur's dead and she was never yours when she was alive. She loved you, I'm sure, but like a brother. Face it, even if she'd lived that was how she'd always have seen you. And I don't. I've no sisterly feelings for you at all.'

She pulled him unresisting to the ground and somehow, afterwards she never quite knew how, her clothes and his were lying in a tangled heap and they were clinging together, too lost in a sudden storm of love to pay any attention to the prickly grass beneath or the occasional walker passing by on the beach.

Betsy and Michael made no formal announcement of the fact but from that afternoon on it was very much apparent that they were a couple. He went on the Jacaranda outing, sitting in the crowded mini-bus with his arm around

Betsy, her blonde head against his shoulder. He appeared in the kitchen more and more frequently until Chef said he never wanted to see his moonstruck face there again. He relented of course and Michael was allowed to come in and pick Betsy up at the end of every shift.

She was in seventh heaven and her cooking went from bad to worse. After a particularly disastrous incident when she dreamily tipped over half a bottle of the best Napoleon brandy into Chef's famous Tipsy Trifle – rendering a party of three spinster sisters comatose at the dinner table – Chef felt he had to act. He approached Sarah in her office one day.

'It's about young Betsy,' he said, straight to the point as always. 'It's going to have to stop, I'm afraid.'

'What is? Her seeing Michael? Over my dead body!' Sarah declared. 'I never thought I'd hear myself say this but I don't care what they get up to so long as Michael stays as happy as he is now. He's his old, dear self again. Betsy's given him back to me and I'll always be grateful to her for that.'

'Yes, yes, I know all that,' Chef put in brusquely. 'But see here, love's young dream is playing merry Hades with my menus! I won't put up with it much longer. I've already told you, she'll never be a chef, hasn't the patience. Can't you put her back at the work she *is* good at? Everyone likes Betsy, the girl's got a way with her. Put her front of house, please, before she does any more damage in my kitchen!'

'You know, you old fusspot, sometimes you have very good ideas. All right, I'll have a word with Michael and we'll break it gently to Betsy. She going on the front desk whether she likes it or not.'

Betsy liked it, and the guests liked Betsy. At this work she was a consummate professional, never a hair out of place, always seeming to have the time to pass a pleasant remark or help solve a problem. Akward guests never bothered her. 'After Chef, how could they?' she replied breezily when Sarah congratulated her. But she was more than just a pretty face. With Sarah's permission, she streamlined the booking system that had bedevilled the office staff for years. She made life a lot less complicated for her co-workers, who loved her for it.

Michael was completely besotted, spending every spare minute of the day with her – and the nights too if Sarah wasn't very much mistaken. He fondly imagined she couldn't hear him creeping out every night, each tread groaning in protest and the tell-tale roar of Betsy's sporty little car starting up just after he carefully closed the front door behind him. They would drive off to her flat but Sarah somehow doubted that they got much sleep there – judging by Michael's hollow eyes and permanently distracted air.

She said nothing to him. She couldn't even find it in herself to be shocked, though, thinking about it, she knew that Gerald would have been. A true believer in the sanctity of marriage, he would never have countenanced any grandson of his entering into such an irregular relationship. Once she would automatically have supported him.

But in the words of one of Michael's favourite songs: 'The times they are a-changing', she decided. And Sarah felt herself to be changing with them.

CHAPTER 35

In the first relief of Claire's departure, when Sarah felt as though a big black cloud had been lifted from the horizon, she had not noticed any significant increase in her workload. True, they were one manager down, but the newly promoted Clive, ably assisted by Michael, seemed to make up for Claire's absence.

Things were rather different in June when, out of the blue, Clive slipped a disc while helping to relocate the hotel's wine reserves in the new store room. He bravely tried to carry on, bent painfully over his desk in the office, but Sarah would have none of it.

'You can't go on like this, Clive,' she told him firmly. 'You'll do yourself permanent damage. What did the doctor say you should do?'

'Go to bed,' he said gloomily. 'Lie down and stay virtually immobile for three months at least. But I can't do that! We're practically in peak season and the hotel's at capacity. I can't let you down like that.'

'And I can't allow you to risk your health on our behalf. I mean it. We'll manage without you. Now, you could stay here in your hotel flat and we would do our best to look after you, but I think it could get pretty boring for you. Is there anywhere else you could go?'

'My parents have offered to help out,' he admitted. 'They were in the business themselves, in a small way, but retired last year. They bought a house in Scarborough. Mum would love me to go and stay there even if I'm going to be a damned nuisance for a few months.'

'Then that's settled,' Sarah told him. 'Don't worry about us, Clive, we'll be fine.'

And for the first month or so they were. Michael rose to the challenge, just as Sarah had hoped he would. Since meeting Betsy and finding happiness with her, he had a new maturity, his grandmother noted approvingly. He addressed even the most mature and distinguished guests as an equal. He was no longer 'young Mr Michael', the boss's grandson, finding his feet in an unfamiliar setting, but Michael Renton, equal partner in all but name in the running of Renton's Royal.

Nevertheless, the habits of a lifetime die hard, Sarah found. With so much extra work to tackle, she drove herself harder than ever.

She had hoped to take a short break in spring or early summer. Sefton had asked her most particularly to visit him again at Le Clos Rozelle. Once Clive left them it was impossible, of course, but time and again during that long, hot summer, as she found herself sitting behind her desk till all hours, Sarah would realize that her thoughts were drifting to that foreign house with its queer, steeply pitched red-tiled roof and brave blue shutters. The rose garden had been so beautiful, she remembered. Strange how she could feel nostalgic for a place she had only visited once. Strange – and a little unsettling.

'I'm worried about Gran,' Michael confided in Betsy one night as they lay together in her narrow single bed, wrapped in each other's arms – not so much from passion, though there was plenty of that in their relationship, but for fear that if they did not huddle close together, one of them would fall out.

'She says she's fine but she's been looking really drawn lately,' he continued. 'I asked her if she was feeling okay and she told me not to fuss over her. Got quite shirty, in fact, which isn't really like Gran at all.'

Betsy nodded. 'Yes, she's been pretty sharp with the receptionists lately too. Had Sandra Gibbs in tears last Thursday about a mix-up over a reservation, and it was the guest who was at fault, not writing to confirm. In fairness to your gran, as soon as she found out she apologized to Sandra, but a few months ago it would never have happened. She'd have checked it all out before leaping to conclusions. Do you reckon it's all getting too much for her, Mike?'

'I don't know,' he said slowly. 'I used to think that she'd happily stay in harness till she dropped – and that wouldn't be till she was eighty at least. Now I'm not so sure . . . I think she's probably ill but too infernally proud and stubborn to admit it to anyone, least of all herself. I'm going to have to keep a careful eye on her.'

'And I'll do the same,' promised Betsy. 'I'd hate it if anything bad were to happen to her. She means almost as much to me as Grandfather does.'

'And speaking of the devil,' Michael teased, 'have you had word from him lately?'

Betsy sounded puzzled. 'No, and that's unusual. I know he had to go down to Torquay for a month or so – problems at the leisure complex there – but he must have come north again because one of my friends said they saw him in Liverpool a few days ago. But he hasn't been in touch with me himself. Strange.'

'Wonder what the old devil's up to?' Michael mused.

'I expect we'll find out,' Betsy sighed. 'When he's good and ready. And in the meantime we must look after Sarah. He'd never forgive me if I let anything happen to her.'

* * *

One golden September day Rachel and Mark arrived at the hotel to pay a visit on Sarah. They'd asked her over to the Hall several times recently but she'd always been too busy to accept. Sarah invited them to lunch in her private dining room. The meal of prawn tartlets, Shewsbury roast lamb and lemon mousse was delicious, but Rachel noticed with concern that her mother barely touched hers.

'Aren't you very hungry, Mummy?' she asked finally.

Sarah glanced down at her plate and frowned. 'Not really. Too much on my mind, I expect. But I see you enjoyed yours, Rachel. You really tucked in.'

Rachel looked down and a warm tide of colour swept over her face. Mark swiftly took hold of her hand.

'I think it's time we told Sarah our news, darling.' He looked her in the eye, practically begging her to be pleased. 'Rachel and I are expecting a baby early next year – February or March. We're both thrilled and we hope you will be too.'

Sarah's eyes filled with tears. She got to her feet and hugged Rachel, and then, after only a slight hesitation, kissed Mark's cheek.

'I couldn't be happier,' she said sincerely, 'but are you sure you're all right, Rachel? I don't want to sound like an interfering mother, but aren't you a little – '

'Old?' her daughter said plainly. 'Well, yes, but this isn't my first child.' There was a momentary pause and Sarah's eyes turned involuntarily to the silver-framed photograph of Fleur standing on a small side table. 'Don't worry, Mother,' Rachel reassured her. 'We've done this absolutely by the book. Mark took me to the top man in Harley Street and he thinks there should be no problems. I'm in my prime, according to him.'

'I'll second that,' laughed Mark, sliding his arm around her affectionately. He was a different man since their reconciliation, thought Sarah, and prayed in her heart that no misunderstanding would interfere in his relationship with this precious second child as it had so tragically with Fleur.

Sarah called for some champagne and she and Mark toasted the new arrival. Rachel only sipped hers, for form's sake.

'I find any wine makes me feel really queasy nowadays,' she confessed. 'Tea and coffee too – but it'll all be worth it when I have a baby in my arms again.'

Sarah waved them both off later that afternoon, feeling more hopeful and relaxed than she had in months. She wondered at first how Michael would take the news but needn't have worried.

'That's absolutely marvellous, Gran,' he told her. 'I'll drop Rachel and Mark a line to say how pleased I am for them both. Oh, and Gran – do you think perhaps Ramiro would like to know? We haven't written to him yet, have we? Maybe now's our chance.'

'A kind thought, Michael. Yes, I'll make time for that tonight. Now, if you've got a minute, perhaps we could finish going through the wholesaler's invoices? There's something wrong with the figure for cleaning supplies but I can't put my finger on it.'

She never lets up, he thought admiringly, forgetting that by placing herself under such strain Sarah could one day suffer the consequences.

Late in September Sefton paid a flying visit to oversee the wine store and arrange for new stock which would be shipped over later in the year.

He had arranged to stay for a couple of nights. To his barely concealed disappointment, Sarah was too busy to dine with him on the first night but promised faithfully that they could have a tête-à-tête the following night, his last.

376

He was waiting in the bar that evening when she arrived, smartly turned out as ever in a midnight blue Duchesse satin two-piece and the sapphire and diamond earrings Gerald had given her on Paul's birth.

Sefton held out his hands in greeting and squeezed hers. 'My dear – ravishing as always.'

But seeing her closer too, he thought there had been some changes in her, and not for the better. Her skin had lost its radiance and her hazel eyes seemed tired and dull. Nevertheless she made a valiant attempt at smalltalk over the cocktails he ordered for them, and later over a delicious meal in the hotel dining room with which they tried a couple of the vintages which Sefton was recommending for the hotel's list.

'So shall we make it two dozen of the Crozes-Hermitage and three of the Château Potensac?' he asked after they had finished tasting the wine and were sitting over coffee and brandy.

Sefton smiled at her ruefully. 'Dash it, Sarah, I'm sorry to have to discuss business over dinner like this. Damn bad manners.'

'Don't be, Sefton. And we'd no other choice. If I hadn't been so tied up we could have done our wine tasting last night and just enjoyed ourselves this evening. But I am very pleased to see you. You know that, don't you?'

'Are you?' His keen brown eyes studied her for a moment and then he said, 'Something's up, isn't it, Sarah? You're not your usual sparkling self. Do you want to talk about it?'

'I don't know what you mean. I'm a little tired, that's all. It's been a long season, and rather gruelling for us with Clive out of action for so long. I expect I'm just run down.'

'More than that, I'd say. Look, Sarah, at your age don't you think – '

She slammed her hands down on the table. 'At *my* age? Hateful words! I'm sick and tired of having every remark anyone makes to me prefaced by them. Am I really so different, less of a person, than I was thirty years or so ago?'

'Not at all,' he soothed. 'You know quite well that you were and always will be my ideal woman. I'm simply concerned to see you looking so tired and fraught. Have you had word from your manager chap – Clive, isn't it? He must be better now. When's he coming back?'

She frowned. 'Actually we haven't heard from him for the last three or four weeks, and that's a bit odd. He was never off the phone at first. He was meant to be back by the beginning of next month, all being well, but hasn't been in touch to confirm.' She sighed. 'Yet another problem, waiting to be solved.'

He took her hand across the table. She did not shrug him off, he was pleased to note. But maybe she was too preoccupied even to notice the way he caressed her fingers as he spoke, softly and persuasively, telling her how much he had looked forward to her trip to him in summer.

'I know you couldn't get away then but if Clive's coming back next month and the high season is over, why don't we fix a date for some time in October? Please, Sarah. Even a weekend would do you good.

'And maybe – who knows? – if you do manage to stop working for a few days, you'll discover it's a habit you could easily grow out of.'

'Stop humouring me, Sefton,' she snapped, and angrily snatched her hand away. 'I know exactly what you're thinking: the old girl's past it but still reluctant to hand over the reins. Needs a little coaxing.

'Well, I'll thank you to stop meddling in my affairs. How I run the hotel, and for how long, is my business, do

378

you understand? Strictly mine! When I want you advice I'll damn well ask for it. Till then, please stay out of what doesn't concern you.'

By now her raised voice and obvious agitation had caused several diners to look their way. Sefton was mortified.

'Very well, Sarah,' he said stiffly. 'If that's the way you want it. I'm sorry I presumed on our long years of friendship by expressing my concern for you. I do know, of course, that you are more than capable of taking care of yourself. You've made that plain often enough. Once too often, perhaps.'

He got to his feet.

'I hope you won't think me even more remiss if I make my excuses and have an early night. I've a long journey ahead of me and want to start as early as possible.'

'Sefton, I – '

'No, Sarah. You have a perfect right to express your feelings. If at any time they change . . .' He smiled sadly. 'Goodbye, my dear.'

It took her a long time to fall asleep that night, and when she did it was only to be woken again in the early hours by the awful drumming in her head and feeling of breathlessness which signalled the onset of another attack of high blood pressure. It was her sixth episode in the last few months and her doctor had made her promise to go back to him if she suffered three attacks. But she wouldn't. She hadn't the time to be ill. She swallowed her pills and waited for them to work. A little sleep and she'd be fine . . ..

The next morning, for the first time in years, she slept right through her alarm. By the time she was dressed and had reached the hotel, Sefton had gone. He left no message.

Sarah shut herself in her office, told Marian she was not

to be disturbed, and for the first time in many years shed tears over a man.

The following week Sarah suffered a body blow when a letter from Clive finally arrived. In it he said that he had been considering his future carefully while laid up and discussing it with his parents.

They felt that their own retirement from the hotel business had been rather premature. Both of them were itching to get involved in another venture, but this time as backers and part-time participants rather than bearing the brunt of the work themselves. They had made a proposal to Clive: they would purchase a small private hotel on Scarborough's South Cliff, and he would manage it in return for part-ownership, his parents to be assured of a home there for life. It was a splendid offer, he wrote, and after much heart-searching he'd decided to accept.

'I hope you won't feel I've let you down, Mrs Renton,' he wrote. 'But with your customary generosity and clear-sightedness, I expect you'll feel as I do that I would be a fool to turn down the chance of becoming my own boss. I've learned everything from you, and will remember my time at Renton's Royal as some of the happiest years of my life.'

'You can't blame him, Gran,' Michael said when she showed him the letter.

'I don't, not really. But we could have done without this, couldn't we?'

He looked at her shadowed face. 'Look, I've a suggestion to make. It's a bit embarrassing, what with Betsy and I being so close, but I really think she's management material. Look at the way she revamped the booking system, and the staff all admire her.'

'You mean, make her under-manager?'

'And officially promote me to manager, yes. I think I'm ready for it, don't you?'

She saw the confident set of his shoulders, the way his once skinny body had firmed and filled out. Michael was a man now, and a man to be proud of.

'I do,' she said with a smile. 'And I think you and Betsy will make a great team.'

'We already do,' he said with a teasing smile.

Betsy's promotion was accepted by the rest of the staff with no adverse comment. She took the following Sunday afternoon off to visit her grandfather who was staying in his Liverpool home for a few weeks while conducting some business in the area. Betsy wanted to break the good news to him personally.

On her return she came to the cottage where Michael was sitting with his feet up reading the Sunday papers before going back on duty.

'What is it? What's the matter?' he asked as she came rushing into the cottage like a hurricane. Ricki ambled over to greet her but Betsy was too preoccupied to lavish attention on him as usual.

'Mike, promise you won't be mad at me! I didn't know, I swear. The old rogue's practically avoided me all summer and I had no idea – '

'Hey, hold on. I don't know what you're talking about.' He caught hold of her hands, which she was twisting together in her agitation, and held them down by her sides.

'I think you should calm down, Betsy, and tell me what this is all about.'

'Is Sarah here? I think she should hear this too.'

'Well, okay. She's upstairs resting, I'll give her a call.'

When Sarah came down in her housecoat and mules, her fine hair loose about her shoulders and face even paler without its customary discreet application of make-up, Betsy felt her heart thud with sympathy and shame.

'Sarah, I think you'd better sit down,' she said, leading her to the sofa. 'I've something to tell you. It's Grandfather – he's bought Clifford's Hotel. Says he's going to turn it into the best venue in the north-west.'

Clifford's was situated only three miles away and had a similar seaside setting. It had once been a thriving concern and a real rival, but bad managers had let it run down until now it posed no threat to Renton's. With refitting and a half-decent manager, it could well be a different story.

Sarah clutched her throat but made no reply to the announcement. Michael exploded in fury.

'That's all we need. Charlie Mullins pouring hundreds of thousands into our closest local competitor. Damn the man, he's always held off before out of friendship for Gran. Why's he suddenly decided to cut our throat now?'

Betsy looked to be on the verge of tears. 'I'm afraid that's not all,' she said tentatively. 'The new manager – it's your daughter, Sarah. Claire will be running Clifford's Hotel.'

'I see,' said Sarah faintly. 'When she left she said she'd be back but I thought she meant at Renton's. I never thought that even she would try and damage us by working for a direct competitor. And Charlie . . .'

'Yes, what the hell is your grandfather playing at?' Michael demanded.

'Don't shout at me like that!' Betsy defended herself. 'I'm not responsible for his actions, you know I'm not. I was so horrified when he started to talk about it this afternoon, I ran out of the house. He knows how happy I am here – and he knows about us, Michael. I just can't believe he'd set out to ruin things.'

'Neither can I,' said Sarah slowly. 'I've known your grandfather all my life, Betsy. He's never done me down so far and he's had every chance. You say you ran out on him? Maybe you didn't hear the whole story. Maybe . . .'

There was a knock on the front door. Michael muttered angrily and went to answer it. They heard a heated exchange of words and then a familiar voice, calling: 'Sarah, call off your guard dog. There's something I want you to hear.'

'I think we've already heard it, Charlie,' she said as he came into the room, turning the brim of his hat between his hands, eyes fixed anxiously on her.

'Not all of it. If that silly lass beside you hadn't gone off half-cocked, she wouldn't have put you through this.'

'*I* wouldn't!' exploded Betsy. 'What about *you* – you . . . you . . . rotten old snake in the grass!'

'I think you'd better go,' Michael began, while Sarah tried to make herself heard.

'All right, you've all said your piece. Why don't you listen to me and BE QUIET!' roared Charlie. 'It's nowhere near so bad as you thought, Betsy. Yes, I have bought Clifford's, but no, it will not be run in direct competition. I'm aiming for a different market entirely.'

'Oh, yes. With a comparable building and practically identical location?' said Michael sceptically. 'Pull the other one, Charlie.'

Sarah waved her hand at him. 'Pipe down a minute. Let Charlie speak for himself. What else were you going to say?'

'Conferences,' he said briskly. 'They're going to be big business for hotels – already are, some places.'

'Yes, cities,' Betsy put in. 'You're not going to tell me that hordes of businessmen are going to come trailing out to Clifford's, because I don't believe it.'

Charlie shrugged. 'Why not? By the time we've finished refurbishing it, Clifford's will have the best facilities in the conference business. Three lecture theatres with overhead projection and sound system. A suite of smaller meeting rooms. Specially trained conference co-ordinators. Re-fitted bedrooms. A dining room that can cope with banquets while simultaneously serving the rest of the clientele. Personally, I think they'd be mad not to come to us, don't you?'

There was silence for a moment, Michael and Betsy guiltily aware that they had overreacted and misjudged Charlie. But Sarah, who had not been so quick to condemn her old friend, still had one major worry.

'And the manger? Or should I say manageress?'

He met her eyes unabashed. 'Yes, it's Claire. I've offered her the job and she's accepted. She'd very much like to be back in this part of the world. In fact, she already is. She's been staying at my place while we've been going over the refurbishment details with the architects and contractors.' For the first time he began to look uneasy.

'I've brought her with me, Sarah. She's outside in my car.'

'No, I'm not,' said a well-remembered voice. Sarah looked up. There in the doorway, immaculate as ever in a military-style coat and long shiny boots, stood her daughter.

'Aren't you going to say how pleased you are to see me?' Her voice was as caustic as ever but Sarah caught a glimmer of uncertainty in her manner.

'Of course I'm pleased to see you, Claire,' she said shakily. 'I was terribly upset when you went off like that without a word.'

'But you managed without me, I hear.' She turned to Michael. 'Manager now. Congratulations. And you must be Betsy. Charlie's told me all about you.'

'And I've heard all about you,' Betsy retorted.

'None of it good, I daresay,' drawled Claire. 'Look, I'd really like to have a word with my mother alone. Would it be asking too much for you to leave us together for a few minutes?'

'I'll stay if you want me, Gran,' Michael put in.

'Thank you, dear. I'm sure that won't be necessary. Why don't you take Charlie over to the bar and give him a drink? He looks as though he could do with one. If I want you, I'll phone you there.'

When the door had closed behind them, Claire came over to stand before the fire, rubbing her hands before the glowing coals.

'I'd forgotten how cold it can be here,' she said conversationally. 'Paris, like all big cities, shields you from the passing of the seasons. I liked it a lot at first. Then I started thinking about home.'

'Renton's, you mean?'

Claire looked into her mother's eyes. 'Not especially. It was the beach I missed most of all, to be truthful – long walks with the the wind in my hair and spray on my face. And trips to the cottage in fell country. Misty mornings . . . The pavements and rooftops of Paris just couldn't compete, I'm afraid.'

'I can understand that,' Sarah said softly.

'I wonder, Mother. Can you? Will you give me the benefit of the doubt after everything I've said and done?'

'It wasn't so terrible. I've had time to think since you went away and I've decided I wasn't very fair to you, Claire. As I told you, I never stopped loving you, but somewhere along the way I seriously underestimated you. Lydia and Charlie put a whole lot more faith in you, to their eternal credit. It was foolish and wrong of me not to have done the same.'

There was silence for a minute. The coals shifted in the fire. When Sarah looked up at Claire she was still standing before it, her back half-turned. Slowly she faced her mother and Sarah saw with astonishment that there were tears in her eyes.

'You don't know how much it means to hear you say that, Mother, but I was wrong too. I was selfish and greedy, trying to ride roughshod over you. You and Father built up Renton's from nothing. You invested so much of yourselves in it, it was foolish of me to suppose I could just step in and take it over, even if I am your daughter.

'Renton's is your creation, and yours to do with as you want. You'll have no further arguments from me on that score. I'm going to be too busy trying to create something of my own. Charlie's been so generous to me, Mother. When he recruited me from Lydia – she was *furious*, by the way, spitting tacks – he offered me a stake in Clifford's, a good one.

'I'm going to make it the best hotel of its kind anywhere. I've got such plans! A swimming pool, health spa, maybe even a golf course one day. Our guests will be there to attend conferences but they'll still be able to enjoy themselves in their off-duty hours.

'And the more successful I am, the more shares I'll be able to acquire from Charlie. We've agreed on my right to buy in my employment contract. I intend to take over in due course – but don't tell Charlie!'

'Do you think he doesn't know?' chuckled Sarah.

Dear Charlie, what a wonderful friend he was – and how it must have gone against his every business instinct to offer such a prodigally generous deal. He had done it for her, Sarah knew, for with Claire estranged from the family, nursing her grievances and silently resenting them, Sarah could never have disposed of Renton's as she saw fit.

Now there was no need for her to worry. Claire's future was assured and for the first time in many years she was behaving with open affection towards her mother. Sitting beside her and after a moment taking her hand as she said:

'Thanks for what you did for Jim. I'll take over that responsibility now. He was my mistake. It's only right I should pay for it.'

'We all make mistakes,' Sarah told her with a squeeze of the hand. 'I'm just so glad we've been able to put ours behind us, Claire.'

Later that evening Sarah hosted a celebration meal for them all in the dining room of the hotel. She had a private word with the sommelier who brought out the very best Krug '65 to mark the celebration. When their glasses were filled, Sarah proposed two toasts.

'To my darling daughter Claire – wishing her every success in her new venture.'

The toast was repeated and glasses held expectantly for the next.

'And to my grandson Michael. For now he will manage the hotel. When he is twenty-five he will become its owner.'

Michael could hardly believe his ears. 'Are you sure, Gran? It's all a bit sudden, isn't it?'

'Not at all!' she laughed. 'Do you really think I haven't been studying you like a hawk these last two years? As my old dad used to say: "You'll do, lad. You'll do."'

'Thank you very much, Gran. I won't let you down. And now, at the risk of overdoing the toasts, I'd like to make one of my own.

'Betsy and I . . . well, we've decided to make it legal. Oh God, that's not how I meant to put it at all! We . . . I . . . why do I always make a mess of these things?'

Betsy laughed and leaned over to give him a kiss. 'Because you haven't yet learned to let your wife do the talking.'

'You will, lad,' boomed Charlie, red in the face from champagne and bonhomie. 'My Betsy will teach you.'

The rest of the meal was a roaring success with Claire offering sincere congratulations to her nephew on his eventual acquisition of Renton's, and to the happy couple on their forthcoming marriage.

'Maybe we'll be able to make it a double celebration,' she said. 'Margaret and Peter seem almost ready to tie the knot. She finally stopped seeing him as her best friend when Peter spoke up and told her he didn't want to be. They seem very happy together.'

'Oh, I'm so glad,' Sarah exclaimed. 'He's a lovely young man. And you will remember your cousin, won't you, Michael, when you're giving some thought to how you'll handle the hotel's finances?'

'Of course, Gran. Couldn't do better than Margaret,' he assured her.

Charlie caught Sarah on her own later that evening as she'd known he would. Before he could say anything, she kissed him on the cheek.

'Thank you, Charlie. You are a dear, good, generous man. You took care of me when I was just a little lass and you're still doing it. Thank you for bringing Claire back. You don't know what it means to me.'

'I think I do,' he said gruffly. 'Sarah, I wanted to ask you . . .'

'No, Charlie. Don't. I want there to be nothing but good feelings between us.'

'There always will be, you know that.'

'Will there? Do you promise?'

He could see from the anxious light in her hazel eyes what she was really asking. 'Yes, I promise,' he said, though his heart weighed like lead inside him.

'That's good, Charlie. I never wanted to hurt you. Think of me fondly when I'm gone, won't you?'

'Gone! You're not going to die?' he said in alarm.

Sarah threw back her head and laughed. 'Not if I can help it! No, I'm not dying, but I have been having some trouble with my blood pressure lately, and I think the time has finally come for me to leave Renton's. I'll look in from time to time to see how Michael and Betsy are faring, but I know they'll do a fine job.'

'What will you do? Buy a little house somewhere, take up gardening? I can't see it somehow, Sarah. Not your style.'

She held her breath for a moment. 'Well, I'm not sure, I haven't even discussed this with the person most closely involved . . . but I do have a longstanding invitation. I think I'll be going to France.'

It was all she needed to say.

'Then I wish you the very best – both of you.'

She knew he would not argue or try to dissuade her. Her decision was made and Charlie would respect that.

She phoned Sefton later that night. He sounded drowsy until he realized who was speaking.

'Sarah! Is everything all right?'

'Couldn't be better,' she laughed.

'Then, good God, woman, what are you doing ringing me at this time of the night?'

'Well, that's very welcoming, I must say.'

'Welcoming? You mean – '

'Sefton, does your invitation still stand? Am I welcome at Le Clos Rozelle?'

'For ever and always. Nothing's changed.'

She clutched the receiver for a moment, fighting back tears of happiness.

'Thank you, my love. Then I might just take you up on that.'

THE EXCITING NEW NAME
IN WOMEN'S FICTION!

PLEASE HELP ME TO HELP YOU!

Dear *Scarlet* Reader,

As Editor of *Scarlet* Books I want to make sure that the books I offer you every month are up to the high standards *Scarlet* readers expect. And to do that I need to know a little more about you and your reading likes and dislikes. So please spare a few minutes to fill in the short questionnaire on the following pages and send it to me. I'll send *you* a surprise gift as a thank you!

Looking forward to hearing from you,

Sally Cooper

Editor-in-Chief, *Scarlet*

P.S. Only one offer per household.

QUESTIONNAIRE

Please tick the appropriate boxes to indicate your answers

1 Where did you get this Scarlet title?
Bought in Supermarket ☐
Bought at W H Smith ☐
Bought at book exchange or second-hand shop ☐
Borrowed from a friend ☐
Other _____

2 Did you enjoy reading it?
A lot ☐   A little ☐   Not at all ☐

3 What did you particularly like about this book?
Believable characters ☐   Easy to read ☐
Good value for money ☐   Enjoyable locations ☐
Interesting story ☐   Modern setting ☐
Other _____

4 What did you particularly dislike about this book?
_____

5 Would you buy another Scarlet book?
Yes ☐   No ☐

6 What other kinds of book do you enjoy reading?
Horror ☐   Puzzle books ☐   Historical fiction ☐
General fiction ☐   Crime/Detective ☐   Cookery ☐
Other _____

7 Which magazines do you enjoy most?
Bella ☐   Best ☐   Woman's Weekly ☐
Woman and Home ☐   Hello ☐   Cosmopolitan ☐
Good Housekeeping ☐
Other _____

cont.

And now a little about you –

8 How old are you?

Under 25 ☐   25–34 ☐   35–44 ☐
45–54 ☐   55–64 ☐   over 65 ☐

9 What is your marital status?

Single ☐   Married/living with partner ☐
Widowed ☐   Separated/divorced ☐

10 What is your current occupation?

Employed full-time ☐   Employed part-time ☐
Student ☐   Housewife full-time ☐
Unemployed ☐   Retired ☐

11 Do you have children? If so, how many and how old are they?

_____

_____

12 What is your annual household income?

under £10,000 ☐   £10–20,000 ☐   £20–30,000 ☐
£30–40,000 ☐   over £40,000 ☐

Miss/Mrs/Ms _____

Address _____

_____

_____

Thank you for completing this questionnaire. Now tear it out – put it in an envelope and send it before 28 February 1997, to:

Sally Cooper, Editor-in-Chief

SCARLET
FREEPOST LON 3335
LONDON W8 4BR
Please use block capitals for address.
No stamp is required!   REROY/8/96

Scarlet titles coming next month:

CARIBBEAN FLAME Maxine Barry
Revenge is what RAMONA KING wants and she'll allow
nothing to stand in her way – until she experiences true passion
for the first time in her life. Damon Alexander can't resist
Ramona, even though he already has a mistress and 'Alexan-
dria' is far more demanding than Ramona will ever be . . .

UNDERCOVER LOVER Sally Steward
Allison Prescott knows one thing for sure: the person with
the wealth calls the shots. Never again will she allow a man
to take over and dictate how she should live. So she needs
money – lots and lots of lovely money! What she _doesn't_ need
is a man like Brad Malone! Brad, too, has other priorities
and they sure don't include falling in love with a woman
who has dollar signs in her heart.

THE MARRIAGE SOLUTION Julie Garratt
When Amy Weldon discovers that her uncle expects her to
marry a man she's never met, she's understandably reluctant. Then she meets Richard Boden and her uncle's plan
suddenly seems very, very desirable.

WIVES, FRIENDS AND LOVERS Jean Saunders
Take three friends: Laura had married Nick Dean after a
whirlwind romance and was still madly in love with her
husband . . . or was she? Gemma wanted stardom at all costs
. . . even if it meant denying her love for the one man who
was perfect for her; while Penny longed only for success and
had no time for romance at all. Friendship, love, marriage or
ambition . . . the choice was vital for all three women.